Praise for

Mary Dyer Illuminated

by Christy K Robinson

In *Mary Dyer Illuminated*, Christy K. Robinson brings Mary Dyer into vivid existence. Christy weaves superb fiction with what is known of Mary's life before her martyrdom into a penetrating novel. Christy's research and depictions are flawless, and her engaging characters invite you into their brilliantly imagined world. Bravo, Christy! (5/5 stars)
She also did a terrific job with *Mary Dyer: For Such a Time as This*. I can't compliment it enough without sounding like a full-tilt book publicist. The historic detail is right on, the story-telling is superb, and Mary Dyer's story is utterly heart-wrenching. The author handled Mary's experiences and beliefs with great sensitivity; they made sense, and so did Mary's actions.
—**Jo Ann Butler**, author of *Rebel Puritan, The Reputed Wife,* and *The Golden Shore*

Mary Dyer Illuminated is an example of historical fiction at its finest. A biographical work spanning the first forty years of Mary's life, this novel paints beautiful descriptions of old England and old London. The history is amazingly well-researched yet the story is smoothly, clearly drawn on the page. Part of Christy K Robinson's charm in writing this novel is her use of primary sources. Quotes from the Bible, from speeches of John Donne, from letters written between the characters pepper the novel with pieces of the living past, drawing the reader deeper into it. I am looking forward with pleasure to book two of this duet. *Mary Dyer Illuminated* is a beautiful novel. (5/5 stars)
—**Christy English**, author of *To Be Queen, The Queen's Pawn, How to Tame a Willful Wife, Love on a Midsummer Night, Much Ado About Jack*

Mary Dyer Illuminated is an absolutely amazing book! Once I had a grasp of the context, I couldn't put it down. As I finished this one and read the notes at the end, I began to fathom the full depth of research and how many hours/years the author has put into this story. The book reaffirmed that history indeed repeats itself, and people today, while pretending to be more sophisticated than those of Boston in the 1600s, can be just as vicious with their words and actions towards those with whom they disagree. The book not only entertained me, but moved me deeply. I look forward to the next one!
—**Don R. Keele, Jr.,** minister and educator

Front cover images:
Detail from *Lady Writing a Letter With Her Maid*, by Johannes Vermeer, National Gallery of Ireland. Public Domain.
Detail from Mary Dyer letter to Massachusetts General Court, courtesy of Massachusetts Archive.
Cover design: Christy K Robinson

Mary Dyer: For Such a Time as This

http://ChristyKRobinson.com

Mary Dyer: For Such a Time as This

Christy K Robinson

"It is not the glorious battlements, the painted windows, the crouching gargoyles that support a building, but the stones that lie unseen in or upon the earth. It is often those who are despised and trampled on that bear up the weight of a whole nation."

JOHN OWEN, English Puritan minister
1616 - 1683

DEDICATION

To those who have
borne the weight of persecution
to bring light to the darkness and
liberty and rights to the oppressed.

To my mother,
Judith Anson Robinson,
1937-1993,
for exemplifying and teaching
the most important
virtues and values in my life:
spirituality, honor, commitment,
love of history and literature,
how to make music,
and how to love the unlovable.
And for transmitting to me the DNA of
William and Mary Barrett Dyer.

ACKNOWLEDGMENTS

There are hundreds of people to thank for standing behind me, lifting my spirits, spurring me on when I was discouraged, and who gave me gifts both spiritual and temporal while I researched and wrote. Their mannerisms, temperaments, and hair color show up sometimes in the characters I've drawn.

Some are friends of many years who insisted that this magazine and book editor should produce a novel and not only pieces for others' books, and they provided counsel in my plotting and devising (Nancy Yuen, Patty Froese Ntihemuka, Stacey Sellards Robinson).

Some are researchers who have spent years studying seventeenth-century New England and who have shared their resources or research with me (Johan Winsser, Jo Ann Butler, history and genealogy authors and bloggers).

Some are published authors whose research methods and writing styles I've admired for years and with whom I've enjoyed a frequent contact in social media and in person (Sharon Kay Penman, Elizabeth Chadwick, Jo Ann Butler, Christy English).

Some are friends, teachers, and pastors I've learned from over many years in churches and university classes (Roberta J. Moore, Stephen Lillioja, Hyveth Williams).

Some are critics, readers, and proofreaders who had the gumption to edit the editor, me. God bless them for finding the errors I'd become blind to (Doreen Sutton, Susan Hicks Arbogast, Jo Ann Butler).

Some are university educators who downloaded and emailed me the documents whose titles and descriptions were tantalizingly dangled before the unwashed public's eyes if we used just the right search terms (Matthew Koehler, Susanna Calkins).

Some are friends who provided gift cards, groceries, restaurant meals, computer support, dental treatment, freelance editing work, and gifts of money while I worked on this two-

MAPS

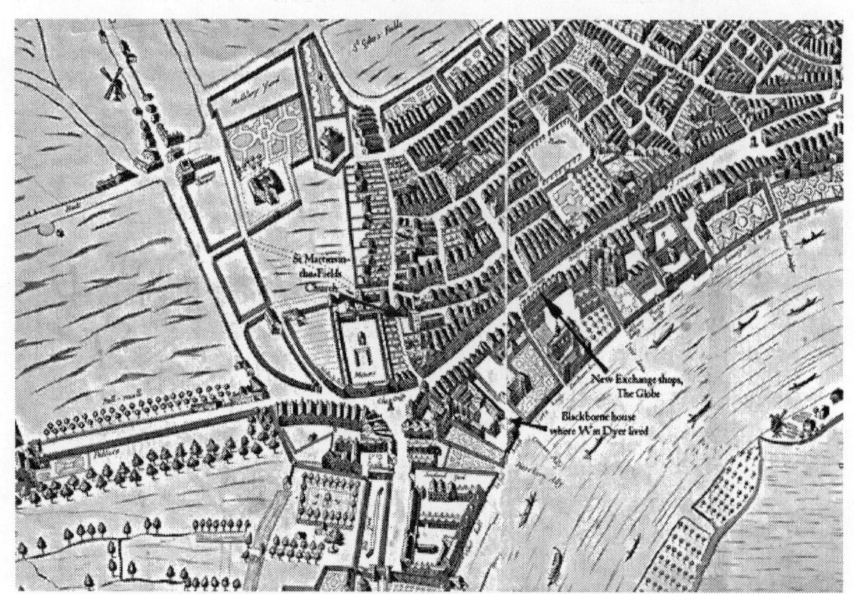

1658 Newcourt map of St. Martin-in-the-Fields parish

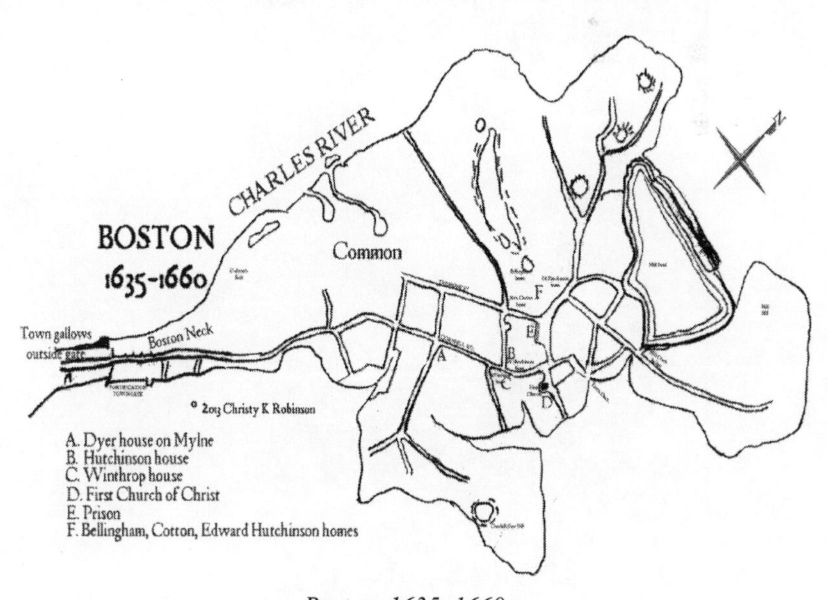

Boston, 1635–1660

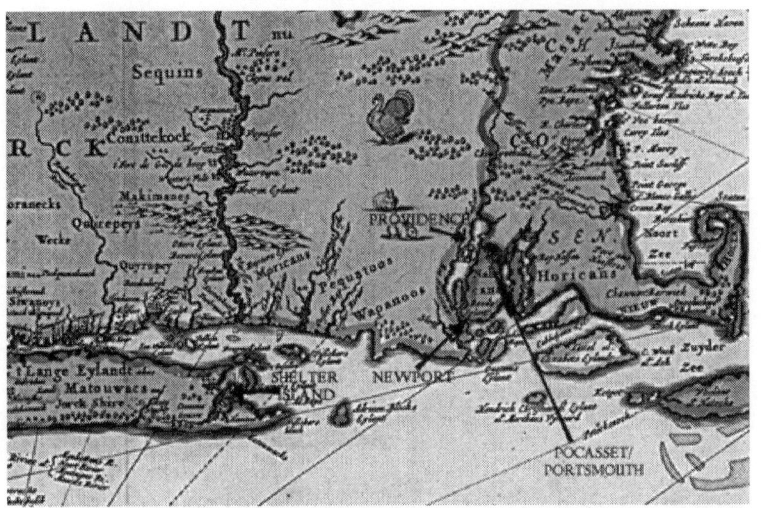

1685 Dutch map of southern New England with labels for Rhode Island.

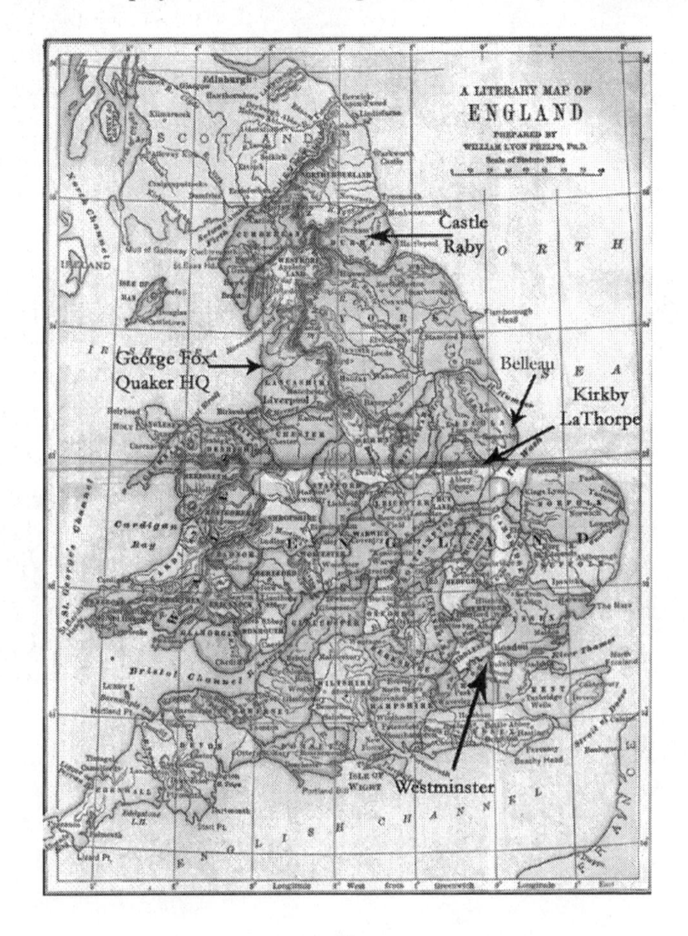

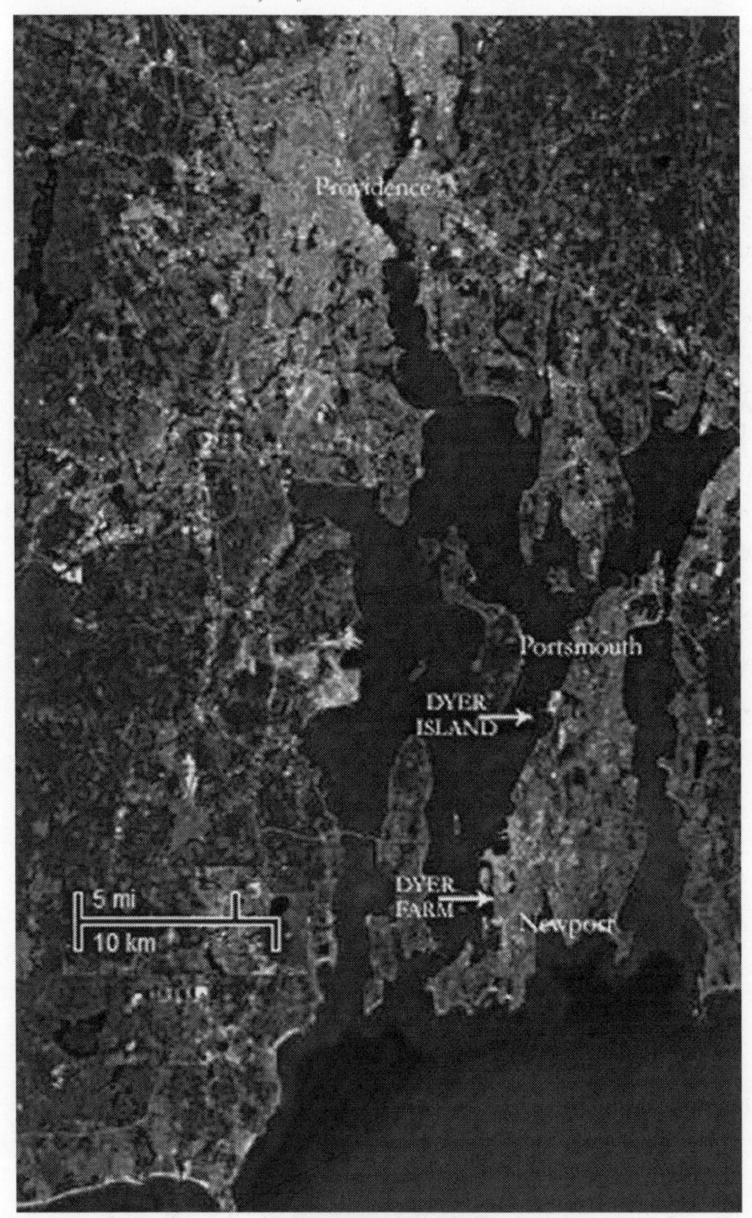

Narragansett Bay

Cast of characters

(F) = fictional character

Mary Barrett Dyer, ~1611-1660, married William Dyer in 1633, mother of "monster," heretic Antinomian, one of Rhode Island's founders, Quaker, martyr for religious liberty.

William Dyer, 1609-1677, born in Lincolnshire, son of prosperous farmer, apprentice to a milliner in a London guild, emigrated to Boston in 1635, one of Rhode Island's founders, surveyor, farmer, government official and first Attorney General in American colonies.

Walter and Elizabeth Blackborne, milliner-haberdasher, member of Worshipful Company of Fishmongers, William Dyer's master during apprenticeship.

Sir Henry "Harry" Vane the Younger, eldest son and heir of Sir Henry Vane, household treasurer to King Charles I; Harry was elected governor of Massachusetts Bay for one term (1636-37), then went back to England to take up a government career. He was knighted in 1640, and an important member of the Council of State until his execution in 1662. His descendants own Raby Castle to this day, and the current Lord Barnard and his son are both named Henry Vane.

John Winthrop, Jr., eldest son of Gov. John Winthrop, Sr., entrepreneur, physician, governor of Connecticut.

Gov. John Endecott, governor of Massachusetts Bay Company, lived at Salem, Mass. As a religious extremist, he was reprimanded by the government several times for acting rashly. He was elected governor again in the 1650s and '60s.

William and Anne (Marbury) Hutchinson, wealthy merchant and midwife from Alford, Lincolnshire. Anne was well-educated by her minister father and outspoken about her beliefs. When they followed their pastor, John Cotton, to Massachusetts, Anne held religious meetings in their home which resulted in two trials and her expulsion from Massachusetts Bay. They were among the first founders of Rhode Island.

Capt. John Underhill and wife Helena, militia commander who emigrated to Massachusetts Bay with the Winthrop Fleet in 1630.

Edward Hutchinson, eldest son of William and Anne Hutchinson, emigrated in 1633 with Rev. John Cotton, militia captain, attorney, merchant.

Richard and Katherine (Marbury) Scott emigrated from Alford in 1634 with the Hutchinsons, settled in Boston, and then moved to Providence Plantations in 1637. Richard was a wealthy landowner in Providence, and Katherine was youngest sister of Anne Hutchinson. They were Baptists, and their minister was Roger Williams. They became Quakers in the mid-1650s, and their daughters accompanied Mary Dyer to Boston.

Nicholas Easton, 1593-1675, one of ten co-founders (with William Dyer) of Newport, president and governor of colonial Rhode Island, an admiralty court judge along with William Dyer, and one of several Newport men who worked tirelessly to unite the Aquidneck Island towns with the mainland towns to have one united colony of Rhode Island.

Herodias Hicks Gardner, a Newport wife and mother who walked from there to Weymouth, Mass., to protest persecution of Quakers. She was whipped while holding her infant daughter.

Rev. Roger Williams, "Puritan of the Puritans" for his extreme fundamental beliefs, he was a maverick from his emigration in 1631 until his expulsion from Boston in 1636. He founded Providence Plantations and made friends with the Narragansett Indians there after purchasing (not appropriating) their land. He wrote a glossary of Indian words, and is considered the founder of the Baptist denomination in America—though he didn't continue in those beliefs for very long.

Rev. John Wilson, one of Massachusetts' first founders, senior Puritan minister at Boston First Church of Christ.

Rev. John Cotton, former senior minister at Boston, Lincolnshire, then Teacher at Boston First Church of Christ in Massachusetts. Father of Rev. Seaborn Cotton and grandfather of Rev. Cotton Mather.

Rev. Dr. John Clarke, Oxford-trained theologian and physician, later Baptist minister in Newport, Rhode Island, and architect of the Rhode Island charters granting separation of powers and religious freedom.

Gov. William Coddington, one of Massachusetts' first founders, one of first purchasers of Rhode Island, governor of Rhode Island (Aquidneck), plantation owner.

Lawrence and Cassandra Southwick, Salem residents who became Quakers and suffered some of the worst persecution of the period. They fled to Shelter Island and died there just before Mary Dyer left there for her final journey to Boston.

Nathaniel Sylvester, owner of Shelter Island, had run-ins with New Haven Colony authority, and became a Quaker in about 1659 or 1660, concurrent with the stays of the Southwicks and Mary Dyer.

Cathy (F), housekeeper at the Dyer farm. They must have had servants, but no names are recorded. I chose this name because after Mary died, William married a Catherine for whom no last name is known. In 1662, William and Catherine had a daughter, Elizabeth, who grew to maturity.

Children of William and Mary Dyer. Precise dates aren't known for William (II) through Charles because there are no vital records of Newport, Rhode Island for those years.

William, b. and d. 1634
Samuel, 1635 - 1678
Unnamed girl, miscarried 1637
William, 1640 - 1688 (perhaps 1693)
Maher, 1643 - 1669/70
Henry, ~1647 - 1690
Mary (called Marie in novel), ~1648 - 1679
Charles, 1650 - 1709

October 30, 1651
Newport, Rhode Island

Crack! Thud. Splash!

Mary pitched stones off the cliff on Dyer's Point as if she were stoning an adulterer in ancient Israel. Curses she had heard but never mouthed formed in her mind, and her breaths came in short, furious gasps. She looked around for a larger rock because the handheld stones weren't large enough to do the damage she wished to inflict on the beach below. Yes! The perfect rock, the size of her head, was part of the low wall, and she was able to pry it out. With two hands, she lugged it to the edge, and slung it down, where it bounced off a boulder and splashed in the surf.

The bloody court at Boston had once again shown the extent of their mercy and understanding when it was needed the most.

Alice Lake, a young mother of five, had lost her youngest child to a childhood disease or birth defect, just like nearly every family in England and New England had. She claimed that she had seen its spirit, which had come to comfort her.

"You've seen the devil," declared her minister, Richard Mather. "Satan has drawn you in by appearing to you in the likeness, and acting the part of, your child."

Someone in the town accused Alice as a witch, and she was tried and convicted because she would not recant her belief that the child's spirit had come to her.

During her interrogation, Alice insisted that she had never practiced witchcraft, but under pressure, she admitted that while she was a bondservant, before she and Henry Lake had married ten years ago, she had played the harlot, and being with Henry's child, used means to destroy the fruit of her body to conceal her sin and shame. Although she did not effect it, she said, yet she was a murderer in the sight of God for her endeavors, and showed great penitence for that sin; but owned nothing of the crime laid to her charge.

She had been given the chance to admit her witchcraft and live, but Alice was hanged at the gallows on Boston Neck, insisting to the end that she had seen her child's spirit, and not the devil.

Mary remembered the vision of her youth, long ago and far away in England, and that she stood on the gallows, innocent, surrounded by hate. And that somehow, John Endecott was involved. Now there was poor Alice, murdered by the magistrates and ministers of Boston for loving and grieving her dead child and seeing a vision.

Alice left four motherless children behind, the youngest of them still in his clouts. Henry Lake had abandoned them and run to Portsmouth on Rhode Island, to stay with his relatives. The little children, under ten years old, were put out as servants to four families in Boston, and the town paid money for their keep, up front. The Lake toddler taken by the Tolmans had just died, and netted a profit of twenty-one pounds for them.

Mary couldn't decide who was more at fault and deserving of her symbolic stoning: Alice and Henry who both abandoned their children, the tattler who had carried the tale to the bloodthirsty minister, the pitiless court, the foster parents… So she pitched another rock down to the shore and stood there, sobbing into the cold onshore wind for Alice Lake, the dead children, and the dark, vicious hearts of people who were dead in their religion. Wolves in priests' clothing, leading their flock into the valley of death and devouring the wounded sheep.

Only misery and death can come from a government wedded to religion, she thought, for therein is no mercy. Jesus came to be savior of individual human beings, not of societies or political systems or kingdoms. He came to heal the brokenhearted, deliver the captives, give sight, and set free the bruised. But who killed him? The religious leaders who had sold their principles to cooperate with the Roman Empire.

As she stood there looking out over the bay, she saw a procession of those people who had had a positive influence on her life, who lifted her out of a quiet obscurity in London suburbs, and gave her an education and a future. Her father, her foster-uncles John and Edward, Liza, Anne and William Hutchinson, Katherine Scott, Harry Vane, John Clarke and Obadiah Holmes, and most of all her husband William—had loved her and treated her tenderly and respectfully, and best of all, honestly. They provided the support that stopped her in her tracks if she was wrong, and gave wings to her heels when she was right.

Mary felt in her bones that she must go to England, but she'd been stopped by war, by her small children, and by her husband. Maybe she was wrong about her desire, and truth be told, she wasn't even sure why she felt such urgency.

"Mary."

"Yes, Lord?"

A shaft of sunlight pierced the heavy overcast and illuminated the water of the Narragansett Bay, making of it countless pinpoints of light that twinkled as they were driven by the stormy blast.

"Be at peace. Your vision is for an appointed time, but at the end it shall speak. I will go with you to England, and I will bring you back."

The Light retreated behind a pillar of cloud.

Mary laid down her fistfuls of stones and walked home.

Newport, Rhode Island
November 4, 1651

"Mary, I've brought you a gift," announced William Dyer, as he hung his cloak on the hook by the door.

She looked up from where she was kneeling at the kitchen fire, pulling the meat pie's baking kettle from the coals and ashes at the side of the fireplace. She'd served supper for the children and servants already, a seafood chowder in rye bread trenchers.

One of the cats lay stretched out as if to claim every degree of heat for a thickening winter coat. Mary liked to pick up and hold a hot cat whether it was in July sunshine or a winter kitchen—it was like holding a bag of jelly.

She smiled slightly, remembering the hundreds of gifts Will had brought her over the years: casks of nails to carry to America, seeds and saplings, game for the larder, fabric for clothing, imported dishes, even window glass for the house. It wasn't so much the item or its value she enjoyed, as the spirit and generosity of the giver.

"Well, are you expecting me, a forty-year-old matron, to play the 'going through your pockets' game?" she asked.

"You may want to play that game later tonight," her husband leered comically, "when you know what I've got you this time."

Now her attention was fully on him.

"First, the anticipation must build. The gift can wait," he smirked.

She feigned indifference. "Go ahead. Can you tell me around bites of your supper?"

Mary brushed the ash from the small kettle's exterior, and set it on the rough wood of the kitchen table. Using their everyday wooden plates, she served a generous helping of meat and vegetables with part of the pastry crust.

"Mmm, it reminds me of my mum's pie," he said through a mouth stuffed with tender pork, thick sauce, onion, and mushrooms. "I've just come from a historic day in the Assembly. Mr. Coddington, Nick Easton, and others shouted and argued, and Providence and Warwick men have accused

Portsmouth and Newport men of seceding from the colony, which is Mr. Coddington's intention, and legal according to his charter.

"The landsmen of Providence and Pawtuxet have hung on to their 1643 charter. The Rhode Island men, forty-one from Portsmouth and sixty-five of Newport, have broken from Coddington and thrown their support to Roger Williams and John Clarke. We voted to send them immediately to London."

Mary set down her spoon. "I thought that was voted two weeks ago."

"Yes, that's true, but with this schism, and one hundred six Island freemen rebelling against Coddington and standing for Mr. Williams and unity, we've resolved that we can't waste time talking about it while Coddington's faction builds its power. And this is where your gift comes in."

William, a mature, cultured man, husband of eighteen years and father of six children, attorney general of Rhode Island colony, stuffed his mouth with a huge spoonful of meat pie and chewed slowly and noisily, smacking his lips with relish—just to annoy his wife and drag out the suspense. Finally, he swallowed and licked his teeth.

"You, my dear, are taking passage separately from me, whenever his turnaround takes place, on Mr. Nicholas Travice's ship."

Mary was stunned. "What changed your mind?"

"The finances have eased. The Providence and Warwick men were so incensed at Coddington that they spontaneously pledged £10 and £20 a man and £100 from the town of Shawomut to hasten the cause and send Williams and Clarke on the first ship to England. They need passage money and funds to set up households in London. They'll be there for at least a year, and will be expected to entertain members of Parliament to win their favor.

"And I want you to go to England to fulfill your destiny and satisfy your longings. I want you to be happy. I'll arrange for you to stay with the Vanes or Blackbornes until you return to Rhode Island."

All her days, Mary had hidden her emotions, not willing to show her vulnerabilities, nor her strength of intellect.

Even now, alone with her husband, her eyes brimmed with tears which did not fall, but her hand crept across the table until William covered it with his own.

They sat like that for a few minutes, until Will whispered, "Do you still want to search my pockets?"

*****

TO KATHERINE SCOTT AT PROVIDENCE PLANTATION
This 6th of November 1651
My dear sister Katherine,

I have the greatest news to impart to you, that William has consented for me to sail to England for a visit. But first, we must arrange for our children's care during our absence. (He is going immediately, and I will follow as soon as possible.) I would be honored if you would foster my youngest along with yours. Please consider this carefully with Richard and don't rush to a decision.

Grace, mercy, and peace to you.
MARY DYER

February 1652

Boston, Massachusetts Bay Colony

William Dyer stood at the rail of a three-masted frigate, despite the biting winds coming off the mainland of Massachusetts Bay Colony. The long, low ship carried forty-four guns, so its form as it sailed into the bay and then Boston Harbor was cause for alarm. The guards posted at the fort on Castle Island, which had been designed and built with the advice of Captain John Underhill, came to attention at the sight of the frigate in the channel between the islands. Tensions were always high, from hostilities escalating with the Dutch and the French. After the beheading of King Charles three years ago, Boston authorities weren't as worried that England would demand their charter and autonomy.

Of course, no one knew what Dyer carried with him on this journey—a directive for Rhode Island that revoked the Coddington charter and guaranteed their rights to democratic government instead of the government William Coddington would have imposed: a government by magistrates and deputy governors without elections, and with himself as lord governor for life. This was not an act of Parliament or the Council of State which would come later, but Dyer bore letters from Roger Williams and Sir Henry Vane, promising their support.

After saluting the fort with the boom of a cannon, the frigate sailed slowly through the channel islands lying nearer the town. Harbor hands took boats and heavy lines with which to pilot the ship into the deep channel that led to the Long Wharf and slowly, she was guided into a place at the wharf.

Will's trunk came off the ship with him, and he gave directions for the short-term storage of his trade cargo. The post road from Boston to Providence would be snowed in, and he planned to hire a smaller ship to sail around Cape Cod and into Newport's harbor.

He headed uphill on King Street, making for Edward Hutchinson's home, and overtook another man striding toward Tri-Mount. The black-coated cleric turned, recognized Dyer, and spoke.

"Will Dyer! It's been years! I'm pleased to see a Lincolnshire boy again, even if that sprinkling of silver hair at your temples reminds me of my age."

"Ah, Reverend Cotton, your appearance hasn't changed a bit in, what, fourteen years? But I have heard your name as recently as two months ago, in England. Harry Vane's children were reciting the catechism you wrote, *Milk for Babes.*"

"It sounds like we have much to discuss. Will you turn aside for a pint with me?"

The two men turned right, onto Merchant Row, and entered Samuel Cole's tavern. Cole had opened the first tavern in New England in 1634 and been a signatory to the Wheelwright Remonstrance in 1637, but, like William Dyer and many others, had apologized to the Boston government and rehabilitated his reputation in the community and the church. Cole's son John had recently married Susanna Hutchinson, who had been an Indian captive for several years when her mother and some of her siblings had been massacred by Siwanoy Indians.

The church teacher and the attorney took seats by the great fireplace and quickly shed their winter hats, coats, and gloves.

"After two months in icy gales on the North Atlantic, I feel ready for a good toasting," said William. He added some small sticks and pine cones to the log fire to make it flare hotter.

Cotton asked, "What made you chance a winter crossing?"

"Business for the colony, trade goods and wine, and the need to come home before the French and Dutch pirates and privateers leave the sun-drenched comforts of the tropics in the spring."

"Home? Which England do you favor?"

"My life is here. My children, farm, business, companions are here. My wife, the exception, has gone to visit the Vanes and Blackbornes and others in England for a few months, and will sail home in the summer."

The minister nodded. "I thought for several years that I'd like to return for a visit, particularly for the Council of

Westminster when our reformed creed was being decided. I had offers of employment, including back at the old Boston. But John Winthrop, Thomas Dudley and others made sure I stayed here. It was a great disappointment that I learned to overcome with the grace of God. I will trust that he has accomplished his will."

"Your children are here," said William, "and soon you'll have grandchildren. Your teaching on the Covenant of Grace has probably moderated the extreme viewpoints and practices of other ministers in New England. You've published books. No one, even God, could accuse you of slackness of purpose, nor of fading into obscurity."

"My son Seaborn, not quite nineteen years old, has recently entered the ministry after his education at Harvard. I consider him the first fruits of my American work." Cotton paused and the wrinkles at the corners of his eyes deepened with a sly smile. "And I've fought bloody intellectual duels with your colony's Roger Williams in our ongoing publishing battle. What think you of our series on *The Bloody Tenets*?"

William shot back, "I'm a prosecuting attorney, not a judge, so I won't be dragged into deciding the winner of your theological debates!"

Both men smiled. They swallowed the last of their pints and William went back to order some warm, mulled cider. He was finally feeling the warmth of the room and the drink.

"You've done well, William. I remember meeting you when you were a London apprentice and I know exactly where you came from, even the church where you were christened. My old friend William Hutchinson thought you were a worthy boy and recognized your potential. And now look at you: militia captain, surveyor, trader, public servant, an attorney who drafts laws and acts as legal counsel, father and husband."

The older man sighed and bent forward to speak to William in an undertone. "I can say to my regret, now that Mr. Winthrop and the Hutchinsons have met their Maker, that I was the principal author of the antinomian controversy, though I never meant to be, and that when taken to its conclusion, I consider it to be heresy. I had preached the Covenant of Grace for years in the old Boston, and like the tower on St. Botolph's, it was a beacon of hope for many, including the Hutchinsons. But Anne tried to rise from her proper place as a woman—even an educated, wise woman—and while it could be tolerated in a village like Alford or even in old Boston, it could not be allowed in Massachusetts Bay. New England is a haven for reforming firebrands, and they're concentrated here as they never were in England."

Will thought about this for a moment. "As I remember, even though you were popular in Lincolnshire, there was a time when you had to flee Boston Stump and hide for a year while the Anglican bishops sought to arrest you."

"Yes. The strain was so great that it broke my health. And it killed my first wife. When I came to America, I could do or say whatever God placed on my conscience. When John Wilson doubled his efforts on the Covenant of Works, I was able to bring moderation to his ministry. But the pressures of the ministers' and magistrates' councils to conform to their rigid structure forced me to change. I can't say that it was against my will. At the ministers' council in 1637, just before Anne's first trial, I saw how it would be for those who were considered lenient about the law or too merciful with sinners. I turned away from her. It was the correct decision for the church and the colony, but I'm sorry that it hurt Anne."

The older man's voice was steady, but his eyes were bright with tears.

"Mr. Cotton, I don't believe that pragmatism is better politics than standing on principle. My wife's guardian, John Dyer, told me before we were married that I should bend in the wind if necessary to protect my family. When we came to this Boston, I bent to the church and the governors and made the expected responses when I didn't fully espouse your tenets. When I was disfranchised and disarmed for taking Mr. Wheelwright's part—the side you once took—I bent again to apologize and submit to your authority for the good of my family."

William was warm now. In fact, the heat of the fire and the cider were nearly intolerable. But he kept his voice low so only the minister could hear and understand.

"In Rhode Island, where we have a democracy, and church and state are set apart, I have the liberty to follow my conscience and stand tall on principle, something I couldn't do in England or here in the Bay. When Mr. Winthrop and his council tried to annex our colony, we fought back and obtained a charter of our own. When Mr. Coddington attempted a takeover of Rhode Island government, we fought back—and I'll tell you this: our cause has prevailed and will shortly be revealed. God created the individual man with liberty of conscience, and those men come together as a body politic, to order society.

"The Rhode Island assembly engaged me to prosecute wrongdoing by individuals and government alike, on behalf of the peace, safety, prosperity, and well-being of the people of the colony. What is good for one is good for every 'one' in the colony."

William stopped. He felt uncomfortable disagreeing with or lecturing a man of Reverend Cotton's stature or years. It was one thing to face him in court; this was not the time or place to air his old grievance or to teach a man of God.

As both men fell silent, the sounds of the tavern rose up and swirled around them. The one being sung now was written as "The Good Fellows Resolution of Strong Ale that Keeps His Nose from Being Pale."

Be merry my friends,
And list a while Unto a merry text.
It may from you produce a smile,
When you hear it exprest.
Of a young man lately married
Which was a boon good fellow,
This song in his head he always carries,
When drink had made him mellow,
'I cannot go home, no I will ne'er go home,
'It's long of the oil of Barley:
'I'll tarry all night for my delight,
'And go home in the morning early.'

Will stood to leave. "It was good to see you, Mr. Cotton, and hear the accent of the shire again. I wish you and your wife prosperity and health."

"One more question before you go, Will. Mistress Dyer? Tell me about how she fares."

"I left her well a few months ago when I sailed to act as agent in London, and in the meantime, she has sailed with my blessing to England for a short stay. I assume you mean her spiritual welfare?"

Cotton nodded once.

"We sometimes attend the Baptist meeting led by Mr. Holmes, the man who was beaten to near-death by order of Governor Endecott. But Mary holds closer to the teachings of Anne Hutchinson. Goodbye, sir. I have business, and the winter sunset will not wait for me."

Reverend Cotton stood, and leaned on his stick. "Goodbye, William. I'll pray for you and Mary."

William redressed in coat, gloves, and hat, and stepped out the tavern door into a rush of freezing wind.

*****

Edward Hutchinson was not at home when Dyer knocked at his door, but his wife Abigail received him. Rather than entertain him in the chilly parlor, she brought William back to the large, warm, fragrant kitchen, the heart of the home. William was considered a family member to the Hutchinsons of Boston, and he stayed here whenever he passed through on business.

Samuel Dyer, now aged sixteen, worked for Edward in his textile business, and was beginning his militia training under Ed's command.

"Sam is working at the shop, Mr. Dyer," said Abigail. "I'm sure he'll be thrilled to see you when he comes home for supper."

She pointed at the cradle in the corner, which was occupied by a pile of baby blankets, as far as William could see. "That one will sleep all day and scream all night—won't you, my pet?" Baby Edward, only two months old, Abigail's first child since marrying Edward, slept on.

Ten-year-old Elisha Hutchinson was seated at the table, puzzling over mathematics problems. William sat next to the boy, saw the difficulty, and proceeded to review the multiplication tables until Edward came home half an hour later. After a significant look from Abigail, the boy thanked Mr. Dyer and went out to start his evening chores of looking after the milk goat and securing the hens.

To allow Abigail to give the children their suppers, the two men, friends since boyhood, took a lamp into the parlor and sat to talk.

Edward spoke first. "I'm surprised you had the land legs to walk up the hill from the port, after all the time you've spent at sea recently."

"It does feel good to stand still without bracing against a wave or the wind. The voyage outbound was quick—only eight weeks—but coming back, the frigate's master was fighting the westerly gales, and it took two weeks longer."

"Did you encounter any trouble along the way? Pirates? Privateers?"

Will shook his head. "No, I think they must be assaulting one another in their winter grounds, or perhaps in the East Indies. The Dutch and French were too loving with one another, which upsets powers in Europe and their empires. Shortly before I arrived in England, Parliament passed a Navigation Act, ordering that only English ships could import goods to England."

"That will cut their own noses off, as far as trade goes!" Ed complained. "How are we to trade with Italy, Spain, France, the Dutch—ah, there's the rub."

William nodded. "Colonel Monck said, 'The Dutch have too much trade, and the English are resolved to take it from them.' And their ships along with it."

"How much is too much?"

"Any trade in the western hemisphere is too much trade. One proposal that offended the Dutch was that they could keep their routes in the East Indies, Africa, and Mediterranean, but they must give over all interest in the West

Indies, Brazil, and New Netherland. They considered the English to be arrogant in that demand."

Ed frowned. "Except for being rivals in commerce, the Dutch have been England's allies and Protestant cousins for decades. I suspect this will mean war. Amongst privateers, if not navies."

William sat forward and said, "The war, if it happens, could come to Long Island, where there are English and Dutch citizens alike. You could be called up for action."

"I'll keep that in mind when I meet with other officers to plan for trained band maneuvers."

They fell silent for a moment, absorbed by the flame in the lamp.

Hutchinson stretched his long legs and yawned. "Pardon. The short nights and overcast winter days make me sleepy. I sometimes dream of making a run for Barbados on days like this. But they have no love for the warm, scratchy woolens I import from Lincolnshire and sell here. You've come straight here from England, have you? And not been to Newport yet?"

Will nodded.

"And now that you're here, have you accomplished your mission? Do you have word from the Council of State regarding Mr. Coddington's ambitions?"

"In a few words," William said, "the Council will uphold our 1643 charter and keep the Providence Plantations and Rhode Island together under one government. They'll answer our complaint formally later in the year. He had given them to understand that he was the sole purchaser of Rhode Island, and he was given full power and authority to issue land grants, raise defense forces, and use all lawful means to settle, improve, and preserve the islands in peace and safety. There would be no elections, he decided who could vote, and the towns could not select their own representatives to his council."

Ed snorted. "No one will stand for that for long, with or without a command from England. Coddington had better keep bodyguards with him."

The door to the hall opened and banged shut. "That would be your son," said Edward. He called, "Samuel, come in here."

A tall lad of sixteen, with sandy-colored hair that had escaped the ribbon tie in the incessant wind, came into the semi-dark parlor. "Yes, sir?"

Then he noticed the other figure. "Father!"

William grinned. "Are you learning your Latin, maths, and all your master's secrets, boy, so you can share them with me?"

"Yes, Father. Mr. Hutchinson has withheld nothing. He's a kind master. For instance, he taught me only yesterday that…" Samuel gave a sidelong glance at Edward and stopped, knowing that lads didn't usually tease their elders.

"I do believe it's time for dinner," groused Edward. "It's a shame I have to fill your mouth with costly foodstuffs to keep you from gossip."

March 1652

London, England

Despite the chill and heavy, wet fog, Mary Dyer stood at the side of the ship as it eased into its slip in east London, controlled on huge, thick ropes by dock hands. To the west, the Tower of London, a huge fortress and castle complex, rose on Tower Hill. Beyond that by several miles, though she couldn't see it from the ship, was St. Paul's Cathedral, where her father's print and book shop had been. And around the bend in the Thames lay Westminster and St. Martin-in-the-Fields, where she'd been married, and buried her firstborn son eighteen years before.

Did she miss her son, whom she'd known only long enough to have him baptized before he died? Yes, she thought. Every day, in the same way she remembered her stillborn daughter, whom she'd never seen, only heard described. But Mary trusted that she'd be reunited with her babies in heaven someday. With five boys and a girl awaiting her return from England, she had an idea of what her other two children might have been like if they'd lived.

Her other children were on the other side of the Atlantic, in Boston and Newport. Samuel, sixteen, was learning the mercantile trade in Boston, though by all reports he was more interested in training days with the militia. William, eleven, and Maher, ten, were enrolled in school, and had embraced their father's industries, to his delight. William showed interest in trading, clerking, and politics, and Maher was more at home sailing on Narragansett Bay than in a house, Mary thought. Henry was five, and little Marie was four. Her youngest, Charles, was eighteen months, and she'd weaned him only last autumn, in preparation for this journey, her first visit to England since she'd left eighteen years ago. Now Henry, Marie and Charles were under the care of Katherine Marbury Scott in Providence, and the boys were staying and working with friends. The custom of fostering children was an ancient practice in Britain.

Her longtime friend and housekeeper, Liza Stansby, had died of a summer fever several years ago, and Mary had employed a bondservant, Cathy, to learn housewifely arts and improve her chances of a good marriage when her service was completed. Cathy would do the manual labor of the household in Newport, but Katherine Scott would provide the spiritual instruction and the mothering in Providence, while Mary was in England for a few months.

Several books had been published, libeling Anne and Mary as the mothers of monsters, notoriously infected with heresy, and unfaithful to their husbands. Ministers like Thomas Shepard and Thomas Welde had written that the antinomian teachings of Anne Hutchinson and others had brought forth monstrous, deformed bastards of evil behavior and beliefs. There were rumors that women who had preached, or had listened to women teaching or prophesying, gave birth to monsters, and that they usurped the God-given order of life. A more direct reference to Anne Hutchinson and Mary herself could not be made. Anne's teachings had even been blamed for the great New England earthquake of 1638.

Mary hoped her return to England would refute those accusations, and finally set Anne's and her reputations to rights. She'd read broadsheets from England about the highly-charged religious atmosphere, and was curious about the sects that somewhat resembled what she'd learned from Anne. She wasn't quite sure how she'd overcome the dishonor, but trusted that God would show her the path. Perhaps she could publish a pamphlet under a pseudonym, but only God knew the plans he had made for her. Her own plans were a distant second to the direct command of God to go to England for a time. Here she was, and she had no idea yet of her assignment or what she must learn or experience to fulfill her destiny.

Before she'd sailed, the Dyers' friend of many years, former Governor Nicholas Easton, had acquainted Mary with the political news out of the home country that she'd need to navigate London society.

The young King Charles, who had been born at the time of the noonday comet in 1630, had fought Oliver Cromwell's New Model Army for several years after his father had been captured, tried, and beheaded. But a few months ago, in August 1651, Prince Charles' ragged army limped into Worcester, where he had been proclaimed King of Great Britain, France, and Ireland. Twelve days later, Cromwell's forces defeated Charles, who fled the city and country, hiding for six weeks before turning up at the French court to be greeted by his mother, brother, and youngest sister Minette, who had also taken refuge with their relatives.

Cromwell's armies had invaded Ireland during the last two years, and committed atrocities at Wexford and Drogheda. His officers offered mercy to those women and children who would surrender—and then murdered them or cut off their hands and feet. Some Irish children had been spared to be shipped to the West Indies as slaves to die of work and fever on the sugar plantations.

"The Puritan Parliamentary forces justify this in the name of religion," said Easton. "Ireland is Roman Catholic, and antipathy runs deep for the papists who are known to carry the Mark of the Beast on their souls. A hundred years after Bloody Queen Mary, the Protestants are still exacting their revenge. While John Winthrop was governor of Massachusetts Bay, he kept the worst zealots like Richard Bellingham and John Endecott on a tether. But now that he's gone to whatever fate God a-judges him, we've seen the beginning of an American reign of terror with their prosecution of John Clarke and Obadiah Holmes. "

Mary answered, "The marriage of religion and government brings forth nothing but the most virulent, poisonous hate and violent passions. Jesus' ministry avoided politics of the Jews and the Romans, though the Jews did everything to win him and harness his popularity and power. When they understood that he would not be used by men, they plotted to kill him."

"And they crucified him," said Easton. "God does not require a government to adhere to a religion. He requires individuals to do justly, and to love mercy, and to walk humbly with their God. If that takes place, there *will* be true justice, mercy, and humility in government.

"Mary, I promised Will before his voyage that I'd watch out for you and get you safely installed on Travice's ship. As I see it, part of that promise is to prepare you for what you'll find in England. You left a culture of music and art, courtly manners, and high learning. But that's all gone. It's been repressed and destroyed by the Roundheads' uneducated, uncultured religious zeal. They have all the education and refinement of a flock of wild goats. Now, you'll see famine and the disease that attends it, fatherless children, angry widows, and great poverty.

"You are a woman of steadfast convictions, possessed of an intellect and great advantages. I've never known you to act or speak rashly, or indeed, in any manner but a godly wife. But you will be entering a different country than you left seventeen years ago. You'll be sorely tempted to speak out, and to effect change. But it will require your utmost discretion to survive there, and to navigate through shark-infested waters."

Mr. Travice's three-masted tall ship traveled slowly up the Thames, and stopped in mid-river near the docks and wharves lying west of the London Bridge. With ropes and pulleys, dock hands and sailors brought her slowly into her slip.

Because her ship had called in at Portsmouth before sailing around to the Thames estuary and then to London, Mary had been able to send a message about her imminent arrival. Down on the London dock below the ship, Mary recognized Walter and Elizabeth Blackborne, Will's master during his apprentice years. She hadn't seen them since she'd moved to Rhode Island, though they'd written letters and Will occasionally did long-distance business with Mr. Blackborne. They both looked healthy, though much aged in the war-torn years since 1638.

And oh, my, that feathered hat on the richly-dressed, ginger-haired man must belong to thirty-nine-year-old Sir Henry Vane! He'd come to the docks with the Blackbornes to greet his friend, Mistress Dyer. Mary remembered when they'd first met: in 1630 at Uncle John Dyer's, before her marriage, her children, and the floodwaters of controversy and the placid streams of domestic life had slid under the bridge; before Harry had spent two turbulent years in Boston, and the rest of his life in English government during the Civil War. Now Harry—she must remember *not* to call him Harry—was, like his father before him, on the Council of State, with a rotating presidency. At times, Sir Henry was the head of state for the realm—England, Scotland, Ireland, and the colonies.

When she disembarked after taking her leave of Captain Travice, Mary had no time to properly curtsey to Henry before she was crushed in the arms of her friends. Then, with her trunk strapped to the footman's bench on the back, they rode in Henry's carriage back to his townhouse at Charing Cross. Mary was accustomed to saddle-riding and wagons, but an enclosed carriage was a bone-jarring luxury as yet unknown in Rhode Island. As they rode through the East End, Elizabeth passed a sprig of rosemary to each passenger, to hold to their noses and distract from the putrid smells of the docks, the streets of London, and the gutters of Westminster.

Over her seventeen years in America, Mary had forgotten how close the old city of London could feel. The blocks of houses rose four and five stories overhead, and because they were wider than their bases, they leaned over the street and seemed likely to crash against each other someday.

Coal smoke from homes, shops, and blacksmith forges eddied through the streets and settled in low, enclosed areas like a malevolent mist.

There were piles of rubbish everywhere: broken wagon wheels, crates, hogsheads, and barrel staves that had been salvaged to feed cooking fires. Children picked over mounds of broken pottery, shreds of stained bedding, and offal, looking for something they might sell for a ha'penny. Barely-alive drunks wearing rags that hadn't yet been stolen from them slouched against walls. Once their clothes were gone, stripped from them while unconscious, they would die of exposure.

What a contrast, she thought, to the new, smaller towns of Massachusetts and Rhode Island, with wide streets that by law must be swept daily. Their buildings were less than twenty years old, and the sea breeze swept the stench and disease away. When she was a young girl, she'd never thought about the unhealthful crowding and filth of the city because she didn't know any other England—only the Stansby farm at Willesden.

Mary answered questions about the children and about her voyage while she watched London go by outside the carriage, and she asked about her husband because they had seen him more recently than she had.

Vane replied, "Roger Williams sent a letter to Rhode Island this week, in which he said, 'I hope it may have pleased the Most High Lord of sea and land to bring Captain Christen's ship and dear Mr. Dyer unto you, and with him the Council's letters for the confirmation of the charter until the determination of the controversy.' So you see, William's mission will ultimately succeed, and he has probably been received in the colony, by all but Mr. Coddington's party, as a hero. The Council has yet to make a ruling, but I assure you that it will be made official at the proper time.

"Mr. Coddington spent several years here in London," said Vane, "persuading members of the Council of how unruly the colony has been, and that if it should not be brought under the authority of Plymouth Colony, that he ought to be governor of the Island, by virtue of his founding of the place, and his financial holdings, and that he was among the members of the

Winthrop emigration, long before the rest of us. Why should Mr. Coddington not enjoy the status and honors enjoyed by Mr. Winthrop?"

Mary responded, "He and Will have been in and out of court for three years already, making accusations of trespassing, moving fences, stealing cattle, and the like. Our farms share fences, you know. I wish we could live together not only by treaty, but in harmony."

There was St. Paul's, there she could see Westminster Abbey, and as they rode along the Strand, she remembered the ducal residences along the Thames, and the New Exchange where Mr. Blackborne and Will had been proprietors of The Globe. Down that tiny lane leading to the river was the house where the Blackbornes and their apprentices had lived, and where she and Will had spent their first year and more of marriage.

Here in the upper-class district, the buildings were much finer, at least at the street level. The walls had a veneer of herringboned brickwork, and the bow windows' small panes glittered in the sun.

Under her warm cloak, Mary was dressed in black, with a flat, white lace collar over her shoulders like a shawl. Though she wasn't a Puritan, she was relieved to see through the carriage windows that her wardrobe would blend easily with the other prosperous women of London and Westminster, where the Puritan-majority Parliament was based. She'd need to do some shopping in the Strand, especially for evening wear. In Boston in the 1630s, she'd had textiles available from William Hutchinson, but the prescribed styles were severe—nun-like, really. Massachusetts women had only just escaped an order to veil their faces when John Endecott and Thomas Dudley had proposed a law, but the ultraconservatives had succeeded only in prohibiting jewelry and decorative embroidery. In Rhode Island, where she could obtain fine fabrics from Mr. Coddington's shop or from Edward Hutchinson, fashions were also sedate and modest, though as colorful as a woman wished. Women with a higher social standing dressed in the more expensive black-dyed fabrics.

But here in London, Mary thought she'd splurge on a dark satin stole and replace her practical fitted sleeves with some puff and flair. She was certainly not the worldly woman who bared her breasts right down to the nipple, as many society ladies did, nor did she wear jewelry to attract attention. But well-made, moderately-expensive clothing was considered a mark of respect to her husband's position and abilities, and Mary understood the value of taste and modest restraint. If a woman respected her husband, others would easily follow her example. By extension, they would respect a woman all the more.

London had changed little in the nearly two decades since Mary had left. But as they neared Henry's townhouse in Charing Cross, which was a stone's throw from St. Martin-in-the-Fields, Mary noticed that the cross monument, erected by King Edward I four hundred years before, had been dismantled. It was a place where official notices were read, and had been the center of an open area and a crossroads, a whipping post and gallows, even. "What happened here?" she asked Henry.

"Parliament ordered that it be demolished as an unholy relic of the papacy," he answered. "There was also a bronze statue of King Charles mounted on a horse, but that was ordered destroyed after the King's beheading. When you visit churches, you'll notice that the judgment scene and saint paintings have been painted or plastered over with white, and much of the stained glass has been destroyed. It's a shame to our noble ancestors and to the generations who come after us, that many tomb effigies and memorial decorations were vandalized or removed, condemned as graven images. Churches are very plain these days." Henry sighed at the memory of five hundred years of high art and rich colors, lost to whitewash and hammers in the hands of common (*very* common) soldiers.

"Why, Sir Henry," Blackborne chided, "You don't miss those pagan idols and the worship of statues, do you? Surely you prefer the purity, plainness, and austerity of England's houses of worship. A good Parliamentarian such as you, often in the company of Oliver Cromwell?" He looked pointedly at

Henry's hat that matched the dark blue velvet doublet, though there was a smile playing at the corners of his lips.

Henry reached up to his hat, stroked the ostrich plume, and shot back, "Of course not, Blackborne. I mourn the loss of beauty in churches. Did God create the world in gray and white and black? Did he not array the birds and the lilies of the field in brilliant color? As for me, am I not worth 'many sparrows?' And may I not,"—Henry winked—"when in a pinch, make practical use of this plume as a writing quill? At least that's what I would answer if a Parliamentarian dared criticize."

"You're the naval commissioner, president of the Council of State, and intimate of the Lord Protector Cromwell—which man in his right mind, who wants to keep his head—would demand that *you* conform to plain apparel styles?" Blackborne laughed. "I think what you need are a pair of Milanese cuffed boots from my shop. I'll have my apprentice bring them 'round tomorrow. Would you prefer blue or red silk lining?"

"Mr. Blackborne, you haven't changed a bit," laughed Mary. "And neither has Sir Henry."

The party alighted from the carriage and entered Vane's luxurious townhouse. Servants followed with Mary's trunk, and she was introduced to Lady Frances Vane, Henry's wife of twelve years. Lady Frances had borne a child every year of their marriage, and this year she bid fair for another, as Mary could see by the perhaps seven-months bulge under the beautiful silk gown. Frances was a gracious woman in her thirties, and it was obvious that she adored her husband.

Lady Frances's hair was pinned up, but in the fashion of the times, one auburn ringlet, a love lock, fell over her shoulder. Mary was just a little surprised to note that Lady Frances wore pearls over a low-cut bodice, and used cosmetics on her face when the "godly elect" were so adamant about women's adornment. Perhaps it was only the Massachusetts people who had gone to such extremes.

Still, Henry Vane was known to be broad-minded about religious practices, including the Seekers, the new sect of Quakers, Scottish Presbyterians, and the Anglican-Puritan relations. There was a range of tradition, doctrine, and practice in each sect and its believers. Conservative to liberal, moderate to extreme. Puritans in London were more liberal in lifestyle than those in New England. And in the same way Mary dressed to enhance her husband's reputation, Lady Frances dressed for her part.

"Mistress Dyer, what a pleasure it is to finally meet you. My dear husband has spoken of you so often, and holds you in high esteem. How do you find your old neighborhood?"

"It is at once no different, and changed significantly," Mary replied. "The prostitutes and sailors, the beggars and tradesmen, the goodwives and mothers look the same. The buildings, St. Paul's, Westminster, and the river look similar, but I see no familiar faces. I suppose that in the years since I left, many died of plague, or age, or have removed to America, and they've been replaced by new generations. The city seems much more crowded than I remember. Two decades ago, the royalists and Anglicans were in power, but now, at least on the surface, we see mostly Roundheads."

"Well, speaking of faces, yours is beautiful. You have a grace and confidence about you that would make a spectacular portrait. While you're here in London, perhaps you'll sit for an artist? Even Mr. Cromwell's wife, daughter, and mother have had portraits made, so you needn't worry about an accusation of vanity or of making a graven image."

"Oh, no," said Mary. "I don't worry about such things. I came to England for other reasons—matters of the soul, and of repairing a good name. Over the last years of religious and political controversy and a war that split our England, what I seek is simplicity, peace, and renewal."

"From what I hear, you left peace behind in Rhode Island. England is weary of war and want," said Frances with a sigh.

As they chatted, Lady Frances conducted Mary to her chamber and called her maidservant to allow Mary her first immersion bath in weeks, and dress Mary's hair for the evening. Then she disappeared for a few minutes and came back with a spectacular piece of cream lace for Mary. It was made for a Spanish lady's veil, she explained. A mantilla.

Draped gracefully around the mass of pinned-up hair and over Mary's shoulders, it was a work of art, Lady Frances declared.

The Vanes, the Blackbornes, and Mary sat at the dining table in Henry's townhouse that evening, with an empty place set for one more guest who would join them later. Mary couldn't help but count the number of dishes being served: though they'd only begun, she thought they were on course for the minimum recommendation of thirty-two offerings at a gentleman's board. She hoped she'd have the stamina to sample all of it, after weeks of stale and limited ship fare.

The last guest arrived and was shown to the table. He was a young man of perhaps twenty-four, with light-brown hair curled in waves to his shoulders in contrast to the short, straight cut of current mode. He wore a severe black coat and a fine linen white shirt in the Puritan fashion.

"May I present Mr. Thomas D'Arcy," said Sir Henry. "He had a late speaking appointment today, and I know you'll forgive his tardiness to dinner. D'Arcy, I present to you Mistress Mary Dyer of Newport, Rhode Island and of this very city where she was born. You know Walter and Elizabeth Blackborne and, of course, Lady Frances."

D'Arcy swept off his fashionable large-brimmed hat, bowed at the waist, and then sat in his place. He lowered his head in a brief silent prayer, then looked up at the dinner guests.

"Mr. D'Arcy, you bear a striking resemblance to Sir Henry, as we knew him in London and Massachusetts twenty years ago," Mary remarked. She didn't know what she'd said, but Henry and Thomas both blushed.

Henry answered, "My mother was a D'Arcy, so we share that blood. D'Arcy, why don't you tell Mistress Dyer about your employment?"

The young man swallowed a thin slice of cold ham and set down his knives. "I am often invited to teach at churches and meeting houses on lecture day. Though I have no parish or appointment of my own, it is my honor to give the ministers a helping hand. Most recently, I've been conducting a series from the book of Isaiah. In the uncertain times of the war, want, and establishment of the Commonwealth, hope is in short supply. People are seeking peace, compassion, and comfort, and Isaiah's prophecies of destruction are followed by promises of peace and plenty for those who obey the Lord. But forgive me for preaching at table."

D'Arcy took another bite of his supper and chewed industriously so as to let others speak.

Mary said, "That's an interesting interpretation of Isaiah, Mr. D'Arcy, one with which I agree. War, famine, and disease do afflict all of us, and how terrible it is that for some people, it's all they'll ever know in their short lives. The Lord bless you for giving people not only the hope, but the assurance of eternal life."

D'Arcy blushed again, trying to restrain his outburst. "But Mistress Dyer, no man knows if he is saved, and salvation is not open to all. Only God has predestined whom to save: those who obey. 'If you love me, keep my commandments,' he said."

Lady Frances glanced at Sir Henry, who understood her look. "Thomas," he interjected, "perhaps you'll be so good as to recite that sonnet that's going around of late. While you taste the roast beef, I'll tell Mary who composed the sonnet."

"John Milton is a man of most excellent learning, having received his Master's of theology at Cambridge. He's a valuable man for his brilliant mind and his gift with languages, and the Commonwealth has kept him busy by commissioning translations and religious-political apologies. Knowing that I, like him and my cousin D'Arcy here, desire the purification of the Anglican Church, by which we're called Puritans, he also appreciates my advocacy for freedom of conscience, and religious liberty for all: Seekers, Quakers, Catholics, Jews, and Mohammedans. Therefore the poetry."

D'Arcy was ready to recite without notes. He stood up and bowed toward Sir Henry from the waist before beginning.

"*To Sir Henry Vane the Younger*, by John Milton.
Vane, young in years, but in sage counsel old,
Than whom a better senator ne'er held
The helm of Rome, when gowns, not arms, repelled
The fierce Epirot and the African bold,
Whether to settle peace, or to unfold

The drift of hollow states hard to be spelled;
Then to advise how war may best, upheld,
Move by her two main nerves, iron and gold,
In all her equipage; besides, to know
Both spiritual power and civil, what each means,
What severs each, thou hast learned,
Which few have done
The bounds of either sword to thee we owe
Therefore on thy firm hand Religion leans
In peace, and reckons thee her eldest son."

Mary clapped with delight as Harry swelled with pride for a moment, then resumed his dignified manner.

"Oh, Harry! I mean Sir Henry. I'm sorry." Mary blushed.

"In private quarters, I'm still Harry."

She continued, "Mr. Milton has captured you so brilliantly, especially the couplet about being one of the few who understands the severing of civil and spiritual powers!" Her eyes twinkled. "Whatever would Governor Winthrop have said about that?"

Vane's eyes twinkled. "Perhaps we could arrange for the poem to be sent to Governor Dudley and Reverend Wilson."

He continued, "Milton is working on his next apologetic, with a sonnet to Oliver Cromwell. It's Milton's belief, he told me recently, that God doesn't save the state, even a Commonwealth in his name, but that he saves the individual believer. That I can agree with wholeheartedly, but he also denies a Trinity, and on that matter we part company for civility's sake."

Walter Blackborne spoke: "Sir Henry, with a decade and more of war behind us, and Ireland still being subdued, is it your belief that England will have yet another front in war, with the Dutch? Can England afford such a thing?"

Henry answered, "Many believe that keeping foreign ships—and that would mean Dutch ships, given their superiority in international trade—out of our English and colonial ports will increase this country's wealth, and that exports should exceed imports. We need to protect our colonial trade and keep it out of the way of the greedy Dutch, who already control the Orient. There have been several incidents of violence between Dutch and English traders."

"Between the French in the north and the Dutch to the south and west, the greater wealth of furs from New England has given England a miss," said Blackborne. "New England's colonial lands in Connecticut are continuously encroached upon by the Dutch from New Netherland who row upriver and trade with Indians. Anywhere they can sneak in and put up a trading post, they claim as Dutch territory. Will Dyer's letter to me said that the word going around is that the Dutch are bribing Indians to kill the English settlers."

Mary sighed, remembering the massacre nine years ago, when the Siwanoy slaughtered Anne and her household, who lived in a Dutch settlement.

Vane stabbed at the meat on his plate, agitated. "Men in the colonies are angry at the restrictions England has imposed since the Navigation Act. They freely trade with the West Indies and Europe, and wink at the rules that their vessels' crews must be composed of at least half English or American men.

"What we need," he continued, "are colonial traders who are loyal to England, who can be trusted to scrupulously obey our laws and stand with us against the Dutch. We can't trust the men of the Bay colony, who think first and only of their precious charter and of course their properties, not of the greater good of the community."

Blackborne considered this for a moment. "What about Will Dyer? He's loyal to you personally, he's a trader, and he's a captain in the militia. He knows his way around a ship, though not as a commander. It's the top man you need, not the ships' captains. He could organize the mercantile traders as a fleet to defend New England, if necessary."

Both men looked at Mary expectantly, waiting for an answer of some kind. Mary looked at D'Arcy, Elizabeth, and Lady Frances and saw no help forthcoming.

"Perhaps you'll write to William and explain your plans when you've taken counsel of other members of government,"

Mary said neutrally. "He doesn't hold orthodox Puritan beliefs, but most assuredly he is a man of honor and I've never questioned his loyalty to England, to Rhode Island, or to me."

Suddenly, Mary felt a sharp pain in her head, and for a heartbeat, she saw a vision she hadn't seen or remembered since the days she was a maiden: William Dyer commanding a ship with cannon, sailors working silently under moonlit sails while another ship lay nearby. A target ship.

"Lady Frances, please accept my apologies," Mary said, hoping her voice was steady. "The supper was delightful, and I've so enjoyed the conversation, but I've had full day, as you know."

"I'll help you, dear. Good night, gentlemen."

*****

TO WILLIAM DYER IN NEWPORT, RHODE ISLAND, IN NEW ENGLAND
30th of March, 1652
Dear of my heart,

Greetings of deepest love to you and our children.

By the grace of God and the skill of Mr. Travice, the ship has safely landed in England. Though we passed through some heavy winter gales in which the sails were lowered, otherwise, the strong seasonal winds filled our sails and the journey was shortened. Mr. Travice joined a fleet of English ships near Cornwall, which provided protection from Dunkirk pirates. He assured me that you were correct in saying that the pirates are less active here in the winter because they're lying thick on the waters of the Caribbean. But the ships of the fleet, some merchants and some navy, nevertheless, maintained vigilance throughout the passage on the Narrow Sea and up the Thames.

The Vanes and Blackbornes met me at the eastside docks and we have passed several pleasant days seeing the city landmarks like St. Paul's and its publishing district nearby, the Tower, Whitehall, and Southwark. The wars have taken a terrible toll on London's women and children. I've seen desperately poor women and children who have nothing to sell but their bodies, and nothing to eat but the eels they can catch in the river mud.

Here is a curious thing that was predicted by astrologers four years ago. The day before yesterday, the wealthy of London fled the city in coaches, just as they did for the plague. They went to country houses and farms to escape the panic and the possibility of riots. Here at the Vanes' house, the street windows and the doors were boarded closed for that reason. At the appointed time on Monday morning, the 29th, we went out into the walled garden to behold a near-total eclipse of the sun. We couldn't look at the sun, of course, but we watched the progress in the shadows cast through pinprick holes in thick paper. Harry estimated that more than nine-tenths of the sun was obscured as the moon passed over it. The sky was not dark as I expected, but a light twilight fell at half-past ten, and then gradually the light returned.

The effect of the eclipse on the people was fascinating. Laborers left their plows in the field, saying that they'd seen birds fall from the sky. Those in London would not work or stir from their houses. Some stood weeping in fright, knowing that their sin-guilt would cast them into the lake of fire at the soon-coming of the Lord. There was a thriving trade conducted in cordials to allay the effects of the eclipse. Preachers and prophets for various sects stood out in the marketplaces and street corners, crying out the day of wrath of God. They named the day Bugbear Black Monday, and by today, broadsheets littered the town. One of them called the eclipse a natural event and scolded those who had been terrified, saying,

What if Eclipse so great, it was no more than has been seen and told some years before.
Of only One 'tis best to stand in awe, to steer his course, and to obey his law.
God is the Guide, His Son, our Way, our Light, till he was once eclipsed, we had cause of fright.
Sin interposed 'twixt us and grace does strike the eclipse's horror on our face.

There can be no doubt that such a great natural event is ordained by the hand of God, but we have no reason to fear. "Learn not the way of the heathen, and be not dismayed at the signs of heaven; for the heathen are dismayed at them." Jer. 10:2. What remains is the interpretation of the sign, and what he expects us to learn from it. The next total eclipse will be in 1715 in our grandchildren's prime, and to be able to observe such a wonder once in my lifetime was a gift.

Of gifts, I'm shipping a small parcel for our children. There are books, mathematical instruments, and collars for the boys, and poppets for the little ones. Though I wish I could visit every market and purchase gifts for everyone in Newport, I remember the horrid poverty here as a result of war, and contrast it to the peaceful prosperity there, and resolve to do my utmost for the children of God whether they know him or not.

I pour my love for you into this letter and commend your health and safety to God.

MARY DYER,
At the Vane house in Charing Cross

*****

As soon as Mary was ensconced in his household, Henry Vane left his family to perform several missions for the Council of State. There was a journey to meet a republican-minded cardinal in France, the cardinal who was subsequently arrested and imprisoned by the king there—the king whose exiled nephew, Charles II of England, was his guest.

Then, as spring warmed to summer and Vane took his family north to Raby Castle in Durham, Henry was needed in Scotland to negotiate terms between the Scottish Presbyterian kirk and government, and the English Parliament under Oliver Cromwell. Between his journeys, Henry directed a committee which drafted new articles of war and codified naval law in order to make the navy work together as a whole.

The naval war with the Dutch expanded from the English Channel to the West Indies, where privateer George Avscue captured twenty-seven Dutch ships at Barbados, and his English privateer colleagues captured another hundred Dutch ships trading with the English colonies in the Indies in contravention of a Commonwealth embargo. The many Dutch losses caused the Dutch West India Company to equip one hundred fifty merchant ships as ships of war. They were not only losing to England, but to Spanish and French privateers in the West Indies and the Brazilian coast.

In New Amsterdam, the West Indies Company residents were unsettled. They were carrying out raids on some Indian tribes, living uncomfortably alongside others, and trading goods for Indian furs coming south on the rivers of New England. There were communities of English settlers among them, and pirates were thick in the waters around Long Island.

July 16, 1652
Narragansett Bay

"I thought fishing was supposed to be relaxing!" exclaimed Edward Hutchinson. He'd just pulled in his second striped bass, and both of them promised to weigh more than thirty pounds each. The silvery fish was so heavy and the suspense was so high that he'd land the monster before he lost his tackle, that his hair was plastered to his head with perspiration.

"You have the Sabbath tomorrow to rest. Good thing you've got a large family to relieve you of the burden of having to eat bass so often and in such quantities," said Richard Scott, who had caught a flounder and thrown it back for being too small. "I'm trying a new tactic with these wily fish."

Will Dyer had had no luck until Ed reeled in his striper, and then all of a sudden, the three men were overwhelmed with bass hitting their lures. Their rods dipped and rose as they reeled in the heavy lines with bass that seemed to want to be caught.

When they'd filled their baskets with fish that were the size of a child, they sat in the shade of the shallop's sail and poured out some cool beer and unwrapped the meat pies Katherine Scott had sent with them.

They were drifting a bit in the calm waters of a cove in Narragansett Bay, with the low, rocky cliffs of Dutch Island off to their starboard side, and Conanicut Island to their stern. The larger craft in the bay, the barques and sloops, sailed in the channel between the main and the islands, making for Providence. Narragansett men paddled their canoes to Dutch Island for Abraham van Deusen's trading post there, and the three fishermen could see a Dutch sloop tied up. Though the season was wrong for pelts, the natives brought wampum, venison, and fish to trade for cloth, farm implements, kettles, and liquor. The island, like many of the thirty or so islands in the bay, belonged to the Narragansett tribes. It was no wonder that the signature mark of their former chief sachem, Miantonomi, had been a small boat.

At other nearby trading posts, it was rumored that Indians could purchase arms, powder and shot from certain Dutchmen. This was extremely dangerous for every Dutch and English settler in New England, even Rhode Islanders and Providence men who had purchased land from the Indians. The old sachems were dead and a younger generation wanted their ancestral lands returned.

"Will, what is your experience of William Coddington's move to make himself governor for life, and take Aquidneck with him into Massachusetts or Plymouth colonies?" asked Edward. "And how could Harry Vane have allowed Coddington that charter?"

Will washed down the last of his pie with a swallow of beer.

"Harry wrote to me that Mr. Coddington, who possesses all the court books that I so carefully recorded over the last ten years, deceived—or at least misled by omission—the Council of State into thinking that it was he who made the transaction with Miantonomi and the tribes, he who owns Aquidneck and Prudence, he who should be lord of the bay islands. The deed of sale listed Coddington, not every investor or founder of the colony."

Richard added, "Mr. Coddington has interests in the usual channels like sugar and timber, but also in the slave trade in the Dutch West Indies. He trades heavily with New Amsterdam and he could expose the whole of Rhode Island *and* Providence Plantations to the tender mercies of the Dutch by using their ships to move his goods, and flouting the provisions of the Navigation Act."

Edward said, around a bite of apple, "Maybe even Massachusetts Bay. Coddington is staying on one of his properties there in Boston after the riot at his tenant's farmhouse and resulting chaos with his actions as governor. He certainly lost a great friend and ally when Governor Winthrop died."

Richard took off his hat and fanned himself in the afternoon heat. "I'm at a loss to figure how Coddington gets away with it all, when he has a minority of support."

"He suspended elections," said William. "He has disfranchised freemen. He and his council of six men have replaced the lawful court system with his own. He has money and land, and he holds leases with tenants. But most of all, he has had the authority of England to do it, by terms of his commission. Knowing Roger Williams, though, I trust it has been overturned by now, and we await the new or renewed charter for our colony."

"Hear, hear. Time we got our business back in order," Richard said.

"Do you think the war with the Dutch will come to New England?" asked William. "I'm wagering on it."

"You're a pessimist, Will," said Richard. "On the other hand, we may already be at war with the Dutch here, but haven't declared it. The Dutch towns and farms of Long Island and the mainland shores of New Netherland have suffered from the pirates coming up from Virginia and Maryland. And the French and Portuguese traders and pirates have harried the Dutch ships coming from Recife."

Will let a short silence fall over the boat. Then he said quite casually, "In two weeks, I'm going to England to bring my wife home, and to solicit the Council of State for a privateering commission."

His friends looked at each other, thunderstruck.

"Other men will try. I will succeed. I have the connections on both sides of the sea. I can stop the piracy and protect our own bay, at least, and expand the protection to the Sound and to Cape Cod with the right men. In taking ships and cargos of the Dutch, there are fat profits to be made, even after dividing the spoils with the Council, the Assembly, and the men of the fleet."

Edward said slowly, "You do know that after the wars are over, governments have difficulty distinguishing their own privateers from pirates. They'll turn on you. Hang you."

Will nodded. "I will be operating in familiar waters, and defensively rather than offensively. There is no temptation to work on my own as a rogue, and I'll propose that there will be oversight by an admiralty court, and full accounts made to the Council. And I anticipate support from the United Colonies. They'll be happy to be rid of the Dutch traders who sell arms to the Indians."

Ed was skeptical. "They already think your colony is Rogue's Island. This will only confirm it. If there's to be a privateer navy, they'll get commissions for their own. I could see you getting support from Johnny Winthrop, but Endecott? He'll either get his own ship and take charge of the slaughter, or send to England for a fleet."

"That's why I'm going to England now. They can call me the Chief Rogue of Rogue's Island if they like, but I'll have the license—and the prizes—before they do."

October 3, 1652

Westminster, England

Mary waited just inside the door of The Old Globe shop in the New Exchange for Walter Blackborne to conclude his accounts and for his apprentice to shutter and lock the millinery shop for the evening. The sharp scent of fine leather goods was one she'd nearly forgotten, after so many years in America.

The merchandise he showed on tables or hanging from hooks on the walls included capes, pouches, French and Spanish gloves, ready-made boots, leather-upholstered tables, and knives, daggers and swords with leather handles or scabbards. Mr. Blackborne also carried silver decorations for fancy saddles.

The New Exchange had become even more exclusive over the years, and catered to the aristocracy of Europe, and foreign diplomats who came to Westminster on state affairs. Though King Charles II and his retinue were in exile in France, it was plain to see that the English Commonwealth cavalry officers who patronized The Old Globe were anything but common.

Mr. Blackborne, for she could not bear to call her husband's old master by his Christian name, wrote the day's take on his ledger with the flourish of a feathered quill, and came from behind the bench to take Mary's arm.

"My dear, you are more beautiful as a wife and mother than you ever were as a girl of twenty," said the old man. "In your sober colors you have a sense of dignity and great worth, and there's a light in your face that never came from a candle."

Mary blushed and curtseyed. "As I stood here waiting for you, I remembered that you once carried silk, gold and silver thread, and ribbons that I used for embroidery. Where did you import them from?"

"Probably from right here in England, along with bolts of kersey and frieze and other textiles for overcoats. As a haberdasher and milliner, I often trade with the other guilds: the cordwainers and cobblers, the tailors, the mercers. Why do you ask?"

"Oh, just something that William teased me about long ago. Are you ready to escort me to supper with the Vanes?"

They went out into the Strand and he hailed a coach. It was only a short distance to Charing Cross, but he was no youngster, and the streets were full of carts, carriages, animals, and people. And among the people were thieves and rogues. They detoured to bring Elizabeth Blackborne with them in the coach.

William Dyer and Henry Vane were already celebrating the day's events with fine Bordeaux when they arrived at the Vane townhouse.

Will had clearly had more than one glass of wine, though he wasn't slurring his speech. "Harry did it! He greased the wheels and got my petition into the Council of State. Didn't you, Harry?"

"Indeed, and I could not be more proud of you. Ladies and gentlemen, we count among our number a new naval commander, the commissioned Captain William Dyer. He's the first in all of America to hold this esteemed position."

"Huzzah!" came the chorus from the Blackbornes, Mary, Pastor Thomas D'Arcy, and Lady Vane. A servant poured glasses of Bordeaux for all of them, and they drank toasts to Sir Henry and Will.

Harry held up his glass. "Sir Walter Raleigh said this many years ago: 'Whosoever commands the sea commands the trade of the world; whosoever commands the trade of the world commands the riches of the world, and therefore the world itself.' That is the fascination I find as a commissioner of the navy."

Again, everyone raised their glasses and took a sip.

"Tell us what the order says," said the elder, Mr. Blackborne.

Will read the gist of it: "The New England colonies and Rhode Island in particular, are to 'raise such forts and otherwise arm and strengthen your Colony, for defending yourselves against the Dutch, or other enemies of this Commonwealth, or for offending them, as you shall think necessary; and also to take and seize all such Dutch ships and vessels at sea, or as shall come into any of your harbors, or within your power, taking care that such account be given to the State as is usual in the like cases. And, to that end, you are to appoint one or more persons to attend the care of that business; and we conceive the bearer hereof, Mr. William Dyer, is a fit man to be employed therein; and you are to give account of your proceeding to the Parliament or Council."

Vane concluded, "It's signed by Major-General James Harrington, president of the Council this month, and John Thurloe, clerk of the Council, but Oliver Cromwell and I were parties to the decision and the subsequent order."

"What comes next, Sir Henry?" asked Thomas.

"It's my place to secure the funds to outfit William properly, but that can't be done in haste, especially when the Navy is desperate for ships. It may take a few weeks to find the money, and to find an American-built ship or ships to fill the requirements."

There were many congratulations and suggestions, laughter, and serious talk of the war with the Dutch. Mary smiled at the appropriate times, but didn't add to the conversation.

October 27, 1652
London, England

Will thought he hadn't done badly at planning the day's outing: a stroll from Henry Vane's townhouse up to St. Martin-in-the-Fields to recall the day exactly nineteen years ago when he and Mary had been wed at the church doorway, and the same day the following year, when he'd buried their first child. He'd bought the midday meal at Covent Garden, including a bowl of exotic and expensive pineapple chunks, the fruit having been imported from South America via Portugal. He'd hired a boatman at Whitehall Stairs to take them on a sightseeing cruise on the Thames.

The barges and ferries, ships and small boats, were thick on the water's edges, and boys with baskets of stinking lampreys picked through the muck for shellfish to supplement their catches that they'd peddle to cook shops.

His wife was nestled under his arm for pleasure, not because of the cold. There had been several terrific storms the last several weeks, and the Thames still ran muddy from flood runoff. This day was overcast and cool, and there was an occasional mist, but Mary was a native Londoner and took no notice. They pointed at landmarks like the Tower, St. Paul's, and as they were paddled westward, the ducal palaces of Somerset, Durham, and York.

His wife seemed pensive and melancholy, and a song came to mind that he thought would lighten her mood. As he sang to her, she nestled closer into his coat and closed her eyes.

The water is wide, I cannot get o'er
Neither have I wings to fly
Give me a boat that can carry two
And both shall row, my love and I.

A ship there is and she sails the sea
She's loaded deep, as deep can be
But not so deep as the love I'm in
I know not if I sink or swim.

Oh love be handsome and love be kind
Gay as a jewel when first it is new
But love grows old and waxes cold
And fades away like the morning dew.

When cockle shells turn silver bells
Then will my love come back to me
When roses bloom in winter's gloom
Then will my love return to me.

"You left some verses unsung," Mary reminded him.

"They were too morbid. This is the anniversary of our wedding. We should be rejoicing."

William changed the subject. "I've got my commission. In a few weeks I'll be invested by the navy, and then I hope for the grant of ships to outfit and sail back to defend our waters."

Mary squirmed, sat up straight, and spoke sharply. "This war on the Dutch, which began with greed for foreign ports, is only about money, and the power that money buys. *You* have money, honestly gained by your hard work. You have the money that I brought to our marriage from Uncle John and from my father and brother. Why isn't that enough? Will, please, I'm begging you: don't make war on innocent Dutch traders and farmers. Don't make up charges so you can steal what they've gained by honest work. Go home, make just laws in the Assembly, and run the farm."

He replied, "This situation is much larger than me and the farm, or even about our trade routes and ports. Privateering is an indispensable weapon of war, and as you know, the realm needs the prizes to finance the navy, thereby saving our own people from crippling taxes. It defends our liberties to trade and import what we need to feed our families."

"Oh, it's patriotism now?" she retorted. "War is noble and glorious when it's not our English fathers and sons and breadwinners dying before cannon and musket shot, and it's only the filthy, greedy foreigners who lose their lives and their women and children die of want."

"Mary! Is this something you've learned from street preachers? Disloyalty to your country? Rebellion to proper authority? And yes, it *is* patriotism. The Dutch on Long Island have been caught supplying Indians with arms to kill English men and women. We're not starting a war. The war has been forced upon us."

Mary lowered her voice so the boatman wouldn't hear. "Do you go so far as to call Oliver Cromwell 'proper authority?' I've never met George Fox, though I've listened to his followers and respect what they have to say about the peace of God, and making time and place to listen for his direction. If the Spirit speaks, I must obey, though men might call it rebellion."

"Well, I've had enough of this uneducated rabble-rouser Fox, and the Seekers, and naked Familists, and so have you. I've spoken to a ship's master about your passage back to Newport. There's a ship that leaves the first week of December, and goes by way of Barbados, so you can have a holiday there while cargo is exchanged. Just think of palm trees and warm sand in January!" He smiled.

She crossed her arms. "I'm not ready to return."

"How can you say that? You have six children who need their mother. Not to mention, your husband loves you and wants you home where you belong."

"I'm staying in England for a while longer."

"How much longer do you propose?"

"I don't know, honestly."

"If I allow you to stay—" at this, Mary glared at him, "what would I say to the children? Or anyone in Rhode Island? How do I explain a mother's reluctance to return to her own home and children?"

"You can say that you weren't willing to risk my safety while there's a naval war raging, and privateers lurk in bays or under cover of fog banks to snatch away safety, security, and personal property. You can say that Rhode Island and Providence Plantations are in an uproar and can't even govern their own affairs."

"Sarcasm doesn't become you, Mary. What is your real reason?"

"I've told you before, and my story won't change because it's the truth. God has called me to England for a time. He's only shown me one step at a time on the path, and I don't know the destination. But he's put it in my heart that I should be here now, and he will reveal the time and circumstances of my journey here, and when it's time to go back home."

Will was silent for a few moments. "Sweetheart, you've plunged a sword in my heart. How can I fight for you when my adversary is God?"

*****

TO WILLIAM DYER IN NEWPORT
31 December 1652
My dear old friend,

Knowing that you and Mary must inevitably return from Old England, I'm sending this letter to Newport. I trust your petition to Harry Vane was successful. Surely Mary will be glad to be back home with her children. My aunt Katherine recently sent me a good report on your youngest three.

Samuel is a faithful lad as he goes about his duties here, though for his own edification and in prevention of pride, I would never say it to him. His chief topic of conversation is marksmanship on training days, and I admit he does very well.

For three weeks in October and November the Bay experienced several severe storms that prostrated houses and barns and drove vessels ashore in the wind and waves. I haven't heard if they affected your lands at Narragansett, but perhaps the Lord stayed the worst damage.

Two significant events have got the ministers here furiously writing and preaching reformation and revival sermons, the like of which will not be heard again for years. From the 9th to the 22nd of December, from the waxing moon to the waning moon, a comet blazed forth from the foot of

Orion. It was perhaps 16 inches from sparkling head to fiery tail, and people trembled to see it, for comets have been known as omens of war, plague, and momentous occasions ordained by God. The comet faded away into the sunrise, even as we wondered at its meaning. The next day, the 23rd, John Cotton died. He was 67, so he lived longer than some other men, but one thinks, somehow, that he should have gone on another fifteen years. Perhaps the comet was a divine message about the loss of the great man.

Mr. Cotton was much beloved of my parents for years before he turned away from the covenant of grace—but with that turning, my mother and your wife were trampled. He became ever more conservative over the years, and more in harmony with Mr. Wilson. Yet flashes of the younger Cotton, the Cotton I emigrated with, and lived with for a year, came through in a wedding he spoke for. He said, "There is no stricter or sweeter friendship than conjugal," and he certainly loved his wife Sarah and their children, though he raised them very strictly. All in all, I'm sorry that Boston has lost the man. Except for a short time when I was in Rhode Island, he was my church teacher from my earliest childhood until now.

I pray that your voyage was uneventful and swift, and that your cases with Rhode Island courts, your farm and trading business, are prospering under God's watchful eye. My best regards to your wife, and a warm welcome home to both of you. I look forward to our first fishing expedition of the spring.

LT. EDWARD HUTCHINSON
Boston, Massachusetts

Newport, Rhode Island

February 18, 1653

William Dyer huddled in his coat against the stiff, icy wind as he rather drunkenly lurched down the gangplank from the frigate on which he'd traveled from England, to the wharf at Newport. He had not been drinking—he just didn't have his land legs yet, and this had been a harrowing crossing of the Atlantic. Few ships crossed in the depth of winter because of the raging storms and monstrous waves of icy seas that could send even a large and stable galleon to the bottom of the ocean.

Because of the rampant piracy—not only the Dutch, but French, Spanish, and English—and attendant kidnappings in the Caribbean, this ship, even though heavily armed with cannon, had made straight for New England instead of taking a triangular course for Recife, Barbados, or another balmy port before sailing north to Boston or Newport. Indeed, William had urgent business in New England, as much as he longed for turquoise lagoons and white sands, and he couldn't afford a delay.

On the quay, he recognized a young man, Edward Hull, who was master of his father's and brother's frigate, the *Swallow*.

"Mr. Hull," William called. "May I speak with you?"

The man, recognizing the famous Captain Dyer, hurried over. Hull looked a bit nervous to William. As he should be, meeting the colony's attorney general. Edward Hull was becoming infamous for his shady business dealings in the Long Island Sound.

"Yes, Mr. Dyer, sir?"

"What are your plans for trading in the next several months? New England? Virginia? The Caribbean? I may have some business to throw your way."

"Thank you, sir! With all the piracy and privateering in the South, I hadn't planned on the islands unless I went with a convoy. I'd prefer to stay on the American coast."

"From what I hear," William said severely, while giving Hull the up-and-down measuring eye, "you and Tom Baxter are pirates yourselves."

"Just the talk of dissatisfied tradesmen, probably."

"Cheeky boy. Nevertheless, I would like to meet with you and see how we can mutually benefit each other. Next time you come in to Newport, let me know."

Hull nodded eagerly. "Yes, Mr. Dyer. Thank you, Mr. Dyer."

Now that Will was in Newport, he made for a tavern on the square where he could warm up with a deep bowl of stew, and fresh bread, and red meat. He couldn't stand one more night of cold, hard, stale rations on the ship, and his own household didn't know he was home.

He took his luncheon alone in the corner, not by the fire with its rowdy drinkers. He spread a letter or two about the table to signal that he was not available to join the songs.

Having finished his meal and warmed his hands and feet, William gathered his belongings and stepped out into the town square.

His cargo wouldn't be unloaded and ready for him until morning, so he collected his small trunk and hired a riding horse from the hostler, and set off down the road to Dyer Gate, and then onto his own land.

William had left home in late July, when his fields and orchards were at their best, and the breeze bent the hay and wheat in deep ripples, as if Mary were shaking out a freshly-laundered bed sheet. Flowers had scented the hedgerows, and the salty brine from the beach freshened the air, so unlike the fetid smells of decay and ordure in London, and even on the ship. Now, everything had been harvested and the land plowed in neat furrows, silent and frozen. Behind Conanicut Island, the sun lowered into a fog and disappeared. The snow, ice fog, dark earth, and black tree bark robbed his world of color, leaving only black and white patches and stripes.

But now William was home again. *His* home, and beautiful it was. No English manor house—it was closer to a farm house or a cottage—but it was his. He took a turn around the nearest paddock and was pleased to see that his mares looked healthy. The cattle and sheep looked well, too, and the ewes would be lambing soon, he could tell from their girth. He dismounted and pulled open the barn door to find one laborer mucking out stalls and one oiling and polishing the horse tack. The mucking should have been a morning job, and the boy knew it, so he blushed and attacked his job with vigor at the sight of the master come home. Will addressed the older boy, "See that this horse is groomed and fed, and you may return him to town in the morning," and gave a stern look at the slacking boy before he turned to go to the house.

He lifted the latch and the housemaid, Cathy, looked up from dicing vegetables, surprised. "Mr. Dyer! We never expected you until April or May! Where is the mistress? Coming along in a moment?"

"Mrs. Dyer is still in England. You just continue what you were doing. I'm going up to get some work done. I doubt I'll want supper—well, maybe some beer and cheese in an hour or two."

"Your bed linens will need airing and I'll heat a brick to warm the bed. Let me light a lamp for you, to banish the gloom of the fog." Cathy bustled around, fussing around the master until he was annoyed.

"All right, all right. I'll work in the sitting room while you take care of all that. I'm tired of travel and glad to be home, but there's urgent work ahead of me. I'll want no distractions tonight, nor in the days to come." Not when he had all the carefully-worded letters to write!

"Mr. Dyer, one more question: will you be bringing the children home?"

"Yes, but not immediately. Samuel, William, and Maher may be in and out as I or their masters have need of them. And I expect to be coming and going at odd times with my government responsibilities."

He took an unlit candle and settled at the table in the sitting room. It wasn't dark yet, but would be soon. He set out his writing implements and the folio of expensive paper and wrote first to the Scotts about his younger children, that Mary was remaining in England, and his new duties would require frequent movements about the colonies.

William Dyer, attorney general for Rhode Island, wrote to the assemblies of the island faction, asking that they meet at Portsmouth "upon Tuesday come seven-night," to discuss the order from the Council of State that revoked William Coddington's governorship for life, and put an end to the schism that threatened to put the island under Plymouth rule and Providence and the mainland, including Warwick, under Puritan Connecticut's tender mercies. Instead, he contended, the two governments, torn apart by Mr. Coddington's policies and departure, should reunite for strength and common good of all.

He wrote to the men in Rhode Island who he could count on for favorable votes in confirmation of his appointment as commander. He wrote to the young man he'd seen at the wharf today, the most important rogue on Long Island Sound, Edward Hull, the brother of the Boston silversmith and ship owner, John Hull. Edward and his pirate friends would be a ready squadron for the war on the Dutch.

Then there was the issue of his Council of State commission to oversee the naval war against the Dutch. He wasn't sure how it would be received with such a diverse group of Assemblymen. But he carried orders from the Lord Protector Oliver Cromwell, directing the governors of the New England colonies to vindicate English rights and extirpate the Dutch from Manhattoes Island and New Netherland. He, William Dyer, was the man designated to carry out the orders and desires of the Commonwealth.

He reread part of his assignment from John Thurloe (though he'd all but memorized it on the voyage): "You are immediately to deliver or send away the letters committed to you, directed to the several governors of the colonies of the Massachusetts, Plymouth, Connecticut, and New Haven, with intimation to them from yourself of your arrival, and expectation of a sudden answer to the contents of the said letters."

> THE PROTECTOR TO THE GOVERNORS OF THE ENGLISH COLONIES IN AMERICA
>
> "Gentlemen,
>
> "We are assured you have been long since acquainted with the hostile attempt of the Dutch, and their injurious proceedings in reference to this Nation; whereby the long continued amity betwixt us and them hath not only been disturbed, but an open and fierce war raised and prosecuted, to the shedding of much blood; which yet continues, through the averseness of their spirits to ways of peace."

Cromwell chided the colonies for failing to meet the expectation that they would defend English rights and stop the Dutch traders who invaded their chartered lands, and that they'd been non-compliant with English policies and previous directives. He said that they knew by experience that the war with the Dutch was a just war, and that God's blessing would therefore rest upon the English cause. "However," Cromwell wrote,

> "we have added to the number and strength of ships designed for those parts upon another service, and in them sent such proportion of ammunition, powder, &c. as may be helpful to your stores in that kind, for furnishing a competent number of land soldiers; as also given commission to Mr. William Dyer, that if there be a concurrence in your colonies to the work (whereof we see little reason to doubt their utmost assistance may be given), for gaining the Manhattoes or other places under the power of the Dutch. We have referred to such as are to be trusted by us in this service, to consider with yourselves or others, to whom you shall commit the managing of that affair; and to determine what number of men may rationally be sufficient to carry on the design; that being fittest to be concluded upon the place, where the numbers and strength of the enemy, with his condition in other respects, may be best understood."

Cromwell said that although some of the colonies are more immediately concerned in this work than others, that their union should engage them in a mutual assistance each of other.

> "We see no considerations that may hinder any of your colonies joining readily and vigorously with the rest in this work, which concerns the common welfare. We desire all possible expedition may be used in carrying on this design, and our ships dismissed, that they may seasonably attend that other service, to which they are appointed; and so commending you and your affairs to the goodness of God, we rest, &c."
> OLIVER CROMWELL
> JOHN THURLOE, Secretary

Below the text of the letter, there dangled on a wide ribbon the wax imprint of the Great Seal of the Commonwealth of England: an engraving of scores of Parliament men centered around the throne of the Protector. The words around the edge of the disk were: "1651 IN THE THIRD YEAR OF FREEDOM BY GODS BLESSING RESTORED."

*****

CAPT. JOHN UNDERHILL, TO THE GOVERNOR AND ASSISTANTS IN THE GENERAL COURT AT NEW HAVEN
25 February 1653
Most Reverend Governor John Davenport and assistants,

The English natives on Long Island living under the double sovereignty of English and Dutch rule are in desperate hazard. They are subjected to the bloody plottings of Director-General Pieter Stuyvesant. All indications are that the governor has paid bribes to the Indians here and promised to set off and destroy the English natives in these parts. They are in continual fear to lose their lives and their lands unless some speedy and defensible remedy is so provided. Some believe that the Dutch here are selling ammunition to the Indians.

I pray that you will keep this message close, considering my employment with the Dutch and the turbulence which Governor Stuyvesant has brought to his office and the plantations.

I seek your prayers and your counsel as our English citizens live in the valley of the shadow of death.
CAPT. JOHN UNDERHILL
Flushing, Long Island

*****

TO CAPTAIN JOHN UNDERHILL AT FLUSHING ON LONG ISLAND
1st March 1653
My old friend,

I pray that you and your family continue in perfect health and prosperity and that God blesses your magistracy in Flushing. Regarding the Dutch and Indian unrest on Long Island, I am confident that you're well able to keep your family safe by transporting them to the mainland if necessary.

The order of the Council of State, appointing me to oversee the defense and offense against the Dutch, has been made known to Rhode Island assemblies, though they claim that they would prefer I limit my activities to the duties of the attorney general, saying that my commission would deprive them of my services, and evade and frustrate "justice in diverse weighty causes pending in our courts." By this, they seek to delay or deny the actions that the Council has ordered. Nevertheless, they have agreed to study how best to proceed.

Please consent to meet with me in a place you suggest that is quiet and inconspicuous, perhaps on the eastern reaches of Long Island, or at Newport, and as soon as you are able. With your experience and connections, and my communications and commission, I have a proposal for you to consider. My messenger will wait for your reply.
WM DYER
Newport, Rhode Island

William folded and enveloped the letter, and sealed it carefully with wax. He would send a messenger to Captain Underhill. The letters to the governors he would take in person.

May 15, 1653
Newport, Rhode Island

"I must say, Dyer, that I wasn't sure the commissions would pass the Assembly, notwithstanding the will of Cromwell, Vane, Thurloe, and the rest of the Council of State. As it is, we only have the support of some of the Aquidneck men, and not even the landsmen of Providence Plantation."

John Underhill's gravelly voice was a contrast to the soft tendrils of fog drifting in from the Narragansett Bay. The three-quarters moon shown low in the eastern sky to their right.

"Yet they did pass, perhaps from the weight of Mr. Cromwell's orders," said Will, "and I have no doubt that Providence and Pawtuxet will follow in a few days. Once they get a whiff of the profits to be made, they'll swarm like ants to honey. They'll argue and threaten, but in the end, we'll prevail."

The men were walking William's two horses from the town, where they'd had dinner in a tavern, back to the Dyer farm. There was no hurry on such a fine spring night.

"I confess my worry that the landsmen will not commission the rogue Edward Hull, after his high-handed antics two weeks ago," said William.

The young Massachusetts man had not asked permission or commission, and had launched his own opportunistic war on the Dutch.

A captain of the Dutch West India Company, Kempo Sebada, had worked for several years as a privateer in the West Indies, taking ships, cargos, and passengers from English, French, and Spanish captains. Lately, he'd made a home at an Indian trading post on Block Island, formerly Pequot and then Massachusetts Bay Colony territory just south of Narragansett. Some of the items he traded were drinking glasses, beads, Jew's harps—and ammunition for the Indians. Last month, Sebada's ship had been lying in the Connecticut River's mouth when Hull pulled his surprise attack, and took the Dutch ship and Sebada himself for ransom. Next, pressing his advantage, he made for Block Island, and raided Sebada's trading post for £96 worth of goods. Connecticut fined Sebada for selling weaponry to the Pequots and other tribes, and released him to Dutch authorities, but Sebada's ship had been impounded until a decision could be made about its ownership.

William snorted. "What was Hull thinking, acting without a commission or letters of marque? Surely he'll be tried for kidnapping and theft, if not piracy."

"He's a valuable captain and he made the most of his opportunity, but what the Assembly or the United Colonies will covet most is use of Hull's frigate. He'll be confirmed," averred Underhill. "If there's a trial in New England, he'll win. But he'll be a 'marked' man in New Netherland if he's ever caught there."

William chuckled at Underhill's pun. "Tell me about this fellow Baxter, who lived so recently in New Amsterdam."

Underhill answered, "Tom Baxter is another young rake in his twenties. If we were back in England, he'd either be an apprentice clerk to an unscrupulous lawyer, or a highwayman. In America, he has a chance to prosper and he thinks the fastest way to riches is with the Dutch. New Amsterdam fears what will happen to them in this war, exposed as they are on three sides of the Manhattan Island, and on the north from English like me, and those of New Haven. Stuyvesant and his colonists are disturbed about the Indians turning on them, as the Siwanoy killed Anne Hutchinson ten years ago, thinking she was Dutch, because she lived on a Dutch farm. And it's understandable because Dutchmen like Kempo Sebada and some farmers are stirring up the native Indians in the present day. So the council allocated six thousand guilders' worth of wampum to purchase oak posts from Baxter to build a wall to protect lower Manhattan. He did fulfill that contract, and the wall was finished on May Day, I understand. But his insolence has got him in trouble. He had to flee before Stuyvesant arrested him. He abandoned his wife, baby, a small house, and his catboat at Schreyers Hoek, the southern point of the island."

"Where is he biding now?" asked Dyer.

"He's at New Haven—when he's not playing the pirate game with small farms on the coasts of the Sound."

"We can use his knowledge of the waters and farms around the Sound in our fleet. Perhaps we'll be able to teach him some discretion."

Underhill snorted in derision and replied in his gravel voice, "William, you're too idealistic. Men like Hull and Baxter were always fated to be pirates. As de facto admiral, you'll call them privateers, and use them as long as they mind the laws, look away when they break the laws, and denounce them when it's expedient to cut ties. Meanwhile, your admiralty court and the Council of State will profit handsomely. This is the way of all military commanders."

"Should I really take advice from a man who still has a prison pallor to his skin?" William asked, on the edge of laughter.

Two weeks before, when Edward Hull had been pirating the pirate, Kempo Sebada, John Underhill had been cooling his temper in the New Amsterdam jail. His suspicion that the Dutch were plotting with the Indians to kill the English had been confirmed. Underhill had publicly rebelled against Pieter Stuyvesant and raised the English Parliamentary colors over Flushing, which prompted Stuyvesant to arrest and jail Underhill for a few days in New Amsterdam, before his charges were dismissed. Upon release, he'd settled his wife, children, and mother-in-law in New Haven at his properties there, and made for Newport.

"You may trust me, Dyer, for whilst in the Dutch cobhole, I learned more precisely what kind of prideful, tyrannical man the enemy is, and I recruited several more rogues for the cause."

The two men had reached the gate to the Dyer farm, and after stabling the horses, they talked long into the night.

*****

TO CAPT. WILLIAM DYER AT NEWPORT IN RHODE ISLAND
17th March 1653
My dear friend and elder brother,

Upon receipt of your letter last month, I was saddened to learn of your wife's necessity to stay in England for the present. However, in light of present circumstances, I must say I agree with your decision to delay her return.

You will, of course, have heard of the Dutch plot to kill the English on Long Island. I will add my account of the affair so you may know it first-hand. The Dutch West Indies Company had sent a ship laden with arms and ammunition for the specific purpose of laying waste to the English. They hired four Indian sagamores to burn and slay whatever they could on a Sabbath day, when all the English families would be at church meeting. But one Indian informed the magistrates of Boston as to his colleagues' intentions. I was sent, with Mr. Gardner, Mr. Hooper, and Mr. Severn, as well as a company of men, to defend the settlement and see what we could discover. At the first wigwams we searched, we found them full of arms and ammunition, with muskets charged with powder and ball. Some Indians confessed that they were hired by the Dutch to be instruments of a bloody massacre on the English.

Salem alone sent 154 men, and besides, most men of the southwest part of Massachusetts holdings volunteered their service in defense of their countrymen in peril. May the Lord deliver the oppressed from their terror and grant victory to the defenders, and may he crown their efforts, at the end, with peace.

I suppose that until the war is concluded, we must forgo our pleasant reunions and fishing. Richard and Katherine will seek refuge here in Boston if hostilities by Dutch or Indians threaten their family, and your little children will be safely cared for, as well.

God grant you peace and well-being.

CAPT. EDWARD HUTCHINSON
Boston, Massachusetts

*****

Newport, Rhode Island

June 30, 1653

William was grateful that the Sabbath was past and he could work without disapproval of his colleagues, in these last days before the official volleys were to be fired in the war on the Dutch. The frigate in Newport Harbor had been fitted with cannon and stocked with firearms, powder and shot, grappling hooks, and block and tackle rigging to transfer crates from another ship or a dock into the hold of the galleon.

The ship itself had been supplied by Sir Henry Vane, naval treasurer, as the admiralty flagship for Captain Dyer in the war on the Dutch. Though it was owned by the navy, it had been built in New England, of strong American woods.

William thought secretly that when the war ended and he had to send this beauty off to England, it would be like losing a limb—perhaps like Pieter Stuyvesant losing his right leg to a cannon ball, and hobbling around on a wooden peg.

William's fleet was quite small, but experienced for the task. Edward Hull had his letters of marque from the Rhode Island Assembly, and Thomas Baxter had also brought his piratical skills and personal grudge against the Dutch. They had their own ships, and had pledged to take Dutch vessels to add to the English cause.

But for what William and Captain Underhill had planned, they didn't need a navy. There would be no blockades or battles at sea, only a show of force.

TO HIS HONOR, SIR HENRY VANE, AT WESTMINSTER
30 JUNE 1653
Greetings to you and the esteemed members of the Council of State.

It is most humbly prayed that your honors' most considerable advantages are to be made in Your Plantations, as shall be demonstrated by the fulfillment of the commission you made to go against the Dutch. The Assembly of Providence Plantations and Rhode Island, and the United Colonies of New England have confirmed your order of October 2nd, 1652.

In addition to my commission as Commander-in-Chief Upon the Seas, Captain John Underhill has been confirmed as Commander-in-Chief Upon the Land. Sir Henry well knows his capabilities and history. Letters of marque have been made for Captain Edward Hull and several other men.

An admiralty court, consisting of myself, attorney general, John Sanford, president of the Rhode Island Assembly, and Nicholas Easton, former governor and moderator, shall comply with your order to take care that the state's part of all the prizes be secured and account given. Sir Henry has known these men during his governorship in America and through correspondence, and can vouchsafe their abilities.

The Rhode Island Assembly, sitting at Newport, voted that "for the trial of prizes brought in according to law the General Officers with three jurors of each town shall be authorized to try it. The President and two assistants shall have authority to appoint the time, but if any fail at the time appointed, either officers or jurors, the jurors shall be made up in the town of Newport when they shall be tried. In the case that any of the officers fail, then those that appear shall proceed according to the law of Oléron," ancient maritime law.

Newport voted a further action, that 20 volunteers and cannon and small arms be sent to the English on Long Island, the better to defend themselves against the Indians who had been incited to violence by the Dutch.

As you know, the Providence Assembly has accused the Newport Assembly of collusion with Mr. Coddington to partition the colony. Nothing can be further from the truth, as you know after granting the colony—the entire colony—the charter with your full approval, and revoking Mr. Coddington's lifetime appointment. Nevertheless, certain men continue to agitate from the other side of the Bay. Men at Warwick and Providence made a vigorous protest to Newport's commissions, made in accordance with your decree, saying that "for aught we know, it will set all New England on fire, for the event of war is various and uncertain." Mr. Samuel Gorton declared that they would petition to England in case of trouble (such as if they dislike and defy our execution of your orders). However, on 27 May, Providence Plantations finally confirmed the commissions of Newport's Assembly.

As for setting New England alight, the Connecticut government has not prevented our mission, but has petitioned that Captain Underhill and I take action on the Dutch fort and trading post at Hartford, called the House of Good Hope, and claim it and its goods for England and the colony. We are even now preparing for that action, and you may expect a report as soon as the matter is concluded.

With your honors' leave, your petitioner shall ever pray, &c.

CAPT. WM. DYER
Newport, Rhode Island

July 1653
Raby Castle, County Durham, England

Had she wanted to go back to Rhode Island after a year and a half away from her children, Mary could not have done so. The English Channel was not safe for passenger travel, as Zeeland pirates and privateers hid in coves to attack English convoys plying the waters. The war with the Dutch continued with the taking of ships in privateer and navy actions.

More battles raged in Westminster. The Rump Parliament had been in the act of passing a bill sponsored by Harry Vane on April 20, when Oliver Cromwell, who disagreed with the act which proposed sweeping electoral changes, called guards into the chamber and dissolved Parliament, much like the hated King Charles had done twenty years before. Vane described the conversation to his wife and Mary.

"This is not honest; it is against morality and common honesty," protested Vane in the chamber.

Cromwell shouted back in annoyance with a mocking tone, "O Sir Henry Vane, Sir Henry Vane; the Lord deliver me from Sir Henry Vane!"

"In that," Vane recounted, "Cromwell repeated something similar to the impatience of King Henry II in 1170, when he wished aloud to be rid of the 'turbulent priest' the Archbishop of Canterbury, and four knights rushed to relieve Thomas Becket of his head."

Though he was asked to serve on a Parliamentary committee, Harry kept his head by removing himself and his family to their summer home, the medieval Castle Raby; but he and his radical colleagues in Parliament and the Council of State lost all political sway. Cromwell declared an end to the Commonwealth and that the new era would be ruled by the Lord Protector, himself. Cromwell was now either a dictator or a commoner king, depending on the perspective of the viewer.

The castle, which Harry's father had bought from King Charles in 1626, was situated in the countryside of Durham, a county between Yorkshire and Northumberland. Unlike most castles in England and Scotland, which had been reduced to rubble and ragged curtain walls by cannon fire, Raby had suffered only moderate damage, and reparable at that, because the Vanes were on the "right" side in the civil war struggles between the royalists and Parliament.

Like his brothers and sisters year after year, Christopher Vane was born at Raby. Sadly, several of the Vane babies had died during infancy. The strong, healthy baby, named for his grandfather Wray, came screaming into the world on May 21, and Mary Dyer was there to keep Frances company during her confinement, delivery, and lying-in after her eleventh child.

Harry Vane continued his moral support and interest in nonconformist, fringe religion groups, most notably the Seekers, who believed like Puritans that the Church of Rome was corrupt, and because of its Catholic heritage, the Church of England by extension. The Seekers held their meetings in silence, with no rituals or liturgy, and expected that the worshipers would receive divine guidance through inspiration from God. Women as well as men could receive and interpret the grace they found in their hearts, and could speak of their revelations, though not in public if they feared the wrath of the religious leaders.

Mary had seen broadsheet cartoons that showed the approved, orthodox religious meetings, where men and women heard a short-haired man in a cap, which indicated a Puritan minister, surrounded by church pillars and diamond-paned glass windows; in contrast with the dissenters, who crowded around an open window of a tavern, and a man perched in a tree, the better to see and hear the "false minister" preaching from the window.

It was in the company of Henry and Frances Vane that Mary met some of the Seekers. In the nearby village of Staindrop, Henry owned the Old Lodge, a three-story building where he allowed the Seekers to meet. Mary attended some of the convocations and waited in silence for the Lord to speak to her heart. Though she felt peace, somehow she knew that God wanted her to continue her journey.

Mary walked back up Keverstone Bank road from Staindrop village to Raby Castle. To the right were fields of barley behind the hedgerow where wild roses bloomed. To the left were the woods and meadows of Raby's park, where large herds of deer browsed. Above, tall columns of clouds scudded across the blue dome.

She was glad of the solitude of the walk, for she'd heard something different at today's meditation. Not God's voice in her silent reverie, but the voices of a man and two women who had stood on the village common and spoken of standing in awe before God. They used old-fashioned language of perhaps forty or fifty years ago, when "thee" and "thou" were words used with social equals or family members, instead of the more modern, formal, flattering, and respectful "you" used in courts, and with people of higher social status. The colloquial dialect used in Cumbria and Yorkshire, where the speakers were most successful in their proselytizing, made upper, middle, and lower classes equal—and Mary knew that was not likely to attract the privileged members of society.

The man had said, "Christ is the Light of the world, and lighteth every man that cometh into the world; and by this light they might be gathered to God." Mary wondered that no one but her seemed to notice the light around the speaker, as if Christ's presence within could not be entirely veiled by human flesh.

He stood on a large stone and opened the scriptures. "The scriptures are the prophets' words," he said, "and Christ's and the apostles' words, and what they enjoyed and possessed, and they had it from the Lord."

But now, the preacher said, "Now, we have something better than scripture: we are children of Light, and we walk in the Light, and the word we hear is inward, from God. It is written that God spoke in times past by the prophets, but in these last days has spoken unto us by his Son, who is the bright radiance of the Father's glory. It is promised in the new covenant that God himself will teach each man. The presence of God in thy heart is better than reading about him in a book of scripture."

The women also testified that Christ had opened their eyes to his Light, which poured into their souls. One of them said, "When I learned this, that Christ the Living Word is life, and the words of scripture had been surpassed in his glory, it cut me to the heart, and then I saw clearly that we were all wrong. We have taken the scriptures in words, mere words, and know nothing of them in our hearts."

The man reinforced the message: "You will say, 'Christ saith this, or the prophets and apostles say this,' but what canst *thou* say? Dost thou have the Living Word in thee, or only a book of words in thy pocket?"

The preachers invited their listeners to a worship meeting in a hired room at the coaching inn before the constable cleared his throat loudly and the crowd melted away like a dew drop in the noon sun.

But Mary stayed to have a private talk with one of the women, named Dorothy Waugh. Dorothy, an uneducated young woman who had been a house maid, described how she'd seen George Fox, the farmer's son, at a church in Ulverston, in Cumbria.

"Brother George went to the steeple-house and waited until the priest had finished. He preached the truth by declaring the Word of life amongst them. The priest was angry and went to the magistrates to get rid of George—to make him leave the steeple-house. The magistrates shouted and threatened to bring the guards, but George wouldn't stop declaring the way of the Lord to the people. He said he came to speak the Word of life and salvation from the Lord.

"The power of the Lord was dreadful among them," said Dorothy, with a joyful glow on her countenance. "The people trembled and shook, and some of us thought even the steeple-house shook and would fall down on our heads! But the Lord was our strong and mighty defender, and though the magistrates' wives strove to scratch out Brother George's eyes, the soldiers—yea, the soldiers of the magistrates!—and the people stood thick around him. He walked safely away from the town with protection of the people on whom God's glory had fallen."

Now, as Mary walked alone on the Keverstone Bank coach road, she pondered the words of the Quakers, for that is what they were. It was a pejorative term disliked by them, for it was spoken in derision, of the times in silent worship when the Holy Spirit came upon them and they quaked in awe at the Lord's majesty. They had no name for their adherents but called one another "Friends."

The logic of the Quaker message did not escape her. That God, a spirit, could mystically inhabit a believer was something she could accept on faith and experience. She could not prove it scientifically, of course, but she had been given manifestations of divine providence and blessing in her life, and observed miracles in the lives of those she loved most. But to say that the spoken word of God now supplanted the written word of God—that was something to study. Perhaps she misunderstood what these untrained preachers were saying. Scripture was not null and void, and it was God-breathed; how, then, would one know the difference between personal desire and the leading of divinity? Perhaps the same way that she knew the vibration of her house was from a high wind, or the trembling of the earth.

*****

The next morning, before the household could awake and notice her absence, she took her Bible with her and left the crenellated castle through its gatehouse with the statues of medieval warriors on the top of the battlements.

Mary crossed the grassy park outside the walls and sunken formal garden, and entered the edge of the wood. She sat on a tree stump and listened to the birds chattering in the trees. Having been a city girl in her youth, she was unfamiliar with which birds sang which songs, but she thought she recognized the goldfinch by its plumage.

Only because the eye blinked did Mary notice the head of a doe that had settled down to ruminate in a stand of leafy saplings. The deer seemed little concerned with Mary's presence, for they were nearly as tame as cattle.

With the sunrise came a slight breeze and the leaves trembled on a wide-spreading oak. Almost as if she could see the wind, she sensed tendrils of sweet summer herbal-scented air riffling the pages of her open Bible. When she focused her eyes on the words there, she read,

For I am persuaded, that neither death, nor life, nor angels, nor principalities, nor powers, nor height, nor depth, nor any other creature, shall be able to separate us from the love of God, which is in Christ Jesus our Lord.

Then slowly, as the invisible tendrils of air caressed the ends of her hair and her cheeks, she relaxed, submitted to its ministrations, and inhaled, and with the intake of breath, she began to be filled with the love of God. Mary could feel it traveling from her heart through her core and to her limbs, and it was not unlike the butterfly flutters of a child quickening in her womb. As she was gradually filled with the love and Light, strength and power, Mary began to tremble with joy. No love in her life had ever filled her like this. Not her parents or dear friends, not her beloved husband William, not the joy of new motherhood, and not her teacher, Anne. She rose to her feet in reverence and lifted her hands.

Nothing could separate her from this love, for now it had become part of her. It was not *in* her blood—it *was* her blood. It was not the flesh of her arms or legs—it was the power that made them move. It was not the English summer air she breathed—it was the very life-breath of the Creator.

It was not an audible word in her ears, but an orchestra in her spirit, which said, *"Mary, my child, I have ordained you to be a light in the world, a friend to the sick and imprisoned, a balm to the persecuted, a voice for the silenced, a banner to rally weary warriors."*

Mary replied without speaking. "Yea, and joyfully I go, Lord."

Gradually, over a few minutes, the trembling faded away, but she felt no sense of loss or emptiness, for the love remained. Everything in her life had a purpose and a destination, which she did not yet know, but she was ready for the journey.

September 17, 1653

Newport, Rhode Island

William Dyer sat at the bench with Nicholas Easton, after adjourning the Court of Admiralty, and organized his notes and papers before leaving for home. Easton was working on a letter to the Commissioners of the United Colonies regarding Captain Thomas Baxter, the young privateer captain.

Two weeks before, Baxter had seized the *Desire*, a barque owned by Samuel Mayo and three other men of Barnstable in Plymouth Colony. Baxter claimed that the *Desire* was carrying on trade with the Dutch, though Mayo was only carrying goods from

Reverend William Leverich of Sandwich to a new farm at Oyster Bay on Long Island, within English limits.

Baxter had put Mayo and his captain off the *Desire* at West Harbor, a larger and deeper harbor about ten miles west of Oyster Bay, claiming he had a commission from Rhode Island to offend the enemy Dutch, and all who did business with them.

Mayo and Lt. William Hudson of the Honorable Military Company of Massachusetts, on duty at the English outpost there, had come to Newport to investigate Baxter's privateer claim.

Dyer and Easton called the Admiralty Court to session, and made a response to Mayo's claim of Baxter's actions.

Now, at the conclusion of testimony, Easton dictated a letter to the court clerk.

TO THE MAGISTRATES OF OYSTER BAY ON LONG ISLAND
16 Sept. 1653
Loving friends,

Having received your complaint regarding Captain Thomas Baxter, I hereby affirm that Mr. Baxter has been authorized by Rhode Island, under a commission of the English Council of State, to offend the enemies of England, and all who treat with the Dutch. He is bound to bring his prizes into Newport for trial, that the state may get its share.

Mr. Baxter tells us that he knows of no English patent or charter for the lands at Oyster Bay or the West Harbor, where he seized the sloop *Desire*, and that the place is known as Martin Gerretson's Bay, in Dutch territory.

However, Mr. Mayo testifies that he, Mr. Wright, and Mr. Leverich purchased the land from the Indians, and he requests that his ship be brought to Connecticut or New Haven if it must be held for trial.

We regret the inconvenience this has caused Mr. Mayo and the other owners of the barque, and assure you of a speedy hearing with the commissioners of the United Colonies when it meets at Hartford.
NICHOLAS EASTON
NEWPORT

He signed the letter and its copies, and the original was given to the fuming Samuel Mayo, who said through gritted teeth that he would appeal to a higher court.

"That would be my advice to you, anyway, sir," said Dyer. "The *Desire* could remain impounded until the case comes up on the court calendar, probably six months from now. That will be a severe hardship for its owners, unless you post a bond with the court and reclaim your ship for the interim. If you win the suit, you'll have your bond returned, and Baxter may be assessed damages."

Samuel Mayo and William Paddy became sureties for the bond and filed a suit against Thomas Baxter, and left the meetinghouse.

Dyer and Easton remained at the bench, talking.

"Meanwhile," said William, "Baxter, eager to make his fortune, sailed off to Connecticut's Fairfield harbor and seized a Dutch ship there, which caused the Dutch to fit out two more ships to go after Baxter."

Easton sat back in his padded chair and toyed with the gavel. "The commissioners of the United Colonies will renew their warning that the Dutch keep out of the rivers, harbors, and bays, and cease all Indian trading in our territory. Baxter and Hull, if they dare to make raids or to engage with the enemy, will run to Connecticut inlets for refuge—and perhaps to cache their prizes if we're not vigilant."

"I have no doubt," Easton continued, "That in the matter of the *Desire,* the commission will find for Mayo and Leverich, and Baxter will be censured or fined. Legally, Baxter had a right to raid the Dutch waters and take the ship and its cargo as prizes on mere suspicion that it was trading with the Dutch. The lands and waters won't be under New Haven, Connecticut, or Massachusetts control without a patent for its founding."

Will nodded. "But morally, Baxter knew it was an English ship with English cargo, and he was a fool to set a blaze like this. It's exactly what Gregory Dexter protested would happen in the Providence assembly in May."

November 18, 1653

Providence Plantations

Richard Scott poured another tankard of Katherine's small beer and handed it to William Dyer, who was lounging before the kitchen fireplace without his boots—just his stockings between the hot fire and his cold feet. For the last two days, the two men, and Edward Hutchinson, had been stalking the woods with an Indian guide, and had come back with a stag that would supply meat for many meals to come this winter.

Though the calendar indicated the autumn season, most of the leaves had fallen from the hardwoods, the swamps and ponds were nearly frozen through, and snow lay in every place the sun didn't reach in its short hours.

Edward sighed with pleasure as he wiggled his stockinged toes between the porridge kettle and the stone sidewall of the fireplace. He was nursing his bowl of syllabub, making it last as long as possible by dipping his spoon and licking it slowly. Syllabub was made from cider or white wine, sugar, and whipped cream. "I shall not relish the ride home to Boston tomorrow," he said, "knowing the life of luxury and hedonistic pleasure that could be mine by staying with the Scotts."

"Edward Hull, the pirate—oh, sorry, Will, the *privateer*—won't be browning his feet at a fire for some time," said Richard. "When he was served notice of Kempo Sebada's suit, he abandoned his young wife and newborn son, and hied himself to England. Just as the winter storms set in." He grinned.

"He disappeared so quickly that I wondered if he'd attired himself in a sugar sack and hid on an outbound ship," said William. "It wouldn't be a bad idea to travel in disguise, with the collective fury of the Dutch, French, and English pursuing him."

Edward said, "The Dutchman Sebada's lawsuit will be heard in Salem on the 29th of this month, but I'm quite sure he'll lose. He's a Caribbean pirate himself, and Hull making a prize of Sebada's ship and trade goods exposed Sebada as an arms supplier to the Indians. He wants Hull's frigate in recompense for his seized ship, but the *Swallow* is co-owned by his father and brother—Robert Hull, the silversmith minter, and it's illegal for them to give title to a foreigner even if they wanted. No enemy pirate can surmount those odds, especially in Endecott's Salem."

William shifted in his chair and unintentionally disturbed the Scotts' cat as it melted by the fire. It stalked away with lashing tail and ears laid back.

"Edward Hull was always a man to keep on a short tether. When Underhill and I raided House of Good Hope at Hartford, the threat of our small fleet was enough to scare the Dutch out of their rabbit holes. They left some trade goods in the warehouse, but we didn't have to fire a shot or take prisoners because they'd slipped away in the night. Johnny Winthrop and the assembly at Hartford are glad to have the Dutch fort in Connecticut possession now. They'll happily assume the fur trade, and put a stop to smuggling guns, powder, and balls to the Indians."

"However," said Hutchinson, "the Cape Cod and Vineyard men were apoplectic with rage over Hull taking prizes of their English ships and cargoes, and accusing without proof that they had traded with the Dutch. After he interfered with their trade—a mortal sin to them—he hid in the coves and inlets of Connecticut. Whether they did or did not unlawfully trade with the Dutch, it was colossally stupid of Hull to go by the letter of the law with his own countrymen."

"Yes, taking offenders who dealt with the Dutch was included and allowed in my commission from the Council of State," said William, "but Hull knew better—I had warned him from the beginning not to offend the English."

"And that's the true reason he ran," said Richard. "He knew he'd never survive the suits of New England captains and ship owners, and his father and brother would be bankrupted and have their ship seized. He was foolishly greedy."

William agreed with a nod. "Hull's inflammatory actions put an end to our—Underhill's and my—planned operations against the Dutch on Manhattoes and the Hudson River. We needed the full cooperation of the United Colonies to do the job properly. They refused to comply with the orders from Mr. Cromwell for militiamen, ships, and other support by simply withholding them. So rather than carrying out raids on Dutch shipping, we blockaded them. The United Colonies sent to the Council of State for a commission for their own commander-upon-the-sea, Major-General Sedgewick, and if he's coming with forces, I haven't heard.

"But I have heard from the Council, a letter from the Protector. I'll read it out to you, and see if you don't think the Council of State is stalling Rhode Island!"

William went to his leather case and pulled out the letter from England, then returned to the fireplace. "It's long," he said. "I'll condense it for you."

"Order of the Protector of the Commonwealth of England, Ireland and Scotland."

"Will," interrupted Hutchinson, "was it written to Rhode Island, Providence, or all the colonies?"

"This one was specific to the Newport and Portsmouth assembly because it concerns the war against the Dutch. Apparently, someone in Providence or the United Colonies has complained to England about the very idea of privateering. It's not possible that the latest exploits of Baxter and Hull have reached England, been discussed in committee, and then an order returned to us. It would mean at least six months' delay with travel time."

He cleared his throat and held up the paper as if he were a herald in an English village and not a middle-aged man who needed brighter light to read the secretary's handwriting.

"'A representation having been made to his highness and his council, that some differences are depending betwixt some of the New England governments and yourselves, about bounds and other matters… You will best provide for your own comfort and quiet, and give the clearest respect, both to the honor of your country and to religion…'"

"In other words," said William, "they were tattled to, and promise to discuss the matter later, but in the meantime, we are to take care of our own business.

"Mr. Cromwell continued: 'All such of you as are not under the censure of banishment, by the sentence of any of the former governments of New England, may enjoy the freedom of ingress, egress, and regress, in, to, and from their several plantations, for trade with those other colonies, and upon other necessary occasions; you demeaning yourselves peaceably and inoffensively…'"

Richard interposed himself. “That bit is welcome news. Rhode Islanders have long experience with Massachusetts, particularly, forbidding our travel in their colony, stopping our trade on the roads and in the ports, and constantly disputing boundaries. You don’t feel it on Aquidneck Island, but we Providence men who own properties in nearby Massachusetts sometimes are charged with trespassing while traveling to our own lands, and their men steal our cattle and drive them across the lines. It’s intolerable!”

William took a swallow of his beer, scanned the document for a moment, then paraphrased: “In case they—the United Colonies—shall determine a war with our neighbor natives, seasonable notice shall be given us of such their resolution, that we may the better prepare for preventing of danger and surprisal to ourselves.” He paused, reading ahead. “And if we shall by our own industry discover any new banks within ten leagues of Rhode Island, we shall enjoy the benefit of the fishing there, without the intermeddling or interruption of the Dutch or French.”

He laughed. “I suppose my men will have to patrol those waters to keep off the enemy, and if we drop lines or nets into those banks during a quiet moment between sea battles, the catch will belong to the Council of State.”

“Mr. Cromwell finishes by urging us to preserve a friendly and faithful correspondence with the neighbor plantations, and our affection to the honor of this commonwealth, whereof we are members. He charges us particularly not to harbor, entertain, or countenance any malefactors, who after misdemeanors committed shall for declining the justice of any of the said four governments, make escape, and fly to us for shelter and protection; but to render them up to the law. Surely he’s speaking of Captain Hull, but I’m afraid that shark has broken through the net. Perhaps Mr. Thurloe will send agents around London to bring Hull to justice.”

Richard stood up and stretched and yawned. “Ed, are you still licking your syllabub spoon, or would you like a splash of aqua vitae before bed? Medicinal use, of course, to warm our joints.” The three men toasted the Council of State in general, and Harry Vane in particular, and sipped the Irish whiskey.

It was long past the time the family and servants had gone to bed. Richard used a tongs to drag the bedwarmer bricks out of the coals and put carrying buckets and wrapping towels there for his friends to take their bricks to their floor pallets in the parlor.

"In the morning, gents. Good night."

February 1654
Belleau, Lincolnshire

Mary, toasting her icy feet before a parlor fire in Henry Vane's manor house near the coast of the North Sea, opened the packet of letters from Rhode Island and began with the one in brown ink, written by her husband.

TO MARY DYER IN CARE OF SIR HENRY VANE THE YOUNGER
20 November 1653
My dearest love,

Your husband and children implore you to return to their loving arms, remembering your tender love for us. We worry for your safety as we hear of terrible events and misery because of the wars in our home isles. Our only hope is that the mercy of the Lord will extend to you, for the mercy of the Parliamentarians surely will not. You may think yourself safe under the protective wing of Harry Vane, but even he could fall prey to the whims of government opinion or public disapproval.

I hold a grave concern regarding your consorting with those religionists known as Quakers. They allow their emotions to overcome their intellect. Surely you know that even their women have been beaten and committed to prison. How our hearts would break to learn of the slightest mistreatment toward you. My influence, my legal pleadings, my bond for your release, would mean nothing at this distance and the months it would take to respond. Remember your station, and give up this degrading business.

Please return to Newport, my darling. The war against the Dutch is all but over after only a few skirmishes, and we suppose that a treaty will be concluded in the winter. Though the southern tip of the Manhattan Island is protected by a fort, John Underhill, being familiar with the lay of the land and its former defenses, instigated English and Indian attacks against the Dutch from the north of the island, and Captain Edward Hull and Mr. Baxter raided a number of Dutch farms along the North and East rivers. Governor Pieter Stuyvesant, knowing of the military actions Captain Underhill performed on the Dutch farms which lay nearby, ordered a timber wall built from one side of New Amsterdam to the other. The palisade wall has several guard towers and a gate, and a supply road for its building is called, brilliantly, Waal Straat. That was wasted effort, as we had no intention of raiding the town anyway. You may think of Captain Underhill and me as aggressors, but in truth, the treacherous Dutch have provoked the English on Long Island and Manhattan, and have paid the Indians with muskets, to kill the English. My role would have been significant if the United Colonies had complied with orders of the Council of State. Instead, it was my lot to be a politician and admiralty court judge more frequently than a commander who blockaded Dutch and French interests in the Sound.

Perhaps you will have heard that Governor Thomas Dudley has died at the age of 76. It is said that in his pocket there was a paper with the words, "Let men of God, in court and churches, watch o'er such as do a toleration hatch." How very rigid of the old man. I smile when I imagine that at the end, he was perhaps thinking of the Hutchinsons, Roger Williams, the Clarke brothers, and the others like us. (And I wither under your disapproval of my unforgiveness.) Governor Dudley has deeded his stubborn, harsh temper to his son-in-law, Simon Bradstreet.

Our friend and brother of nearly two decades, John Sanford, died last summer, while still holding the office of president of Rhode Island, and committed to the unification and harmony of the towns after the disruption caused by Mr. Coddington. He left Bridget with nine children and a valuable estate, but she is considering marriage to William Phillips because her children are so young: all of them under seventeen, needing need a man's governance. Surely, with the wit and heart of her parents William and Anne Hutchinson, Bridget will land on her feet. If not, her brother Edward will advise her well. John Sanford had lived in Alford and came over on the *Lyon* in 1631. It would be a great favor to me if you would visit any relatives of that name, and tell them what an outstanding man he was, and how dear and valuable to his community, and that he has left a legacy of greatness for his children to be proud of.

As you well remember, two years ago, Rhode Island considered a law banning African slavery. John Clarke and Roger Williams, who supported the idea, are in England for the charter, as was I on two occasions. But between the former troublemaker Samuel Gorton and I and several others, we wrote and approved the law. I'm sorry to report, my dear, that the Aquidneck towns, Portsmouth and Newport, have refused thus far to accept the law under firstly John Cranston, Henry Bull, and now John Easton, my successors as Attorney General. Mr. Coddington is certainly unwilling to give up his own Negro slaves. The economic and shipping center of this colony is here in Newport, and without support and enforcement here, I fear that the law is dead. I'm sorry to grieve you with this news, which you will take very hard. Perhaps the law's time will come again.

Providence and Warwick, and Portsmouth and Newport on Aquidneck Island, are much divided these last two years, mostly related to Mr. Coddington's attempt at making himself lord governor. The educated and affluent men are here, while the men who hold most closely to their religion, such as Mr. Williams and his followers, take a different side. The mainland men, particularly Mr. Dexter, have disapproved of our military actions against the Dutch and preach that Underhill, Hull, and I are apt to set New England afire, but they seem happy enough to account for and claim a share of the spoils that we reclaim from the Dutch.

Our son Samuel learned a useful skill from an Indian last year. The Indians drill holes in maple tree trunks, and when the sap rises in the spring, they catch the liquid in a vessel. They boil the slightly-sweet sap to a sugar syrup that gives a curious flavor. They sweeten corn cakes or meat with the syrup. There's such a small yield that I doubt its usefulness as an export.

Our children are well, and growing nearly as fast as the weeds in the tobacco field. Keeping them in decent clothing may beggar me, despite the ventures I've embarked upon. (That is a jest, my dear.) I am rebuilding our humble home to make space for loft storage, bed chambers, and a larger kitchen and parlor on the ground floor, similar to a large English cottage. Even the outbuildings will be enlarged for our stock. You won't recognize it, but you'll have a home you have long deserved. If you'll only come home.

With a husband's full esteem and love,
WILLIAM DYER

Mary refolded the sheaf of papers that made up Will's letter. She was annoyed, if she allowed herself to think it, that her husband didn't understand her, even after twenty-five years of friendship and twenty of marriage. There was no doubt that he loved her, but if *he* didn't hear God's call for himself, he couldn't fully respect her own calling.

What would it take to make Will understand? Even Mary was confused at times. Anne Hutchinson's calling had been clearly seen and understood. She was charismatic, and theologically, she was better-trained than many clergy. Anne had followers by the hundreds. Mary was still uncertain as to why Anne went publicly silent after the exodus from Massachusetts. Had she said all she'd been commanded by the Lord? Had she finished the race? Had she lost her strength after her difficult journey through life? And then, before she could make a new beginning after her widowhood and move, she'd been cut down.

Mary was staying with Harry and Frances Vane at their Lincolnshire estate of Belleau, a gift from Oliver Cromwell before his break with Harry. Today, Mary had walked along a narrow cart track between fields on the gently rolling hills. Though in February everything was white and the frost off the North Sea fogged the air, the fields were a riot of color in summer: the golden yellow of rapeseed flowers here, the green of barley there, and a field of red poppies. She'd heard that the oriental poppies came to England with the Romans, and time out of mind, the potent juice of the seed heads had been used to treat pain, severe coughs, and to make patients sleep so broken bones could be set.

The Belleau deed included several manor houses, with ten acres of land, meadow, pasture, and wood. On these lands, Henry Vane had the advowson, the right to appoint a minister to the parish church. He'd installed a learned Puritan man whose beliefs were similar to Vane's, especially regarding liberty of conscience.

The moated, walled, and gated manor of Belleau was four miles northwest of Alford, where the Hutchinsons had lived for generations, and about twenty-five miles north of the Dyers' old farm in Kirkby LaThorpe. William's brother had been forced out by the high taxes and the Earl of Bedford's scheme to drain the fens and drive farmers out so he could buy the land cheaply. As for Alford, Mary had visited it on one of her longer walks in the summer, and had laid flowers on the graves of Anne's children who had died in childhood. After twenty years, only the old people there remembered Anne and William.

Though Anne's calling had flared up brightly for three or four years two decades ago, Mary's calling seemed to be lost in mist off the North Sea. She could see a glow in the distance, but no details in the cloud. She had faith that God indeed had a plan and a time for her, but she wondered how much longer she'd have to wait for its realization. At the same time it was frustrating not to know how to plan her life or her family's, she knew a Sabbath-rest in waiting on the Lord's pleasure as his handmaiden.

Having no specific Light, no matter how earnestly she prayed, Mary studied the Bible, and attended meetings of the Friends. The meetings were most often segregated, women from men. As Anne had taught her, Mary attended at births, and used the long hours of waiting for the baby to teach and learn. The Friends movement was much stronger here in the northern midlands of England because of the concentration of work in the counties further north by George Fox and his followers. Mary enjoyed the protection and fellowship of the Vanes, but had ready access to meetings with others of similar beliefs.

As she had learned long ago, she kept her activities and thoughts to herself for the most part. Especially now, it was important to keep silent, with the fiery Roger Williams also staying with the Vanes for a week before he returned to America. Mr. Williams did not approve of women expressing opinions or taking part in conversations. He most certainly did not approve of the Friends, either.

The daylight was gone by half-past four, and she'd never even seen the sun in the frozen fog. Not uncommon in English winters, she thought. Mary pulled her slippered toes away from the fire, gathered her letters, and went upstairs.

Having been a mother, and mistress of farm laborers for nearly twenty years, it seemed strange not to be involved in meal preparation at this time of evening, knowing she had hungry and healthy appetites clamoring to be satisfied after the daily work. Here with the Vanes, and dinner served fashionably late, she had plenty of time for… what?

Kicking off her slippers, Mary brought a folder of papers and candle to the high, canopied bed and lifted the down cover, snuggling amongst the layers of luxury in wool or feather-stuffed pillows and mattress. Only her fingers and her face from the nose up were visible as she held a paper before her and her body gradually warmed the fibers surrounding her.

Mary was reading a draft of Harry's work-in-progress, *A Healing Question,* and though she agreed with some of it, she believed it would cause serious political damage to Harry's career for its criticism of Oliver Cromwell's and the Puritan Parliament's current policies.

> *For when once the whole body of the good people find that the military interest and capacity is their own, and that into which necessity at the last may bring the whole party (whereof, of right, a place is to be reserved for them), and that herein they are so far from being in subjection or slavery, that in this posture they are most properly sovereign, and possess their right of natural sovereignty, they will presently see a necessity of continuing ever one with their army, raised and maintained by them for the promoting this cause against the common enemy, who in his next attempt will put for all with greater desperateness and rage than ever.*

This was more than an argument about the need of a militia to conquer or maintain order, thought Mary. It was about ownership of a principle, and a determination of liberty for every individual to form a union of like-minded citizens. It was a challenge to every man to ennoble himself by his participation in a righteous cause for all of the community, rather than reserving power for those born to a privileged class looking out for their own interests and effecting the economic enslavement of everyone else.

Though Harry was one of the privileged class, he advocated that the general populace should have a right to work their way up, and take ownership in their own government. Oliver Cromwell, though he'd abolished the House of Lords, and the House of Commons ruled the country, would not be at all happy with Harry's beliefs.

In fact, thought Mary, Harry had said privately that he might be a suspect in the vast espionage network headed by John Thurloe, Cromwell's Secretary of State. He was certain that the letters of his brother, Sir George Vane, had been intercepted along the way. There were spies all over Britain, in the West Indies, and even in America, who were seeking royalists and reporting on the threat potential—perhaps there were pockets of sedition plotting to bring young Charles II out of exile and return him to the throne.

Wouldn't her husband love to know who the English agents were, operating in New England, thought Mary. William preferred the royalist faction mostly because it, like him, was anti-puritan, but he understood the importance of appearing neutral, for the good of his family and his business.

Harry Vane wasn't a fearful man, nor had he been a royalist for more than a decade: he was bold and outspoken in his politics, and his loyalty to the Republican cause was impeccable. But with the Civil War just behind him, a falling out with his own father (who had retired from politics to his estate in Kent), and the volatility of the Protectorate, he had discreetly moved his family northward from London. The men uncovered by Thurloe's spies were tortured, and one man was trepanned to death—his skull was bored, little by little. Now was the time for Henry Vane the Younger to settle into a more local leadership role, to write about religious toleration, to meet with representatives of religious sects, and correspond with colonial government.

Now that she was warmer, Mary set aside the manuscript and dozed into a cat nap, dreaming of being held in her husband's arms, and her children tucked in for the night, their faces as innocent in sleep as pups in a basket. Tears spilled from her eyes as she dreamed.

Mary awoke to the scent of roast fowl wafting up from the kitchen in the crofts below the hall. She reluctantly left her warm nest, washed her face with icy water from the bowl, and tidied her hair before changing to her nicer gown and donning a woolen stole.

Servants had lit candles in sconces on the stairs, and the hall contained several candelabra on the table and sideboard. Even after two years back in England, and staying with the wealthy Vanes, Mary remembered the economy of light on which she'd existed for twenty years. Candles had been very expensive in Boston when they first emigrated, and even after chandlers began making cheaper tallow candles a few years later, most reading or socializing had taken place at the kitchen fire, or by the light of an oil lamp.

Mary joined Frances in a smaller family dining room, where the children had just finished their dinner. Lady Vane stood at the head of the table and opened a Bible to the evening's reading.

"In the fear of the Lord is strong confidence: and his children shall have a place of refuge. The fear of the Lord is a fountain of life, to depart from the snares of death."

"Albinia, explain what the first verse means, please."

The tow-headed ten-year-old piped in her treble voice, "It means that all people who reverence God may trust his love and desire to save them."

"And Mary," the mother addressed her eight-year-old, "What is this place of refuge in the proverb?"

"Our refuge is the bosom of the Lord."

"Very good, dear."

"Rich, what is the fountain of life?"

A boy, the same age as Maher Dyer, eleven, replied, "Jesus Christ, the well of water springing up into everlasting life."

"Well said, my son. You answered with a gospel text." The boy beamed.

"You may be excused to get ready for bed, my loves."

The other children, Thomas and Dorothy, kissed their mother's cheek, bowed or curtsied to Mrs. Dyer, and went with their nurse to be put to bed. Christopher, almost a year old, was already tucked in, having been fed by his wet nurse.

Mary's heart constricted, thinking of her own family in Newport. Two years of her children's lives she'd never get back. It was her own stubborn fault. Or maybe God's fault, taking her on this endless road, blindfolded. Or something of both.

"Right, then," said Frances, who had noticed Mary's sadness and guessed its source. "Shall we go in for dinner?"

The men were already seated at the table, but rose briefly when the women came in. In addition to Henry and Roger Williams, there was a familiar face Mary hadn't seen since he sailed with Mr. Williams to England: Dr. John Clarke, the physician and Baptist minister of Newport.

Though the Friends didn't remove their hats or bow to other men because they reserved their respect for God alone, Mary chose to live according to good manners, for after all, the apostle Paul had determined to be all things to all men, so that he might win men for Christ. Showing disrespect would not have been the Lord's way, either, and she knew that these men were submitted to the Lord. Therefore, she readily curtsied to each man, which they acknowledged with a nod.

"Dr. Clarke, what an unexpected pleasure to see you, sir," said Mary.

"You're looking very well, Mistress Dyer. The soft, sweet airs of England agree with you. And, I suppose, your extended holiday from establishing a garden and a house full of children." He chuckled.

She knew he meant it as a compliment, but it was like a pebble in her shoe to be reminded that women were thought incapable of intellectual pursuits, independent action, or advanced education. Men in Connecticut and Massachusetts said that the Connecticut governor's wife, Ann Yale Hopkins, had gone mad from too much reading and writing—not because she'd inherited madness or been driven to it by illness, injury, or unbearable events. Men seemed to value clear thinking, and a modicum of education in their own wives was desirable, but there was a threshold beyond which women must not pass.

In fact, Mrs. Williams was in Providence Plantation, and Mrs. Clarke was in London. Women almost never traveled with their husbands. And they *never* traveled alone, for any reason.

As the courses were served in turn, talk between the men reverted to what they'd spent the afternoon discussing: the state of affairs in Rhode Island. Roger Williams was intending to sail back to Boston, and then to Providence, having accomplished his mission of obtaining both a revocation of Coddington's governor-for-life appointment (a copy of which William Dyer had already taken back to Rhode Island), and a replacement charter granted by the Council of State. Dr. Clarke was the author of the charter, but over weeks and months, he'd had considerable guidance and counsel from Roger Williams and Henry Vane. Even William Dyer, their Attorney General, had had a say in some of the clauses.

Sir Henry was a member of the Council of State, and its presidency rotated to him every few months, at which time he was the head of state for all of England, Scotland, Ireland, and the American colonies. His experience in Massachusetts had given him an edge when it came to dealing with the needs and concerns of the New England colonies, in particular. He was a member of the Committee for American and West Indies Plantations. Though it was nineteen years since he'd been present in Massachusetts, he was still well-acquainted with scores of men through correspondence and their journeys back and forth to England.

Rhode Island still had a divided government, with Portsmouth and Newport at odds with Providence and Warwick on the mainland. It was an embarrassment to Sir Henry that his charges were proving troublesome. While Dr. Clarke and Reverend Williams were here at Belleau, they had hammered out a letter to the colony.

Henry had brought his copy of the letter to dinner, and offered to read it to Frances and Mary, both of whom were very interested in the contents.

So he took his horn-rimmed spectacles from a small box, set them on the bridge of his nose, and tilted his head back slightly to rest the lenses on his face. He held the letter high, near a candelabra, and read aloud in a dramatic voice he reserved for special occasions:

> TO THE PROVIDENCE COLONY AT RHODE ISLAND
> Loving and Christian Friends:
>
> I could not refuse this bearer, Mr. Roger Williams, my kind friend and ancient acquaintance, to be accompanied with these few lines from myself to you, upon his return to Providence Colony; though, perhaps, my private and retired condition, which the Lord, of his mercy, hath brought me into, might have argued strongly enough for my silence; but indeed, something I hold myself bound to say to you, out of the Christian love I bear you, and for his sake whose name is called upon by you and engaged in your behalf.

How is it that there are such divisions amongst you? Such headiness, tumults, disorders and injustice? The noise echoes into the ears of all, as well friends as enemies, by every return of ships from those parts. Is not the fear and awe of God amongst you to restrain? Is not the love of Christ in you, to fill you with yearning bowels, one towards another, and constrain you not to live to yourselves, but to him that died for you, yea, and is risen again?

Are there no wise men amongst you? No public self-denying spirits, that at least, upon the grounds of public safety, equity and prudence, can find out some way or means of union and reconciliation for you amongst yourselves, before you become a prey to common enemies, especially since this State, by the last letter from the Council of State, gave you your freedom, as supposing a better use would have been made of it than there hath been? Surely, when kind and simple remedies are applied and are ineffectual, it speaks loud and broadly the high and dangerous distempers of such a body, as if the wounds were incurable.

But I hope better things from you, though I thus speak, and should be apt to think, that by Commissioners agreed upon and appointed in all parts, and on behalf of all interests, in a general meeting, such a union and common satisfaction might arise, as, through God's blessing, might put a stop to your growing breaches and distractions, silence your enemies, encourage your friends, honor the name of God which of late hath been much blasphemed, by reason of you, and in particular, refresh and revive the sad heart of him who mourns over your present evils, as being your affectionate friend, to serve you in the Lord.

H. VANE

Belleau, the 8th of February, 1654

"What think you of the letter, Mistress Dyer?" asked Williams. "Do you believe Mr. Dyer can be persuaded to heal the wounds between the island and the mainland? The privateering raids of the men under his command have, as Providence men predicted, set the colonies around the Long Island Sound alight with strife."

Mary considered her answer. Williams was asking two questions, but pointing particularly at Will. On one hand, she abhorred privateering, which she considered thievery, and a stain on his otherwise-honorable career. On the other, he was her husband, and she loved him in spite of her broken heart—there could be no disloyalty. They were one flesh.

"I've received letters from William as recently as this week, in which he tells me of his great disappointment with Mr. Coddington's politics and business dealings over the years."

Mary paused for a moment to sip her wine and think how best to word her next statement.

"William, in his letter to me about Rhode Island politics, spoke of being ready to make good, to avoid devouring one another with hypocrisy, dissimulation, and back-biting. He desires that all who love the Light come forth and show their deeds."

True, she thought. Those were exactly his words. But he was speaking in layers not about the colony in general, but about William Coddington specifically, demanding that Coddington admit he was trying to cheat his neighbors, including the Dyers, by moving pasture fences and making the public pay for roads that benefited him by ending on his property.

Roger Williams took the bait and seized on one word.

"You said 'Light.' Is it your understanding that Mr. Dyer has embraced familism, or perhaps this Quaker nonsense?"

"Sir, I cannot think so. It's unlikely that he's read any Friends tracts, and as for religious beliefs, my husband attends Dr. Clarke's and Mr. Holmes' church when his affairs allow."

Williams made a sound that could have been a "humph" or a snort.

John Clarke smiled into his beard, and only Mary observed it.

"Will Dyer is a good man," said Clarke, "and I value his support and his intellect. He defended Obadiah Holmes, John Crandall, and me after we were arrested in Salem and taken to Boston nearly three years ago. Crandall and I were released after paying heavy fines. But Holmes, who had once lived at Salem, refused to submit to Endecott, and he was given thirty stripes."

When Dr. Clarke had sailed to England, Holmes became the pastor of Newport's Baptist church. He referred to his terrible scars, which Mary had helped tend, as the marks of the Lord Jesus.

"Governor Endecott is a madman who revels in inflicting pain, whether of the body or the conscience," Clarke continued. "He derives personal pleasure from violence, and cloaks it dangerously as zeal for the Lord. It is not the will of the Lord than any one should have dominion over another man's conscience. Conscience is such a sparkling beam from the Father of lights and spirits that it cannot be lorded over, commanded, or forced, either by men, devils, or angels."

There was silence for a moment as the guests, all of whom had experienced persecution or flight from it, considered Clarke's statement.

Again, Clarke smiled slyly. "That was a line from my book, *Ill Newes from New England*," he said. "I'm just a little wounded that you didn't recognize it."

The tension eased as they laughed in embarrassment.

"And to set your heart at ease, Roger, William Dyer seems to be a creature much like you: he doesn't subscribe to a particular creed or fellowship, and he awaits a personal revelation of the Savior."

"Sir Harry," Mary asked, "Were you speaking only to my husband in the letter, or do you address all the government of the colony?"

The fowl course was served then. The rich smell of roast turkey filled the room. Turkeys were native to the Americas, but had been brought to Europe more than a hundred years ago, and were well known at the table. Mary liked this domestic variety more than the wild turkeys she'd cooked in her Rhode Island years.

When the servants had withdrawn, Harry Vane answered. "I addressed the letter to Providence, not to Newport. I'm not a man easily fooled. Among the accurate statements, I recognize some flattery and puffed-up words in Gregory Dexter's letters to me, and adjust my judgments accordingly. His most recent complaint says that Will Dyer is 'a great disturber of the peace of the Colony, making him a partner with others of most unnecessary and unrighteous plunderings, both of Dutch and French and English.'"

At this, Mary flushed a bright red, not of embarrassment, but of defensive anger. How dare Dexter blame the unrest on her husband—the unrest that had its origins in Providence—when Will was attempting to bring the factions to harmony.

But Roger Williams noticed her discomfort and lifted his hands to command Mary's peace.

Sir Harry continued, "Providence squabbles with Warwick, and both trade barbs with Massachusetts and Plymouth. Newport and Portsmouth are not guiltless, either. One should think that adversities of colonial life would bring all the parties together for strength, but instead they strive against one another. But Providence is Mr. Williams' destination, so Providence will experience my remonstrance first.

"And you need not worry about my esteem for Will. The Council of State, Mr. Thurloe, and I have our agents in the Caribbean and New England. We know what is happening."

He smiled, speared and dipped a chunk of turkey in its own liquor thickened with bread crumbs, put his eating knife to his mouth, and took a bite. "Mmm… You must try the turkey, Dr. Clarke. This one is from my own farm, of course."

Lady Vane had followed the conversation all along, only murmuring politely when expected. But now she spoke up.

"Dr. Clarke, I understand you've recently sat for a portrait. Would you describe it to us, please?"

The ginger- and silver-haired man answered, "There's not much to say, really. I wore my physician's black robe and a close-fitting cap over my hair as befits a clergyman. A square white collar and white cuffs completed my dress. On my lap was a human skull with trepanning and scalpel instruments to signify my profession."

Frances Vane shuddered. "A skull. How does one obtain such a thing? At an apothecary?"

Clarke reassured her, "I borrowed it from a wealthy surgeon. How he obtained it, I can't say. Because of a royal grant of only four bodies a year for study, there's a lively trade (if I may make a pun) in grave-robbing, to supply medical classes with subjects for study and practice of surgery. As many executed criminals as there are, there are never enough corpses for autopsy."

He realized, too late, that this was not the best dinner topic. His dinner companions looked rather queasy.

"I'll spare you the details of how it's done," he said drily. "Here's a change of subject, though I'm not sure how much more pleasant it is."

Mary thought to herself that during times of war and economic uncertainty, there seemed no end of unpleasant news.

Dr. Clarke reminded them first of Rev. Thomas Welde, who had written the vicious preface to John Winthrop's book about Anne Hutchinson—and made liberal mention of Mary's poor "monster" a decade before. Thomas was also the brother of Joseph Welde, who had been Anne's jailer during that terrible winter.

"Welde, as you know, was sent to England on an errand of the Massachusetts General Court. He's made one excuse after the other, when recalled, and I think he has no intention of returning. He found a calling to a parish in Yorkshire, and surely he'll stay there or attempt to climb the ladder of preferment. But he and his parishioners have been exposed to the Quaker ranter, James Nayler, and he's lost some of his members."

Mary had heard about the fiery young preacher from Dorothy Waugh, but had never met him, and she refrained from comment. What had been repeated of Nayler's sermons was unintelligible. She could imagine the man had flecks of foam on his lips.

Roger Williams spoke up: "Welde has published two rather violent anti-Quaker tracts, *The Perfect Pharisee under Monkish Holinesse*, and *A Further Discovery of the Generation of Men called Quakers*. As much as I disapprove of Welde as a man, I confess that I agree with his theology in this instance. Nayler must be a shipwreck of heresies, if I must take the side of Welde."

Sir Henry said he'd seen a draft of another book that would soon be distributed, this one by another Boston acquaintance of them all, Captain Edward Johnson. This book spoke of all the wonders and miracles God had performed to show how much he favored New England's method of religious reform over the English way; and the marvelous providences and mercies by which Jehovah had shown up the heretics of Rhode Island. According to Sir Henry, Johnson had reiterated the Hutchinson massacre and even dredged up the story of Mary's monster, and implied that witchcraft was the root of their heresies.

"With apologies for mentioning it, dear friend," he said. Mary inclined her head in acknowledgement.

"This horrible slander would never have been allowed in Rhode Island," Mary said. "The General Assembly passed a law about slander at the same time Will was engaged as Attorney General. I read the law for myself: 'Forasmuch as a good name is better than precious ointment, and slanderers are worse than dead flies to corrupt and alter the savor thereof, it is agreed, by this present Assembly, to prohibit the raising or spreading of false reports, slanderers and libels throughout the whole Colony.' It went on to cite specific examples."

"That is a righteous law," said Williams. "The principles of a good name and how it's spoiled are taken from the Book of Ecclesiastes."

But under Mary's serene exterior, she seethed about Johnson's book. There was a sharp pain behind her eyes. It just never stopped: the slander, the accusations. Not for Anne, who couldn't speak for herself these ten years, and not for Mary.

John Winthrop was a dragon who had breathed deadly fire. Even in death, his barbed tail made deadly swipes at his enemies. If not for Governor Winthrop and his spiteful prosecution, and Thomas Welde and his lurid preface to Winthrop's book—their tragedies and their sorrow might have been healed and there would exist the communion in the Body of Christ that they purported to long for. And now, years later, Captain Johnson raked coals Winthrop had lit, and fanned them into fresh flames.

The rest of the evening passed with the three men vigorously debating the points of religious liberty versus an almost-inevitable entrée of licentiousness. If society relaxed laws based in religious principle, men would take advantage of the liberality and civilization would become chaos—just what the Bostonian Puritans feared.

Lady Frances and Mary, after exchanging lifted eyebrows, left the table after the fruit pudding, and said goodnight to each other at the top of the stairs.

July 1654

Newport, Rhode Island

"Nick, I need your help. I must write a report for the Council of State, and don't know where to start."

William Dyer felt like a fourteen-year-old student, with blank paper before him, sitting for examinations. And that image didn't escape Nicholas Easton.

The two men were taking refuge from the intense heat of noonday, by catching up on correspondence in the shade of William's farmhouse, hoping for a breath of cooler air off the bay.

"I can hardly complain of the Council's tardiness and lack of provision in fitting out ships or supplying the colonies with powder and ammunitions, as they promised."

"True," said the older man.

"Rhode Island and New Haven, and even Connecticut, were ready to act, as we're most closely associated with the Dutch along the Sound. But Massachusetts Bay has dragged everything down. I have no proof, but I suspect they've sabotaged our efforts to treat with the Council of State and therefore to fight the Dutch. I've heard rumors that Endecott and Stuyvesant are peas in a pod."

"Probably."

"I've taken a mistress, and made over half my estate to her."

"Yes, obviously."

"My best mare foaled hound pups last month."

"Mmm-hmm."

"Nick!"

Easton glanced up from the letter he was writing. "Just make sure your mistress doesn't drop any foals while Mary is in England."

"I was sure I'd lost you."

"Look, Will, just write the damned letter, saying everything you want, then cross out the bits that would make you look petty or ineffective, and copy out the rest on good paper. It's an important letter, but it won't get written chattering at me."

Without sympathy, Easton went back to his letter-writing.

The waters of Long Island Sound might have resembled the crowded streets and alleys of London, William thought, with the addition of troops and ships from Plymouth Colony added to those of his privateer fleet and the trading ships coming into Newport in convoys. Fifty men conscripted from the Plymouth towns had been ready to march down to Sandwich with the venerable Pilgrim Captain Miles Standish, their commander in chief, and take ship with Major General Robert Sedgwick, who had been promised four ships and two hundred Englishmen by the Council of State, for them to take over Manhattan Island for the English.

Like William Dyer before him, Sedgwick held a commission from the Protector Oliver Cromwell to reduce the Dutch to obedience to the state of England. His promises had never come to fruition, and his flotilla had yet to appear when the news of the treaty of peace between England and the Netherlands came to the colonies in April. Sedgwick had taken several malcontented captains and their ships north to the French provinces of Acadia and Canada, and harassed French traders there, saying it was an efficient use of England's resources. He'd taken St. John from the French, and had moved back down the coast to Acadia.

When the afternoon breeze came up from the water, the men finished their letters, and went into town for some cool refreshment.

So much for dreams of wealth and conquest, and fame as a commander of a fleet.

*****

William received a reply from Secretary Thurloe some months later, reassuring William of his favor in the Council. "The assistance of the Southern Colonies was not wanting in carrying on that design" of taking over New Netherland, wrote Thurloe, "but Massachusetts did not act with that life that was expected, supposing they had not a just call for such a work."

TO WILLIAM DYER IN NEWPORT, RHODE ISLAND
August 1655
My dear husband,

Greetings of grace, mercy, and peace to you and our children. I pray for you moment by moment of every day, that you're growing in grace and wisdom.

This has proved a difficult summer for Sir Henry and his family. The elder Sir Henry died at his estate in Kent, having once been comptroller and adviser to King Charles and then putting his loyalties with Parliament and Oliver Cromwell during the war. Father and son fell out over a political matter ten years ago, and their relationship was strained. As you surely remember, the elder man was desirous of being a member of the Council of State five years ago, but was passed over. His son, our friend, was named instead, and there has been ill feeling. When the father died last May, members of Parliament whispered none too softly that he made away with himself. The four sons and five daughters attended the funeral service, and he was entombed at Shipbourne. Harry is his firstborn and heir, so he inherited most of the estate and all of the responsibilities.

Harry, no longer in the good graces of Oliver Cromwell, wrote a small book called *The Retired Man's Meditations,* in which he attempts to join the many jagged fragments of religion under the Commonwealth, and still provide for liberty of conscience and separation of civil and religious powers. The Lord bless him—because without divine intervention it will not come into being if one considers all the factions. Harry has proposed a convention to write a constitution guaranteeing liberties and deciding the limits and extensions of government of the Commonwealth.

His former friend, Oliver Cromwell, has ordered on one hand that all Catholic priests to leave the country; on the other hand, he has selected new members of Parliament based on their piety and loyalty to the reformed church. In their zeal, they have outlawed the celebration of the Christ Mass and its frivolities, which has caused much grief among the people of London. The Protector has met George Fox, and while not convinced of the gospel, he was convinced of Mr. Fox's sincerity and personal austerity, which are chief qualities of reforming Puritans. That may protect Fox from arrest in the City, but he is loath to stay here while his Friends are persecuted around the country.

Here at Raby Castle, we have peace. The occupying Parliamentary forces in the last decade damaged property but didn't destroy it, as they did at countless other houses, castles, and monumental churches, possibly because Harry's brother George was active in its defense. Harry has presented the government with a demand for reimbursement for the timber in his forests and the repairs he's had made because of their vandalism.

Through Sir Henry's friends, I've learned of the great loss of life in the English navy, due to fevers and flux in Jamaica. Hundreds of men who were eager to take advantage of free land grants have died. If our son William is intended to sign on to one of the trading ships going to the Indies, I pray you will intervene.

My dears, I treasure your letters and notes, and ask that you continue to remember me with your messages and tokens of love. As your mother, I remind you of your duty to study your lessons and apply your best efforts to your work, as unto your master, Christ.

I leave you with confidence in the providential and tender hands of our Father in heaven, and remain your loving
MARY DYER

*****

October 27, 1655
Westminster

Mary picked her way through the offal and debris in the warrens of Westminster Yard. The wet fog from the Thames and the coal smoke from thousands of homes combined to make an oppressive atmosphere in which one could hardly tell the end of afternoon from the evening. As a matter of fact, it was only mid-afternoon. She was grateful for her water-repellant cloak.

There was a stinking dead cat on the pavement that was so close to a cook shop, she wondered how the cook had any customers. A sailor was using a prostitute, both of them standing under the overhang of a tenement building, with no regard to lookers-on. A cluster of tough-looking young men eyed the bag that Mary clutched close, but then melted away into shadows. She caught a few of their words in a gust of wind off the river: "It is a ghost. She glistens."

Smiling to herself, Mary straightened up with an odd sort of pride—that she was the daughter of the King of heaven. She silently thanked God for protecting her with a veil of light that the unbelievers feared.

She found the door she was seeking. After her knock, she was let into the building, and directed up the stairs. She wished she had God's light to show her which stairs were sound and which broken, but it didn't work that way.

She arrived at the flat, knocked again, and let herself in to a room with perhaps fifteen women, several toddlers, and a wailing baby. The laboring mother, a woman in her early twenties, was sitting on the edge of a cupboard bed, laughing with her friends. So the labor had hours to go, yet.

"Mrs. Dyer," said the young mother, "I welcome you to my home. I'm called Hester. My chaplain, Thomas D'Arcy, told me you were visiting London, and recommended you as an excellent midwife, and full of wisdom."

"My dear," said Mary, "There are many midwives more qualified than I. I'm only here to assist should I be required. I suspect that your chaplain invited me here to speak with you of spiritual matters, for as you know, death sometimes stalks the birthing chamber, and you must be ready to enter the kingdom of heaven, and if your babe does not survive, that it will be safe in God's presence until you are called there yourself."

Hester swallowed hard. "My mum bore eight children, and all lived, so I hope that I'm like her. She died of hard breathing, not childbirth."

"Ah, yes. This London air is poison. Is your midwife here?"

"Not yet, Mistress. She sent word that she'd come as soon as she could."

Mary asked Hester's friends to acquire the clean sheets, the baby's swaddling, some unlit candles if more light were to be needed, and buckets of clean water for washing. "Not Thames water, mind! Well water, and that well-boiled after it's drawn," she said.

One of the girls built up the fire in the tiny grate, and they set the water to heat. Mary rubbed Hester's shoulders and back to relieve tension as the cramps came and went.

When they had finished, Mary asked, "Now, Hester, I expect you've witnessed many childbirths over the years." The young woman nodded. "Are there any questions about your labor, or about your new babe, that you'd like to ask while we wait for the child to come?" She explained what would happen during the lying-in, and how she'd help Hester to endure the pain of the contractions with breathing, crouching, and walking about, and herbal infusions to calm and strengthen her.

"To take your mind off your travail and to keep your friends calm and settled, I like to tell stories. Would you like that?"

A chorus of yeses answered her.

"Then I shall tell you my favorite, the story of Queen Esther. Hester is named for her. Esther wasn't always a queen. She was a Jewess, the daughter of parents who had been taken captive by the Babylonians, who in turn had been conquered by the Medes and Persians. But she was orphaned as a young girl, and became the ward of her relative, Mordecai, who worked in the citadel of the king, Ahasuerus.

"The king was fabulously wealthy, and after several extravagant banquets for his ministers and even the common people living at the fortress of Susa, where he displayed his abundant riches, he made a terrible error: he commanded his wife, Queen Vashti, to display herself, her raiment, and her crown, to the men of his kingdom, for she was beautiful and she wore his gifts well. Vashti was his most valuable property."

At this, the women in the birthing chamber nodded, knowing that any dowry or inheritance belonged to a father and then a husband, never to a woman. But to be commanded to expose herself as a prized concubine or caged tigress instead of an empress, was more than any woman should have to bear, for it stripped away her humanity.

"Vashti was having none of it," Mary said. "She refused the king's command. Though you may hear sermons that she was wicked for disobeying her husband, Vashti was correct to protect her modesty, and therefore her husband's dignity in front of his ministers and subjects, when her husband's judgment had lapsed in a drunken stupor. But Vashti's righteous actions had consequences. The princes and magistrates of Ahasuerus' empire were incensed that a woman, even of Vashti's stature, would disobey her husband's order, and said in their council of state that soon the commoners would hear of her rebellion, and there would be anarchy—the fabric and foundation of society would break down.

"The council decided that a decree should be published that a man was the master of the house, that Vashti should lose her position, and that the king should have a new virgin every night—and the king was pleased with his wise men, as you might imagine."

The London birthing chamber erupted in laughter. "Dogs will be dogs," said one of the women in waiting.

Mary continued, "This is where young Esther comes to the story. She was probably only fourteen to sixteen years of age. All the virgins in all the provinces were required to be inspected for their beauty or lack of it, and of course the exceptionally beautiful were sent to the king's harem to be prepared with a year of skin treatments and cosmetics. After they spent the night with Ahasuerus, they were given a gift and moved to the concubines' harem, from which they were sometimes called, but they could not ask to be recalled. At Esther's turn, she accepted the advice of her eunuch, which was to decline a gift so as not to look greedy—or imply being paid for her favors like a prostitute. The king was intrigued, and she was recalled several times, and Ahasuerus loved her for her kindness as well as her beauty. He set Vashti's crown on Esther's head and held another vast banquet in her honor, not knowing that he loved a conquered Jewess, for Mordecai had told her to keep silent on the matter.

"Meanwhile, outside the palace, Mordecai had overheard a plot to assassinate the king, and through a message to Ahasuerus passed through Esther, had prevented the murder. Now when Haman, a counselor of the king, passed in the streets, the custom was for every person to bow down to him—except that Mordecai refused to bow down, and this enraged Haman. Haman knew that Mordecai was a Jew, and that there were thousands of Jews across the empire. He decided he would find a way to exterminate every man, woman, and child, even the elderly and frail. The way he proposed it to Ahasuerus, the Jews kept different laws and were therefore a danger to the peace and order of the state." She paused for a moment, remembering her short years in Boston and the conflict between the Puritan church-state, and the followers of Anne Hutchinson.

She went on. "Haman offered to pay for the extermination, and put a fortune in silver into the treasury for the opportunity."

Hester's contraction interrupted the story, and when the groaning was over, the women passed sweetmeats and cups of cider and beer around the chamber. It was a celebration of new life, with gift-giving and guessing games.

When they settled down again, Mary continued her narrative. "Ahasuerus and his counselors discussed this offer of Haman's, and issued an irrevocable decree that on such and such a day, every Jew in the empire was to be killed and their goods confiscated. Perhaps some Jews fled or melted into the population—we aren't told. But the observant ones, who kept God's laws, put on sackcloth and ashes in mourning. Mordecai himself wailed and howled in the citadel, though he was forbidden to come to the palace in mourning clothes. Esther heard of his great distress and tried to comfort her cousin. But now Mordecai had an idea: Esther would be his agent at the royal court. She should go in and plead the lives of her people. Remember, Ahasuerus didn't know she was a Jewess, though more than six years had passed since he'd made her queen consort of the Medes and Persians.

"Esther reminded Mordecai that there was a law that no one entered the king's presence without an invitation, for it meant death unless he extended his scepter; and furthermore, the king hadn't called her to his bed for more than a month. Maybe after six years, a younger, more exotic girl had captured the man's fancy, and Esther's bloom had faded.

"But Mordecai sent back this message: 'Do not imagine that in the palace, you can escape any more than other Jews. For if you remain silent now, God will send relief and deliverance for the Jews from elsewhere, but you and your father's legacy will perish.' And here was Mordecai's lesson for Esther, and for all of us who hear God's voice in our conscience: 'Who knows whether you have not come to your position *for such a time as this?*'"

As Mary spoke the familiar words, she trembled inwardly at their importance. There was no fear, only a sense of awe, thanksgiving, and humility, knowing that God had spoken those words especially to her, at this time, reminding her again of her importance in his plan.

She paused and collected her thoughts. The women and girls had broken their trance-like attention.

"Hester, how do you fare? Shall we walk around for a bit?" It wasn't a suggestion. Two friends helped Hester to stand, and the expectant mother waddled around the room while another woman took this opportunity to put her toddler down on a rug for a nap. Hester had another contraction, harder this time, and she moaned in pain as her pelvis expanded in anticipation of the birth. But it would be a while, yet, Mary estimated.

She finished her story of Esther. "In a turn of authority, Esther commanded Mordecai to have the Jews fast and pray for three days and nights, and she did the same with her maidens. She said, 'Then I will go to the king, and if I perish, I perish.'

"During the time of fasting, Esther commanded that a feast of wine be prepared, and though she didn't know if she'd live to host it, she knew that her lord was magnanimous in his cups and would be likely to grant her requests. Then she did the reverse of what Queen Vashti had: she prepared herself in the most beautiful raiment and her royal crown, and entered his throne room with its ministers and court, to seduce him, at risk of her death.

"He held out his golden scepter to indicate his pleasure at seeing Esther, and she invited him to the banquet that night. When he had enjoyed the evening, he offered her whatever gift she pleased, unto half his kingdom. But again, she made no demand—only invited him and Haman to another banquet with music, entertainment, and wine.

"Haman went home to his wife and ten sons, sure that he had the trust and esteem of the king and his lady. He ordered that a seventy-five-foot gallows be built to hang Mordecai, and then went to the banquet the next evening.

"When the second feast had everyone in high spirits, the king asked again what he could do for Esther, and this is when she sprang the trap. She begged for her life, and the lives of her people. 'For we have been sold, to be slain. To perish. If we had been sold to work as slaves, I would have held my tongue, but the enemy could not have repaid the king's losses.'

"'Who is he that presumes to do this?' asked Ahasuerus, and Esther answered that it was Haman. The king was so furious that he stormed out to the garden to think. Haman threw himself on Esther's couch, begging his life. The king came back in and shouted that Haman was forcing himself on the queen in his own house, and had the guards carry Haman out with his head covered—perhaps to stifle his screams for mercy.

"Haman was hanged on the gallows he'd built for Mordecai, and Mordecai was elevated to second place in the empire, after Ahasuerus. Because even the emperor could not revoke a law, he and Mordecai wrote a new one, that the Jews were to arm themselves in defense, and that they could kill and plunder those who had persecuted them.

"This is how the girl Esther, an orphan in the care of her cousin, used her wit and her obedience to God's word in her heart, to save her people from oppression and death. When the moment comes, as it will to all of us in one way or another, will your eyes be open? Do you understand the urgency to be prepared for that day? Will you know that that time, that place, that turn of events, great or small, public or private, is the moment for which God has prepared you? Will you train your children to recognize the Shepherd's voice?"

All were quiet for a few minutes. The mood changed when the women heard through thin walls, the noises and cries of a couple having marital relations. Though they'd all heard the sounds countless times before, from earliest childhood, it broke the solemnity of Mary's teaching, and they all laughed. One of the girls imitated the cries and pants loudly enough to be heard through the walls before her friends hushed her, covering their laughter.

"Crying and panting, plus nine months, and the result is crying and panting!" observed another friend.

Then Hester's waters broke, and the stories stopped amidst the excitement. Her friends supported her as she walked around the room, held her hand as she groaned, screamed, and pushed, and they wept for joy when, hours later, Mary finally caught the healthy baby girl.

"Your babe has a lusty cry," said Mary as she cleaned, inspected, and wrapped the infant before handing her to Hester. "See how tenacious she is to grasp your finger? She'll need no instruction to learn the nipple from the touch on her cheek—though you may need help in the first days."

Hester's gossips gathered around the new mother and cooed at the baby as Mary delivered the placenta and bathed Hester. There was a knock on the door, and Hester's midwife, Prudence, rushed in and slammed the door.

"Oh, I'm sorry about that noise," she sighed. "I'm sorry to be so late, too. And you've already delivered the babe. I've just come from another birth, and I suspect there will be one more in the parish by noon tomorrow!"

"Sit down, my dear. You need to rest," said Mary. She signaled for one of the guests to bring a mug of cider. "Hester has brought a healthy girl into the world, and I'll sit with her through the night to be sure she's all right. But you're threadbare with exhaustion."

"Yes, I'll admit to that."

"Why don't you go home and sleep until you're called again. I'll make sure Hester's husband pays your fee to you. You'll register the birth and continue with her for her recovery. What do you say?"

"I'll just examine Hester, and accept your gift of rest with thanks," Prudence sighed.

They allowed Hester's anxious husband to enter and meet his first child, then shooed him out, and Prudence chose to stay the night and sleep off her weariness in the corner with the little children.

But the younger women lounged around the cupboard bed of the new mother, and listened to Mary Dyer's stories of America and its wild, foreign ways.

"Many people have called the Indians 'savages,'" said Mary after she'd described the Narragansetts of Rhode Island, "but what is a savage? A barbarous, cruel person or beast. That description fits no Indian I ever met, though some tribes have committed atrocities on other tribes and on European colonists. But here in England, I've met a woman who was treated barbarously and savagely in the name of religion."

Mary's listeners weren't surprised. The prisons were full of Anglicans, Quakers, Familists, Catholics, and suspected witches. Even in this time of Puritan supremacy, there were plenty of Puritans in prisons, as well.

"Have you heard of George Fox, the leader of the Quakers?" asked Mary. The women nodded, for Fox had been to London in the summer and had spent time with Oliver Cromwell. But Quakers were notorious for breaking up church meetings and courts with shouting and testifying, criticizing ministers and judges, and calling for God's judgment to be visited on them. Some people considered them to be mad.

"Fox says that before sin entered the world, men and women were equal, and that with rebirth in Christ, this equality returned. God's spirit does not dwell in stone or wooden temples made by man, but in the hearts of his people—both men and women."

A bold young woman spoke up. "Mrs. Dyer, you're a married woman? With children?" Mary nodded to both. "Yes. Hester has borne her babe tonight, on the twenty-second anniversary of our wedding."

"Do you go about the marketplaces, preaching and shouting? What does your husband think about his wife speaking forcefully, as a man does?"

Mary smiled. "My husband has encouraged my education and allowed me liberties that other women do not enjoy. But I honor my husband by acting soberly and respectfully as our society demands. I do not preach to men, but obey the apostle who wrote that older women should teach the younger. I learned from a very dear friend that the birthing chamber is a perfect place to do that! You are the age of my oldest sons, born in America. Now, shall I tell you about savages?"

"Yes, please. Your stories are more interesting than the preacher on Sunday."

"All right, then. Dorothy Waugh was a serving maid in Lancashire, younger than you are, when she heard the gospel teaching of George Fox, himself a young man from a farming family, and became convinced that God had called her to testify to the truth of the gospel. Because being outspoken is forbidden in our society particularly for women, she has suffered arrest, prison and its privation, and whipping all over this country. Whenever she stands in a marketplace and speaks with her usual zeal, the local minister berates her both for her lack of formal training and for daring to declare that God speaks to her, an ignorant and blasphemous woman. As usual, the constable arrests her, or she's driven out of the town.

"Recently, Dorothy, and a woman called Anne Robinson, were committed to prison at Carlyle by the mayor of the town, Thomas Monke, because they testified against sin and wickedness of the minister and council of Carlyle."

"But Mrs. Dyer," said one of the mothers, "The minister? How would a servant girl with no education have the nerve to go against a university man? Begging your pardon, but that's just foolish!"

"Dorothy and Anne told me that God filled them with strength and boldness and the conviction that the truth must be said. Scriptures say there is neither Jew nor Greek, there is neither bond nor free, there is *neither male nor female*: for all are one in Christ Jesus.

"Some ministers are not called by God as we would expect, but by personal ambition that masquerades under godly guise. You know that in your hearts, and you may have discarded the idea, but it's true. The women, on the other hand, having heard the call of God, took the risk of punishment with full knowledge of the consequences that might follow. Even as Queen Esther did.

"Dorothy's speech in the Carlisle marketplace resulted in their arrest. Mr. Monke ordered an iron instrument of torture, called a bridle because it somewhat resembles the horse bridle, be locked in place around Dorothy's head as she was the speaker that day, which they kept on for three hours the first time. The bridle is not merely a cage. It has an iron bit in it which is placed on the tongue, and contains spikes to bite into the flesh of the tongue and mouth, to punish the woman for her former speech—and to show her her place as a dumb animal and their mastery over her. The ability to speak distinguishes humans from beasts, but with this iron cage, a woman is forced to be as silent as an animal."

"Mrs. Dyer, I've never heard of such a thing!" said one of the women in the birth chamber. Her voice betrayed her shock.

"No, I'm sure not. They're not used here in the south, where we have prisons and ducking stools. They're used in Scotland and the Borders to control scolds. In addition to the bridle, the authorities are accustomed to chain an offender to the pillory to expose the criminal to human and animal dung, rubbish, even men urinating on the woman's skirts. Sometimes onlookers are able to land blows on the bodies of the offender, too.

"Dorothy described what it felt like to wear the bridle. The mayor's man violently plucked off the hat that had been pinned to her hair, and it tore her scalp to do so. Then they put the bridle on her head, which weighed fourteen pounds, and tore her clothes to fasten it about her neck and shoulders. Her hands were bound and she was forced to stand for three hours with that heavy weight on her head and the bit in her mouth. The mayor announced that it was to make of her an example, and charged two pence of every person who came to stare at her.

"Afterward, she said, it was taken off and they kept her in prison for a while. Was this a merciful reprieve to Dorothy, or was it because some in the crowd were angry at her evil treatment merely because she'd quoted the Bible? Many people wept at the cruelty shown her, so I think the mayor was worried about revolt.

"But Thomas Monke was not finished with Anne and Dorothy. He ordered that the bridle be replaced on Dorothy's head, and he sent them out of the city, tied to the back of a cart like a donkey or ox, using vile, unsavory words that a Christian ought not use. The executioner whipped the women ten stripes as they walked out of the town gate, and after he removed the bridle, they were released."

Hester stirred, and hitched herself up to a sitting position. In a cross voice, she asked, "Why would anyone knowingly put themselves in the way of prison and scourging? Everyone knows that Quakers make their own trouble by their outrageous words and acts."

Her friend suggested, "Perhaps, like the martyrs in Foxe's book, there is no pain in persecution. Some of them sang as the flames licked their clothing."

"That could be," said Mary. "I hope it was so. Or the Lord may give them visions of what their martyrdom accomplishes, as he did to Moses on Mount Nebo. The beatitudes explicitly state that those who are persecuted in Jesus' name are truly happy. But because we've all seen death, we know that dying is sometimes painful and lonely. And no one we know has come back from heaven or hell to describe how it feels or what it's like. Indeed, if someone claimed that, they'd be hanged for heresy or witchcraft. And there's the possibility that the martyr feels every lash, every blow, every cold wind on her bare breasts, swallows her tears in thirst or starvation, hears every insult, sees his family in the crowd and mourns. But as is written in the book of Hebrews, he or she has only one view in sight: the cloud of unseen, but felt, witnesses to Truth, which is Jesus."

By unspoken agreement, the women settled down to sleep for the rest of the night. They left only one candle burning.

Mary's quiet, measured voice came from her place at Hester's side.

"My charge to you this night as we watch with Hester and her babe is to always stop and listen for God's voice in your heart. If you walk in the counsels of godly men and women, your salvation shall be sure, whether temporal or eternal, because the Lord offers grace to cover your sins and your errors. But at times, God will call you to obey him when it goes against the ways of the world. You must choose now that God will be your guide and your strength to overcome, and that he will provide a way through. That way, when the persecution inevitably comes, you'll be well on your way, with a disciplined, mature, muscular faith, like the Bible greats, who, with no firm evidence of God, still reached out and caught his hand—and now live forever."

TO MRS. KATHERINE SCOTT AT PROVIDENCE PLANTATIONS AND RHODE ISLAND
21st March 1656
My beloved friend,

Greetings in the Lord, who loves us with an everlasting love; and from Lady Frances Vane, who is a most charitable friend and hostess, and has taken me into her family as if I were a sister. Between Sir Harry and me, your virtues have been sung to her, and she has declared that if you visit England, you must be her guest and friend.

I cannot count the times I've wished you here, as much for your friendship, as for your midwifery and herbal skills, and to share the opportunities for enlightenment in our thinking, the renewing of our minds by the Holy Spirit.

Although I haven't met him face to face, I have heard several lectures by George Fox at a London meeting, and know that you would greatly enjoy his fiery temper and prophetic manner, as of an Old Testament prophet crying out. Yet in his quiet moments, he speaks warmly and intimately of the Light and love of God that causes us to tremble in awe that we should be so favored. At one time, Fox condemns vanity and he prophesies that God's vengeance will fall on the persecutors of the Friends; and at another, he opens man's sinful condition, and leads the sinner to the Light of the world.

Another man, only in his twenties, is a powerful and persuasive preacher. I'm not yet convinced of his teaching and must think on it carefully. He declares that there is one saving baptism, that of the Holy Ghost and fire, but they do not use water baptism, neither sprinkling nor immersion. They also do not administer the bread and wine of Communion as a Christian ordinance, but instead, take up the inward (spiritual) body and blood of Christ and abide in him and are nourished. Likewise in other emblems of worship, in singing, or preaching, or public prayer, there is the will of man. It is carnal and traditional. This man, Burrough, says, "Prayer with the Spirit of Truth we do own, for that is not in word merely to be seen of men; not by custom, form and tradition, but by the Spirit, which has free access to God, and which He hears, and accepts."

Some Friends are preparing to go to New England, New Amsterdam, and Virginia to preach the gospel and have sought my recommendations. For myself, there is no call at this time, but the Lord knows it is my desire, and I await his word.

Countless thanks are due you for keeping my little children and for supervising their education, when William is upon his business. When the Lord called me here, I had no idea of the length of the journey, and in truth, the end is not yet in sight. Some women and men have left their possessions and all they love, to take up the cross and follow Christ through trials and persecution, perhaps unto death. We desire that all people may be saved, and come to knowledge of the glorious gospel which has shined in our hearts, and shown us the Father because we know the face of his Son.

I send showers of kisses to my children, adding to the mother's tender care that you have so richly bestowed. Greetings to your husband, and to your nephew Edward. May the Lord bring us all together soon, is my fervent prayer.
MARY DYER
Written from the Strand, Charing Cross

*****

August 20, 1656
Mt. Wollaston, Massachusetts

"She's a beauty, Will!" shouted Ed Hutchinson, from the top of his wooden gate to the pasture. "Take her around again. I want to watch her gait."

Only a quarter-mile to the north, the sun glinted off the waves of the bay north of Ed's farm at Mt. Wollaston, inherited from his parents.

This area about six miles from Boston had been a thorn in the side of Governor Winthrop twenty years ago, with disaffected Pilgrims nearby, Anglicans setting up a pagan maypole, Ed's uncle John Wheelwright preaching antinomian salvation by grace here, the Anglican Reverend Hull having to be silenced, and the town being plagued by wicked, profane sailors, fishermen, and boat builders at Weymouth.

William Dyer brought the chestnut mare back to the gate and dismounted, tossing the reins to Edward. "Your turn. See if she isn't the smoothest ride you've ever had, smoother than a boat on a glassy pond. You could put an infant to sleep in your lap while she's trotting. Go on!"

Edward opened the gate, mounted the mare, and tried her for a short distance on the wagon road that ran from Weymouth up to Roxbury and on to Boston. He pushed her a bit, and she didn't appear winded or reluctant to keep her speed.

"She can go all day without flagging," Will said with obvious pride upon Edward's return. "I've supplied some like her to the Rhode Island militia, and some to Barbados, too. They all have nothing but praise for our pacers. So I'll take your order today for—how many?"

"Don't make me mortgage my farm at Pullin Point. If we can agree on a price, I'll take this lady for myself, and will demonstrate her at the training day. You and your partners will undoubtedly have a market greedy for your older colts."

So the two old friends struck a bargain of cash and barter, and then walked along the beach of the small bay where they were able to talk privately with only the gulls to hear. William wanted to know about the Quakers who had arrived in Boston so recently. He had reason for his curiosity, because of his wife, naturally, but also because it was the most interesting topic in New England right now: would the mad Quakers of England bring their odd beliefs to America, and what would Massachusetts Bay's theocratic courts do about it?

"The *Speedwell* came into the harbor," said Edward, "and was stopped as usual in the deeper waters until her business could be discerned and she be carried in to the proper slip according to her cargo. The passenger list contained four men and four women with 'Q' before their names, and Governor Endecott ordered them brought directly to the court and examined. As is the Quakers' wont, apparently, they gave personal testimonies of their conversions and used the occasion to proselytize even the Boston ministers, if they could!"

William mentioned that he'd heard a Quaker ranter in London once, and their beliefs and emotional behavior held no appeal for him. "What came next?" he asked.

"Endecott and the ministers Wilson and Norton were most offended, of course. The eight were committed to the jail until a ship for England could be found. But one of the men, a Christopher Holder, immediately demanded their release on the grounds that no law existed that justified their arrest and imprisonment."

"He spoke truly, and Endecott's fellows were infuriated. The Bay's charter does not permit imprisonment on the grounds of religious belief. So Endecott's court began what I think will be a series of laws meant to catch up with what is happening at the time. Perhaps he thinks they won't know that the laws to convict them are so recent—or in some cases, not yet written!"

William sighed. "It's Endecott's inconsiderate, rash way to jump into a situation and make it worse without properly considering every angle. In England, a law is written by heated but reasonable discussions, negotiations, and honing by many men with experience in the law and consideration that the law could be repealed or overturned by future actions. It takes time, time that is useful for the cooling of hot tempers and for wise heads to prevail. Here—there's no process unless you count a dictator's floundering around like a child in a tantrum."

Edward agreed that the court's practices were not conventional by home country standards. "The laws of England must apply in an English colony," he said. "But, of course, they don't."

"The new order requires Quakers in custody to be considered 'dangerous persons' who are 'working to reduce the people of this jurisdiction to their abominable tenets.' They're to be kept close prisoners, not allowed visitors, or to confer with defenders, or to have paper or ink to communicate their beliefs or experience."

"The problem with that, or one of the several problems with that," said William, "is that there is no evidence of a crime by the accused prisoners. Based on a presumption by the ship's master, or a suspicion of Boston's very suspicious court members, any person could be arrested, hauled off to the cobhole, and forgotten for months until it's convenient to try them before a panel of ministers—not a jury of twelve men following procedure refined over hundreds of years."

"And if the verdict goes to their guilt," said Edward, "I doubt they'll have the recourse of appeal to a higher court in England, because they haven't had a proper trial in the first place. With the distance and time involved, their sentence, whatever it may be—fine, hanging, hard labor, banishment—will be executed immediately."

"Further," he continued, "there was an order to the jailer to search, as often as he sees appropriate, the prisoners' possessions, especially for pen and papers, and seize them. In this way, they cannot make notes or write letters for their own defense."

William kicked an empty sea shell out into the shallow bay surf. "We've worked very carefully to preserve our liberty of conscience in Rhode Island, and the separation of civil and ecclesiastical powers. If not for fighting against the oppression here in the Bay, we might not have cared very much, and I suppose our colony's body of laws might have been constructed the same way as Plymouth, Connecticut, or New Haven."

"Ah, Will, you're forgetting the unquenchable Roger Williams. He would never allow Providence or Rhode Island to conform to anything expected! For him, it has ever been soul liberty, and separation of powers. He won't even countenance such decrees as public days of feasting or fasting.

"As for me, I'm beginning to think that perhaps God's purpose in sending me back to Boston after their persecution of my mother was to place me here to speak for the cause of liberty of conscience," said Edward.

The men turned and walked back up to the pasture to admire the young mare. It was much more relaxing than talking politics.

September 1656

Raby Castle, Durham County, England

"Mistress Dyer," said the minister Thomas D'Arcy as Mary walked through the ornamental garden, stooping to sniff the lavender and the last roses of summer, "A messenger has delivered letters, and there's a parcel for you from America. I thought you'd want to know as soon as possible."

"Thank you, Thomas, I'll come inside in a few minutes."

Thomas turned and strolled to the stables and carriage house, and Mary watched him go. She had recently learned from Lady Frances why Thomas so strongly resembled the Vane brothers Henry and George and the others: Thomas was no maternal cousin. Thomas was their *sister,* Katherine Vane! She had been such a bright student that she'd insisted on enrolling in university—except that universities did not admit women.

The twelve-year-old Katherine had begged her father, who was a Privy Councilor to King Charles, to support her desire and aptitude for higher education, and eventually she wore him out with the asking. It was no light decision or indulgence: as a woman, she'd have been a valuable asset to marry to a noble family for political and business alliances. If she became a man, she'd never be able to marry, and there was the danger that her deception would be discovered, in which case she could be executed. And she'd have to lay aside her Vane family identity forever.

Katherine had donned men's clothing, taken the name of her maternal grandfather, and been reborn a university student, now free to travel unmolested, move unhampered by skirts and petticoats, become educated, find work and be useful—and at this last bit, Mary giggled—become a Puritan preacher. What an abomination to those legalistic Calvinists!

What delicious irony: the pious, righteous, Elect of God, who called women the evil daughters of Eve who led Adam to sin; who said that too much reading or intellectual stimulation of women would cause madness; who forbade "weak-minded" women to speak in public or contradict a man, who believed that in the Resurrection, the saved would take the physical form of men—should be ministered to, interpreted scripture and taught by, a sheep in wolves' clothing. *A ewe sheep!* At this, she burst out laughing, and hastily covered her mouth lest a groundskeeper observe her own temporary madness.

Katherine Vane, born 1628, was no longer. Thomas D'Arcy now lived amongst the crowded tenements of London, visiting the sick, teaching and interpreting scripture, and comforting the dying. Mary could see only good about that. There was even a portrait of Thomas, made about the time of his university commencement, and kept by his sister, Lady Margaret

Vane Pelham. Thomas' living was provided by his family, with whom he kept some distance for the safety of all concerned. Mary's heart warmed to see the deeply-rooted love that ran through the Vane family.

Mary knew why Henry's and Frances' latest child was named Katherine, and why Thomas D'Arcy had journeyed so far north to Raby: it was to baptize his—her—his—namesake. He was beloved of his family, those to whom he ministered, and his God. Though his appearance was altered, the same spirit shone through.

Besides, Mary thought, the human spirit, which has no gender, is created in the image of God. The body is only the housing of the spirit, and the manner in which the body was clothed had the least importance.

While Thomas hoped to reconvert Mary to Puritan thinking and salvation, Mary hoped to reveal to him the glorious Light of God, and knew that she'd never go back to the condition of dark slavery perpetrated by the church-state in Boston.

By now, Mary had reached the Neville Gateway, and she entered the deep shade of the twin battlements to skirt the small courtyard and walk into the great hall. There were carpenters at work on several of the rooms, maintaining the three-hundred-year-old structure and modernizing it according to the plans of architect Inigo Jones, the same architect she'd met twenty-some years ago in London. She gave a friendly smile to the workmen as she stepped around their tools and sawdust.

One of the servants brought her parcel to her room. Mary sat on a cushion under the new window recessed in the ten-feet-thick stone wall. The window had been enlarged from a quatrefoil arrow slit and the window seat enlarged from the space where an archer once knelt. She began to read her lengthy missives, mostly in Will's hand. One was addressed to Sir Henry, and she set it aside for Lady Frances to decide its disposition, for Harry was imprisoned at Carisbrooke Castle on Wight.

TO MARY DYER AT RABY CASTLE, DURHAM
1 June, 1656
My most dearly beloved wife,

O, be merciful and fly home to me: I long for you, and beg you with tears to speed your return to New England, where your children languish without their mother. I enclose their notes, childish drawings and a sample of Marie's embroidery—how it reminds me of you!—to call to mind their love and need of your watch-care and teaching.

Samuel is engaged to work with Ed Hutchinson, as you know. But here is some gossip: he has cast his eye upon little Anne Hutchinson, and perhaps when he becomes his own master and she is older, there will be a marriage.

You may be amused to learn that our William, a lad of nearly sixteen, has found his calling. He heard the Siren song not of the sea, to which I'm training him to be a trading captain, but of the courts and assemblies. The boy would aspire to be a magistrate like Mr. Winthrop, or an attorney like his father, if I did not curb this tendency. He may tread the paths of government after he has completed his apprentice service in shipping.

Young Maher is only twelve, but the boy has a spine and a sense of justice and equity that is more of you than of me. From me, he gets the thrill of the well-executed trade.

Henry is a green sprout of nine years. I struggle to keep him at his studies when he'd prefer to be running with the horses and learning hunting lore from the Indian lads. Henry has bravely suffered my application of the strap not a few times, but he's a good boy in ways that matter.

Marie, at eight years, is an obedient girl, and in addition to her housewifely duties learned from Katherine Scott and our maid Cathy, I've taught her to read and write so she'll have every advantage available to her curious mind. She reads more advanced works than Henry does. Patience Scott, who has the strength of her Aunt Anne Hutchinson, has become almost a twin sister to Marie. Mistress Scott tutors both girls daily when our girl is biding with them at Providence.

Charles, a boy of six, has begun his schooling, and though he is our youngest, he seems to be a fatherly, nurturing sort who loves the turning of seasons, the cycle of crops, and the husbandry of animals. My duty every evening is to find the kittens and puppies he smuggled to his bed, and send them back to the barn where they belong. I've not discovered skunk or squirrel kits in his quilts, but can they be far behind? Charles is the living image of my father.

Children teach us who our parents were, and remind us of our own formation. The traits I see in them that were not from the Dyers of Kirkby LaThorpe must be from the Barretts of London, and I respect your father the more, though I never knew him in life.

I am well, as usual. The only concession I make to my 46 years is my hair color and the shape of my hairline.

Captain Underhill has been living on Long Island, variously at Southold, Setauket, and Oyster Bay, where he is developing a large estate called Kenilworth, after the Warwickshire castle where his father served Queen Elizabeth and Robert Dudley, Earl of Essex. (I daresay he chose the name also to flatter Lord Rich, earl of Warwick and patron of New England.) This Kenilworth is near New Netherland, on the edge of English territory. It should provide him a peaceful retirement from conflict, and rest from those blood-thirsty crusaders in Boston. Mrs. Underhill sends her greetings, but she has been ill, and prays that you'll return in time to see her again ere her death.

Political matters between Rhode Island and the Providence Plantations remind me of the fens of Lincolnshire and Norfolk: strips of fertile soil, bearing abundant corn and cattle, and peat bogs in the lowlands between them. I never dreamed, when I signed the Portsmouth and Newport Compacts, and helped carve our towns from nothing into the second-most port in New England, that I could rise to be a militia captain, attorney general, or commander-in-chief on the seas. (You knew it, though, my dear.) Nor did I know that one could lose respect cultivated for many years, in a space of moments. Those lords and proprietors of the mighty empire of Massachusetts said that I was ineffective and tried to rise above my meager calling as a farmer's second son. But with the advantages of education and connections offered by the Hutchinsons and Blackbornes, your family's legacy, Harry Vane, and many others who built me up, I've risen in the world. It would not have been possible in Old England.

The people of Rhode Island resent my avarice in the late war with the Dutch; and there is the Coddington faction who resent my adherence to the principles laid out by our 1643 charter, the laws we've written and tried, and my loyalty to Roger Williams and John Clarke.

I've laid suit for £500 to Mr. Coddington regarding property boundaries, but also have publicly and politically reconciled to him as of 14 May, when the records of the Assembly (that I so carefully wrote for many years and that he stole away and returned under duress) pertaining to Coddington were ordered destroyed. The Assembly also refuses to hear complaints against him in an effort to repair his reputation and restore his authority. Yet I have not vacillated or betrayed one faction to take up another, but only acted upon my conscience in individual matters rather than taking the easy road to popularity by siding with the powerful. You understand well how that would stir up adversity. For the time being, I will attend courts and Assembly, but choose to remain silent. Perhaps my detractors will think I've grown wise. Perhaps they are finally correct.

Newport is a haven for religious dissenters of all sorts. Portuguese Jews are planning to move here from Barbados, and there are a few Catholics who live quietly. There are no Quakers here yet, but rumors have them preparing delegations for Maryland and New England. Most dissenters to the Massachusetts and Connecticut regimes are Baptists, but some claim no religion at all and have come here for respite from the Pharisaical actions of John Endecott and Mr. Wilson, whose lash can't have too many knots or draw enough blood to quench their hot rage. Surely they are bloody brothers with Bishop Bonner and Bloody Mary of the last century, and the High Priest Caiaphas.

I've heard that Walter Blackborne is ailing. Surely one last visit from you to convey our respects and my lifelong gratitude would be welcome to him. If you do see him, you may read parts of this letter to him.

Once again, I remind you of your home here, the children who long for a mother's arms, and your husband who holds you in great esteem as well as tender love. In this packet there is a letter of credit for your comfortable passage on a ship—promise that you'll take a private cabin, or share with one companion if you must, but do not go below decks or associate with the rough seamen.

As I did so many times when you were present, I do now in my dreams: I hold you close and cover your face in kisses. Let it be so again.
Your loving husband,
WM DYER

Mary's eyes filled with tears, which splashed on her dark gown and disappeared. Will had grown during her absence. He seemed to see for himself now what had separated them: his reckless disregard of moral principles for selfish gain and worldly approbation. He was as persuasive as ever, too: Mary would love nothing better than to leap onto a horse, ride like a Valkyrie to Bristol, and sail back to America. She still had a few more responsibilities, but yes, it was time to go home. She thought she felt approval when she was in her quiet time with the Spirit.

And that surprised her just a little. Hadn't she spent more of her life in England than America? England, with its mist and green, its massive cathedrals (steeple-houses) and castles, its history, culture, and creature comforts—not home? Yet there was nothing left to do here. She'd found what she hadn't been looking for, and she was finished preparing for life and death. It was time to accomplish the purpose the Lord was revealing, bit by bit.

Mary read her children's short letters next, then picked up another message in Will's hand, from Herod Gardner, her friend in Newport.

TO MARY DYER AT RABY CASTLE, DURHAM
My dear friend,

I send warm greetings, praying that you are well, and that the next ship brings you safely back to your family. Your husband is kind to write this letter for me. Surely his letters speak of your children, so I shall tell you a story or two (if Mr. Dyer does not tire of scribbling or the ink run dry) of New England. Both stories are in regard of Governor John Endecott, that you may know what darkness fills his heart, and be warned of how to act upon your return. Yes, your return. I feel it coming, as if the first warm breezes of April are trembling in the birch leaves.

The first is that Mr. Endecott, in defiance of his own Parliamentary party in England, has directed the minting of shillings and sixpence in Boston, with the date of 1652 stamped thereon—every year, 1652. If England asks how these counterfeit coins appear, the governor can claim that they were made before the order to cease. The coins, made of silver plate and Spanish coin, are alloyed and known to be light in silver. Roger Williams said of Mr. Endecott, it is a dangerous combat for the potsherds of the earth to fight with their dreadful Potter. Oh, to have the courage to say those words myself, though I am a woman.

The other story concerns Mr. Endecott's second son, Zerubbabel Endecott. Two years ago, the young man of 20 years was named the father of a servant's child. The indentured servant, Elizabeth Due, testified—and I will rely on Mr. Dyer to write this story in correct form though I speak the events out of order—that coming over alone, having been sold from England as a girl in 1650, she had only fellow-servants for acquaintances. She was a lace-maker for Mrs. Endecott, whose son Zerubbabel was nothing like the righteous high priest after whom he is named. The governor's son pursued the unwilling Elizabeth at every occasion with unseemly words and carriage, and fathered a child on her in 1654. When she was tried for fornication at April General Court, a fellow-servant, Cornelius Hulett, was accused as the father, though Elizabeth denied he'd ever so much as kissed her. She insisted that Zerubbabel was to blame, and for her troubles she received 13 lash-stripes (some say 12 only, saving one for mercy's sake). The governor set her at liberty though there were three years remaining on her indenture, and gave her in marriage to Cornelius. However, Elizabeth persisted in her explanation that Zerubbabel had forced himself upon her and fathered the child, and she and Cornelius were innocent of fornication and of slander. At the December court, Cornelius received ten stripes for his supposed fornication with Elizabeth, and she herself was stripped to the waist and received twenty more on lecture day, so all of Salem could see her shame. Then she was made to stand at the pillory, though it was freezing, with a paper pinned to her forehead that was inscribed in capitals, "A SLANDERER OF MR. ZEROBABELL ENDICOTT." Zerubbabel, being the governor's son, was never ordered to provide for the babe nor punished, unless you consider that Zerubbabel was hurriedly married to one Mary Smith.

If this is how the governor treats with an orphaned and friendless servant, brutally tortures the naked and nursing mother of his first grandchild, covers the lies and fornication of his son, and treads the razor's edge of treason regarding the coinage, is there anything he will not do in his zeal to persecute those he hates? He exults in torture of his enemies. When you return to New England, I pray that you'll consider landing at Newport, Barnstable, or even New Amsterdam. Boston is a viper's nest, and Plymouth is as savage.

George Gardner and I expect our sixth child in a short time. The other children are content.

With my respects to you and to Sir Henry Vane, I am your faithful friend.

HEROD GARDNER per William Dyer
Newport, Rhode Island

Dear Herod, Mary thought. She has overcome so much adversity in so few years. It was kind of her to warn about Governor Endecott. He was so cruel that his reputation was known even in England. John Endecott, that dangerous man Mary had had a premonition about so many years ago, who had so viciously attacked Anne Hutchinson at her trial, and who was responsible for the near-fatal beating of Rev. Holmes, the Baptist minister in Newport. The proof was in the pudding, she mused, then she chuckled at the idea of food when she remembered Geoffrey Chaucer's *Canterbury Tales*: "Therefore behooveth him a full long spoon, That shall eat with a fiend."

Mary wished she'd kept a journal during the turbulent years of Boston and the settlement of Rhode Island, but excused herself when she remembered the difficulties and dangers of the time, the eighteen-hour days of hard work and mothering—not to mention the great expense of imported paper. Ah, if Anne had kept a journal, how wonderful to have captured her genius for the generations to come. Anne was a creature of the Light. She hadn't spoken often in those terms, but she understood the filling of the Holy Spirit.

Mary's journal, begun during her voyage to England, contained a summary of her experiences in those years, the hurricanes and earthquakes, the miracles Mary had witnessed, the accounts of the Lord's direct revelations to her. After composing the summary, Mary had written at greater length of her encounters with Anne Hutchinson and Roger Williams, William Robinson, and Christopher Holder, and her thoughts and experiences filled many pages in the folio. Among the most treasured pages were those which contained the testimonies of the women Mary had introduced to the Light.

Criminals, vagabonds, and Quakers were severely and savagely treated in England, and Mary documented the sufferings and the testimonies of her Friends. They were tortured to extract false confessions and give up names to the authorities, mutilated by nailing an ear to the pillory, had their tongues bored with a red-hot awl, whipped until they were near death, were slowly hanged until they strangled. To be imprisoned or thrown down a thief's hole often meant starvation, deadly disease, or madness, unless loved ones could bribe guards or judges to provide food and speed the trial process. George Fox spent months at a time in prison and had been beaten numerous times for preaching inside and outside the steeple-houses, as he called them. The "church" was a body of believers, not an inanimate building.

Mary had managed to avoid persecution thus far by ministering in the way she'd learned from Anne Hutchinson: to attend births with her midwifery skills, and talk on an intimate level with the women in labor and the gossipers sharing the birth chamber. Teaching women in private homes was also an effective ministry that was difficult to criticize from a biblical stance because she wasn't upsetting the societal expectation that a woman should not be permitted to teach a man. But anytime she was in a crowd of people listening to a Friend preaching in a marketplace or barn, she was also at risk of arrest and beating. Being the wife of a Rhode Island official wouldn't matter a bit to an English sheriff.

She sighed at the Friends' ordeal, but was frustrated about the theatrical demonstrations by those who walked barefoot in the snow or stripped nude to show their innocence before God and man: they made more of their cause than they did of their Master. It tainted all the Friends' reputations.

Here at Raby Castle, Henry Vane's massive residence in County Durham, she was surrounded by the deer park and the stream winding below the castle walls. The tiny village of

Staindrop lay a mile down the carriage road, and its six-hundred-year-old steeple-house contained the stone effigies and remains of some of the Neville lords and ladies of Raby. It was a serene and beautiful refuge, but Mary wasn't hiding. She'd soon be on another of the Lord's errands.

Lady Frances Vane was the chatelaine of Raby, and she kept their children here in the fortress their grandfather Vane had purchased from King Charles thirty years ago. The castle was only sparsely furnished with furniture two centuries old, because of its renovations program and because the Vanes had other, more comfortable manors where they preferred to stay. Raby was where their children were born and baptized, and Mary had come here to attend as a midwife at the birth of little Katherine.

The family had stayed here for safety because Sir Henry had been recently arrested and taken to prison at Carisbrooke Castle on the Isle of Wight. He had refused a summons to council regarding his writing that the British military headed by Cromwell ought to submit to the authority of Parliament. He'd as good as called Cromwell a dictator. Carisbrooke was the same prison where King Charles had been imprisoned before his 1649 beheading, so they feared for Henry's life as well.

Her present surroundings blurred, and somewhere deep inside, Mary saw Henry Vane, his attire as rich as ever, with a paper in his hands. He stood on a platform with strong stone towers and walls around him, trying over a trumpet fanfare to read the speech he'd composed, but the paper was snatched from his hands and thrown into the crowd. From memory, then, Henry spoke with dignity, confidence, and some heat of the cause he had stood for, and of presently being at the right hand of Christ. "For my life, estate and all, is not so dear to me as my service to God, to His cause, to the kingdom of Christ, and the future welfare of my country. How much better is it to choose affliction and the cross than to sin or draw back from the service of the living God into the ways of apostasy and perdition."

Ah, no, thought Mary, with a stab of pain in her heart. It was the future she saw: Harry's execution.

Another entry for her journal. Another martyr of Christian conscience, only this man had been one of the foundation stones that bore up the weight of a great fortress. A fortress that could only be seen with eyes of faith, and touched with hands that knew from experience that there was something there to grasp.

That fortress of believers was the true Zion, not the plantations of New England, and not the Saracen lands of Palestine. Mary saw what Winthrop and Dudley, Wilson and Cotton had not: the Holy City was not a geographical location in heaven or on earth that could contain God, nor was it a steeple-house that could contain the Eucharist, but a community of souls gathered close to the heart of God. Believers are the temple of God, and sacred to him, the apostle Paul had written. Mary was comforted that sometime, probably sooner than later, both she and Harry Vane would be part of that cloud of glorious light.

Mary ran her fingertips affectionately over her husband's familiar, artistic quill strokes, folded the pages of her letters together and set them with her books, to be packed for her voyage back to New England.

Though she'd been in England for nearly five years, she still had only the one chest to send back. Her clothes were simple, plain, and serviceable from her travels with the Friends, and the few bits of evening finery she'd owned had been given away. She needed only a change or two of clothes and a warm cloak for winter. Most of the books she'd purchased had either been given away or, like his gift, *The Compleat Angler*, shipped to Will in Rhode Island. She would take with her only a few cherished books and her journal of her experience with the Friends.

Yes, it was time to go back to America. The Word in her heart was strong and clear about that.

*****

TO WILLIAM DYER AT NEWPORT IN RHODE ISLAND
14 October 1656
My dearest William,

Your letters and gifts are most welcome, and received with joy. I closed my eyes as I sat in a ray of sunshine, and felt the warmth of your embrace and the heat of your kisses.

If it be the Lord's will, and when he reveals the time, I shall indeed return to New England. I confess that it can't be soon enough, for I long to see our children and know the state of their hearts and minds.

I feel a great void of darkness and fear when I think upon Massachusetts and Connecticut. Not my fear, mind, but the fear of those who have no assurance of eternity, no joy in their hearts. They thought to build Zion, but their priests led them instead to Babylon. The people living in darkness are crying out for the Spirit of the Lord, for he is Love and love casts out fear. He is Light and casts away darkness with a word. Yet he will not force man to accept his grace. He has shown me that there will be much suffering as the Devil defends his stronghold, but Christ will prevail. Indeed, he has already prevailed, from the foundation of the earth.

It will be my pleasure to visit the Blackbornes, convey your respects, and say goodbye for the last time.

Sir Henry Vane is detained at Carisbrooke, as you may have heard. I pray for his comfort and for consolation for Lady Frances and their children—and that he may be freed or released to house arrest. Though we do not share exactly the same beliefs, I have observed the Light resting in him, even since the days of Anne Hutchinson. I heard this said of Sir Henry a few months ago: "Shall we say he is a scholar? Nay, but a rabbi, a doctor in the knowledge of Christ, in whom a greater fullness of the riches of wisdom and knowledge were treasured up than in most, like that disciple that lay in Christ's bosom."

I have no recent contact with Dr. Clarke, whom I believe to be in London, but if we meet, I shall greet him for you.

My dear William, do not fear for my safety as I journey back to America. There are Friends along the way who will extend their care and hospitality, yes, but ultimately I am in God's hands. You and I shall be reunited in his time and place. Until then, may the Light of his love fill you with perfect peace and trust in his goodness.

You are continually in my heart and my prayers. Embrace our sons and daughter for me.

MARY DYER, written from Raby Castle, Durham

*****

TO MARY DYER, IN THE CARE OF SIR HENRY VANE FROM KATHERINE SCOTT AT PROVIDENCE PLANTATIONS, THIS 10TH SEPTEMBER 1656

My dear sister in Christ,

I received your most sweet letter of April, by your husband, and praise God for the continuance of your health, and of the family of Sir Henry—to him give greetings of love and remembrance from my husband. I thank the Lord we are also in good health, and we long for your coming home.

Our farm prospers with Richard's expert husbandry, and our children grow like the mustard bush in the parable. John is 16, and a good mate with your William and Maher. Mary and Hannah are excellent tutors for your Marie, and Patience astounds me with her innate knowledge of the Bible—like the boy Jesus in the temple. Deliverance and Rich are learning to read.

My sister's son Edward Hutchinson and his household are also well. When his tribe, his sisters' families, and mine meet for fishing, sailing, and berry-picking, you cannot imagine the speed with which the cellar is laid bare, or the extra barrels needed for laundry day. The horses roll their eyes and lay back their ears at the swarm of children which descend like mosquitoes on the fields.

Mr. Bellingham, the Bay's former Governor and magistrate, has been strangely silent, Edward told us, regarding the trial of his sister, Mrs. Ann Hibbins. William Hibbins was a merchant and magistrate, and the Bay's agent in England for two years. Ann, if you remember, was censored in 1641 in a dispute with church members, but it seems that William Hibbins' position and money was enough to protect her from other charges. He lost £500 in an investment two years ago, and died thereafter. Because of her censorious, bitter spirit, always quarreling with her neighbors, she was brought to the Court of Assistants who acquitted her. But the people wanted her death, and the General Court tried her for witchcraft. Even the ministers Wilson and Norton supported Mrs. Hibbins. Norton was heard to say that she "unhappily guessed that two of her persecutors, whom she saw talking in the street, were talking of her, which cost her her life." Edward was one of her will's executors, and tells us that her will and her speech were quite reasonable and there was no evidence against her. Governor Endecott delivered her sentence, that she be hanged. The people there at the Bay, including the magistrates, are mad. The combined civil and ecclesiastical power is too great a burden for any man or community to bear, and it corrupts entirely.

There was a curious and tragic story that came to our ears a few months ago, and I relay it to you that you may exercise all caution when you return to this country. The ship *Charity*, mastered by John Bosworth, left England for Virginia, and encountered a stormy passage. Several weeks before they entered Chesapeake Bay, the sailors wondered if their bad fortune was the result of a witch in their midst. One Mary Lee, a small, quite aged woman traveling on her own, was suspected, and they demanded of Mr. Bosworth that she be examined. The captain at first refused, but the sailors clamored all the more. He consulted with two young merchant passengers, and foolishly yielded to the demand. Two sailors searched Mrs. Lee's body for witch marks and declared they had found them. They left her overnight, fastened to the capstan, during the storms, but in the morning light, when they could not prove their claims of witch marks, they declared that the marks had shrunk into Mrs. Lee's body. The 25-year-old passenger examined her again, and the terrified old woman, her nakedness on display to the crew, still tied up in the storm, confessed she was a witch. Though Mr. Bosworth opposed it, the crew hanged her, and when her life was gone, they tossed her body in the sea. One might wonder who took possession of her worldly goods.

The unholy union of church and state is the chief evil of the papacy, the Church of England, and of the Massachusetts Bay Puritans. They do not see the image of the beast in the mirror.

I trust that the Lord our God, who has kept us in health and safety, through storms of summer and snows of winter, through trials and grave threats to our freedom, through perils of childbirth and monsters of the deep, will preserve us and ours until we meet in joy and peace.

KATHERINE SCOTT

February 26, 1657
Barbados

Ah, this is the life I could have chosen, though at age forty-five, it's late to make a change, thought Mary Dyer as she and Anne Burden luxuriated in the private garden of her host, John Rous, a sugar planter who had grown up here. Rous had become a Friend during a stay in England. Last year he'd published a book about the depravity of the Anglican priests and their parishioners on Barbados, *A warning to the Inhabitants of Barbadoes Who Live in Pride, Drunkennese, Covetousnesse, Oppression, and Deceitful Dealings.* Henry Fell, a judge's clerk from Ulverston, Cumbria, was staying there while evangelizing the planters of Barbados.

Rous's home lay on the south coast of the island. Just a few yards away from the grass lawn, the blinding white-sand beach stretched out to a shallow turquoise lagoon where empty rowboats floated gently at anchor.

The palm fronds overhead rattled in the late afternoon's breeze, and the sun lowered toward the soft pillows of a distant squall. Exotic birds in the tones of royal jewels squawked noisily from nests under the porch eaves. Anne dozed on a settle made of wicker. Mary kicked off her shoes and felt scandalous to remove her hose under her long skirts—but it was her intent to walk barefoot across the hot sand and cool her feet in the tepid waves of the lagoon. She left her companion and headed for the Caribbean waters.

Mary's hostess in Bristol had been Mrs. Anne Burden, formerly a follower of Anne Hutchinson, who had moved back to England with her husband and children from Boston in 1651. They'd become Friends in the last few years. Her husband had recently died in Bristol with property and rents owed him by Massachusetts colonists. Anne had had no success in having agents settle her husband's estate, so it was her intent to sail to Boston, sell the Boston land parcels, and go back to England.

Anne was leaving her youngest children, aged six, ten, and twelve, with Friends in Bristol. Her older son was apprenticed to tanners, as his father had been. All eight of her children, including twin boys and a son who had died shortly after birth, had been baptized by John Wilson in the First Church of Boston. One of the factors in the Burdens' departure from Boston was that Anne had given birth to twins. Some people believed that twins were God's judgment, proof of a woman's adulterous liaisons: because a man could only implant the seed for one child in her womb. That her babies were identical was a point in favor of Anne's honor, though.

Mary only vaguely remembered the Burdens from their few years in Boston. Anne reminded her that George had signed the Wheelwright Remonstrance, as William Dyer had done. He'd been made a freeman in the first actions of the General Court in New Towne on May 17, the same day that Henry Vane had unleashed his furies and John Winthrop had been reelected governor. In November of that year, George was disarmed along with scores of other men, but he had apologized and after a period of probation and distrust by the Court, was allowed to remain in Boston. In the privacy of their home, however, Anne and George were dissatisfied with the church and its application of justice without mercy. The Lord had spoken to her heart one day, said Anne, and told her to keep silent about her beliefs, but to leave Puritan fellowship and move back to England with the children. George, who was surprisingly content about this major development, would follow in a few months.

As she settled into a house and waited for George to join them, Anne met women in Bristol who invited her to a home for a sewing party, making warm clothes for the poor. The hostess was a Friend. As their relationships grew, Anne remembered God's word to her in Boston, to keep silent, and that it must have been a prophecy about finding him in silence, a practice of the Friends.

Mary and Anne took ship in January. They'd had their scant belongings taken to the ship at Avonmouth, and they boarded and settled in their cabin near the captain's quarters in the stern, awaiting a favorable wind. While there, they praised God for the news they heard that Henry Vane had been released from prison at Carisbrooke.

They were companions in a tiny cabin above decks, as Will Dyer had insisted. They were treated with respect by the captain, and the rude sailors curbed their obscene and profane words around the women.

The first mate ordered the sails to be set, and the ship moved away from the frosty docks and into the Severn estuary. The winter storms, even hundreds of miles away, blew up gales and towering waves from the beginning of the journey.

Once out in the open sea, the ship had been violently tossed by such wicked storms that Mary and Anne had inquired of the Lord in their silent reverie, if they were doing God's will by returning to America. The calm assurance came that they were held securely in his hand, and to persevere.

But the screaming, icy winds that reminded Mary of the hurricanes in Boston and Newport, had broken icebergs away from the pack ice around Iceland and Greenland, and great deadly icicles hung from the ship's rigging. Sailors attacked the ice on the rails and deck with huge mallets and knocked it into the raging seas. The sails froze and were in peril of shattering like glass. The captain's every effort was defensive. After weeks of this, the ship was in danger of being driven upon the shoals off Newfoundland and Acadia. Finally, the captain gave up the fight, sailed past Cape Anne and Cape Cod in a howling blizzard, and made for Barbados to wait out the winter's fury.

By the skillful navigation of their ship's master, and the intervention of their Savior, they'd escaped all danger of pirate attacks. They'd arrived yesterday in the same port Mary remembered from her first Atlantic voyage, and they'd asked to be conducted to the home of their brother in the faith, Mr. Rous. They'd never met him before, but of course he was well known to Margaret Fell, and was a great supporter of George Fox and the Friends of England, so their hospitality was assured—and it was safe haven compared to an inn.

There was no winter here in the tropics, only the dry season. Mary and Anne would have sweltered in their woolen clothes, all they carried with them in the ship because they were traveling in winter, but Rous had asked the neighbor women to loan them linen and cotton garments to wear.

Mary thought Barbados was what Paradise must feel like. Between the fog, rain, and snow of England, and the blizzards and hurricanes of Massachusetts and Rhode Island, Barbados was a carefree, lovely dream where the sun stood high in the firmament. Perhaps this balmy island, for the few days or weeks they would be here, would be the calm eye of a swirling hurricane of persecution and extreme danger. In England, to which there was no returning, was the possibility—nay, the probability—of imprisonment, beatings, torture, and death. In New England, her home and mission field, she faced the same. Some Friends had already been persecuted in Connecticut, New Netherland, and Massachusetts, she'd heard.

Only at a seemingly great distance did she remember the last months of 1656 after leaving Frances and Henry Vane in County Durham.

Mary had completed her business in London, including visiting the Blackbornes for the last time and praying with them. She had assisted at the births of several Friends' babies and participated in women's meetings. She'd walked around Westminster, remembering her youth and visiting the graveyard at St. Martin-in-the-Fields where her firstborn son was buried. There were no tears for the son who would have been twenty-two years old now, for she trusted that his spirit was safe in God's presence, and someday soon, she thought, she would meet her first son William.

Then she had taken a coach across southern England, seeing the beautiful countryside along the Western Road for the first time. Through Reading, Newbury, and Marlborough, the coach jolted and stopped at intervals to change horses and passengers. A mail coach could make the trip in eighteen hours, but with passengers, freight, and muddy roads, overnight stops were required.

The woods, which had been gold and russet a few weeks ago, were now bare on hilltops, and hogs snuffled in the oak-leaf carpet for acorns. The fields below the fells had been harvested and the stubble plowed under with manure, awaiting the first snows. In the hedgerows, the vines had turned the color of dying embers. Flocks of sheep and herds of cattle grazed, blissfully unaware of the impending autumnal slaughter. School boys exploded from the door of their classroom and chased one another or threw balls on their way home for chores, and girls drove geese from the ponds to the barnyard.

In Wiltshire, the Western Road ran past the conical Silbury Hill, constructed by long-forgotten pagans. The coach descended

Labour-in-Vain Hill and came into the market town of Calne. They passed through Bath, where hot springs fed pools within Roman ruins. The coach followed the River Avon's course, crossing it several times at fords and bridges, until they entered Bristol's city gate and pulled up on King Street across from the cathedral green.

Mary arrived in Bristol in November to make arrangements for her voyage. There, the previous month, Quaker radical James Nayler had ridden through the city gates on a donkey, with several followers casting their coats before him as if he were the Messiah in triumphal entry. The Bristol sheriff seized and imprisoned Nayler, and some of the Friends had hastened to disengage from association with him.

Nayler was tried in London for blasphemy and impersonating Jesus Christ, and found guilty in December. Some Members of Parliament insisted that he be stoned to death, echoing the divine mandate in the Israelites' law. Instead, Nayler was whipped through London streets, exposed to December's freeze and the hurled rubbish and feces while his head and hands were locked in the pillory, had his tongue bored through with a red-hot awl, a letter "B" for "blasphemer" branded on his forehead, and made to repeat his Bristol ride as an antichrist, while facing backward on his donkey. He was again whipped through the streets of Bristol. However, that was not sufficient punishment for the Puritans who held political power: Nayler was committed to hard labor for two years in London prison.

Mary knew this beautiful tropical island, though it was a hotbed of evil in the towns, was a temporary haven, one last place to rest and gather her health and strength for the struggle before her. Though she'd told no one, she had again seen her end on the gallows. The Lord had laid open the path before her, and she felt no fear. Mary returned to the shaded porch of Rous's home, and took her journal, an inkwell, and a pen, and sat down to write.

She thought of the storm-tossed voyage, and of her desire to reunite with her husband and children. And she wrote,

> "When I perceived only darkness, oppressed as we were in the storm, and the ship turned on its side as if to spill its contents into the freezing sea, in a dream I saw a Light break forth. It danced along the rigging and masts, and at first its sparks trickled like a spring, then gushed

forth in a flood to envelop the little ship. This Light was no candle fire or reflection of starshine, but the Light of the Holy Ghost. It reached out for me, and took me in its arms as a lover, and warmed me but never burned. It convicted me of my sin of faithlessness, and gave me power to confess my unworthiness of forgiveness. When God had emptied me of selfishness, I was filled with Light, obtaining from the very Source, compassion, mercy, peace, forgiveness, and love.

"There is a new law in Massachusetts that prohibits the entrance of Friends, and from providing succor or hospitality to Friends who travel. Some of the Friends have already suffered beatings and are held in jails in the dark and cold. The Lord has shown me that he is the way and that he will be the Light unto my path, through the dark valley of Puritan New England. My destination is Boston, to come face to face with the ruthless persecutors of the faithful, John Endecott and John Wilson."

*****

TO MARGARET FELL AT SWARTHMORE HALL, CUMBRIA
19 March 1657
My dearly beloved in the Lord Jesus,

I was expecting to come away with the next ship. But truly at present the Lord hath ordered it otherwise, and, though it was contrary to my own will, yet by his eternal power, I was made willing to give up all to Him who hath laid down his life for me. Upon the 9th of February, the word of the Lord came to me that I should go to New England, there to be a witness for Him; so I was made willing to offer up my life and all in obedience to the Lord, for his word was as a fire, and a hammer in me. Though then in outward appearance there was no likelihood of getting passage thither, by reason of a cruel law which they have made against any Friends coming thither.

About the 25th day of February, a ship came in hither, which was going to New England, and was upon that coast, but the storms were so violent that they were forced to come hither, while the winter there was nearly over. In this ship were two Friends,

Anne Burden of Bristol, and one Mary Dyer from London; both lived in New England formerly, and were members cast out of their churches. Mary goes to her husband who lives upon Rhode Island, (which the Puritans call the island of error). In this ship the master hath permitted me passage. He saith he will endeavor to put me ashore upon some part of New England, out of their power and jurisdiction. The Lord hath a great work to do in that nation, and the time is hastening, wherein He will exalt his own name and his power over all the heathen that know him not."
HENRY FELL
Barbados

*****

Boston, Massachusetts
March 30, 1657

The heap of filthy snow where a lazy servant had spilled a chamber slop, pushed up against the east side of the prison, was the last thing she saw of the outside world before the door slammed behind them. With a rude shove from the jailer, Anne Burden was hurried from the office, through a short passage, then down the slimy, stinking steps to the damp earth floor. Mary Dyer received no such push, but the below-ground cell was also her destination.

The window above their heads was boarded up, and only slivers of light showed between the planks. At their feet was some straw that stank of human waste and crawled with vermin.

Both Anne and Mary were soaking wet from the day's drizzle. They'd been roughly handled when harbor officials inspected their ship's manifest and learned from the first officer that they were of that disdained group, the Quakers. The few belongings in their ship cabin had been confiscated, and they'd been rowed to the wharf and escorted straight to the courtroom for arraignment.

Deputy Governor Richard Bellingham, who had been a Member of Parliament for old Boston, was on duty, Governor Endecott being at his home in Salem, when Mary and Anne came before him. The women were made to stand before the bench while the Secretary, Edward Rawson, was called to attendance.

"Are you Anne Burden, whose husband George Burden was a tanner and shoemaker, a freeman and member of Boston Church? Are you the woman who deserted the fellowship of the church at the Lord's table after fifteen years, and dissented from Mr. Wilson's teachings?"

Anne answered, "I am Anne Burden, widow of George Burden. My husband and I and our children removed to Bristol, and lived there six years until he died."

Bellingham ignored her as if she had not spoken. "And you, you are Mary Dyer, who was banished in 1638 for sedition and heresy, and removed to the Isle of Error?"

Mary stood straighter by a quarter of an inch, and answered, "You reproachfully say so, though I was never excommunicated. My husband, attorney general of Rhode Island, would show you your own errors of geology and nomenclature."

Something about Mary Dyer caused Bellingham and Rawson to catch their breath. There seemed to be a cloud of light gathered about her head and shoulders, and they shrank back slightly in superstitious fear. Then Anne choked in a long series of coughs. She used her apron to cover her face until she could control herself.

"Mistress Burden, do you carry a plague from Barbados? Will you infect Boston with your fever, as well as your Quaker rants?"

She shook her head as she tried to suppress the fit, and her eyes watered. "No, I was ill from the journey. I am here lawfully to collect my children's living and inheritance."

Bellingham glanced at Secretary Rawson with one lifted eyebrow, then addressed the two women. "By the order of the governor of Massachusetts Bay, I declare that you are plain Quakers and must abide the law, which requires" –he consulted his paper– "that 'whatever Quaker shall arrive in this country from foreign parts, or shall come into this jurisdiction from any parts adjacent, shall be quickly committed to the House of Correction, and, at their entrance, to be severely whipped, and by the master thereof to be kept constantly to work, and none allowed to converse or speak with them during the time of their imprisonment, which shall be no longer than necessity requires.'

You are hereby committed to the House of Correction until the Court sets a trial date."

"Mr. Bellingham," repeated Anne, "I have not come here to prophesy or testify, but to lawfully settle my husband's estate and return to my children with their inheritance. You well know that there were no buyers for our properties when we moved back to England."

"It matters not. You have returned as cursed Quakers. Because I am a man not without mercy, and in consideration of occasional business with Mistress Dyer's husband, I will suspend the whipping you heretics deserve, and the hard labor, but you will be kept in close confinement, your goods are forfeit to pay your costs until your court date, and your books and papers will be burned as befits devilish doctrines."

Mary blanched. Her journal, her notes—to be ashes. She recovered slightly, knowing that the testimonies of her Friends would not fall into Puritan hands to bring down destruction on their heads. Though she would have protested, and would have suffered a whipping for Christ's sake, yet for lack of a word from the Seed within, she held her peace, knowing that Anne was ill and did not have the same calling as Mary did.

The jailer bound their hands before them, and tied them together, then pushed them as much as he dared, on the short walk to the House of Correction. Several score of Bostonians stopped to stare at the women prisoners, who by their dress seemed to be women of merchant class, as they were led by a slack rope to the jail.

The late-afternoon sun slanted under the last of the overcast as it pushed eastward, out to sea. Patches of muddy snow lay in the shade of structures, trees, and fences, and the unpaved road was slick with a layer of mud from the rain. It was cold enough to see one's breath, and Mary missed her heavy cloak that had been confiscated.

This was not the way Mary had imagined her return to Boston, after nearly twenty years away.

Jailer Salter untied the women and tossed some tatty woolen blankets in a corner. "There's your slop bucket, here's your water bucket. Try not to get them confused," he laughed. "The governor has ordered bread and water for prisoners, and your ration will come in the morning. Make it last. I won't get much money for your tiny heap of belongings, so you won't get much bread."

Anne Burden choked in another fit of coughing. When the jailer left, without so much as a candle or oil lamp to shed a glimmer or give off a little heat, Mary used her boot to scrape away the filthy, crawling straw. She put the two blankets together, put them over their shoulders like a shawl, and huddled close to her friend on the cold mud floor of the cell. Anne wept quietly but didn't complain.

Mary felt the cold and the wet clothes. She scratched the places that the fleas and lice bit her. She heard the rats tunneling through the straw only a few feet away, rats that might bite her and Anne if vigilance were not maintained throughout the night. It did not escape her that she had left the familiar comforts of England, and the earthly Paradise of Barbados, to take up the Cross and follow her Lord.

It was a marvel to her that though she felt the discomfort in her body, it couldn't touch her soul. As she had read so many years ago in Foxe's *Book of Martyrs* about the Protestants under the Inquisition and papal persecution, there was a kind of spiritual ecstasy within, that numbed the pain of the physical world.

But the ecstasy could not be maintained forever. Mary longed to see her children, and her Will. It had been five years, and Charles only a toddler when she left for a short journey—would they know her, or would they shy away? Would she and William be able to pick up their marriage as it had been in happier days, or would they be strangers? Tears seeped from Mary's eyes when she considered the latter to be more likely. True, they had exchanged warm, sweet letters the last year over long distances, but flesh-and-blood reality, and the decisions she had made to put Christ's mission above even her husband and children, portended heartbreak.

Mary dragged her gaze away from the home and life she'd once known, and turned her mind inward. She prayed silently that God would strengthen her mind and body to be able to endure the road she must travel—in fact, she was even now engaged on the journey of no return. "I give the care of my children and my husband into your tender hands, Lord. You promised your people when the enemy advanced against them, 'Your children I will save.' Show mercy to my husband, and open his heart to your Light, and save his soul, for I want to spend eternity with the man you gave to me when I was a girl. Here in this foul prison, I'll cling to the hem of your robe of righteousness, anticipating healing and the fulfillment of your promises."

Anne coughed again, and Mary held her closer and pulled the blankets up over their heads to capture the slight warmth of their breath. It would be at least twelve hours until a sliver of light would enter their cell, and they couldn't sleep that long. So because it was at the top of her mind, Mary recited the beatitudes to Anne and herself. The gospel was spoken just for them, she whispered to her friend: "Blessed are they which are persecuted for righteousness' sake: for theirs is the kingdom of heaven. Blessed are ye, when men shall revile you, and persecute you, and shall say all manner of evil against you falsely, for my sake. Rejoice, and be exceeding glad: for great is your reward in heaven: for so persecuted they the prophets which were before you."

"Say it again, Mary, please?" Anne croaked from her ravaged throat.

"Blessed are the poor in spirit, for theirs is the kingdom of heaven."

March 30, 1657

Newport, Rhode Island

William relaxed in a cushioned chair at the home of Nicholas Easton, and took a deep pull on his mug of beer. Between spring planting, lambing and calving and foaling, and their work with the courts and government, March was a busy time. Newport was the second-busiest port in New England, and the courts carried a full calendar of hearings. As their city grew, so did the cases of marital disharmony, infidelities, theft, property disputes, non-payment of debts, public drunkenness, and assaults.

But the case they discussed this evening was the talk of all four towns of the colony, and one of the hearings had been here in Newport, though the crime had taken place at Providence, because Newport had a jail and Providence did not.

Easton cracked a walnut with a hammer and picked out the nutmeat. "Who would have thought a case of buggery would lead to a case of high treason?" he asked.

"Those three men have been trying to secede for months, and deliver Pawtuxet to Massachusetts Bay's jurisdiction. Are they mad? Now they've called our duly-elected president, Roger Williams, just another one of us, and say that he has no authority. And Mr. Williams calls Thomas Harris, William Wickenden, and Thomas Angell 'ringleaders' for creating new divisions in the colony."

Will was angrier than he'd realized. "They're plotting rebellion and longing to return to the welcoming arms of John Endecott and his loving companions at the Bay, when they were the very faction of men who unjustly accused me of dividing Rhode Island when I chose the side of Roger Williams instead of William Coddington."

"Ah, Will, calm yourself," drawled Easton, as he ladled another serving of beer into Will's mug. "We'll sort it out, you'll see. Because it's connected with Long Dick's buggery case, and their support of that perverted heifer-lover, I will prophesy that this case will be buried deep in the records—if a record is indeed kept. Williams will be vindicated, of course, and that's all that matters. Cheer up!"

William snickered then. "Richard Chasmore, alias Long Dick. What is that—his Indian name? Two Indians witnessed him buggering his cow on more than one occasion. His wife substantiates their story, saying he's done it with other animals. Long Dick even *admits* to attempting, but not consummating, his adultery with the heifer. I can't imagine his wife would take him back to her bed, no matter how long his sword is."

Nicholas said drily, "If Chasmore is found guilty of buggery, it'll be his neck stretched in a halter, not his dick. Pity."

"Long Dick can't decide who to put the horns on: his wife or his cow."

Easton's beer spurted from his nose as both men burst out laughing like adolescent boys.

May 30, 1657
Newport, Rhode Island

William Dyer looked up from his ledgers at the sound of someone pounding on the door of his new house. Three years ago, he'd replaced the farm house and its additions and lean-to, with a fine home with painted, planed siding and a brick facing around the base, with some of his profits from farming, breeding horses for sale—and privateering against the Dutch.

He was annoyed that one of the servants hadn't opened the door, but got up and did so himself. Standing at the top of the steps was a travel-stained young man he didn't recognize.

"Are you Mr. William Dyer?" When Will affirmed that he was, the young man handed him an envelope. "I'll stay for your reply, sir."

Will unsealed the bundle and found a letter and a scrap of paper with charcoal markings on one side. Naturally, he was curious to read that first.

"To William Dyer at Newport, Rhode Island. We are in Boston prison since 30th first month. Please come. Mary Dyer."

What? It seemed that every drop of Will's blood rushed to his head. Like a guard dog, his hair stood on end, as if it would eject from his scalp as the rage filled him.

With shaking hands, he unfolded the letter.

MR. WILLIAM DYER, NEWPORT, RHODE ISLAND
27 May 1657 Boston
Dear Sir,

Information has come to me from my wife, who wishes to remain anonymous and avoid prosecution by the Massachusetts General Court. I assure you that my wife is virtuous and not given to gossip, or to carrying false or inflated tales. As she passed the prison in Boston, she heard two women's voices lifted up in prayer, the sound coming from a boarded window. Seeing no guard nearby, she crept to the window and listened for a few moments. She called softly, "Who is there? Why do you pray?"

A voice answered her. "We are Anne Burden and Mary Dyer, formerly of this town. Will you carry a message to someone who can help?" But then a guard came and sent my wife away with a warning to keep away.

My wife slept badly that night, and had a dream in which she believed she was commanded to go back to the prison. She told me her dream in the morning, and I decided that she ought to stay away, but I would go in her stead.

When the guard went indoors for his noon meal, I crept to the boarded window and listened for a moment. A voice was singing a Psalm. I asked who it was in the cell, and the answer came back, Anne Burden and Mary Dyer. One of them asked for paper to send a message to her husband, and I slipped the scrap of paper I had, through the cracks. I promised to come back later and consider forwarding the message. I made discreet inquiries in the town and discovered something of your experience 20 years ago, and made the connection with your Court positions in Rhode Island since then.

Mr. Dyer, that night I also had a dream. A voice told me to help the women in prison, for they were unjustly suffering for Christ's sake. In the morning, I waited in secret again, and when I could, whispered through the boards that I had come for the message. The paper was slipped through, and now you hold it in your hands.

I pray earnestly that God will use you and your estimable experience to speedily free the women in their distress. I'm a young clerk who wishes to both obey God and stay out of trouble with the authorities, though the first will take precedence over the last if it comes to that.

Your friend in Christ.

There was no signature.

Though his blood was boiling, Will felt a cold rage inside. This was the work of John Endecott, that pox-hearted devil. Rawson, Bellingham, Bradstreet, and Reverend Wilson were also waist-deep in the shit, he thought.

He turned to the messenger, who waited on the steps, having watched Dyer's face as he read the messages. "Thank you for your speed. You've been paid for your journey, I trust? Good. Take these coins for your trouble and the return. There will be no return message. I'll take it in person."

Endecott's counterfeit shillings. Good riddance, Will thought.

Calling sharply for the stable boy, he ordered his favorite pacer and an extra riding horse to be saddled and prepared for a fast trip to Boston. Cathy, the housekeeper, also came running at the sound of his voice.

"Cathy, I'll need my court suit packed, and some venison and corn cakes for my pouch. Also a flask of ale. I'm going to Boston to fetch my wife home. Tell the boys I expect them to greet their mother with their best manners when I return. I'll probably be back in two or three days with Mistress Dyer and we'll stop in Providence for our daughter on the way home. Oh, and pack my wife's clothes that are suitable for riding and whatever grooming articles a woman needs for traveling."

*****

It had been a hard ride, and he'd stopped to explain the situation to the Scotts, and changed horses in Providence. He intended to exchange the hired horses for his own on the way back with Mary.

Will reined in his horses and stopped at the town gate on Boston Neck. Behind him, on a small hill, stood the town gallows. Tidal marshes stretched on both sides of the isthmus between Boston's almost-island peninsula and the mainland. The guard at the fortification opened his eyes a bit wider when he heard the identification of the rider as Captain William Dyer. Will was allowed through, and he slowed his speed so as not to arouse attention. He looked over his shoulder at the house he'd built more than twenty years ago, as he trotted by.

Once in Boston, he rode slowly past the House of Correction and tavern with its courtroom and pillory outside, arrived at Edward Hutchinson's residence with no trouble, and surprised its occupants at supper.

June 1, 1657
Boston, Massachusetts

William meant to make plenty of noise as he pulled up the horse in front of the governor's residence the next morning. He hadn't needed a horse for that short distance, but he wanted the effect. Looping the pair of reins over the fence post, he ran up the steps and pounded on the door, which was opened by a servant.

Without introduction or explanation, he barged into the house and turned the corner into the parlor, where the governor was going over papers while nursing some affliction of his back.

"John Endecott, you bastard!" Will thundered. "Where is my wife? Produce her, whole and unharmed, or I'll have you keel-hauled out of your own harbor, all the way to London's justice courts."

"Now, Mr. Dyer, surely you can calm down, and we can discuss the case rationally, as officers of the court. Your wife was not whipped, as our law allows, nor has she been set to labor, and she has received food rations while in custody."

"You've molested a citizen of Rhode Island, who, by charter of England's Council of State, has free right of passage through Massachusetts territory. You've kept my wife in prison for eight weeks, with no notice to her husband—or anyone. Though you held court on May the sixth and ruled on the sale of lambs, prohibited liquor to Indians, dispensed thousands of acres of land to yourself and your friends, and made tax assessments, though you held General Court and elections only a few days since—"

William felt himself about to explode, so he intentionally calmed himself. "–you thought nothing of a tender woman—*my wife*, mind you—held in prison, given maggoty bread, eaten by vermin, and subject to the cold of a late winter and spring that has only now come.

"I will not only take her home now, but will forthwith write of your conduct and abuse of power, to Sir Henry Vane and the Council of State."

"Your wife was charged as a heretic Quaker, and her court date has not yet been set. Quakers are ill-regarded in England, as you know. We apply the laws here in the same way as our mother country." Endecott twisted the signet ring on his right little finger.

William lowered his voice to a menacing growl. "Her court date had better be set for this very day, and she will be released immediately, or you will discover just how fast England will recall your charter and set a new governor in your place. Who do you think signed my naval commission, and who has been well-acquainted with my wife these last years? Mr. Cromwell the Lord Protector, Sir Henry Vane, Major-General James Harrington—and Mr. John Thurloe."

At the last name, Endecott shifted in his seat, and quickly looked away to cover his fear. Thurloe, a spider at the center of a vast and sticky web, was known as the spymaster to the Council of State. William Dyer implied that he was one of Thurloe's network of agents in the Americas.

"Call whomever you wish to a session, and do it now. I go now to the prison to meet with her." Will flicked his riding crop down on Endecott's writing table, and Endecott snatched away his ringed hand, the oval *memento mori* with the death's head and crossbones.

"Mr. Dyer," said Endecott, "Our dread of the Quakers' heresy is great, that their insufferable calumnies against God will corrupt the minds and behavior of the Bay's inhabitants. Everywhere they go, they stir up trouble and anarchy—in churches, taverns, homes, even traveling the roads. They just cannot be silent! And we cannot allow those cursed Quakers to get their devil talons in our colony. If you will leave a bond for surety that Mistress Dyer will speak to no one and will leave the colony without taking lodging in any town or home, she may go with you."

William's temper cooled slightly. "Set the bond and I will pay it. But I require witnesses to the contract, and a termination clause, lest you decide to make my bond a permanent part of your counterfeit coin mint. I've noticed that 1652 was a banner year for shillings.

"By the way, do you know that your heavy fines on Quakers are spoken of as a lucrative private enterprise? And that your young minister Seaborn Cotton coveted a heifer and then confiscated her from a farmer who is only suspected, but not proven, of being a Quaker? It puts me in mind of King David and Bathsheba's first husband. If John Cotton were alive today, he would be ashamed of his son's lust for his neighbor's goods."

Endecott flushed a hot red, but restrained a comment. Will stalked out.

He mounted his horse and trotted it around several blocks of house lots to the House of Correction. He tied it to a post at the prison gate and walked in, noticing that some of the prisoners were under guard in the yard, sawing posts and boards from a vast stack of logs.

The jailer on duty, William Salter, was much aged since 1637, when he and William Dyer and others had co-signed the Wheelwright Petition and been disarmed. Will had thought they were of a similar age twenty years ago, and supposed it was the curse of a depraved and violent nature that had aged the man so. His ears looked huge next to his creased, gaunt face, and there were bags under the rheumy blue eyes, which stared out of deep-sunk sockets with no emotion.

"Dyer. Come for your wife, I s'pose," said the monster. "You don't enter without Mr. Rawson's order for release, and you've settled up for her board."

"Oh, you'll have both. Get out of my way, Salter."

But the jail-keeper did not move. Though he appeared old, he was certainly not frail. It took strength and skill to wield the thrice-knotted scourge made of gut.

Will walked around the building then, and called at the windows until Mary answered.

"Mary Dyer! I've come to take you home."

"Will, is it really you? Praise God, you've come! Can you help us?"

"My darling! Yes, I've roused Endecott and his court. Are you all right? Are you well, and able to travel? Who is with you?"

"I'm well enough. My companion is Anne, widow of George Burden, the cordwainer. She's a Friend who is innocent, but being extorted for her husband's estate. She's very ill, and I can't leave her."

Will sighed at this complication—and delay. "Then it's sure that she cannot travel with us, even if they were to release her. I'll inquire about her at the hearing, and try to accommodate her.

Now I'm going, but I swear I'll be back in a short time. I've brought something for you to wear to ride toward Providence this afternoon and evening. Prepare yourself while I'm at the court."

"William. There are more Friends here who are whipped every week. John Copeland and Christopher Holder lie in another cell. Can you help them?"

"Not this time. It will be difficult enough to win your case. But I'll see what can be done by my colleagues."

From his saddle roll, he pulled the bundle of Mary's clothes and soap and cloth and a comb, and handed them to the jailer's wife with a scowl. "When I return, I expect to have a report on my wife's companion, Mistress Burden. A physician will be summoned, this moment. See to it."

As he rode to the courthouse, Will remembered the advice of his mentors, John Dyer in 1632, and William Hutchinson in 1640: to keep his passion on a tight rein and to present a solid, imperturbable appearance to his opponents. For the sake of his family, he must be in control of himself.

He drew a long, slow breath and made his shoulders relax. As much as he loathed Endecott, Bellingham, and Rawson for their extremes in religion and harsh punishments, he must present a rational, calm appearance. If they were heated, he would be cool. After all, King Solomon had said that a soft answer turned away wrath. And if that didn't work, there was a time for everything under the sun—including revenge. Revenge could take many forms. But first things first.

He dismounted his horse, combed and smoothed his hair with his fingers and retied the ribbon on his ponytail. He walked calmly into the courtroom, a place he was familiar with in Rhode Island, of course, but he'd also presented several cases here.

John Endecott and Richard Bellingham, governor and deputy governor, sat at the bench, and Edward Rawson, the secretary, sat at a lower, but still imposing, level. William Dyer removed his hat, then stood before the bench and waited.

Rawson, a square-faced man with a thin mustache and beard so small they formed a T when his lips were closed, spoke: "In the matter of one Mary Dyer. An accursed Quaker as she herself professed, she was arrested on board the ship in which she and Mrs. Burden arrived from Barbados, on the twenty-fifth day of

March, 1657. The women were in possession of heretical papers and books, which were confiscated and burned."

He read the October 1656 law aloud to William Dyer, taking more than five minutes to read the all the provisions. As he did, William looked up through his eyelashes at the governor and his deputy. They looked quite smug, having thought of every way to knock down Quakers, and whenever the negative adjectives came up, their eyes sparkled more brightly. Their chief complaint against the missionaries was this:

"Whereas, there is a cursed sect of heretics lately risen up in the world, which are commonly called Quakers, who take upon them to be immediately sent of God, and infallibly assisted by the Spirit, to speak and write blasphemous opinions, despising government, and the order of God in the church and commonwealth, speaking evil of dignities, reproaching and reviling magistrates and ministers, seeking to turn the people from the faith, and gain proselytes to their pernicious ways."

Rawson went on. Whoever reviled the persons of magistrates and ministers, "as is usual with the Quakers," –and Baptists, William remembered from seven years ago—"shall be severely whipped, or pay the sum of five pounds."

That was the crux of it, thought William. It was about maintaining their power over their citizens, not about a tiny group of people who worshiped in ecstatic silence or preached their strange beliefs on the street corner.

Ship masters bringing Quakers into the land were to be fined £100 or be cast into prison until they came up with the fine. As for the sect of Friends, "Whatever Quaker shall arrive in this country from foreign parts," Rawson growled at William Dyer, "...or shall come into this jurisdiction from any parts adjacent, shall be quickly committed to the House of Correction, and, at their entrance, to be severely whipped, and by the master thereof to be kept constantly to work, and none allowed to converse or speak with them during the time of their imprisonment, which shall be no longer than necessity requires."

Rawson set the book down and glared at Dyer.

Richard Bellingham spoke then. "By my own discretion and merciful nature, though the law commands a severe whipping upon committal to the House of Correction, Mistress Dyer and

Mistress Burden were spared that punishment. I hoped that with time in prison to think on her error, and your strong hand in her correction once home in Rhode Island, Mistress Dyer may be brought to her senses."

William gave no hint of his thoughts. In contrast to his stormy appearance at John Endecott's home earlier, he stood relaxed, though not languid. "My wife was detained in error, sir. She would only have briefly passed through Massachusetts because of its harbor, on her journey to her husband and six poor, grieving children, who have been deprived of their mother. Further, you have burned and sold her possessions, so you have no evidence with which to convict her."

Endecott entered the conversation. "She and her companion admitted to being accursed Quakers. Both of them are well aware, these twenty years, of our laws and ways—and despite their banishment in 1638, we find them again treading our soil. In the last year, New England has been overrun by Quakers who bring disorder, even anarchy, to our churches, and our members have refused to pay the tithes that support government. We will stamp them out—we will cut them off in their infancy."

William said mildly, "And pray, sirs, what is the effect of your suppression? You have said previously that the Quakers are loud and disruptive, that they go naked about the town, or shout their tenets in the marketplace. And yet in Rhode Island, where we have liberty of conscience, and where many Baptists and Quakers have come for refuge, we have order in our churches, and commerce is unimpaired. In fact, I observe that they are loath to accept the peace of our towns, but crave the martyrdom that our brothers in Connecticut and Massachusetts are eager to provide. They seem to delight in your persecutions, as the Lord Jesus said, 'Blessed are ye, when men shall revile you, and persecute you,' because they are more likely to gain adherents as you draw the more attention to them with whippings, heavy fines, and mutilations. People want to know how they suffer so patiently and still give glory to God. Surely you have observed that effect in England."

Endecott muttered, "We shall be glad to help them on their way to hell."

"And now, your honors, to conclude our business. I must take my wife home by Providence, and that is a hard ride in what's left of the day."

"Mistress Dyer is still under her banishment order of 1638. She is not to step foot again in Massachusetts upon pain of death. On your way to Rhode Island, you will not lodge her in any town of the colony, nor permit any to have speech with her on her journey, against which you will leave a bond of twenty pounds," Endecott said. "Mr. Rawson will write a release for Jailer Salter. Mr. Bellingham and Mr. Rawson are witnesses."

"My witness shall be Captain Edward Hutchinson." Edward walked forward from the back bench of the courtroom, where he had observed the proceeding unnoticed.

"Captain Hutchinson will take receipt of my bond upon my notice that my wife and I have complied with your requirements."

"You're free to take your wife away from here, Mr. Dyer."

"One more matter. There's another prisoner, my wife's companion, Mistress Burden. Out of tender consideration of my wife, I would also post bond for her release and transport her away when she has recovered from her illness. Unless you would be the uncaring Pharisee and Levite in the Lord's parable of the Samaritan."

At this, Endecott and Bellingham exchanged uneasy glances. "No," said the latter. "We are releasing your wife because of who *you* are. Anne Burden has no husband and no reason to be here, having left here abruptly with no leave to return."

"Except for her husband's properties," Will noted. "The rents due from the tenants, the furnishings, the domestic stock, the buildings and the plots of land… That must be worth something to the honored sirs, or Mistress Burden would have been allowed to conclude her business and go home to her fatherless children. And yon Salter, the jailer, turns a profit for 'boarding' her indefinitely."

Hutchinson whispered to his friend, "Will, don't push them further. You take Mary home, and you can trust me to see to Mistress Burden's release and departure. If they won't release her property, I'll stir up sympathetic souls to help. And she'll trust me for my mother's sake. Let us go. I have this in hand."

Will turned back to the magistrates and said with a steely voice, "Sirs. Mr. Hutchinson will advocate for Mrs. Burden. I leave the bond in escrow. I leave within the hour with my wife. And I leave you to your own consciences before Almighty God."

Edward came with him to the prison, walking as they led the horses. "Will, I never knew Mary was brought here, or I'd have raised the fort against the governors and the church to get her out."

"I know, Ed," said Will resignedly. "I haven't seen Mary since I returned to England for the charter in 1652. She was living with Harry and Frances Vane then, and our marriage was tense. We've both seen high and low tides, and experienced things while apart, that we'll never be able to explain to one another. The younger children have grown without her, almost as if they were motherless. Samuel, William, and Maher are baffled at a woman who would choose religion over her children, though I strove to honor her at all times. And I don't know what to think, except that I've loved her all my days, but I sense that she'd leave me for God. How can I compete for her affections with God, who has alienated her from me?"

Edward replied slowly, "None of us knows what road God would have us travel, Will. My father and mother adored each other, but Mother was such a vivid, opinionated woman that I wonder how their lives would have fared had they lived longer. When you and I were excited young men coming to America, could we have dreamed of bearing up under the weight of Winthrop and Dudley, being banished, losing our close family members to violent death, and all the disasters that we've survived?"

He sighed ruefully. "And after all that, I moved back to Boston with Katherine, and submitted to the discipline of Pastors Wilson and Cotton—you have no idea how humiliating it was to be the butt of sermons for years, or to hear my mother condemned as a heretic—and pull off the performance of a stoic actor. Even so, God was teaching me true submission such as few men know, and how to accept his grace.

"You don't know which path is the correct one to take. And God isn't giving you any hints—rotten luck there! But it's my experience that all things considered, if you make the best decision you can, God will not count it as sin even if you choose the wrong path. He'll miraculously make it work for good, whether in this life or the next.

"Here we are, though we've dragged our feet. I'll settle your bill with Salter and check on Mistress Burden while you reunite with Mary."

"Ed, how do I look?" Will asked hesitantly.

Edward laughed. "Pull yourself together, man. You look ghastly pale. But you compare favorably against Jailer Salter, I'd vow. Your wife won't mind your bald head and tavern-keeper's belly. Bahahaha!"

Stepping back into his attorney general persona, the very fit and coiffed Captain Dyer strode up the steps to the prison office, with Captain Hutchinson behind him. Slapping Rawson's release order on the table, Will demanded to see his wife.

"There is the matter of her board, Mr. Dyer," said the jailer. "Two months at thirteen shillings each. A bargain for you, considering she should have been at work earning her bread."

William wrote a note of credit, which Hutchinson countersigned, then said with a growl, "You're no innkeeper, Salter. I know about prisons. My innocent wife is nearly starved with your wormy bread. Have her brought out. Captain Hutchinson will be responsible for Mistress Burden, and you had better make sure she recovers, with warmth and light, a bed, and good meat on her menu, or you'll answer for it."

Salter sneered, "I answer to the Governor, and you have no power in this jurisdiction. Take your witch and be gone."

Edward stepped forward and spoke with the icy north wind in his voice. "You're not mighty enough to speak in the presence of a governor, who thinks not enough of you to even say your name. You're just 'the jailer,' the prison-keeper. You answer to the head jailer, Munnings, and he answers to the marshal-general. And he, like me, is a military man. Captain Dyer has stated my wishes, which the marshal will enforce."

At that moment, Mary Dyer entered the office. She was dressed in a white chemise and gray bodice, a voluminous gray skirt, and red jacket that was fitted in the bodice and fell in a short skirt to her knees like a man's coat. Her riding habit from five years ago, when she was healthy and vigorous from walking, gardening, and chasing small children, now hung like a sack on her emaciated frame. Most shocking was her lank hair, hacked off close to her head to ease the lice-picking.

Will's eyes didn't even register the wretched creature the jailer had made of his wife. He saw Mary Barrett—the virtuous flirt in the market, the breathtaking beauty in her court gown, Mary Dyer—the lovely woman who bore his children and bravely dared the wilderness to support his dreams, and Mary Dyer—the woman who inspired him to be more than the sum of his parts, the face he imagined as the graceful figurehead cutting the wind and waves on the prow of his ship.

He walked quickly to her and took her in his arms, whispering, "Mary, my love. You're free now. Come outside without speaking to anyone, not even Ed."

His wife clung to him and he felt her convulse with silent sobs. When he looked again at her face, there were no tears. Just a terrible grief that he must find a way to heal. And protect her so she never experienced that grief again.

Once outside, where she blinked and squinted in the sunshine, Will explained the terms of her release, and assured her that Anne Burden would be cared for, and that they had to ride for Providence without delay.

"Will, I have other Friends in prison here who are beaten twice a week. Is there anything you can do for them?"

His heart skipped a beat. He *must* get Mary out of Boston. Now.

"No, Sweetheart. I'm lucky to win your release. That is all I can do, all I can think about. Ed will try to help Mistress Burden."

Will set the too-frail Mary on her side-saddle and gave her a kerchief to wrap around her head. He left her momentarily in the shade of a building while he hurried in to purchase a coif for her hair, and then they were off, trotting down Cornhill Road toward the fortification at the Neck. Will thought he saw John Endecott skulking on Cornhill Road, but he couldn't be sure it wasn't a visitation from a demon. Once past the town gate and gallows, they chose the road that ran southeast toward Providence.

William didn't notice that Mary's gaze lingered for a moment on the gallows at the Boston Neck.

*****

Mary trembled with exhaustion, making the effort to sit in a padded box with her feet on the planchette, and turn her upper body forward. She had been quite comfortable in the side saddle for years. But two months of prison privation had debilitated her in every way. Will led her horse as she clung to her saddle horn.

It wasn't easy to talk as they rode, no matter which gait Will tried. It was imperative to reach Providence before dark. Even as they neared the summer solstice, there were few enough hours in the day before they lost the light. The release order said she could not lodge in Massachusetts, and she was in no physical condition to camp in the forest, so Providence it must be.

They rode through dark forest, light-dappled stands of hardwood trees, and in the bright sunshine along stone walls dividing farms and fields. The fresh air, though sometimes polluted momentarily by a manure pile or a cloud of gnats, was something she'd taken for granted while living in Rhode Island or at Raby Castle. It helped to take away the remembered stink of prison.

Will stopped a few times to let her rest, and once to take some bread, cheese, and ale. He spread a canvas on the tall grass near a spruce, and cradled Mary in his arms as they made small talk. Mary breathed deeply of the sharp, clean scent of the spruce.

This was the bliss she'd been deprived of for years, by her own decisions, and by unavoidable events like war and distance. She studied her husband's countenance for the first time in four years. At age 46, his face was unlined except for squint lines by his eyes. His broad forehead was only a little expanded by the beginning of hair loss, and the silver hair at his temples blended pleasingly with his sun-bleached light-brown hair, which, having escaped the ribbon, curled gently at his shoulders. When Will walked, he had no stoop of age as other men did, but with his chest thrust confidently ahead of his square shoulders.

She planted her face against his chest and listened to him breathe, and felt the familiar vibrations of his voice in his sternum and ribs. Will's words were indistinct, so far away had she retreated, but now she drew in the masculine tone, the rhythm of his heartbeat, and the strong muscles that expanded on inhalation and speech. The loneliness, the fear, and encumbrances drained from her, and she bathed in his strength and vitality, flowing into her heart and spreading luxuriously to every limb and digit. For now, she didn't have to be courageous or set an example. She could just be.

In this safe, comforting harbor of her husband's arms, she dozed for a few minutes. In her mind, a shower of golden light drifted over her, like October birch leaves on an afternoon breeze. *"Peace, be still, daughter. God is in your midst; you shall not be moved: God shall help you, and that right early. The heathen raged, the kingdoms were moved: he uttered his voice, the earth melted."*

The sparks, insubstantial as feathers, dispersed.

She opened her eyes. Will was looking down at her in wonder.

"You're radiant," he said.

"Yes. I have the peace of God. I'm feeling stronger, too. But much as I'd love to stay here, we'd better get moving."

"Can you ride by yourself, or would you rather ride astride?"

"Let me ride with you for a while. It's been months since I've ridden. Ladies' saddle or astride, it matters not. I'll be stiff as a board tomorrow."

After Will mounted, he reached down and pulled Mary up behind him. She put her arms around him and rested her chin on his shoulder as they rode.

Unsure of how to speak of all the issues that must be said after four years apart, they chatted of everything but themselves.

"Plymouth has lost two of its pioneers recently," Will said. "Miles Standish died in Duxbury last October. For a soldier, or any man, really, he lived to a very ripe age of seventy-two. And Governor Bradford died at Plymouth a few weeks ago, at age sixty-seven. As stern and unbending as they were, perhaps their mettle was exactly what was needed to survive for thirty-seven years in the plagues and famines and upheavals of this land."

Mary agreed. "They lived as they believed God commanded. I admire that. They passed through fiery trials, betrayal, and fraud, years before they came here. They endured and overcame so much, to make a straight road in the wilderness—for people like us. Now, their successors are so toughened that they reject such notions as immersion baptism, and the covenant of grace. Well, God rest Standish and Bradford. I hope that they were able to know the Light of God."

"Their new governor, Thomas Prence, is known to be as rigid, or more so, than Mr. Bradford was," added Will. "I've heard his opinions at meetings of the United Colonies, and he approves of similar resolutions to those of Endecott and the Bay."

Will avoided talk of the Friends, Mary noticed. Even so, she wrapped her arms around her husband's waist and reveled in the physicality.

They rode another mile before Mary spoke. "Last year, Oliver Cromwell, with the advice of Harry Vane, allowed Jews to settle in London for the first time in three hundred sixty years, the better to stimulate commerce. The government hopes that the Jews will bring trade with them. They've been granted leave to practice their Jewish faith in secret, but not to proselytize—I doubt that will last, with the words 'heretic' and 'infidel' being whispered, none too softly. There's been a messianic fervor with Cromwell's government, not seen since we were children. Some people hope that when the Jews convert to Christianity, it will bring in the New Earth."

Will replied, "Portuguese Jews, fleeing the Inquisition, settled first in Brazil, then Barbados. They've financed a number of shipments of New England products—fish, horses, timber—and exchanged them for salt and slaves, but primarily cane sugar. Some of them are considering moving to Newport to live safely in liberty of conscience."

"Will, I nearly forgot. Harry Vane, John Clarke, and Mrs. Blackbourne gave me letters to carry to you. I'm sorry that they were burned with my books and papers when I was arrested off the ship."

He sighed. "Letters can be replaced. I trust that if there were any secrets to be transmitted, they would have written in such a way that interception would not harm the sender or recipient. Still, there won't be any more news from them this year."

Mary dozed again as Will described the changes to their town over the last four years. When she woke, much refreshed by the sun, the air, and the security of her husband's presence, she felt strong enough to ride by herself again.

Once they were cantering in a smooth pace again, Will spoke. "Mary, while you were lying in Boston jail, Roger Williams stepped down from the judge's bench to prosecute a case in Newport. The crime was reported by two Indians at Pawtuxet, who saw 'Long Dick,' Richard Chasmore, buggering a heifer in both winter and spring. Williams was so angry that he tried to arrest Long Dick, but some Pawtuxet men helped him get away. So Williams wrote to Governor Bellingham for help and Long Dick was captured and bound for Boston on this very road—but again he was rescued. He agreed to surrender if he be tried in Newport instead of Boston. So two months ago, the case was brought."

"What happened? Surely he was convicted with two witnesses against him."

"Much to the fury of Mr. Williams, who even threatened to send Long Dick's liberators to England to resolve the case, no man would testify. And the jury would not convict based on the Indians' word, even though everyone knows why Chasmore has the nickname he does. The jury acquitted Long Dick. And the heifer lived."

"Why do you say that?"

"If the heifer's milk or meat were to be consumed by humans when it contains the seed of a man, it would be cannibalism."

Mary had doubts about that, but had no other solution to the moral problem.

And so, as the summer sun set over the Narragansett forest, William and Mary Dyer walked their horses off the ferry barge and made their way to the Scott home at Providence. There was a grain mill on the river near the house, and the dogs guarding the yard came out barking and wagging. The Scott children were finished with supper and taking their evening Bible study when the Dyers arrived, not unexpected.

Katherine and Richard hastened to the porch with a stern look at the children, which meant to come to attention and put on company manners, only a short step up from everyday manners. Marie Dyer, eight years old, swallowed her nerves and stood straight behind her place at the study table, waiting to see the mother she couldn't remember. She was in her best blue dress, and her dark-blond braids hung stiffly down the front of her lace-edged white collar and apron.

William and Mary greeted their old friends outside the farmhouse. Mary was still weak from her prison stay, and she nearly stumbled over her too-large riding skirt as she climbed the steps to the door, but Katherine, who had her arm, grabbed Mary around her waist and helped her into the house.

"Ah, Mary. What has that devil Endecott done to you?" asked Katherine.

"Your sister Anne once said to me, 'The body they may kill,'" replied Mary.

She quoted again: "'The mind is its own place, and in itself can make a heaven of Hell, a hell of Heaven.' So wrote John Milton, whom I met in London. I've learned that it's true. Only when I took my mind from the Savior have I felt privation."

Now they were in the parlor, and Mary's eyes went immediately to her daughter, and understood the fear the girl must feel for the mother she didn't know.

"Marie. You're a lovely girl, and you have the look of your father in your eyes. I'm so pleased to see that you're a student of Scripture."

The girl silently dipped a curtsey before her mother.

Mary tried again. "Your father sent me gifts that you made. The embroidery sample was beautiful, and I kept it in the cover of my Bible. I hope you'll join me in embroidering some new pictures when we're home in Newport. I should love to design a humbird for your apron."

Marie's eyes sparkled for the first time. Mary stooped down and gently hugged her daughter. The little girl was stiff as a poppet, but she obediently embraced her mother's waist, as she'd been told to do before Mary's arrival.

"We'll become reacquainted tomorrow as we ride to Newport, my dear."

Katherine took her cue. "Marie, Patience, Deliverance, Mary—put your books away and get ready for bed. I'll come up and hear your prayers in a few minutes."

Once the girls were gone, Katherine pulled up a chair, padded it with a folded blanket, and set Mary down.

"Last night at this time," Mary mumbled, "I had forgotten what it meant to be loved and cared for in this world. My only succor was the Light of heaven in my heart."

"You should be tucked in bed yourself, and you shall be as soon as I'm finished with you. First, some rich broth and toast, for strength, while I hear the girls' prayers. Then, you will submit to my physical treatments. You won't even need to speak, for I have much to tell you, myself, beginning with this: Richard and I are Friends."

*****

Will and Mary on Dyer-bred horses, and Marie on her side-saddled pony, rode along the Wampanoag trail from Providence, southeast on the peninsula between Narragansett Bay and Mount Hope Bay, in the direction of Portsmouth.

They'd risen at dawn, which was terribly early in June, but having been wakeful most of the night despite their exhaustion, the light came as a relief. After porridge and bacon, Katherine sent them off with a generous lunch tied in a cloth, but not before offering more hospitality.

"Mary, you're still so weak and starved. Stay and recover here: I fear for your life," Katherine had urged, knowing that Mary would refuse.

The well-worn road, an Indian trail enlarged by Englishmen, put them now in forest, now near sunlit marshes that sent up clouds of waterfowl when they rode close. They splashed through freshwater streams and hurried past the corn, squash, and bean fields where Indian women labored at their tasks. These Wampanoag Indians were friendly, thanks to the ongoing ministry of Roger Williams, but just as Indians were scrutinized for motives in Newport or Boston, Englishmen and women moving through Indian lands were noted—and watched.

After thirteen miles of riding, the Dyers reached the southern shore and hired a ferryman to carry them to Aquidneck Island. Just to the south, they could see Dyer Island in the bay. Will had never developed it, but occasionally he moved goats or hogs there to graze for a week or two.

They came ashore within a quarter-mile of the place where Will and Mary had built a small cabin in Pocasset, so they turned aside to show Marie, dismounted their horses, and climbed up a large boulder cleft in two. Comfortable, thatched two-story houses dotted the town of Portsmouth now, and pastures and fields were fenced. Spreading their cloth, they ate bread and cheese and dried venison, and drank cider from a small jug.

"When Samuel was five years younger than you are now," said Mary to her daughter, "there was a great earthquake here, and it was felt all over New England. It was nineteen years ago yesterday, that it happened," she mused.

Marie's eyes went to the broken boulder on which they sat. "Did it do this?"

"No, Sweetheart. This stone was broken hundreds or thousands of years ago. But the earthquake was so severe, and so rare, that everyone knew it was no ordinary act of nature, but the very breath of God, roaring his judgment. Never before and never since, has there been such a shaking that lasted for four minutes. That's a very long time, when one is in fear!"

"Were you afraid, Father?"

"Yes, I was, but not for myself. I was terrified that your mother and brother would be injured," said Will. "Once I knew they were safe, it was very interesting. It felt rather like standing up in a small boat."

Mary spoke again, softly, as she remembered Anne Hutchinson. "Our friend Anne, Katherine Scott's oldest sister, who was like a mother to me, was praying when the earth began to heave and shake. Like a tub filling with water, the movement seemed to rise up from the ground and escape to the sky. Anne cried out, 'It is the Holy Ghost!' and put us in mind of the Upper Room in Jerusalem, where the Holy Ghost filled the room and baptized the believers with miraculous gifts."

"Was anyone killed?" asked the girl.

"No, dear, no one lost their lives. But many men said that the earthquake was another of God's judgments on Anne and me, for our beliefs, for bearing dead babies, and worst of all, for Anne challenging the men's authority."

Will made a sound like a short hiss, and jumped down from the boulder. Mary folded the cloth around the remnants of their meal, slid down and helped Marie in her scramble, and they all mounted their horses. There were nine more miles before Mary would reunite with her sons on their farm.

The road from Portsmouth to Newport lay mostly south, with a slight westerly cast toward the town and its deep-water harbor, just as Will Dyer and his friends had laid it out in 1639. The afternoon sun shone through the trees that lined the road, dappling the road and its riders. Between the trunks, they could see green fields of barley, rye, wheat, hay, and Indian corn that promised life and health for the coming year. Pastures held cattle, horses, and the finest black-and-white sheep imported from England. Some low-lying fields held pig shelters with herds of pigs squealing and snorting about them.

Rhode Island had prospered while she was gone, thought Mary. What a contrast with depressed England, after years of civil war and famine. Only the aristocrats' properties were doing well; thousands of yeoman farmers like Will's father and brother had been forced to sell out and move to the cities.

Mary hadn't thought about it in several years, but Rhode Island felt and smelled so different from England: it was more foggy more often, and the perpetual sea breeze brought a chill even on clear days. But it was fresh and clean, and somehow brand-new, as if there were blessings yet to be unwrapped. England's heritage of hundreds of generations would always be there, but wild and spectacular America was the home of her children and perhaps a hundred generations of them. And she and Will were the pivot point. She smiled.

The Dyers skirted William Coddington's large property, then turned into the lowering sun, onto their own lands. Though they didn't goad the horses, the pace picked up considerably as their mounts recognized the scents of home and fodder.

Mary saw a line of silver sunlight lying across the sparkling bay, and wispy horse-tail clouds lay over Conanicut Island on the far side of the water. The familiar scent of brine, fish, and salt-weeds at low tide came up to meet them in the afternoon sea breeze. Sloops and fishing boats were sailing into port, and a galley was anchored off the long wharf in the harbor to the south. Gulls squawked and flapped about down at the rocky shingle.

On the fields nearest the house, sheep and goats dotted the turf, cropping it close like a gentleman's lawn.

The lavender bush she'd planted at the corner of the herb garden was much larger now, and covered in flower spikes. Mary was delighted to see a pair of humbirds darting between the fragrant branches.

Mary breathed it in, this beautiful place that Will and she had made. Every hour, every minute now was precious. Heaven would come for her very soon.

Rather than riding straight for the stable, Will led Mary and Marie to the front of the rebuilt house. He'd raised the roof by making the attic into a full second story with a ceiling and new attic loft above. The ground floor had a larger footprint now, with parlor and dining at one end, and the original kitchen at the other, where there was a tiny lean-to room for the maidservant. Glass windows faced west on the bay, and both ends of the rectangular house had stonework to a height of four feet. The lapped-board siding was painted white.

"It's beautiful, Will," Mary said, and she meant it. But she was so very tired. And she still must meet her sons after an absence of four and a half years.

The door slammed inward suddenly as if in a gale, and her two oldest sons, Samuel and William, ran out to meet her and help her dismount. Maher, Henry, and Charles, less sure of how to act, came outside more slowly, but they lined up dutifully as if before a schoolmaster, awaiting inspection.

Tears came to Mary's eyes as she saw the growth her sons had attained, taller and more muscular than the English boys of the same age. Untouched by privation and the horrors of war, they had a wholesomeness about them, too. They were sons of whom to be proud.

Samuel was twenty-one, a grown man, and William would be seventeen in the fall. Maher was thirteen, Henry was ten this year, and Charles was nearly seven. She'd missed those four years and would never be able to take them back. She felt a physical pain as if her heart were being squeezed dry.

Mary knelt down and hugged the very stiff Charles gently, then stood up and did the same for each of her sons. Maher impulsively kissed her on the cheek, then quickly pulled back in confusion. Henry was polite and obedient, but distant.

It was young William who noticed Mary's emaciation, gray-faced tension, and exhaustion. "Come inside, Mother. You're home now." He took her hand, and walked her up the steps to the door, tossing a severe look at his family. They quickly arranged their features into pleasant countenances and followed. Will took the packs off the horses, and handed their mounts off to a stable hand.

The housekeeper, Cathy, had, by necessity, become much more than a kitchen servant during Mary's extended absence. Several candles were lit, supper was ready to be served, and the children were well-cared-for.

Cathy dipped before Mary, and told her that supper would be served when Mary had refreshed herself. She led Mary upstairs and showed her that there was a basin of scented water for washing, and that Mary's own clothes had been aired and laid out. "You must be very tired from your ride. I'll hold the meal as long as you need, Mistress," she said before she closed the door and went downstairs.

You have no idea, thought Mary. She wanted nothing more than to strip down and burrow in the bed linens, but her family awaited. She changed out of Katherine Scott's skirt and blouse, and took off the coif that covered her ragged hair. Vigorously rubbing a wet, lavender-scented cloth over her hair and skin, she dressed in a blue calico skirt and white blouse from five years ago, and left her hair uncovered. No one knew yet why her husband had dropped everything and raced to Massachusetts three days ago. The story-telling would begin first with her family.

June 15, 1657
Newport, Rhode Island

Though the day was muggy and the sweat streamed down each strand of his wavy hair, William Dyer and his sons worked alongside field laborers and neighboring farmers, bundling the dried hay and heaving the bundles onto an ox-drawn wagon. It was important to get the hay under cover before it was exposed to rain and then mildew. In the next field over, he could hear shouts and cheering from a speed contest between the best mowers, and not a few men, including Will, had laid wagers on the strongest, fastest mower of the day.

Many of the women and children were raking the sweet dry hay, or spreading the new cut to dry in the sun. Their singing lent a comfortable rhythm to the raking.

In the merry month of June,
In the prime time of the year;
Down in yonder meadows
There runs a river clear:
And many a little fish
Doth in that river play;
And many a lad, and many a lass,
Go abroad a-making hay.
In come the jolly mowers,
To mow the meadows down;
With budget and with bottle
Of ale, both stout and brown,
All laboring men of courage bold
Come here their strength to try;
They sweat and blow, and cut and mow,
For the grass cuts very dry.

Mary had intended to join their neighbors in the field, but Will had restrained her by insisting that she was not ready yet for physical labor, and instead, she should help prepare food for the nightly supper and dance.

As he worked, the song and the shouts faded away and were replaced by the argument he'd had with Mary. So they'd not be heard by children or servants, they'd gone outside to walk along the low bluff above the rocky beach.

"Why must you embarrass me and your children with this foolishness over your 'Friends'?" he asked, emphasizing the last word. "They're just begging to be whipped and imprisoned. It's enough that you take them in as boarders or nurse their wounds. But I will not have you following them or being treated as they are. Your name is Dyer. Your actions reflect on me. On all of us."

Mary was quiet for what seemed like many minutes. "I've lived autonomously for four years, Will, obeying the will of God. When he moves in my heart, I must also move. He has directed me all my life, and now, like Esther, this is the time he has brought me to, to speak for my Friends. Where they are persecuted, I will stand for them."

"And what about my reputation? Secretary. Attorney General. Commander in Chief. Perhaps one day, Governor. Your defiance of authority, and of your own husband, would put an end to any political hopes for me and this family.

"What will become of your sons? Maher's just beginning his training in navigation, and Samuel and William also have to hold up their heads in society as they learn their trades. When you are arrested, stripped, and whipped, as Quakers seem to challenge the Bay to do, how do you think they will feel, with their mother in a common jail with rats and lice, drunkards and thieves?"

Will's voice changed tenor. "Mary, what of *me*? I can't stand the thought of you in pain and filth—you're bone of my bone and flesh of my flesh. How can you put me through that agony? You've only recently come back after years away. There's a vacant place in my heart that only you can fill."

Tears rolled down his wife's face and fell from her chin to her bosom. "Do you think I asked for this? That I want my husband and children humiliated? That I want to leave our comfortable home? This calling is not from within myself. It is God himself urging me to do my duty. This is what I was born to do. This is what he's been preparing me for over the years, both in Massachusetts and England. Why else the education and introduction to society? Why else the connections with Anne, and even with Winthrop, Cotton, and Wilson? It was training, so I could stand my ground bravely, knowing that no matter the battle raging, the war is won. Greater is the Lord's angel host that surrounds me, than the devil in such as John Endecott."

"Look at yourself, woman. You've no more meat on you than a doe in February snows and you're only now getting some color in your cheeks. You need to stay home and gain strength. Get back to the wholesome life you've known here in Newport. Use your calling in healing and midwifery. When those scrawny, starved, and beaten Friends of yours need refuge, treat them here.

You can obey God by being a mother and wife to the family that God gave you before he called you."

"Get thee behind me, Satan! You cannot tempt me away from the Light!" Mary cried, and turned away from her husband.

Will Dyer was cut to the bone. "I see now that in all our years together, I have been too lenient. Perhaps Governor Winthrop, as much as I despised him, was correct in one thing, that a woman who fixes her mind on books and concepts too difficult for her, will lose her reason. Remember Ann Hopkins of Hartford. What is this madness that falls upon you and the Quakers?"

"It is not madness. You blaspheme the Holy Ghost, William Dyer."

"That is not my intention, and not my sin. I'm thinking not only as your grieving husband but as your legal counsel. That is what Endecott and Davenport and Prence think of your Friends, that the Quaker devils must not infect the faithful. They use words like 'devil,' and 'witch,' and my dear Mary—I fear for you! They'll whip and humiliate you for their secret pleasure, and then kill you to assuage their filthy consciences."

"The very reason that I—we—must speak out is to prevent it happening to others. Will, your advocacy would be such a witness to the persecuting Pharisees."

"And I tell you that I won't do it. Your disobedience will ruin everything I've worked for in the last thirty years."

Mary stopped walking with Will, sat on a large stone at the edge of the short bluff, and pretended to look out over the bay. He walked back to the house and sat down to write to John Winthrop the Younger. In it, he asked, for Mary's sake, that Winthrop do all in his power and influence to spare Mary from whippings or other physical harm, and to put out a private word to other magistrates and jurisdictions that Mary Dyer must not be touched.

That's what William Dyer thought on this hot June day, as he participated in the homely acts of haying and evening merriment so familiar to the many generations before him. His joy had gone out of him, but he would carry on as if all was well in his home and his town.

August 21, 1657

Newport, Rhode Island

Mary sat at the kitchen work table, her hands employed with preparing food for her family and guests, but her mind was occupied with all her new Friends had shared over the last week.

She and the maid Cathy had been steaming fruit puddings for two days, to send to laborers at the evening harvest celebrations around the island. It was reaping time for the grains and the Indian corn, and it was hot and humid in the fields, so when the workers came in, they were met with celebrations, music and dance, and special treats for supper.

John Copeland, Richard Doudney, and Christopher Holder had been imprisoned at Boston at the end of July for agitating in churches in Massachusetts. While in the House of Correction, they'd written a creed, organizing the collective thought and revelation of the Friends in America. It had been copied many times over to share. Mary's thoughts turned to a section which resonated most with her: the Light that shone in her heart.

"Turn inward to Christ the Light," they'd written, "which shows you the secrets of your hearts, and the deeds that are not good. Therefore, while you have the Light, believe in the Light, that you may be the children of the Light; for, as you love it and obey it, it will lead you to repentance, bring you to know Him in whom is remission of sins, in whom God is well pleased." But they also warned of how contrary to Jesus' example and teaching was the persecuting spirit of New England. As expected, it gave great offense to the Boston magistrates.

One of the Salem households who turned to the Light were the family of Lawrence and Cassandra Southwick, an older couple who had been cast in prison for merely hosting the traveling Friends, as they had been commanded in the Bible.

Almost as soon as he'd reached New England after the *Woodhouse* voyage, Christopher Holder had gone to Salem, that dark, repressed town of fanatical zealots, and the family home of Governor John Endecott and Simon Bradstreet. There had been a sermon preached at Endecott's home one evening, and Holder stood up afterward to prophesy the words God had revealed to him. Suddenly, a man grabbed Holder's hair and knocked him down, and stuffed his mouth with a glove to suffocate him for his heretical speech. Samuel Shattuck stopped the man before he could kill Holder, but Shattuck was arrested at the same time as Holder. They were taken to Boston and received thirty lashes with the tri-cord whip, until the sight of their flayed flesh caused a bystander to faint. After that, they were put in a bare cell with no bedding, only the straw with vermin. For three days and nights they were allowed no food or drink. And then, by special order of Governor Endecott, Holder was whipped weekly, until his back bore one hundred eighty stripes.

When William Dyer had heard the account, he was moved more to deep disgust than to rage and said to Mary, "Endecott acted in righteous zeal, believing himself to be divinely appointed to safeguard his realm from heresy. I say that to try to understand him, not to excuse him."

Bellingham and Endecott had ordered that any and all Quakers be severely whipped twice a week while in custody. Endecott had never been able to control his outbursts, and this was no exception. He said that Holder deserved to be hanged for his writing, and if he possessed power to execute his desires, the gallows beam would soon have terminated the Quakers' labors.

Cassandra had possessed the same paper that Mary held now, and had been in prison now for more than a month. She'd be there at least another three weeks, another six whippings, until the court met next.

Mary breathed a prayer for endurance and refreshment for the sister she'd never met.

Mary was still curious as to how the Light was manifested to others. Was it a feeling? Could they see it with their eyes? Was it a vision? Could others see the Friend enveloped by the Light?

Young John Copeland, after his release from jail, had come to Newport to recover from his scores of lash stripes before setting out again. Mary had met him and William Robinson in England, so the reunion was sweet fellowship. He had sat outdoors with a quill and ink and paper, writing on a lap desk, and come in to have Mary hear his letter before he posted it to his parents in England.

FROM RHODE ISLAND, THE 12TH OF AUGUST, 1657
Dear father and mother,

My love salutes you and all the faithful in Christ Jesus, who is my joy, and in whom I do rejoice at present. This is to let you all know that I am at Rhode Island and in health, where we are received with much joy of heart; but now I and Christopher Holder are going to Martha's Vineyard, in obedience to the will of our God, whose will is our joy.

Humphrey Norton is presently at Rhode Island; Mary Clark is waiting to go towards Boston; William Brend is towards Providence. The Lord God of Hosts is with us, the shout of a King is among us, the people fear our God, for his goodness is large and great, and reaches to the ends of the earth; his power has led us all along, and I have seen his glory, and am overcome with his love. Take no thought for me, for my trust is in the Lord; only be valiant for the truth upon earth. The Lord's power has overshadowed me, and man I do not fear; for my trust is in the Lord, who has become our shield and buckler, and exceeding great reward.

The enclosed is the voyage as Robert Fowler related it, which you may read as you can. Salute me dearly to my dear friends, with whom my life is, and the Lord's power overshadow you; so may you be preserved to his glory. Amen, amen. Stand fast in the Lord.

We are about to sail to the Vineyard, and having this opportunity, I was free to let you know, by way of a ship going to Barbados, how we are. Farewell. I am your servant for the Lord's sake,
JOHN COPELAND

Mary's heart was full, having been hostess to these apostles of the Light. They'd told their story of the voyage of their small ship *Woodhouse*, straight across the Atlantic from England to Long Island Sound, over the treacherous Hell Gate and landing at New Amsterdam, with God directing the ship safely.

It was remarkable to the Dutch that the *Woodhouse* had arrived by the Long Island Sound and the Hell Gate, instead of through their southern harbor. But Mr. Fowler, the ship's master, had fired no salute or flown colors except from the foremast. A strange ship, unexpected and unidentified, was a threat to their security. And they refused to show proper respect by removing their hats before the fiscal officer or Director-General Kieft, so relations were strained from the beginning.

The men and women had immediately set about preaching in the marketplaces and in the English and Dutch churches—and being ejected from the places where they spoke, often with whips applied to their bare backs. Yet instead of being deterred, they were filled with zeal for God's work. Their mission was willingly chosen, and they were familiar with the consequences from their witnessing in England.

Three women who had suffered for the Lord in England were using Newport as a base for their travels. Sarah Gibbons, Mary Wetherhead, and Dorothy Waugh had learned the gospel in Lancastershire and Yorkshire from George Fox himself. For their preaching, they'd been bridled twice. But despite the abuse most people wouldn't give their beasts, the women offered praise and thanksgiving to God for the honor of being persecuted in his name.

Mary Clark had been beaten and imprisoned in Boston, and her naked body searched for witch marks, moles which might be the teat for a demon.

Each time the Friends were abused to the point of death, they returned to Rhode Island for medical treatment, prayers for healing, and to strengthen the faith of the growing Friends meeting in Newport. Some of the town's most prominent residents, including former Governor Coddington, had professed their adherence to Quaker beliefs.

Nothing could stop the Friends from the call of duty or the "movings of the Lord." The commands or messages from the Lord were clear as crystal in their minds, and the movings felt like a physical draw, as iron to a magnet. If they were led into danger, they believed that God could use their suffering or even death, to advance the truth of the gospel, in a way that their lives never could.

There was another place of refuge, across Long Island Sound on Shelter Island. The owner of the island was not himself a Friend, but in Sandwich and Salem and other towns, even Boston, there were a few who would not countenance the persecution of Christians who acted like Jesus' disciples, nor could they accept the violence and hate of the leaders who called themselves Christian. Shelter Island's owner, Nathaniel Sylvester, had made it known that he wouldn't answer to the authority of New Haven and Reverend Davenport—that he was ruler of his domain, and that he would provide hospitality to dissidents and persecuted heretics if he liked. His partners in Barbados were his brother Giles, and John Rous's father, so the young Quaker missionary and his Friends Copeland and Holder were welcome there.

The Dyer sons Maher and Henry were the first to burst through the door, talking loudly about their wagers on which man could reap more wheat in a day. As they were thirteen and ten, the currency was who would have to do whose farm chores on the morrow.

"Wash up first, before you soil every nice thing in the house!" Mary called. "Or there'll be enough dirt in the hall to plant a hill of beans."

They dutifully turned on their heels and went back out to slosh and splash in a horse trough. Without the application of soap, it only moved the dirt around. But it was good enough, maybe more than enough, for adolescent boys, she mused.

Her children were somewhat reserved around this mother they barely knew, but their obedience and manners were scrupulous. That was one of the benefits of the ancient English custom of fostering and trading children to be raised by trusted relatives or friends. It also served to advance the boys' future trades or professions, and to train girls to manage their own households someday. Keeping a child at home too long spoiled him, for one could love a child too much to discipline or punish when required.

Samuel, who was nearly 22 years old, had returned to Boston and his employment with Edward Hutchinson, and his most recent letter reported that there had been an outbreak of measles in Boston and the surrounding towns. Though it was well known in England and Europe, this was its first occurrence in America. Now that there were several generations born in America who had not had measles when they were children, it struck youth and adults with more violence, and some died of brain fevers and pneumonia. Mary prayed that her son would escape the measles and smallpox, but especially that he would escape the physicians' deadly remedies for disease. Having participated in midwifery for so many years, she knew the physicians were often more harmful than helpful. A popular remedy for smallpox was bloodletting, and drinking a pint of beer every other hour with sweet vitriol. It did nothing to hasten the course of the disease, or lessen the scars, but perhaps it relieved some of the pain.

But the pain Mary felt in her heart could not be relieved by doctors' cures. While she'd been in England, her older children had grown up with little interest in things of the spirit. Not that they were pagans or non-believers, but that they had no firm foundation for their faith. They bent with the winds.

But isn't that what her Uncle John Dyer had counseled for preservation of life and limb? She knew that it would never suit her to hide the light of her convictions under a clay vessel. It must shine as a beacon.

November 11, 1657
Newport, Rhode Island

William rode his horse home from the town along the same road he'd walked so many times as a younger man. The gold and scarlet leaves had been lashed from the trees by a strong storm two weeks ago, and farm laborers were still working to gather the broken tree limbs and shovel and cart the blown beach sand back to its place on the shore.

In his satchel, he carried a letter from Harry Vane, along with a bolt of dark silk sent as a gift to Mary.

TO WILLIAM DYER, GENT., AT NEWPORT IN RHODE ISLAND
29 August 1657
Greetings in the name of the Lord, to you and to your esteemed wife,

You will be interested to know of my encounter with George Fox, the Quaker preacher. My friend and chaplain, George Sikes, approached him and began to compare righteousness of man, and righteousness of the law. Fox answered that Sikes take heed of blasphemy and presumption, and they proceeded to debate Christ's fulfillment of the law. Sikes asked Fox whether he would come to Raby Castle to meet me, but Fox had no instruction of the Lord, so he demurred. But the next day, Fox came down to Raby, and he was brought up to meet with my dear Lady Frances. While he was there, I came up to the drawing room with Mr. Hugh Peter, formerly minister of Salem, as you remember, and later a chaplain to Essex and to an army colonel. I inquired if he was George Fox, and he affirmed it. He seemed surprised at my appearance; perhaps he expected an older man.

He said that he was moved of the Lord to speak of the true light which enlightens every man that comes into the world, and that Christ said, "Believe in the light that you may become children of the light," and that Christ has promised the Holy Ghost and the spirit of truth, which should lead us into all truth. He told how the grace of God, which brought salvation, had appeared unto all in the apostles' days and also now.

I told Fox that I had experience about all that he had said, and he asked, "So how did this come about, if you don't believe in the light as Christ commands; and how can you come into truth, if you have not been led by the Spirit of Truth, and how could you know salvation if it is not by the grace of God? I began to tell him how the word became flesh and dwelled among us, but Fox interrupted and all but accused me of idolatry to a god of flesh, rather than serving the god who was light and spirit. He said that I knew something of God as he was formerly, but that I'd ignored the mountain of earth and imaginations, and from that arose a smoke that darkened my brain, and that I myself was not the man I was formerly. We argued about things on which we agreed but expressed differently, and to mollify Fox, I confessed that I must have made a mistake in my speech (though I had not). In the end, Fox admitted that the Lord's power came over all.

I said later that if Fox's friend Pearson had not been there with us, I might have put Fox out of my house for being a madman. Of course I would not do so, considering that liberty of conscience is a gift of God to all men, and that God, or the Seed, or the Light, had spoken to him. If only Fox were not so arrogant and observed customs, such as the putting off of the hat in respect to others. He is quick to take offense where none was offered.

My Lady sends greetings to you. She wonders what it would be like to visit New England, and though I've told her many stories, she believes my memories to be old and imperfect. I prefer to think that twenty years have passed in an instant, and that reports from our agents in the colonies have kept my imagination fresh.

This dark night and black shade, which God has drawn over His work in the midst of us, may be (for aught we know) the ground color to some beautiful piece that He is exposing to the light. His sons may be manifested and evidently distinguished from those who say they are such and are not. There is a glory to be revealed in them, unto which their suffering is made the needful preparation. They are the seed and offspring which the Lord hath blessed.

You see, Mary, I must have absorbed something of your witness to speak so, of Light and the Seed. Perhaps someday you will recommend me to Mr. Fox.

I rest in the Lord, who is my salvation.

HENRY VANE
CHARING CROSS

William opened the gate from his saddle, and his horse moved through and waited for the latch to be replaced. Then William let the horse, Legato, pick up the pace, knowing that a trough of fodder and a rubdown awaited. William gave a nudge with his heels, and the horse cantered smoothly down the lane to the barn.

"Mary," he called when he entered the house. And it was almost a surprise when his wife answered from the top of the stairs. Between their stays in England, they had been apart for more than five years of this decade. And even now she was back in Newport, she was often out for a Friends meeting or to help heal their lash marks gained in one of the other colonies.

"Yes, Sweetheart," she said. "I've been gathering clothes and linens for the laundress tomorrow. What is it?"

"We have a letter from Harry Vane and you have a gift. I also have news to impart."

She descended the stairs and they sat at the table by the window to make use of the last of the afternoon light.

"Which shall I have first?"

He handed Mary the large sheet of laid paper, the same kind he used for letter writing and court documents because there was only one decent paper maker in England.

It took Mary a few minutes to get into the rhythm of deciphering Harry's spidery handwriting. Her face brightened as she reached the end.

"I can just see it! Both of them are so alike—confident of their own correctness, and proud of their philosophies, though neither would ever admit it. They use similar descriptions and accusations of one another. George Fox and Henry Vane are brothers, and as George said, the Lord's power is upon them both."

She looked expectantly at her husband. "And what is your news?"

"After your young Friend from Barbados, John Rous, ran afoul of Governor Prence in Plymouth, and Reverend Samuel Stone of Hartford, the United Colonies met in Boston last month, to unite their resolve against the Friends, and John Endecott wrote a letter to the Rhode Island assembly, urging us to act consistently with the other colonies, and not give sanctuary or support to people like you."

William restrained himself from calling them Quakers because it was offensive to Mary and most of them in the same way that the Puritan label was offensive to the Congregational churches. But there was no helping what other people called the Friends.

"The letter was read in our Court of Trials held at Providence. It was full of such words as 'pernicious,' 'accursed tenets,' and 'contagion.' We desire to maintain friendly relations with all of New England, but following their orders would violate this colony's laws about liberty of conscience, and banishing men over religion or any other matter would break our 1650 law against banishment."

"Yes, I remember that was one of the first laws you drafted after your appointment as attorney general. There isn't one among the first founders of Rhode Island who doesn't appreciate that protection after what the Bay colony did to us in 1637 and '38."

He handed Mary a copy of Governor Endecott's letter, and watched her face as it first drained of color and then blushed with anger.

> GENTLEMEN,—We suppose you have understood that the last year a company of Quakers arrived at Boston, upon no other account than to disperse their pernicious opinions, had they not been prevented by the prudent care of the government, who by that experience they had of them, being sensible of the danger that might befall the Christian religion here professed, by suffering such to be received or continued in the country, presented the same unto the Commissioners at their meeting at Plymouth; who, upon that occasion, commended it to the general courts of the United Colonies, that all Quakers, Ranters, and such notorious heretics, might be prohibited coming among us; and that if such should arise from among ourselves, speedy care might be taken to remove them; (and as we are informed) the several jurisdictions have made provision accordingly; but it is by experience found that means will fall short without further care by reason of your admission and receiving of such, from where they may have opportunity to creep in among us, or means to infuse and spread their accursed tenets to the great trouble of the colonies, if not to the professed in them; notwithstanding any care that has been previously taken to prevent the same; whereof we cannot but be very sensible and think no care too great to preserve us from such a pest, the contagion whereof (if received) within your colony, were dangerous to be diffused to the others by means of the intercourse, especially to the places of trade among us; which we desire may be with safety continued between us; we therefore make it our request, that you as the rest of the colonies, take such order herein that your neighbors may be freed from that danger. That you remove these Quakers that have been received, and for the future prohibit their coming among you; whereunto the rule of charity to yourselves and us (we conceive), doth oblige you; wherein if you should we hope

> you will not be wanting; yet we could not but signify this our desire; and further declare, that we apprehend that it will be our duty seriously to consider, what provision God may call us to make to prevent the aforesaid mischief; and for our further guidance and direction herein, we desire you to impart your mind and resolution to the General Court of Massachusetts, which assembles the 14th of October next. We have not further to trouble you at present, but to assure you we desire to continue your loving friends and neighbors,
> the Commissioners of the United Colonies."

Mary's expression was downcast. "Just as Brother Rous said, 'Thus may all see how these four United Colonies, as they are called, have agreed to banish Christ out of their coasts by a law. What a brotherhood is this, that thus uses the friends of God; and abuses his servants' sons and daughters by whipping, burning, and otherwise mangling their bodies!' And I would add, what hypocrites to consider themselves to be loving friends and neighbors. They do not remember the parable of the Lord which answered the question, 'Who is thy neighbor?'"

"Naturally, we—the Rhode Island Assembly—wrote a letter in response."

"Naturally," said Mary drily. "How cleverly written was it? I know that look on your face."

"Oh, very cleverly, indeed," William laughed. "We told them that with respect to his highness Mr. Cromwell and the Council of State, we were are not subject to any others in civil matters and we have eyes and ears open to discover if our adversaries seek to undermine us in our privileges. We may not be compelled to exercise any civil power over men's consciences so long as human orders are not corrupted and violated—which our neighbors do frequently practice—and we have large experience because of it. We consider it absolute cruelty, in fact. Though we didn't say it, we implied that we know firsthand of our neighbors' cruelty."

"Yes," said Mary. "Many of us remember those events very clearly."

"Our letter, written by committee and signed by Assembly President Benedict Arnold, then went on to poke Endecott in his pompous, puffed-up breast. We wrote that the Quakers had too much peace and prosperity in Rhode Island, and couldn't get converts to its religion simply by making speeches and sermons—only by being persecuted, which is why Quakers keep going back to Puritan jurisdictions and inviting trouble. We clearly implied that if the Puritans would just leave the Quakers alone as we do in Rhode Island, there would be no trouble at all."

"William, you know that is not why we walk into danger. We have a fire burning within that commands us to preach the gospel in all the world, and release the captives from bondage to their idolatrous religion."

He answered, "Many men see the stubborn Friends as using their martyrs' wounds to gain sympathy and adherents to the Quaker cause. 'Look at their patient suffering,' men say, and wonder what you have that is worth the beatings and imprisonment.

"I had a clerk make copies of Rhode Island's answer. Here, I'll read a portion aloud to you. President Arnold said that Rhode Island will return all who 'fly from justice in matters of crime, but as concerning these Quakers (so called) which are now among us, we have no law among us whereby to punish any for only declaring by words, &c. their minds and understandings concerning the things and ways of God… And we find that in those places where these people … are most suffered to declare themselves freely, and are only opposed by arguments in discourse, there they least of all desire to come, and we are informed that they begin to loath this place, for that they are not opposed by the civil authority… they delight to be persecuted by civil powers, and when they are so, they are like to gain more adherents by the conceit of their patient sufferings, than by consent to their pernicious sayings.'"

"Pernicious?" asked Mary. "God had called us to this road, to take up the cross and follow him, and we are willing to obey unto death if necessary."

"The letter simply turned Endecott's words back on him and subtly mocked him. What we're saying, my dear, is that the principles of liberty of conscience, and separation of civil and religious powers, are more important to us than cruelly persecuting people who have religious convictions that differ from others, even if others are Quakers, Baptists, Jews, or those who deny there is a God. It's more important to uphold freedom for all men, than to cave in to the threat of trade or travel restrictions, or bowing to the wishes of mad tyrants like Endecott. Supporting liberty for the individual man is more important than dwelling in harmony with our neighboring colonies.

"The letter went on to say that 'as to salvation and an eternal condition... And as to the damage that may in likelihood accrue to the neighbor colonies by their being here entertained, we conceive it will not prove so dangerous as the course taken by you to send them away out of the country as they come among you.'"

Having so recently passed through that country, Massachusetts Bay, Mary let the words rest in her heart for a few moments. As she sat there in the fading daylight, Will thought he saw a light in her countenance.

"William Dyer, I want to say something that you should remember always. I love you, and over the years, you have many times honored me with your words and actions, and your constancy and loyalty. You have trusted me to bring honor to you as a wife should. Few will know of your involvement in great matters of religion and state, but many shall benefit from the liberty you and your colleagues have advocated and won, and the foundation stones you lay down for the future. I'm so proud of you and what you have done for Rhode Island and indeed all mankind, for generations to come. God has blessed us through you."

January 15, 1658
Newport, Rhode Island

I'm getting too old to do this in such cold, thought Mary as she and Marie rode double in the ladies' saddle on one of the Dyer mares. They were returning from an all-night childbirth party at the home of a Friend on the south side of Newport. The sky was clear, but the morning sun had little warmth to impart.

The home had been warm enough, especially with a room full of chattering women and small children and food bubbling in kettles at the fireplace. But out on the road, the icy wind off the Long Island Sound seemed to go right through her. Though she'd have liked to gallop home, she had to walk the horse slowly, watching for ice on the road. As cold as it was right now, she thought Newport was usually much warmer than England, even as a tiny icicle of her breath slid off the fur of her hood.

Not like those Friends of hers who had felt the persecuting heat of Boston and Plymouth, and thought it prudent to board a ship for Barbados, to minister there for the winter. William Leddra, Thomas Harris, William Brend, Robert Hodgson, Sarah Gibbons, and Dorothy Waugh would be eating pineapple and browning their arms in the bright sun now, even as they preached to the planters and slaves of the island. And they so richly deserved the warmth, considering that many Friends had lain in prisons last winter with no fire or blankets, and little food. Only the miraculous warmth of God's love had kept them alive, they said.

Though Mary had Friends in Newport, she missed the intensity and the zeal of the missionaries. The plan was that some would return in the spring, while others, like the elderly Brother Brend, would return to England.

Another gust from the southwest hit Mary and her daughter with force, and the mare braced herself for a moment before walking on. Mary thought that this wind storm must be raging just as strongly on Long Island. Captain Underhill's wife Helena had died at their home in Oyster Bay last summer, and he had taken a new wife, from New Haven Colony, only a month ago. He was in his early sixties, and his bride, Elizabeth Feake, was twenty-five. Miss Feake was a Friend. She was also the grand-niece of the late

Governor John Winthrop. What would the patriarch Winthrop have thought of the young woman being a heretic Quaker, or that she was making this match with Captain Underhill? Or that the Winthrop and Underhill bloodlines would be united? Given enough generations, she supposed, the people of New England could have the blood of Anne Hutchinson, Governors Winthrop and Endecott, and John Cotton running in their veins.

Mary and her daughter arrived back at the Dyer farm, and turned the mare over to the stable boys. After a small breakfast, Mary sent Marie to her bed for a nap to recover the lost sleep.

Charles, now seven years old, and Henry, ten, walked to school with their brother Maher as an escort. William was learning the business of commerce, import, and export on a trading ship, and Samuel was in Boston.

William had already been out to check on his sheep, cattle, and horses, to supervise the servants in the husbandry of feeding and mucking out, and laying down fresh straw, then leading the horses around the fields to warm and exercise them.

So it was that Cathy, the housekeeper, brought bread, butter, and sausage for Mary and William. Though her prison stay last spring had left her with a sensitive stomach and little appetite, Mary found she was hungry after being up all night, and buttered her hot brown bread liberally before taking a bite.

The chief topic in Newport the last week had been the uprising at Flushing, Long Island, after the Dutch governor, Pieter Stuyvesant, had declared that Quakers would not be tolerated as residents or as guests in that territory.

"Stuyvesant had orders," William said, "from the Dutch West India Company to permit other religions, like Quakers, Jews, Baptists, and Catholics, to quietly and peacefully practice their traditions and faith as long as they broke no laws. But he holds to his rigid belief that the Elect were purified and sealed to God by perfectly keeping biblical laws.

"According to John Underhill and others of my acquaintance, he has often acted on his own authority without waiting for permission from the Company. A few months ago, he declared that the Friends in his territories had no right to assemble or worship in their Meetings because they were not members of the Dutch Reformed Church."

Mary spoke: "I don't know how he can be so cruel. The first Friends only reached New Amsterdam eighteen months ago, and they were promptly beaten and sent away. Last summer, the *Woodhouse* sailed in and again, they were persecuted and banished, as we well know by their subsequent arrival here."

William took another helping of sausage, as it was obvious that Mary wouldn't take any.

"I'm sure he had heard of their activities in England, and he has cordial relations with Reverend Davenport of New Haven, who is in turn tied to Endecott."

He called to Cathy, "Bring the mistress and me two oranges from the cellar," and then turned to his wife, "I don't want you getting scurvy, Mary. You must think better about the balance of your humors, to regain your health."

When Cathy returned, Mary dutifully peeled her orange and ate the sour sections one by one. "Tell me about the Remonstrance, Will," she said.

"Thirty members of the Flushing community, none of whom is a Friend, wrote a Remonstrance, saying that they would not accept Stuyvesant's command 'because our Saviour sayeth it is impossible but that offences will come, but woe unto him by whom they cometh.' They said further, 'Our desire is not to offend one of his little ones, in whatsoever form, name or title he appears in, whether Presbyterian, Independent, Baptist or Quaker, but shall be glad to see anything of God in any of them, desiring to do unto all men as we desire all men should do unto us, which is the true law both of Church and State; for our Savior sayeth this is the law and the prophets.'"

Like the founders of Rhode Island, William said, the Flushing men saw the division of government and ministry modeled in the Bible by Moses the Lawgiver and Christ the Lifegiver.

"But Will, that is much of what Anne Hutchinson said more than twenty years ago! At Christ's transfiguration on the mount, Moses and Elijah appeared with him, representing the Law and the Prophets of the Old Testament. But they faded away, and the voice of the Father said to the disciples, 'This is my beloved Son. Look at *him*.'

She spoke again after swallowing another bite. "Do you think the people of Flushing are experiencing a renaissance?"

"If they are, they're starting out similar to our beginning. Their Remonstrance is a statement of faith, more than a political stand. They said that Friends are supposed, by some, to be seducers of the people. But the men of Flushing will not condemn them in this case, neither can they stretch out hands against them, for God is a consuming fire, and it is a fearful thing to fall into the hands of the living God. They said they would not judge lest they be judged, and would not condemn lest they be condemned, and that they are bound by the law to do good unto all men, especially to those of the household of faith."

"How lovely," said Mary, "that they would have such courage and conviction to take a stand for the rights of other children of God."

"And from a legal perspective," her husband responded, "it's interesting that they had the presence of mind to state that their charter requires them to be 'bound by the law of God and man to do good unto all men and evil to no man,' according to the patent and charter of their town, given to them in the name of the Dutch States General. They warned their governor that they are not willing to infringe or violate their patent.

"Mr. Stuyvesant was extremely annoyed at that reminder, to say the least. Five of their number, including the clerk who wrote the document, were thrown into jail by Stuyvesant, and the rest were stripped of their freeman rights."

Mary frowned. "Surely they'll stay in the town for the winter and not rush to resettle in New England. I heard at the childbirth last night that even the great rivers have frozen so hard that deer run across them."

"The bay islands at Boston will be surrounded by ice chunks, if not frozen solid."

And so the Dyers continued companionably in their warm kitchen, just as they had so many times in their twenty-three years of marriage.

March 15, 1658
Newport, Rhode Island

"Mistress, you are asked to come into the town, quick as you can," panted a boy who had obviously run the distance from the town center.

"Who is it that asks?" said Cathy, who had answered the door. "And besides, I'm not the mistress."

"My master, of the ship *Golden Bear,* has a sick man on board who has asked for Mistress Dyer."

"You wait here. I'll get her." Cathy shut the door.

Mary was in the parlor directing Marie's studies. When she went to the door, she asked the boy, who looked to be about ten or twelve, why they hadn't sent for a doctor.

"The man asked for you, Mistress. He said to say his name is Norton and he's your friend. You'd better prepare yourself. I've seen dead men in better health."

Though the boy was young, Mary did not doubt that statement. Humphrey Norton had been preaching in Connecticut and had spent the winter in jail there without comfort of fire or blankets.

"Yes, I'll come straightaway. Will you ride with me?" she asked the boy.

"No, Mistress, I was ordered to run and not dawdle," he answered. "You'll find the *Golden Bear* at the long wharf."

She called for the stable boy to hitch a wagon to a cart-horse, and strewed a thick layer of hay and horse blankets on it. Mary and her daughter drove the short distance into the town, and left the horse and wagon at the top of the wharf. The ship's boy waited to direct her to the ship.

She climbed the gangplank and left Marie at the rail. She entered the tiny cabin where Humphrey Norton lay on a cot, senseless.

"When he woke last, he asked for you, Mrs. Dyer," said the master, who identified himself as Captain Peterson. "He must come off the ship here. I'll not take him any further, for he'll surely die at sea."

"You've done the right thing, sir. I don't know him well, but he has friends here."

"Quakers, you mean?"

"Yes. And in the other sense, brothers and sisters who will care for him whether he's to live or die—though we'll pray for life."

"Norton's passage was paid by a Dutchman, for the English would have nothing to do with him, though many were sickened at the cruelty of his punishments."

"What do you know of his wounds?" asked Mary. "Did you see them inflicted?"

"No, I was only told what happened," he answered.

Norton shifted on his cot and moaned, but didn't regain his senses.

Captain Peterson spoke again, in a hushed voice, so as not to disturb Norton. "I was told by the Dutchman that about ten days ago, Mr. Davenport, the minister at New Haven, undertook to prove to the court that this one, Norton, was guilty of heresy. He had already lain through the ice and deep snows of winter in New Haven's jail, without fire or candle, blanket nor bed, and not for breach of the civil laws, only for his Quaker doctrines. That's something far beyond one such as I."

"It's all right, sir. I'm familiar with the doctrines, and with the evils of the marriage of church and the government," said Mary.

Captain Peterson nodded. "I hold to the old Church of England beliefs, not this Puritan, Independent movement. But I must admit there is too much of politics in the English church for my taste.

"Anyway, in spring court session, when Norton tried to reply, Davenport had a large iron key placed in his mouth and tied there, like a scold's bridle, to prevent his speaking in explanation or defense. The trial went on for two days, with many attempts to entrap Norton in his own words. He was sentenced to whipping on the next lecture day and recommitted to the jail.

"Three days hence he was called to his flogging, being stripped with his back to the magistrates and placed in the stocks, unable to move. He received thirty-six blows before disgusted cries rose from the watchers, 'Do you mean to kill the man?' and the executioner stopped at a reluctant wave from the magistrates. Norton claimed not to feel pain, saying it was as if his body had been covered with balm. But you see, Mrs. Dyer, that the pain has set in since then."

She did, indeed. How was it possible for a man to live through that without divine intervention?

"Look at this hand," said the captain. He pulled back the bloody sheet, and Mary recoiled in horror. A deep burn in the shape of an H had been branded on Norton's right palm. She could see the blackened, dry edges of skin, and the angry, red, oozing flesh inside the H. H for heretic.

"The Dutchman told me that Norton lifted his voice in prayer, saying his help came from heaven, to the astonishment of them all. They loosed him from the stocks and as he stood there rocking on his feet, they demanded ten pounds in fines, plus his keep for the winter in jail, and banished him on pain of death. Norton replied that if his discharge cost only two pence, he would not pay it, nor consent for others to pay. The magistrates were eager to be rid of him, and offered to let him go now and pay them later, but he also declined.

"That is when the Dutchman paid the fees and put Norton aboard my ship, and paid his passage. I don't care much for getting involved in politics or criminals, and certainly not dying Quakers. But in my mind, I saw the gospel parable, with the despised Dutchman as the Good Samaritan, showing the Christians how religion ought to be."

Mary felt like the chill, dark clouds of a winter storm had blocked out the Light of the world. Again, she wondered at the evil things that man could get up to. Now she stood up straight and decided, against human reason, to trust that the Light was still shining above the clouds of sin and horror.

"Captain, thank you for sending for me. Humphrey Norton will not die this time. The Lord has preserved him and brought him to his true Friends because there is yet more work for this man. I'll take him home and tend his wounds while he heals."

The captain called four of his seamen to carry Norton off the ship and lift him onto the wagon. Mary put her daughter in the back to steady the wounded man against the rocking or bumping on the roads. Before they left the town center, she found a schoolmate of her sons and asked him to carry a message to Herod Gardner, asking to help her tend Norton when she got him home.

The cold wind, hinting of snow on the mainland across the bay, helped congeal Humphrey's wounds as Mary slowly and carefully drove back to the farm.

April 14, 1658
New Haven Colony

The winter snows had retreated two weeks ago, and the streams and rivers had only just returned to their bounds after the ice dams broke with a crack and a roar, flooded down to the harbors and estuaries, and melted in the brine of Long Island Sound. There was very little spring green yet, as frosts continued for several more weeks.

Mary and her two Friends, William Brend and Mary Wetherhead, stood at the top step at the house of Reverend John Davenport, cofounder of New Haven twenty years ago. Brend, a soft-spoken man in his early seventies, and the young Miss Wetherhead, had both been passengers on the tiny Quaker ship *Woodhouse*.

Brend pounded on the solid wood door of the large house, demanding to see the priest inside. The manservant, alarmed at the noise, stood inside the door as Davenport came to answer his callers.

"What do you mean, raising such a noise?" Davenport boomed. "Guard! Guard! Come here!" he shouted down the street.

Brend, who had already lived twenty years longer than many other men, left his hat on his head instead of doffing it in respect for the chief minister and magistrate of New Haven. His turquoise eyes blazed like a flare from a pine knot. Two months ago, in Plymouth, he'd been called a "man of turbulent spirit and forward to abuse men with his tongue."

"Priest Davenport," said Brend, in a voice loud enough to be heard fifty feet away, "We denounce you and the other rulers for cruelty and bigotry. Having broken no law, you kept Humphrey Norton in your jail through the winter with no blanket or the shelter you'd afford an ox or horse; you caused him to be flogged with thirty-six stripes and would have given more if not for the uprising of your own citizens at the harsh treatment. And then you burned his hand deeper than anyone has ever seen in beast or man, to mark him as a heretic. How do you reconcile yourself to that, when our Lord acted with charity and mercy to known law-breakers? But Humphrey Norton caused no offense to your laws, and spoke only as would Christ."

As Brend spoke, Reverend Davenport's face turned purple and white and Mary wondered if he were apoplectic at being denounced by a heretic on his own property.

"Guard!" Davenport shouted again, and a member of the militia ran to his aid, followed by two others who patrolled the streets of the town to report on law-breakers.

"What is your name, man?" demanded Davenport.

"Henry Bristol, sir!" though he pronounced it "Bristow." "The cooper and meat-packer, I am."

"Arrest these cursed Quakers, bind them, and cast them into the jail. There will be a hearing today."

"Aye, sir."

"You Quakers," Davenport admonished with a sneer, "If you open your mouths to spew your heresy in this town, you'll get the same bridle bit as Norton on your tongue. Perhaps we'll even heat the key to burn you."

Bristol looked meaningfully at his musket as he ordered his prisoners to stay together and then he and the other watchmen escorted them to the jail in the town's stockaded fort.

After they were roughly searched for weapons, Brend was shoved into one cell, and the two Marys were prodded none too respectfully into another. There was no straw on the earthen floor, and it was very dark and cold. At least they had the cloaks they arrived in. Mary Dyer took the younger woman over to the boarded-up window where the air stank marginally less than the corners of the cell, where human waste lay. She began reciting scripture:

We give thanks to God always; Remembering without ceasing your work of faith, and labor of love, and patience of hope in our Lord Jesus Christ, in the sight of God and our Father; Knowing, brethren beloved, your election of God. For our gospel came not unto you in word only, but also in power, and in the Holy Ghost, and in much assurance. And ye became followers of us, and of the Lord, having received the word in much affliction, with joy of the Holy Ghost. So that ye were ensamples to all that believe. For from you sounded out the word of the Lord in every place your faith to God-ward is spread abroad. We wait for his Son from heaven, whom he raised from the dead, even Jesus, which delivered us from the wrath to come.

Brend's voice, strong as a man in his prime, sounded from around the corner, in a hymn.

Mary smiled to herself. No man could bind her spirit. With the Light, it was brighter in this cell than if she sat on her porch with her mending in her lap, facing Narragansett Bay on a summer afternoon. Mary Wetherhead gave her testimony in a voice that projected through the boarded-up window, not knowing if anyone outside heard her. Still, the vocalization was praise to God.

Two hours passed in that manner. And then, similar to that June day of Pentecost twenty years ago, there came a deep rumble that was sensed before it was heard. The timbers of the fort's palisade creaked and groaned, and nails screeched as they popped out of their boards and posts. The floor heaved once, and the rotten boards over the jail windows splintered and fell to the earth outside. The amazed inmates could see outside to stone and brick chimneys crumbling and toppling, and men and women running haphazardly through the enclosure, no destination in mind—just trying to get away from falling walls or masonry.

Though the earth quieted after a minute or two, more tremors and shocks came upon the town, smaller, shorter, and of lessening intensity.

The inmates marveled at the quake no less than the Puritans outside. This was God's hand, judging the wicked. Of course, which party was the wicked one was a matter of perspective.

Reverend Davenport, who had been meeting with the other rulers of New Haven about the Quakers, came to the prison himself an hour later. Henry Bristol and his mates were leading two horses, Mary saw from the open jail window. The Friends could have escaped if they'd wished. But to be honest, they were exactly where they needed to be to bring attention to their cause: public outrage at the treatment of people of conscience.

"You heretics are the cause of this damage," Davenport said. "Your very presence here has prevented God's protective hand from keeping us safe in our God-fearing, obedient town.

When pure praise cannot be heard, even the rocks will cry out to God.

"The council has agreed to your sentence: time served, and banishment on pain of death. Get you gone from our town and take your pestilence and disaster with you. Bristol here will set you on horses and accompany you to the port without your speech to anyone, and a shallop will escort your boat downriver to the Sound, where I hope you founder in the waves as you deserve. You accursed Quakers! Stay out of our province, on pain of death."

Bristol prodded the elderly man to mount a horse, and helped the two Marys astride the other horse for the one-mile trip to the harbor.

William Brend, Mary Wetherhead, and Mary Dyer were released from the wreckage of the prison, grinning that they had accomplished their mission, and exhilarated that the angel of the Lord had delivered them, this time, from persecution. Just as he had the apostles, plucking them from the prison with a mighty earthquake.

On the banks of the river, they saw hundreds of trees broken or uprooted, and the waterline had risen and sunk, leaving some moored boats staved in and half-submerged in mud. Their hired sloop was undamaged, they boarded safely, and waited until the ship's master finished loading the cargo.

Mary Wetherhead shouted as she stood at the rail of their ship, "Woe be unto you for Humphrey Norton's sake! Woe be unto you!"

Brother William's voice rang out again, loud enough to be heard on the wharf as the sloop's sails caught the breeze and sailed slowly down the river. It was the Song of Moses, after Israel's delivery from Pharaoh:

"And in the greatness of thine excellency thou hast overthrown them that rose up against thee: thou sentest forth thy wrath, which consumed them as stubble. And with the blast of thy nostrils the waters were gathered together, the floods stood upright as an heap, and the depths were congealed in the heart of the sea."

*****

But when the three Friends had returned safely to Newport and reported their protest and triumphant deliverance to the Meeting, they learned that their brothers Christopher Holder and John Copeland, who had been witnessing and preaching in Plymouth Colony, had been arrested at Sandwich. Governors Prence's and Endecott's spies took them captive during a Meeting there with the Perrys, Harpers, Trasks, Smiths, and others. The two missionaries were marched twelve miles to Barnstable, stripped of their clothing, and bound to a privy post. The local executioner used the whip with three strands so as to triple the effect of the thirty-three strokes he laid on. The horrified Friends and Puritans who watched the punishment said that Copeland's and Holder's bodies ran with blood.

One of the observers there cried out, "How long, O Lord, how long shall it be ere you avenge the blood of your elect? Did I forsake father and mother and all my dear relatives to come to New England for this?"

June 1, 1658

Newport, Rhode Island

Mary set her satchel of herbal remedies on the bench inside Herod and George Gardner's home. The Gardners had five boys under the age of fifteen, a two-year-old daughter Dorcas, and the infant Rebecca. Mary had helped deliver the older boys, but not all, because she'd been in England for more than four years.

Herod had taken her newborn baby Rebecca, and Robert Stanton's twelve-year-old daughter Mary to help her, and had walked sixty miles to Weymouth, the port town where she and her first husband had lived before moving to Rhode Island. The people of Weymouth were amazed that a woman who had so recently given birth should have the strength to walk so far, but they decided that God had given supernatural strength to Herod. There in Weymouth, she had denounced the vicious treatment of the Quaker Friends, and its author, Governor John Endecott, who was visiting the town. She told them that their governor was the grandfather of a four-year-old bastard and he'd had the mother beaten instead of his horny, rapist son Zerubbabel, yet he had no

Christian compassion in his soul for decent people who only wanted to follow God's voice and live in peace.

Without a court hearing, Endecott in his fury had screamed at them, and committed Herod and the Stanton girl to the jail. They were taken out to the pillory, in public, to receive the standard ten lashes of the whip. They were stripped to the waist and tied by their hands to the whipping post, and the baser sorts of the town leered at their nudity and flung mud and animal dung at them. The whip had multiple flails, which bit into their skin and left them bleeding. While receiving the heavy blows, Herod tried to protect her wailing baby with one arm, and Mary screamed in pain, fear, and outrage.

When it was over, Herod fell to her knees in shock and tears. She managed to croak, "The Lord forgive you, for you know not what you do," before collapsing on her side, Rebecca still clasped to her naked breast.

A witness to her torture said to her neighbor, "Surely if she had not the spirit of the Lord she could not do this thing."

Herod, young Mary, and the tiny baby had been dumped into the jail for two weeks, and the filthy conditions and scant, moldy bread there had exacerbated their wounds. Mary Stanton's father had had them brought back to Newport by a coastal sloop, and they'd just arrived this morning.

With Dr. Clarke still in London, the Newport citizens relied on midwives and healers to mend injuries and treat illnesses. Nicholas Easton's granddaughter, only six months old, had recently died despite, or perhaps because of, the midwives' efforts to keep her alive.

Mary Dyer and her daughter Marie set about gently washing Herod's and Mary's wounds, some of which were infected, and applying poultices and dressings. She didn't give a tincture of poppy because Herod was still nursing the baby.

Herod told the tale to Mary through gritted teeth as her friend worked.

"What made you decide to testify, and why Weymouth?" Mary asked.

"Have I not seen for myself what a devil Endecott is?" spat Herod. "And have we not sheltered the Friends here in our own home, who have come to Newport to recover from their beatings and brandings? Yes. I chose Weymouth because of the church members who judged me as a deserving sinner when I was a mere slave girl being beaten by my former husband."

"But Herod, what possessed you to ask mercy and grace for the jailer who beat you?"

"I've been beaten many times in my life already, some for cause when I was a rebellious girl, and some out of drunken hate. Perhaps I deserved my beating for disturbing their so-called peace. But not young Mary. Not my babe. Endecott is mad with the devil's power."

Herod paused for a few moments, while she struggled to roll onto her side. "The words just came to me, perhaps from God, to redeem some good out of my pain. If my actions, testimony, or those words praying forgiveness take root in Weymouth, it will be worth the beating. Surely there is a little compassion somewhere in that god-forsaken town, that will slow or stop their persecutions of the Friends and the Baptists."

Mary disagreed, but didn't argue the point. "Perhaps the Friends' repeated visits and our patient suffering will cause people to wonder what or Who gives us strength to endure. We demonstrate that in our voluntary weakness and emptiness, there is space for the strength and power of God to fill us to overflowing.

"And Herod, no human being deserves beatings or whippings. It does nothing to correct behavior and only instills fear, which drives out love. A man who lifts his hand against a woman shows his own fear and weakness, that he knows no intelligent or logical way, no skills of gentle persuasion, to accomplish his will."

"You are too charitable, Mary, too naïve, believing that animals like Endecott could be taught peace or mercy. Some people are just wicked, down to the bones."

Mary finished laying the dressings over the poultices of fragrant mint leaves, and helped Herod pull a loose shift over her head to clothe herself. She brought baby Rebecca to nurse, checked Marie's progress with Mary Stanton's wounds and approved, and sat down to rest for a few minutes before starting the evening meal for the Gardners.

No one spoke, and there was a rare moment of peace.

She saw an army with pikes and muskets, led by proud men on war horses, and carrying standards with dragons on them—not the dragon of Wales, but the dragon of the Book of Revelation. When the captains turned to command the soldiers, she saw the faces of John Endecott, John Wilson, Simon Bradstreet, and Richard Bellingham, twisted with hate and fear.

But as her heart chilled, there came a gust of warm summer air, and a familiar wave of love and pure light overcame Mary as she sat there. Out of the almost-substantial light came the Voice:

"I will make you to this people a fortified, bronze wall; they will fight against you, but they will not prevail over you, for I am with you to save and deliver you."

The presence of God shimmered around her, and faded away in what seemed like minutes, but must have been only seconds. She knew not to try to hold on to the Light, only to retain its warmth.

After another few moments, she stood up. "Herod," said Mary. "What would you think of a fish fry to strengthen you in your healing, and satisfy those hungry boys of yours? Marie, dear, all finished? Good. Take this purse and run down to the fishmonger for some cod or bass. Be sure to haggle with him, and remind him whose London guild your father belongs to so he gives you the freshest he has. I'll leave you to estimate the amount of fish to feed the Gardners, Stantons, and the Dyers tonight. Take Benoni with you to carry back the purchase."

June 17, 1658

Providence, Rhode Island

KATHERINE SCOTT TO JOHN WINTHROP, JR.

For the hand of John Winthrop called Governor of Connecticut, at Harvard in New England, there deliver with trust.

Providence, this 17 June 1658

John Winthrop, — Think it not hard to be called so, seeing Jesus, our Savior and Governor, and all that were made honorable by him, that are recorded in Scripture, were called so. I have writ to thee before, but never heard whether they came to thy hand.

It is only out of true love and pity to thee, that thou mayest be free, and not troubled, as I have heard thy father was, upon his death bed, at the banishment of my dear sister Hutchinson and others. I am sure they have a sad cup to drink, that are drunk with the blood of the saints.

O my friend, as thou lovest the prosperity of thy soul and the good of thy posterity, take heed of having thy hand, or heart, or tongue lifted up against those persons that the wise yet foolish world in scorn calls Quakers: for they are the messengers of the Lord of Hosts, which he hath in his large love and pity sent into these parts, to gather together his outcasts and the distressed of the children of Israel: and they shall accomplish the work, let the rage of men be never so great: take heed of hindering of them, for no weapon formed against them shall prosper. It is given to them not only to believe, but to suffer, &c., but woe to them by whom they suffer.

O my friend, try all things, and weigh it by the balance. I dare not but bear witness against the unjust and cruel laws of my countrymen in this land: for cursed are all they that cometh not out to help the Lord against the mighty; and all that are not with him are against him. Woe be to men that gather and not by the Lord, which woe I desire thou mayest escape.
KATHERINE SCOTT

"What do you think of my letter?" Katherine asked Mary Dyer. They were sitting on benches in the shade of the orchard. They had baskets of mending with them, all but forgotten as they spoke. Their daughters were employed at the house, hemming garments while Mary Scott read aloud to them. "Do you think it will change his mind?"

"Johnny is a man of two minds: that of his father, who insisted that God's law is eternal and must be of more importance than human beings, and that of a new generation that sees the law as a good fence to provide guidance and protect people—not a wall blocking them from the fields of grace," Mary replied. "It seems to William and me that Johnny has a larger measure of God's grace and mercy than his fellows in Connecticut or Massachusetts. I pray that he will see the Light and become a beacon in the darkness. But he's firmly entrenched in their ways and it would betray his heritage to leave that life. Perhaps he'll work from within his circles to help us."

"I like John very much," said Katherine. There's a soft heart there under the tough exterior, perhaps from his mother's influence. It's a heart the Lord can work with."

Mary laughed softly. "You sound like your sister Anne. She could be very tough, yet she spoke with conviction and passion—as Johnny Winthrop does. Is there any hope for John Endecott and his band of brothers? They've arrested our Friends merely for withdrawing from their church assemblies and holding their own meetings. After fining them into poverty, they committed ancient people to prison, gave them ten stripes, and put them to hard labor: Lawrence and Cassandra Southwick, and Edward Harnet and his wife. They should be treated with tenderness. They're all old, with grown children!" she cried. "There are many more beside, who suffer the lash and prison. But how Endecott and the others just give themselves over to the Evil One, I can't understand."

Katherine slammed her fist down on the bench for emphasis. "They are whitewashed sepulchers, like the Pharisees of old. They look consecrated and pure on the outside, but inside, they are rotting corpses."

She looked around at the fertile orchards, vineyard, fields, and animals her husband had built up over twenty years, and her voice quieted to a whisper. "Endecott has left the husbandry of their farms to the four winds. What he hasn't taken by fine will be ruined by neglect, starvation of the animals, or the weather. I feel for those Friends and their loss. If they are given so much time on earth, it will take a long time to recover their losses. The Southwicks have another boy living at home, but he won't be able to do it alone."

Mary covered Katherine's hand with her own. "Imagine stripping those old women to the waist and beating them with whips of gut as thick as a viol string. It could kill these grandmothers! It's potentially a capital punishment, for a civil misdemeanor like taking Friends into their homes or not attending their steeple houses.

"Have you heard this?" Mary continued after a moment. "William and others have noticed a pattern in the Bay's prosecutions. The magistrates observe behavior or speech they do not like, then arrest the perpetrator without a law, and throw them in prison for months with liberal whippings and hard labor. When next they hold a general court, they try the prisoner—separately from his friends' trials. If the prisoner demands to know on what charge he is bound, the court somewhat desperately lays new charges on him and soon a new, more cruel law is written. But Will says that laws may not be administered retroactively, as Boston and Salem are doing, nor can they punish prisoners under one law, then change the charges to fit their whims."

Katherine said with a growl of intensity, "I've not had a call from the Lord yet on this subject, but if he does call me to travel, I will go to Boston and face that lot who would whip old, frail, helpless people who should be honored. I'll acquaint them with the woes and sorrows of those who deliberately disobey God."

"They'll whip you, Kathy, and throw you in the House of Correction. They've already done it to my friend in Newport."

"You've been there. If God is pleased to send me to Boston or anywhere, I will go. And so will Richard. Even our daughters will go. We look to the Master as humble servants."

They fell quiet for a few moments before Mary spoke.

"William says that last month, John Endecott published a new law against the Friends, calling us Quakers, accursed heretics with pestilent errors and practices and diabolical doctrines. Can't you just see him spitting foam as he rants?"

"What did the law pronounce?"

"That in addition to their former laws, every person professing our ways by speaking, writing, or by meeting on the Lord's day or any day, shall after conviction incur the penalty of paying ten shillings for each offense. Everyone speaking at a Meeting shall pay five pounds each. If they've been punished by scourging already, they shall be kept at work in the House of Correction until they post a bond with two other men, that they shall nevermore vent their 'hateful errors' or 'sinful practices,' or shall depart the jurisdiction at their own charges. If any return, each person shall incur the penalty of all the laws made for strangers. That's the abbreviation for burning our papers, and committing us to prison for an indefinite time, with regular whippings."

"Well, it was only a question of time before the Boston court added fines to their whippings and imprisonments. Surely the other governments will follow in their footsteps."

"They have, indeed," said Mary. "In addition to the Southwicks, they have taken Joshua Buffum and Samuel Shattock, all of them merely for providing Christian hospitality. Then they added charges based on false reports of townsmen jealous of their prosperity. And in Sandwich at the last court, they fined Robert Harper, Edward Perry his wife's father, and many others, for not taking the oath of fidelity to the colony and to the Commonwealth of England."

"Old England," Katherine sighed. "I'd love to go back for a visit. Though it's been twenty-five years since I left, and surely much is destroyed by war as you've told me, I still dream of it sometimes—the softer climate, the stone manors and churches, the lovely blooming orchards, the flocks of sheep dotting the steep fells, the fields of golden rape and red poppies and green wheat."

"I dream, too," said Mary. "Those places do exist, where war has not destroyed them. But the human misery I saw was immeasurable. Women and children left to starve on burned-over farms, their men conscripted for war. More men died of dysentery, fevers, pox, and plague than they did of battle injuries. I heard that in Ireland, Cromwell's forces massacred most of the men and women, and the starving children and youth were lured to slave ships with promise of food. I suppose that the lucky ones are sold here in New England, but the majority are destined for the plantations of Virginia and the Indies. Over the years, William has bought indentures for servants for the house and farm who have told us terrible things."

"We couldn't husband our farm properly without bond-servants to plant, harvest, and clear the land," said Katherine. "But we treat them well, and they have food and warmth and safety in addition to lessons in reading. That's in contrast to what we've observed on other farms, where the servants are little better than beasts of burden."

Mary sat back and looked up at the changing skyscape, the afternoon clouds scudding by. "When I think of the way the Bay Colony was promoted as the New Jerusalem whose godly residents would bring in the second coming of Christ, and how it was corrupted in such a short time, I'm amazed. We lived under a crushing law of sin and death, not only before God, but before the magistrates and all their spies. Do you remember how they were encouraged to report law-breakers so the community could purify itself by discipline?"

Katherine nodded.

"It was your sister who took the next step beyond Mr. Cotton's teaching about grace, which still depended upon the old covenant of works, which could never be kept. We knew that no matter how we tried to keep the law by actions and in our thoughts, we could not do so, and that meant we were condemned to hell. When Anne taught us that there was no longer condemnation, but that Christ loved and accepted us, what joy opened before us!

"Our Friends movement is still in its youth. It's imperfect and unformed. But in it, I've found fullness of joy, and a love I never dreamed of as a young and earnest woman. Obeying Christ's commission to go into the world and teach this good news, we are hunted down as prey."

Katherine responded, "They are fearful. They fear that we will bring chaos to New England and they'll be forced to receive a royal governor. And they fear that what we teach is heresy and will bring down God's wrath and they'll go to hell no matter how hard they tried to be good or to persecute us in God's name."

"Kathy, do you ever wonder why you were put on earth?"

"I'll know it when I see it. But no, the time is not yet here."

"My time is coming."

October 25, 1658

Boston, Massachusetts

William left his pinnace in charge of its master, and stepped off the gangplank on the city dock. Well, it wasn't strictly *his* pinnace, but he had a financial interest in the ship and its cargo, and he had passed the short voyage between Newport and Boston at the helm with the master. This lovely vessel, formed like a galleon, had a shallow draft, and was square-rigged on three masts. After loading timber and barrels of salt fish in Boston, the ship was bound for the Caribbean; William would hire a horse to ride back to Newport.

Against the biting-cold wind coming from a mass of black clouds to the west, he strode uphill on King Street to Ed Hutchinson's home at Tri-Mount, and was admitted by the young Anne, a pretty girl on whom the sober Puritan garb favored by Boston was somewhat funereal.

"Mr. Dyer! Please be welcome, and come inside. You may wait in the parlor, and I'll call Father."

William looked around the room that contained a writing table, several cushioned chairs, and a case of precious books much like the Dyers kept at home in Newport. On the floor under the table, a bull terrier snored unevenly, not caring that a visitor had recently arrived.

Edward entered the parlor a few moments later. William was the older by a few years, but Edward had aged over the last few months. There were deep lines between his mouth and nose; his close-cropped hair was salt and pepper.

"Ah, Will! Your unexpected appearance makes me a happy man." He clapped William on the back as they embraced. "Can you stay the night? And join us for supper?"

"I suppose I could tolerate one night of your watering the porridge and allowing me a blanket to sleep with the dogs," he replied, as if this were Edward's customary hospitality.

"It may come to that, though not for you. With my wife Abby and eight children, plus my aunt Scott and her daughters, and your son Samuel—we're full. But we'll evict the older boys. As for supper, I apologize that we're living roughly with sea bass tonight."

Will laughed. "Stop twisting my arm. No man can resist bass. How is Sam these days? Earning his keep?"

"Yes, that. And casting puppy eyes at Anne. She's only fifteen. I won't let her go in marriage, if that's what it comes to, for at least two more years." He paused for a moment. "I wonder what my parents would think of uniting Hutchinson and Dyer in marriage, and producing future generations of our mixed blood."

"You don't have the same gift—or plague—of revelations, then, that your mother did?"

"No, but as the years go by, I swear that I know my parents more intimately now than ever, though they've been dead these fifteen years and more."

"If Sam needs to cool his fever, I'll borrow him back and send him on a trading voyage. It worked for your parents, and for my master, Blackborne."

Ed's wife Abigail brought pints of ale, and the two friends from the shire settled back to talk until supper.

"Ed, you said Katherine Scott is here. Just a visit, or is she on a Quaker mission?"

"The latter," Hutchinson replied irritably. "She was caught by Endecott's spies, providing succor to Christopher Holder at the prison. Holder, Copeland, and Rous—do you know them?— "

Will nodded.

"—Holder might as well give his home address as the House of Correction, as he's spent more time in residence there this year. All three of them are walking miracles because they ought to be dead after their severe beatings. I don't understand how they choose conflict and confrontation when they could be safe and free in Rhode Island. But on one of their stays in Providence, with Katherine and Richard, Holder and Mary Scott handfasted to marry when the girl is a bit older.

"Endecott had the men's ears cropped in secret, so as not to arouse the rabble to sympathy, and everyone knows *that* is against the law, because punishments are meant to be public so as to instruct the people. Rous claimed an appeal to English courts, but our magistrates are not eager to have their laws or executions overturned there, or indeed, for their rash actions to be known at all.

"When they heard about it in Providence soon after, Mary would not rest until she came to Boston, and of course Katherine and Patience had to round out the party. Once here, Katherine and the girls were arrested and thrown into the jail—of course on the women's side, where they can't meet or speak to the men, anyway.

"And then they sat in the prison for weeks. Endecott kept their arrest from me—well, from almost everyone, but I'm their advocate here. The jailer, Munnings, died meanwhile, so there was upheaval over his replacement. On October 2, the governor had Katherine whipped ten stripes with the thrice-knotted braided cord for her insolence in saying that Endecott and the court were going to act the works of darkness, because they had not publicly charged the men with their crimes so that all could hear and fear."

William winced and moaned aloud, for the Scotts had been friends for decades and he genuinely cared for her and Richard. And if Katherine had been beaten, could Mary Dyer be far behind?

But Edward continued, "When Endecott taunted her for leaving the safety of Providence to enter Massachusetts, Katherine said that if God called them—the Quakers—woe be to Quakers if they did not obey his commands, and she didn't question the God she loves, nor was her life dear to herself when considering the sake of his cause. At this, Endecott spat after her, 'And we shall be as ready to take away your lives as ye shall be to lay them down.'"

"I petitioned the court," said Edward, "regarding the disposition of fees paid for the release of my aunt and three others from jail. The General Court directed that the fees be taken by the jail keeper until further order. I suppose that's the last I see of that lot of coin. Down the cobhole it went."

Will said, "Wait. Go back to the men's trial. As I understand, they weren't even recovered from their Barnstable beating when they entered Boston and invited more trouble."

"You know Endecott and his magisterial brothers haven't a scrap of pity in their bowels. This is what I learned from another attorney, whose name I shall keep secret. Endecott asked why the men returned to Boston when they knew the law.

"'We remain in the fear of the Lord, who commanded us to come,' said Christopher.

"Endecott was in a fine fury and shouted that it was not God, it was Satan. He commanded that the keeper of the House of Correction take into custody the prisoners, and that they be committed to labor with prisoners' diet only, till their ears be cut off, and that they not be suffered to converse with anyone while in custody.

"My Aunt Scott heard of the sentence, and rushed here to protest with two of her daughters. She said to Endecott's face that it was evident they were going to act the works of darkness in secret, or else they would have brought the prisoners forth publicly to make an example on lecture day as usual, and that secret punishments were contrary to the law of England. She taunted

Endecott that he feared a public execution of the sentence because his own people had become hostile to his personal crusade against the Friends.

"That sealed her fate, a prison stay of more than two months, and a lashing of ten stripes with the three-fold whip at the end of it. Endecott would not hear my pleadings."

William was furious. "The Rhode Island Assembly men will be outraged that Endecott has treated the wife of one of its founders and most prosperous men in such a manner. Endecott has dishonored Richard and the entire colony.

"Do you know that at the Assembly in March, our doctrine of freedom of different consciences was reaffirmed. A letter was sent to the Commissioners of the United Colonies which threatened—or informed—that if trouble arose from harboring Quakers, we would present the case unto the supreme authority of England. Rous knew that and appealed, and it was denied illegally. Even old Winthrop never would have countenanced such a thing!"

"I know," sighed Edward. "And after Katherine's passionate speech, the men were cropped anyway. As they bled copiously, they were asked how they liked it. The reply was a cheerful one. 'In the strength of God we suffered joyfully, having freely given up not only one member, but all, if the Lord so required. We desire from our hearts that the Lord forgive you if you did this in ignorance; but if you do it maliciously, let our blood be upon your heads; and such shall know in the day of account that every drop of our blood shall be as heavy upon them as a millstone.' Then they were whipped again, and their recent wounds opened. They've been beaten twice a week for nine weeks, and recently released only to take a ship to England or Barbados—just not America."

Will shook his head. "Endecott and his court are a brood of vipers, and they are escalating their efforts against the Quakers. My wife hears similar stories from Connecticut, New Haven, and Plymouth, though she has stopped mentioning them to me. I hear them anyway from Nick Easton.

"Robert Harper of Sandwich has refused to take the oath of fidelity, and won't attend church, so Plymouth is getting rich from confiscating his cattle and horses one at a time. Matthew Fuller is the son of a Pilgrim, but that heritage hasn't distracted Plymouth magistrates from fining him for the same thing as Harper. Captain Tristram Hull of Barnstable, with whom I do business, protests the persecution of Quakers and Baptists to his peril. And I've seen a report for myself, thanks to Captain Underhill, from the Dutch ministers at New Amsterdam. They said that the 'raving Quakers' have not yet settled down there, but they never fail to pour forth their venom. They reviled Rhode Island as a *caeca latrina,* the sewer of New England, for tolerating and harboring Baptists and Quakers."

Abigail opened the parlor door to say that supper was ready and the younger children were tucked in bed. As the men walked out, the bull terrier shot between their legs and skidded to a halt at the trestle table, where he resumed the posture of feigned indifference. Throwing a mother's severe look, Abigail said quietly to the waiting young people, "Thurloe will have his supper of scraps later. He had better not enjoy one morsel from anyone at table."

Will laughed. "You named your dog after the spymaster?"

"Why not? He uses his nose to sniff out offending pests," Edward responded.

Once the men were seated, the rest of the family took their places. Elizabeth, Elisha, Anne, and Abby ranged from twenty to fifteen years of age. Anne, learning household management, served the meal, striped bass steamed with wine and vegetables, and Mary took a plate to her mother, who was recovering from her wounds in an upstairs chamber.

"Ed, shall I take Katherine and the girls back to Providence when I return to Rhode Island?" William asked, as he stabbed a morsel of bass with his eating knife, and raised the knife to his mouth. Between chews, he said, "They'd have safe passage with me, more safe than if Richard came and fetched them. He might open his mouth to the wrong person with a 'thee' or 'thou' and be arrested himself."

"Thank you, Will, but I have plans to see them home, myself, when Katherine is more fully recovered."

"The first snow may be at your door within a week or two."

"Yes, and the urgency of their departure is heightened by last week's new resolution passed by the General Court."

Will raised his eyebrows in inquiry and Hutchinson continued.

"They mean to banish those who manifest the evil of their tenets, and the dangers of Quaker practices tending to the subversion of religion, of church order, and of civil government. Of course, that's a reference to Rhode Island's tolerant, liberal government. Here, they say that the necessity of this government is put upon, for the preservation of religion and their own peace and safety, to exclude such persons. Reverend Norton, as one of the most vocal on this matter, has been commissioned to write a book about it. His comment was that even after arrest, conviction, and whippings, they remain 'obstinate and pertinacious.' Endecott tells prisoners to take heed not to break the Bay's laws, or they'd have their necks stretched by a halter."

"The Court's problem," said Will, "is that though they consider themselves magistrates and judges who dispense life and death, they don't understand proper legal procedures. They arrest and charge, hold prisoners for months in that privy shaft they call a prison, then find that the charges don't hold up because they had no law in the first place, to cover that imagined offense. You just can't throw someone down the hole and make a new law for when they're hauled to the bench. They are guilty of being unjust judges."

Edward answered with a pained look, "You've noticed that too, have you?"

"Not only I, but the prisoners, as well. Endecott, Rawson, Atherton, and Bellingham have done the same thing for years!"

By this time, the young people, who had been silent at table as expected, waited to be excused. Edward sent Samuel and Elisha to ready their bed in the storage room and carry in a wool-stuffed mattress for William, and the girls cleared up the food and cooking pots, and prepared for morning.

"Father," asked Elizabeth, "may I prepare a basket of food for the Jacklins? They have the measles, as do so many families, and they're quite overwhelmed."

"You may prepare it, but Samuel or Elisha will carry it over in the dark. Tell them I said so."

He turned to William. "The measles are a plague this year. So many people have sickened and died from the fever that the

Court has called for a day of humiliation and fasting to entreat the Lord's favorable presence to be continued to his poor people and churches. This is yet another opportunity to blame the Quakers for the Lord's displeasure. The Court specifically named "the arrogance and boldness of open opposers of the truth and ways of the Lord," as well as unseasonable rains and the mortality of the measles. Once, it was the devil and his witches that were blamed for every evil thing. Now it's the Quakers."

November 5, 1658
Newport, Rhode Island

William Dyer and Nicholas Easton, his neighbor and colleague in the Assembly, rode home from Portsmouth along the island road he'd helped to survey twenty years before. Easton was about sixteen years older than Dyer, but their paths had been parallel since the days in Boston when they were disarmed for following Reverend Wheelwright.

Multi-colored trees lined the road, but farms lay on both sides and he passed fields of cattle, horses, grain, tobacco, and orchards. The air was salty and chilled, coming off the Narragansett Bay to their right. The grasses and reeds of the marsh stood erect in some places, but in others, they'd been harvested for roof thatching.

Most of the water fowl had migrated already, but some fat geese with white breasts and grey-brown and black top feathers still paddled on the ponds.

Easton broke the quiet. "I wonder why some of that breed flew away in V formations for the winter, and some stayed to brave the storms and ice."

Dyer chuckled. "Perhaps some of them came from Newfoundland or farther north, and Rhode Island seemed like a Barbados to them."

"They leave such a mess. The only things those geese are good for is dinner, grease, and pillow stuffings."

The lowering sun broke through the low-hanging clouds, and made the bay's wave peaks glint like bright golden coins, with the troughs nearly black.

They'd been to the meeting of the legislature today, which had discussed the actions of its neighboring colonies toward the Quakers. The United Colonies had urged Rhode Island several times to adopt a punitive policy against the Quakers that would be consistent with Massachusetts Bay, Plymouth, New Haven, and Connecticut, and to discontinue Rhode Island's toleration of those heretics. Governor Endecott, in Boston, had spearheaded a law only two weeks ago that banished Quakers—dangerous heretics, he said. They certainly seemed harmless enough in Rhode Island, Dyer thought. His wife was a Quaker, as was Nicholas Easton and William Coddington, for that matter. Many of the bruised and broken Quakers had stayed in his home while they recuperated.

After a few minutes of companionable silence, Easton spoke up again. "The United Colonies subtly suggested that to grant sanctuary and allow us Friends to move about freely would result in restrictions on passage through the colonies, and disruption of trade with Rhode Island."

Will asked, "You thought that was subtle? It stood out like a pustule does on a sailor with the French pox! They said that if Rhode Island did not comply, that it would be their duty to take strong economic measures against the Quakers and Rhode Island."

Will had been among the dozen men who resented how the colonies continued to oppose the concept of separation of powers. Some of the men of Warwick and Providence, though, persisted in thinking of putting their loyalties with Connecticut.

"Civil and ecclesiastical matters must continue separately," Dyer had said in the Assembly, on a rising voice. "Our authority and rights are derived from England's rulers, not from our immediate neighbors, who love us not. Do we not remember clearly how, twenty years ago, the Bay drove us away over matters of conscience, and repeatedly attempted to annex us and remove our liberties and put us back into bondage?"

"Hear, hear!" cried the Assembly members.

The Rhode Island General Assembly answered the letter, claiming that separation of religious and civil powers was even more important to them than getting rid of those "pernicious" Quakers, as Endecott and the congress had called the Friends.

The Assembly wrote to the United Colonies, Governor Endecott in particular, that their charter protected their sovereignty in civil and criminal matters: "…may it please you to have an eye and ear open, in case our adversaries should seek to undermine us in our privileges granted unto us, and to plead our case in such sort as we may not be compelled to exercise any civil power over men's consciences, so long as human orders, in point of civility, are not corrupted and violated, which our neighbors about us do frequently practice, whereof many of us have large experience, and do judge it to be no less than a point of absolute cruelty."

While William and his committee wrote the Endecott letter, Easton's working committee drafted a letter to Dr. John Clarke, their agent in England, as insurance against the United Colonies. They asked Clarke to use all his influence on their behalf to make sure that they'd not be compelled to persecute the Quakers.

"We have found," they wrote, "not only your ability and diligence, but also your love and care to be such concerning the welfare and prosperity of this colony, since you have been entrusted with the more public affairs thereof, surpassing the no small benefit which we had of your presence here at home. We are emboldened to repair to you for further and continued care, counsel and help; finding that your solid and Christian demeanor hath gotten no small interest in the hearts of our superiors, those noble and worthy senators, with whom you had to do in our behalf, as it hath constantly appeared in our addresses to them, we have by good and comfortable proof found, having had plentiful proof thereof."

After they discussed the letters, Easton asked if Will had considered attending a Friends Meeting, since he had been supportive of his own wife Mary and the various ministers who passed through their doors over the last year and more.

"No," he replied testily. "I'll have none of it for myself. Not only do I not share your beliefs, but I must remain neutral for my wife's sake, if she requires legal aid—which I am sure she will, as obstinate as all you Quakers are about defying authority. Further, you need an advocate in court matters and appeals. I can best do that for the colony's sake, and you Quakers' sake, without professing my faith and taking the martyrs' road for myself."

"That seems reasonable, Will; nevertheless, I will pray for the Light of God to enter your heart, that you find the joy and the assurance of salvation that we share."

That's nice, thought Will somewhat sourly, but he said nothing for the last mile of their ride. He nodded at the trading ships anchored in the bay. "That'll be Tristram Hull with a cargo of sugar and salt from Barbados. I wonder what else he stashed in the hold that he's willing to part with at Newport instead of Boston? I have a string of horses to send down to the Caribe—what about you?"

They chatted amiably until Easton and Dyer parted ways at the edge of William's property.

June 10, 1659
Providence Plantations

Friends William Robinson and Marmaduke Stephenson had already gone over the side of the sloop to sit in the dugout canoe that would take them from the cove on the Seekonk River, to the shore of Providence, and they assisted Mary as she stepped gingerly on the netted rope ladder. She bunched her skirts in one hand and held the net in the other—with a death grip. In their breeches, men could scramble as much as they liked or needed, but a woman had to protect her modesty even as she was hampered by layers of petticoats and overskirt that could billow in the wind or get caught on splinters or tangled in rope. Mary was helped to sit down quickly and smoothly so as not to rock it over. As her heartbeat returned to normal tempo, she looked around the Indian canoe which had clearly seen better days. There was a bilge sloshing around the bottom, and the hull had cracks in it, as if it had sat out in the weather instead of being covered from sun or rain. To get in as close to the shore as possible, the sloop had come in on high tide, but there was still the distance of a few rods to traverse, to step out on the shore in front of Roger Williams' house.

Next, it was Sarah Gibbons' turn to transfer, and Nicholas Davis would follow last. Sarah had been a passenger on the *Woodhouse*, and she and Dorothy Waugh had preached—and been beaten and imprisoned for it—all over Massachusetts, and had recently been to Barbados and back to minister there. She'd been staying in Newport with the Dyers while Robinson and Stephenson had stayed with other Friends in the town.

It had been a quiet winter, but a tumultuous spring for the Quaker missionaries. Their elderly brother, William Brend, had over a short time sustained nearly two hundred blows from the hand of the Massachusetts Bay tyrants. It was miraculous that he still clung to life. Endecott's court, on May 6, had kept him in prison for ten days after declaring that Brend must depart their jurisdiction or face death. Brend had returned to England.

In nearby Salem, the young Southwicks, Daniel and Provided, tried to keep their elderly parents' farm going while the parents, who had been severely tortured by Boston Puritans, were forced to flee to Shelter Island. But the court had fined the estate so that there was nothing left to sell to survive. And then the most cruel blow of all: Daniel and Provided were offered for sale as slaves, to any Englishman of Virginia or Barbados who would buy them to relieve their liens for non-payment of fines to the court. Daniel would have been worked to death in a sugar or tobacco field, and Provided would have been used as a prostitute until she died. But no ship captain, even African slave traffickers, would buy the Southwicks over a misdemeanor of religious preference, and seeing the outrage in citizens' faces, the court backed down and let them go.

When William Dyer had heard of this, he'd seethed with anger. "Those dull-wits break their own statute in the Body of Liberties from 1641, prohibiting the enslavement of whites unless they be lawful captives taken in just wars, or strangers who willingly sell themselves."

"There is no more intelligence in them than there is milk in a steer! Richard Bellingham is a university-trained lawyer and magistrate who has been in Boston from the beginning—you'd think he'd have the sense and the political weight to curb Endecott. They're a bloodthirsty gang of thieves."

The Friends staying or recovering in Newport prayed and fasted, and sought God's voice. On June 8, after a First Day meeting, Robinson and Stephenson had both had words from the Lord that he wanted them to give up their lives in Boston. Sarah Gibbons and Mary and several others had experienced a powerful moving of the Lord that day, and now, here at Providence, the small company of Friends was less than fifty miles from their destiny. They were to bear witness against the murderous spirit of the Massachusetts authorities. Nicholas Davis was coming along because he had business dealings in Boston.

Sarah gathered her skirts to one side, and grabbed the net ladder on the side. She was young and fit from her foot travels in England and Massachusetts, and an old hand at boarding and leaving ships, and it was only a few feet down to the boat. But then her shoe slipped off the slick rope, and she fell heavily onto one side the canoe, knocking her senseless. The dugout keeled over with the change in balance, spilling its occupants into the cold, deep water.

Mary had no time to take a breath before she pitched into the water. Her skirts billowed around her head as the air was trapped in them, but then they dragged her down as she struggled to kick and claw through the water toward the light at the surface. As soon as she broke the surface, choking and gagging, she was grabbed by the neck and hauled to the shore.

"Ye'll be right, miss." The sailor who had helped her plunged back in to help the others. Robinson and Stephenson staggered out of the water for a few moments, but Sarah was missing, and they tried desperately to feel the mud for her body. All the tramping and splashing only clouded the water further.

By this time, Richard Scott, who had waited for the party on shore, had thrown himself in to the rescue, and others joined in the search.

Finally, though no one spoke the dread words, they gave up, and dragged themselves out of the water one by one. Providence women had brought blankets almost at once, but still, the Friends and their helpers shivered. Mary tried to stand, but her legs felt like an unsteamed pudding.

"You just sit there," Katherine commanded. "You're half-drowned and shocked. We'll get a cart for you and the others."

The Scott house was only a short distance away, backing up to Roger Williams' lots, but a horse cart came to their rescue, and Richard lifted Mary up for the ride. The other Friends clambered up, and the Welsh draft horse plodded slowly around the corner to where Mary and Patience Scott were anxiously awaiting their arrival.

Richard carried Mary into the house and up the stairs, and at Katherine's direction, deposited her on the girls' bed and left. Katherine pulled the curtain, and went to work unfastening the sodden, heavy layers from the trembling Mary, washing her with warm water and a precious scented soap, and combing out her bedraggled hair. The patient, slow, gentle ministrations were calculated to soothe, but still Mary shook with grief, shock, and her own near-drowning. She heard Mary Scott ask her mother if a broth or stew would be needed, but Katherine shook her head.

Katherine pushed Mary gently back onto the down pillows, and lifted her feet onto the bed. She said softly, "You have a fever, dear, but I'll care for you, and you're hardy: you'll be well soon. Would you like me to send for William?"

Mary tried to speak, but couldn't form the words. The look of alarm was enough for her friend, though. Katherine spoke again. "All right, Sweetheart, I won't send for him, but he'll have to know about the accident and that you survived. Richard will write a message saying all is in hand. Now you relax, and I'll read scriptures to you while you go to sleep."

She paused, and her voice broke. "The men will look for Sarah's body at low tide, and will bury her in our orchard. She's our Sister, and she was faithful to the end. Herein we are comforted—that she is now in the presence of God. She has only joy."

*****

When Mary's fever broke two days later, she learned that Sarah had been found and buried, with words and prayer by William Robinson. He and Marmaduke Stephenson and Patience Scott, the precocious eleven-year-old who preached in meetings, along with Nicholas Davis, had left for Boston, taking the most direct road through forests, fields, and villages to the northeast.

"Why couldn't they wait for me?" Mary said in an irritated voice, as she spooned into her chicken stew in the Scotts' guest bed.

"Why can't you eat faster?" asked Katherine. "I counted twenty-eight times you chewed a very tender carrot. How will you heal and strengthen if you won't take my cures? You can't breathe and swallow tidewater and then skip away on a three-day walk to Boston."

"I could have taken a horse, though," said Mary, still annoyed. "I've endured much worse."

"Mary, Mary, stop and think! Perhaps the Lord wills that you are delayed in the journey. 'Be still, and wait on the Lord,' says the Word. Unless I hear a word to the contrary from the Lord, you are staying here to recover for a sennight. If you're well enough by then, you can use one of our horses to go to Boston."

"Four nights, and I'll save you the horse, and walk myself," said Mary, in her market bargaining voice.

"Seven nights, or your husband will hear about you nullifying his bond by appearing in Massachusetts, and will personally drag you back to Newport."

"I will not be threatened by the likes of you, Katherine Scott." But Mary smiled, took a small bite of stew, and swallowed it immediately. Except for feeling physically weak and heartsick at Sarah's loss, this being pampered and forced to rest for a week wasn't a terrible fate.

Mary had finished her stew and set the plate on the bedside table. She settled back onto the pillows, more exhausted than she cared to show.

"If the weather's fine tomorrow and you're strong enough, you can rest in the orchard and gather your thoughts on Sarah," Katherine offered.

She helped Mary change her night shift as she talked. "Richard heard some news this morning that gives a sense of the frustration that Endecott and Bellingham and the rest must be feeling. The false shepherds of the sheep, Norton and Wilson, have commanded a day of fasting, humiliation, and prayer for the fifteenth of June, in all the churches of Massachusetts. They mention the fears, commotions and troubles in England and in Parliament, and in New England, the divisions in many of the churches—especially at Dr. Samuel Stone's church in Hartford where the members are divided according to Congregational or Presbyterian doctrine—the hand of God against us in the unseasonable rain of this spring, and one thing that may refer either to the younger generation, or to the growing influence of our Friends! They said 'the face of things in regard to the rising generation.' Does that not sound like they're worried about us, the Quakers, as they spitefully name us?"

"It could mean the obvious," Katherine said, "which is concern for the youth who question authority instead of accepting it. But I suspect Massachusetts' day of fasting and soul-searching for every unconfessed sin has something to do with us. They won't admit it, even to themselves, but they fear their own people now. They nearly killed poor William Brend, and the Boston people are sick and sorry about it—perhaps even angry. Last fall Endecott and his ministers cut off Christopher's ear in private, which is against their laws, because they didn't want their people to object. When the Court tried to sell the Southwick children at Salem, though the people were afraid to make themselves known lest they also become victims, there was a growing sense that the Court is flailing and desperate to hold on to their power. But God has sparked pinpoints of his Light in the Bay souls. Now is the time to fan it into a blaze!"

Mary felt a blaze flaring up in her own heart, but Katherine soothed her friend by stroking her hand and interrupting. "And that is what Brothers Stephenson and Robinson will do. They'll fan the flames, and bring out a burning brand that will sear the consciences of those ready to hear and accept the Gospel.

"Richard says that the other major concern in Boston is that Parliament has called for Richard Cromwell to resign as Protector and for Charles the Second to come back to the throne. With news traveling as slowly as a ship in heavy seas, it may have happened already. Boston is worried again about its authority and that Parliament or a new king will revoke their charter and send a governor to depose them. The Puritan regime in England is coming to an end sooner or later, and they must fear the upwelling of the persecuted, the countless people they've thrown in prison, the starving widows and orphans whose men were lost in the wars. They must be very distracted, indeed, to pass a law in May General Court, that their people may not celebrate Christmas and other festivals, on pain of five pounds' fine. Christmas is mostly forgotten in this land, anyway."

Mary nodded. "Yes, the poison fruit ripens for harvest on both sides of the sea. Katherine, the Lord is moving me toward Boston, step by step. I feel drawn there, as a flower turns to the sun. It may be to testify about the Light, or to minister to the brothers and sisters in prison, or for some other purpose. But I must go."

*****

To THE KEEPER OF THE PRISON,

You are by virtue hereof, required to take into your custody the persons of Nicholas Davis, William Robinson, Marmaduke Stephenson, and Patience Scott, Quakers; according to the law made in October, 1658: to be sure to keep them close prisoners till the next Court of Assistants, whereby they are to be tried according to law; not allowing any to come at them, or converse with them, without special order from this court; and allow them only prisoner's food, unless it is in times of sickness.

Boston, June 19th, 1659.

Edward Rawson, Secretary

*****

WILLIAM DYER AT NEWPORT IN RHODE ISLAND THIS 19th OF AUGUST 59.

My dear husband,

Again I write to you from the House of Correction at Boston, not for my own sake, for I choose to stay here and continue the cause of Christ as he commands, but for the sake of the Friends who suffer here with me. If you would send certain items to relieve our burdens, such as a copy of scripture, blankets, and the money to buy our food until the General Court meets again, we would be greatly encouraged.

I know that my actions have wounded you, and I grieve for that, but I consider my own life as rubbish, compared to the Day of the Lord and the glory of heaven that is drawing nearer daily, so that I can see its faint glow on the horizon. Let that comfort you if we are parted for a time, until you join me in the Kingdom.

What shall I say unto you, my dear love, of the love of my Father? His love draws me to him as a seedling is drawn to the summer sunlight, and as a daisy flower follows the sun through the day. My Friends and I will be a tree that will bear much fruit in the harvest. In the plucking and devouring, the fruit will give birth to more seed. In that knowledge, none can impart fear to my soul. When you pray for me, in captivity or in death of the body, you are near to me, for God is Love and the source of our love. Never doubt that I have loved you and our children—it has been made so much more because of the intercession of the Savior.

Do not come to rescue me, William. Do not think that in my temporal discomfort I am unsafe or that I've lost my reason. It was my intent to visit the brethren in prison, as Christ asks of me, and return to you and our children. But my life belongs to another now. I see and feel in my own body the great need of the comfort of the Spirit. The sacrifice of my liberty or my life could change the hearts of the court or of the people and stop the wicked tortures of God's people. If the decision were of my flesh, I would teach the Word and assist in childbirths, haymaking, and sailing on fine sunny days, and supporting you in your endeavors. But long ago, God showed me what my end would be. At first I was frightened, but now I see that my end will eventually bring about liberty of conscience not only for Friends, but for countless others over many generations. I must take this position because it is right, and necessary. I do not fear death, for my absence from the body is presence with the Lord.

Farewell, William. You have my love forever, and we shall be reunited.
MARY DYER

*****

August 27, 1659
Newport, Rhode Island

William read the two letters from his recalcitrant wife, and fought the nausea that nearly overwhelmed him. The letters had arrived together. The other, written two days earlier, described the condition of Mary's prison mates, those she'd gone to visit, and those who had been arrested with her, and he knew that it included Mary's own condition. These two months she'd been gone from home, he'd thought her safe with the Quaker friends. But it seemed that the moment she consorted with that lot, their first action was to defy authority.

How could a forty-eight year-old woman think more of her cause than her own six children and husband, and deliberately and willingly defy those bastards in Boston? They showed all the vicious traits of the Catholic bishop of London, Edmund Bonner, during the reign of Queen Mary, a hundred years ago. Yes, there was an obvious parallel between John Endecott and Bishop Bonner. They both were obsessed with crushing religious dissent: Bonner sending Protestants to the fiery stake after extensive torture, and Endecott beating men and women to pulp and slicing off ears, and abusing them in a prison which enriched the government by enslaving the prisoners and charging exorbitant rates for food. He'd even attempted to sell two children from his own town of Salem, as slaves to the planters in the Caribbean. There was no doubt what kind of slave the girl would have been if the sea captain hadn't refused to buy and sell the brother and sister.

Hardly any citizen had ready access to coins, even the tree shillings minted by Endecott's man, John Hull. They had to resort to the Spanish silver cabos, or cobs, to pay for the fines, food, and lodging of their family members in prison. When they paid the fees, they resentfully spoke of throwing their money into the Cobhole, the bottomless coffers of the prison business.

Endecott was a greedy man, and he was the worst kind of religious zealot. He would not hesitate to carry out executions. Anyone could see the escalation of violence in the last year. Endecott's pastor in Salem, Reverend Frances Higginson, had called the Quakers' Inner Light "a stinking vapor from hell," so the judges were arrayed in a solid battle line of intolerance and punitive vengeance.

Will knew that the banishment orders, if defied, resulted in the death sentence. Death by hanging. Hanging wasn't always a quick death as it should have been. If the body was not sufficiently heavy, the condemned could strangle slowly and agonizingly, or until some merciful friend or relative pulled on the victim's legs to hurry the end.

He set out his silver tray with pen, ink, and sand, and took several large sheets of linen paper. He wrote to John Winthrop the Younger, in Connecticut, wished health upon Winthrop's wife and daughters who were ill, and explained Mary's situation.

Then he wrote to the English governor of Acadia, Sir Thomas Temple, and asked for his influence to be expressed in Boston's court. Sir Thomas was a prosperous land developer with large interests in Boston. William knew he'd have no success with the governors of Plymouth, Thomas Prence, or New Haven Colony, John Davenport. They were certainly in Endecott's party, and Davenport had already banished Mary from New Haven even before she'd had a chance to protest their policies.

Finally, he reached for another large sheet and began writing in his fine, artistic hand to Boston's court, John Endecott, presiding governor.

As an attorney, William recognized that the Massachusetts court had no evidence of a crime, for Mary had not transgressed their laws by speaking in church services or dissidence to the authorities. She'd simply gone to support friends in prison, as the Lord had commanded in the Gospel of Matthew. There was that banishment order for which he'd paid a bond, but of course he chose not to enter that in his defense of Mary. He decided to appeal to their professional ethics and Christian spirits (if they hadn't sold them to the devil already).

> Gentlemen:
>
> Having received some letters from my wife, I am given to understand of her commitment to close prison to a place (according to description) not unlike Bishop Bonner's rooms.
>
> It is a sad condition, in executing such cruelties towards their fellow creatures and sufferers. Had you no commiseration of a tender soul that being wet to the skin, you cause her to be thrust into a room whereon was nothing to sit or lie down upon but dust? Had your dog been wet you would have offered it the liberty of a chimney corner to dry itself, or had your hogs been penned in a sty, you would have offered them some dry straw, or else you would have wanted mercy to your beast, but alas, Christians now with you are used worse than hogs or dogs. Oh, merciless cruelties.
>
> You have done more in persecution in one year than the worst bishops did in seven, and now to add more towards a tender woman that gave you no just cause against her. For did she come to your meeting to disturb them, as you call it, or did she come to reprehend the magistrates? She only came to visit her friends in prison and when dispatching that, her intent of returning to her family, as she declared in her statement the next day to the Governor. Therefore it is *you* that disturbed *her*, else why was she not let alone? What house entered she to molest, or what did she, that like a malefactor she must be hauled to prison, or what law did she transgress? She was about a business justifiable before God and all good men.

The worst of men, the bishops themselves, denied not the visitation and release of friends to their prisoners, which myself hath often experienced by visiting Mr. Prynne, Mr. Smart, and other eminent men, yea, when he was commanded close in the town of Boston, I had resort once or twice a week and I was never fetched before authority to ask me wherefore I came to the town, or King's bench, or Gatehouse. Had there not been more adventurous, tender-hearted professors than yourselves, many of them you call godly ministers and others might have perished if that course you take had been in use with them, as to send for a person and ask them wherefore they came thither. What, hath not people in America the same liberty as beasts and birds to pass the land or air without examination?

Have you a law that says the light in M. Dyer is not M. Dyer's rule, if you have for that or any of the forenamed a law, she may be made a transgressor, for words and your mittimus hold good; but if not, then have you imprisoned her and punished her without law and against the law of God and man.

Behold, my wife without law and against law is imprisoned and punished and so highly condemned for saying the light is the rule! It is not your light within your rule by which you make and act such laws, for ye have no rule of God's word in the Bible to make a law titled "Quakers," nor have you any order from the Supreme State of England to make such laws. Therefore, it must be *your* light within *you* is your rule and you walk by. Remember what Jesus Christ said, "If the light that be in you is darkness, how great is that darkness."

When called before you for her act of conscience, the first and next words after appearance are "You are a Quaker," see the steps you follow and let their misery be your warning; and then if answer be not made according to the ruling will; away with them to the Cobhole or new Prison, or House of Correction. And now, Gentlemen, consider their ends, and believe it, it was certain the Bishops' ruin suddenly followed after their hot pursuance of some godly people by them called Puritans, especially when, twenty years ago, Bishop Laud proceeded to suck the blood of Mr. Prynne, Mr. Burton, and Dr. Bastwick's ears, only them three and but three, and they were as odious to them as the Quakers are to you.

What witness or legal testimony was taken that my wife Mary Dyer was a Quaker? If not before God and man, how can you clear yourselves and seat of justice, from cruel persecution, yet as so far as in you lies murder, (as to her and to myself and family), oppression and tyranny. The God of trust knows all this. The God of truth knows all this.

This is the sum and totals of a law titled "Quakers": that she is guilty of a breach of a law titled "Quakers" is as strange, that she is lawfully convicted of two witnesses is not heard of, that she must be banished by law titled "Quakers" being not convicted by law, but considered by surmise and condemned to close prison by Mr. Bellingham's suggestion is so absurd and ridiculous, the meanest pupil in law will hiss at such proceedings in Old Lawyers! Is your law titled "Quakers Felony or Treason," that vehement suspicion render them capable of suffering?

If you be men, I suppose your fundamental law is that no person shall be imprisoned or molested but upon the breach of a law, yet behold my wife, without law and against law, is imprisoned and punished.

My wife writes me word and information, that she had been above a fortnight and had not trod on the ground, but saw it out your window. What inhumanity is this? Had you never wives of your own, or ever any tender affection to a woman, to deal so with a woman? What has nature forgotten, if refreshment be debarred?

I have written thus plainly to you, being exceedingly sensible of the unjust molestations and detaining of my dear yokefellow, mine and my family's want of her will cry loud in your ears together with her sufferings of your part.

But I question not mercy, favor, and comfort from the Most High of her own soul, that at present myself and family be by you deprived of the comfort and refreshment we might have enjoyed by her presence.

Her husband
W. Dyer
Newport this 30 August 1659

William signed the elegantly-penned letter and folded it into another sheet to make an envelope, then applied his wax seal. On the envelope he wrote with a flourish, "To the court of assistants now assembled at Boston this 6th Septemb ano 1659." That was the date of their next court session.

He called his sons Samuel and William to explain their orders to deliver the letters by sailing to Hartford and Penobscot, and when that was accomplished, to make haste to meet in Boston at Ed Hutchinson's house. The Boston letter, a shorter note to Mary, and money would go with him, personally.

Will's nausea had abated as he wrote the letters and planned his strategy. It was replaced now by a cold rage against Endecott and Bellingham and Wilson, and a profound depression surrounding his thoughts of his wife. He had lost her, but he'd vowed his fidelity and tender care for her, for life. Mary's choice was to end her life. And then what? What did Mary care for *his* life after she was gone?

September 13, 1659
Newport, Rhode Island

She stepped from the bath in her own kitchen, her skin and raggedy-cropped hair scrubbed free of the crusted filth of prison. With a twinge of guilt at the self-indulgence, she dipped her fingers into a jar of rose-scented ointment and rubbed the balm into her roughened skin before dressing in a gloriously-clean chemise, skirts, bodice, and jacket. No amount of laundering or stitching would repair the clothes she'd worn for more than two months in Boston's prison, and even the clothes Will had brought to Boston had suffered for their use on the journey home.

Against her wishes to stand her ground against the Boston tyrants, Will had ridden to Boston and presented his written defense of her at the September 6 court session. The court first considered the case of Patience Scott, the eleven-year-old daughter of Katherine and Richard. Patience had gone with three Friends,

Marmaduke Stephenson, William Robinson, and Nicholas Davis, on the errand to try Boston's law and lay down their lives if necessary, in late June. Patience, under a moving of the Lord, had given testimony against the inhuman persecution of the Friends, and had been taken to house arrest at the jailer's home. This was her second incarceration in Boston, having accompanied her mother and older sister Mary last year.

Though only a child, Patience had a supernatural spiritual gift of prophesying the Word, and had amazed the Boston inquisitors with her deep insights in the Bible. The court could not bring a heavy penalty on a young girl, so they declared that she was too young to understand their anti-Quaker laws, and that she was inhabited by an unclean spirit (like her aunt Anne Hutchinson), and had released her to her cousin and legal advocate, Ed Hutchinson, with an admonishment to stay away from Massachusetts.

In turn, the court considered the cases of William Robinson, Marmaduke Stephenson, Nicholas Davis, and Mary Dyer. They were kept closed up in the prison and not allowed to defend themselves at court, but later, Will had told Mary a bit of what was said by the fanatical Puritans: "The prudence of this court was exercised only in making provision to secure the peace and order here established against their attempts, whose design was to undermine and ruin the same."

Securing peace and order by violent beatings, driving old people from their homes and farms, imprisoning young parents and leaving little children to the wolves if not for tender-hearted neighbors, Mary thought. She was surprised at the reasoning that the Massachusetts authorities used to justify their actions, yes, but more astounded that they actually believed their own hypocrisy, their own lies.

William's written defense of Mary, particularly his point that the Quakers had not transgressed a law because there was no law, had been the key that turned the lock on the prison door. The Friends were released on the 12th, but banished "on pain of death" if they returned. However, William Robinson, perceived as a Quaker teacher, was singled out for a public whipping before his release. He was taken into the street and stripped of his clothes, his hands locked in the holes of a cannon carriage. Jailer Salter held him captive while the executioner gave him twenty stripes with a three-part corded whip.

It was a small victory for themselves, they knew, but Boston's persecution would continue for two reasons: because the Friends would not back down, and the General Court would get about the business of writing that missing law.

Among the ministers who sat in on court proceedings was John Wilson. He had baptized Samuel when the Dyers were new to Boston. If anyone had a heart for ministry to former parishioners, it should be Wilson, but he was among the most harsh and vindictive.

Mary remembered every word Wilson had spoken when he'd excommunicated Anne Hutchinson in 1638: "Therefore in the name of the Lord Jesus Christ and in the name of the church I do not only pronounce you worthy to be cast out, but I do cast you out; and in the name of Christ do I deliver you up to Satan, that you may learn no more to blaspheme, to seduce and to lie; and I do account you from this time forth to be a Heathen and a Publican, and so to be held of all the brethren and sisters of this congregation and of others; therefore I command you in the name of Christ Jesus and of this church as a leper to withdraw yourself out of the congregation."

Mary had taken Anne's arm in sympathy and support as they walked out of the church trial. Now, she was in Anne's place, but instead of one woman taking her arm, Mary had a host of men and women who embraced the Light and lifted her up not only in physical needs for food and shelter, but in prayer and solidarity with the cause of Christ.

Sometimes the awe of worshiping together with like-minded brothers and sisters was too wonderful for Mary, and she shed tears for the glimpse of heaven that it was.

Nicholas Davis was banished to his home in Sandwich. Robinson preached to his accusers and was silenced by a handkerchief stuffed in his mouth and then whipped with twenty lashes. Stephenson also chose to stay, though imprisoned, because they were obeying the Lord's command to lay down their lives in Boston.

So William and Mary Dyer had ridden home with their son William, Boston to Providence to Newport, and here she was again, safe. Safe, while her Friends were still in peril from the gathering storm in Boston. She felt encumbered with the role that she had once loved, wife to a prosperous gentleman and mother of six growing children, though the three oldest were young men now.

The sixty-mile journey home from Boston had been no pleasure jaunt for any of them: Mary, Patience Scott, and William Dyer. Few words were spoken, but from her husband's manner, Mary knew that he grieved the death of their years of intimacy, which she had renounced, or in his eyes betrayed, to follow the Voice.

Now clean, refreshed, and well-dressed after her bathing, Mary pulled on her boots and sat the coif on her badly-cropped hair. Taking her Bible with her, she set out slowly for Nicholas Easton's home. It would be a few days before she regained some strength after so long a restriction of motion in prison. Along the wide dirt road that Will and his colleagues had surveyed and laid out twenty years ago, she met her friend Herod walking toward the same destination: a Friends Meeting. They linked arms as comrades, and walked in comfortable silence, the Meeting already begun between them.

*****

TO WILLIAM DYER AT NEWPORT IN RHODE ISLAND
17th of September, 1659
My dear friend,

I write only a few lines to acquaint you with the information that the Lord Protector, Oliver Cromwell, was taken by a malarial fever, and passed into the presence of God on the third of September. On the same day, his son Richard was proclaimed His Highness, by the Grace of God and Republic, Lord Protector of England, Scotland and Ireland. I'm considering standing for Parliament in Hampshire. I pray that your family is well, and that your greatly esteemed wife is recovered from her ordeal last year. My lady Frances sends her deep affection.
SIR HENRY VANE
Whitchurch, Hampshire

September 19, 1659
Newport, Rhode Island

William awoke on his christening day, a half-century old. He felt those fifty years in his body, not because of the aches and pains of a life of heavy work or abuse of his diet or too much strong drink, but because of the state of his family. The younger children seemed to be well in hand, taking lessons in a predictable routine of seasons, times, and society. A week ago, Samuel and Maher had stood before the Portsmouth Court of Trials to face charges of refusing to serve in the militia, which was determined to be a breach of the peace. When they pleaded guilty and assured the court that they would comply thereafter, they were freed without further prejudice.

But it was his wife he worried about.

Mary was still fragile from her summer imprisonment, and her stomach gave her pains, so she ate very little, even in this time of harvest and abundance. Unlike other goodwives, she showed no interest in ruling her womanly domain, leaving all domestic pursuits to Cathy and other servants. What a change from the woman who had so ably stewarded their farm and home for years.

If she assisted with a birthing, she took Marie with her, as other women did with their daughters or little children. She used those many hours of waiting for the birth to befriend the other women and teach them to understand the scriptures—with a bend toward Quakers, naturally.

As for sex with his wife, there had been none of that for many months, between Mary's traveling, prison time, and recuperation. She wanted to be held and to have her hair stroked, but then she turned away as if to distance herself from further attentions. In that way, she seemed as fearful as a poor child who had been beaten regularly. On the other hand, Mary had never been so strong-willed and opinionated—as adult and assured as any woman of education and experience could be.

Will's love for her was sometimes like a spring torrent, and sometimes, when he held her and felt her fragility, it was a calm, deep lake.

On this fiftieth anniversary of his birth, he was more than a little disturbed. Last night, as they talked in bed, Mary had told him about one of her long-ago revelations, which she had remembered during her imprisonment.

"It was the morning after you kissed me for the first time," she had said. "I'd hardly slept, wondering what it meant. I stood at my window as the dawn broke, and the light glinted off the London rooftops. I saw you, Will, in middle age, with a band of children—who I now recognize as our children. They stretched out their arms to me, with tears and confusion and fear. It tore my heart then, though I didn't know who they were, and I was about the age of the oldest boy. I wanted to comfort them in my arms, and heal their sorrow, though I didn't know them."

Mary's voice choked with tears. "But I hardened my heart to their cries. I turned my back and walked away into the forest. God forgive me."

William had been horrified. Who had taken away his wife's love?

She whispered again. "But Will, God has shown me that this moving, this hard destiny he's given me, will be a blessing for countless people, through the ages. It will benefit our children, and bring them freedom from tyranny. Our descendants will be governors and statesmen, and godly men and women."

William was silent and Mary took it for assent. But then he spoke, in low tones that did not pass the bed curtains, but carried ferocity and possessiveness. "If I thought it would change matters, I would bind you to me as a prisoner. I could beggar you, and lock you in a cage to keep you from turning away from your husband, from the children you bore to me. What is it that I should do to keep you here? What do you want me to say? I'll say it. I'll do it. Only don't leave me alone and go running off to a martyr's death—and at the hands of that Boston Pontius Pilate. God can use someone else. He can't have you."

Hot tears rained from his eyes and soaked his pillow. He felt, rather than heard, Mary part the bed curtains, take a blanket from the foot of the bed, and pad downstairs to the kitchen, where she kept her Bible.

She had hardened her heart. It was only a matter of time before she disappeared again.

Sometime during the night, she returned to the marriage bed, but she lay on the far edge, not touching him.

And that is how William's fiftieth birthday began: a sleepless night, followed by his favorite meals that tasted like sawdust.

October 4, 1659

Newport, Rhode Island

She took her writing materials to her favorite table at a south-facing window, for its light and the warm sunshine streaming in. One of Charles's half-grown cats was curled on the chair cushion with its eyes and nose buried in its fluffy tail, like a squirrel. Rather than disturbing the creature, Mary pulled another chair over and sat down. The cat stirred, looked up through eye slits, and went back to sleep, secure and content, unrepentant for its claim on the best seat in the house.

Just like a tiny child with a favorite blanket, Mary thought, and resisted caressing the cat. Besides, the poor thing needed its sleep. Drowsing by the kitchen fire this morning had been so exhausting, she thought drily. She dipped the quill's nib in the ink bottle and began to write.

My dear children,

Though your ages are spread over fifteen years, I shall write you all as if you are of one age, trusting that your father will be able to help you understand my actions and motives. I want each of you to know and remember always that no mother has ever loved her children as much as I have loved thee. I loved you—and the babies I lost—even while I carried you in my womb, and that love has grown immeasurably as I've watched you grow in stature and in wisdom. A mother's love is the most fierce and awesome power in this world, and I have given you what I was given, and more. I've taught you to walk in faith in the Lord's providence in all things. God's love for you is more than we can comprehend. Praise God for the blessing that my children have been to my life, and for the teaching he gave me, in how to trust and obey him, and to stretch out my hand to him for Light in the darkness. When I look into your eyes, I can see the Seed of Christ in thee, which is so beautiful to behold that I feel my heart should burst for joy. I kiss each of you with the love of Christ, and the love of a mother, which I pray you will hold as long as your hearts beat.

I dread what is coming not for my own sake, but for the grief and perhaps shame that you might feel on my account, because for a little while, I must forget that I ever knew you. If I cherished you more than Christ, I would fail to obey his command to forsake father and mother and all others to follow him.

O, how shall I speak of this commission in terms you will understand? The Lord has moved me to go and care for the children of Light who languish in prison, and to testify to the cruelty of their rulers and priests. I am to leave this place of beauty, harmony, and outward enjoyments, and submit to harsh conditions and even death if it be required of me. I do not fear death, for it sets us at liberty from our worldly desires and the faithless pursuit of perfection. In his resurrection call, the Lord banishes the darkness by overcoming us with his Light.

Be not troubled, for if I am asked, it will be to go home to my Father. Death is inevitable for all of us. It takes us out of that mortality which began in the womb of our mother, and now ends to bring us into that life which shall never end. The day which you may fear as my last, is my new birth into eternity.

My will for you is that you do not let the occasional pain and grief of this world harden you against the beauty of God's creation, or the joy of loving your neighbor as yourself. Walk in love. Be at peace with God and man. Do not allow the hatred of others to take root in you, or their bitterness to invade the sweet flavor of your influence. Do not be overcome by evil, but overcome evil by doing good.

I commend each of thee, Samuel, William, Maher, Henry, Marie, and Charles, to the tender care of two fathers, which is better than a mother. William will nurture you as you deserve, and your heavenly Father will shelter you under his wings and will never leave thee or forsake thee. When someday you follow me, I will be waiting with embraces and kisses. Farewell for now, my dears.

MARY DYER
4th of the 8th month, 1659

Mary sanded and cleared the page, folded it in thirds, and wrote her husband's name on the outside, then placed it in the back cover of the large family Bible.

October 5, 1659
Newport, Rhode Island

Mary took only her medical bag of herbs and remedies and dressings, minus the childbirth essentials, of course, thinking that it would be useful to have restorative and curative supplies when she visited the Friends now imprisoned in Boston with twice-weekly beatings. She wore her comfortable walking boots under medium-weight skirts, and her shirt and jacket were dark in color. Over all, she wore a water-resistant cloak, and a large hat to keep off whatever rain or snow might fall along the way.

For she would be walking to Boston from Providence Plantation. She silently let herself out of the farmhouse in the darkness, and walked a mile to the wharf, where her Sister Hope Clifton waited with a hired sloop to sail to Providence; Mary Scott would join them for the journey.

Once on board, Hope and Mary held hands and prayed for God's will to be done. By the time they reached Providence, the sun was rising above the trees in a golden and coppery splendor. Mary Scott joined them, and they set off on the wagon track toward Boston, surrounded by yellow, orange, red, and purple foliage. The leaf showers that fell on them with any gust of wind were gifts from God, their road paved in heavenly coins, and as they talked along the way, their hearts were full of joy.

Mary Scott, a seventeen year-old wise beyond her years, was engaged to Christopher Holder, who had been whipped many times, and had lost his right ear fifteen months ago for defying Endecott, Norton, and Wilson. Mary's mother Katherine had received ten lashes for protesting Christopher's harsh treatment. Now he was about to sail home to England, and Mary wanted to see him off before she and her mother would meet him the next year at the wedding.

Mary Dyer smiled to remember what Anne Hutchinson had predicted when Mary Scott was newly born: that the girl would grow to be a helper and a blessing.

They spent the nights in the farmhouses of people sympathetic to Quakers, and rested their feet for a few miles on the back of a farm wagon carrying sacks of milled wheat flour into Boston. To avoid trouble for the carter giving aid to heretics, they hopped down several miles from the Boston Neck and camped in the forest at the side of a farm near the Pequot Road. The moon, in its last quarter, sank behind the trees mid-evening, but by that time, they were asleep on the carpet of leaves they had gathered for a thin ground cover.

It was Tuesday, the eighth.

October 9, 1659

Boston, Massachusetts

Mary and her two companions arose early, of course. The autumn forest was chilly, though the women had wrapped themselves together in their mantles and a blanket from their packs, one of those intended for the imprisoned Friends. There had been sounds of wild animals, and by dawn, they were laughing at one another for the loud growls of hunger in their stomachs, having missed dinner last night.

She pulled some fresh apples and venison jerky from her pack, as well as some corn cakes wrapped in muslin, and they satisfied their appetites. It was traveling food, as learned from the Indian women who sometimes worked in their fields or gardens.

So refreshed, they prayed for the comfort of their Friends in prison, and for the Friends who traveled through wilderness to hostile towns to carry the gospel to the people living in darkness. Then they packed up and set off again on the road to Boston.

The young man who minded the fortification gate did not recognize the three women as Quakers and allowed them through along with many others who came into the town, for church attendance was required of all, and this was the Lord's Day.

Rather than risk being sighted by someone she might know, Mary took a short detour to Tremont Street to avoid the groups of people on Cornhill Road. When Tremont ended at Court Street, there was the prison on their right. When the well-dressed people of Boston had gone into their church behind a row of houses and gardens, the three women casually entered the prison enclosure and went to one of the windows on the men's side, and softly called for Christopher Holder. He was overjoyed to hear his fiancé's voice, and they promised to meet in England as soon as she could find a ship in the spring.

More Friends quietly entered the prison yard and shook hands or embraced Mary Dyer and her two companions. Mary recognized Daniel Gould from Newport, and met for the first time the Friends from Salem and Plymouth: Hannah Phelps, William King, Mary Southwick Trask and her younger sister Provided Southwick, Margaret Smith, and Alice Cowland. Alice had brought lengths of linen to shroud the dead bodies of those they knew, by revelation of the Lord, were soon to suffer.

They had brought blankets and food for those already imprisoned, and this they handed up over the high window sill to the men inside.

"It is no accident or coincidence that we meet here today," said Mary. "The Word of God has come to our hearts and drawn us together. When John Winthrop brought his fleet from England to these shores, he exhorted his people to remember that they were a City upon a Hill, with the eyes of all people upon them. With the God of Israel among them, he said, ten should be able to resist a thousand of their enemies, and the Lord would make of them a praise and glory.

"Winthrop himself said these words that we should heed, 'Therefore let us choose life, that we, and our Seed, may live; by obeying his voice, and cleaving to him, for he is our life, and our prosperity.'

"But he warned that if they dealt falsely, God would withdraw his help from among them, and they should be made a curse word throughout the world. They would shame the faces of many of God's worthy servants, and they would be consumed."

Mary stopped for a moment and looked in the eyes of each of the Friends.

"This latter prophecy we have seen with our eyes. They have laid hands upon God's worthy servants and caused us to suffer, and perhaps some of us will die. But if our lives are required of us," and here her voice rose in triumph: "we are assured that in a moment, in the twinkling of an eye, we shall be raised incorruptible, and we shall be changed. *They* will bring down judgment on their heads, and go down to everlasting darkness.

"But some of the people of Massachusetts are seeing the dawn of the light. We Friends must keep our eyes on the light, that we may be salt and light to them. When we see unjust laws and decrees, that the judges put our old people, our widows and children out of their homes, that they afflict the just and take our corn and cattle, we must speak as the Lord Jesus did, and say that the Spirit of the Lord hath anointed us to preach good tidings unto the meek, to bind up the brokenhearted, to proclaim liberty to the captives, and the opening of the prison to them that are bound, that he might be glorified.

"He has called you out of this world to bear his name, and he has put his testimony into your hearts, and the same weapons into your hands as were used by the saints of old against the powers of darkness—full faith in the Lord of angel hosts. By faith, you have power given to overcome evil with good."

That was the moment that Captain Oliver and his town patrol clattered into the yard on their horses. He signaled that the Friends should be surrounded. The patrol dismounted at his order, and formed a circle around the small group.

"Well, Mistress Dyer," he said condescendingly. "Here you are at the prison again. You've made it very convenient for me, finding your way back here on your own. Bringing your Quaker friends along is a nice touch, as there might be rewards on their heads, as well as fines and prison fees. You've done us a good deed."

He glanced at the unrepentant, unresisting, eerily-silent Quakers. "You know well that Governor Endecott craves the stretching of your necks only a little less than the Court desires your fines and your estates. Now, if you'll just go along, we'll herd you Quakers into the prison to await the pleasure of the Court, who, as good Christians, are enjoying the Sabbath as they ought to, in sober reflection."

Mary Dyer, holding the hands of Mary Scott and Hope Clifton, stepped forward and walked fearlessly into the prison.

October 18, 1659
Boston, Massachusetts

Mary heard her name called in the darkness of the prison cell she shared with other women Friends. Jailer Salter appeared with a lantern which illuminated his chin, nose, and eyebrows, but left his cheeks and eye sockets in deep shadow.

He rattled the paper and then read it out to any who would hear: "It is ordered that William Robinson, Marmaduke Stephenson and Mary Dyer, Quakers now in prison for their rebellion, sedition, presumptions obtruding themselves upon us, notwithstanding their being sentenced to banishment on pain of death as underminers of this government, etc., shall be brought before this Court for their trials, to suffer the penalty of the law (the just reward of their transgressions), on the morrow morning, being the 19th instant.'

"Furthermore," read Salter, "'It is ordered that Secretary Rawson issue out his warrant to Edward Michaelson, Marshal General, for repairing to the prison on the 27th of this instant October, and take the said William Robinson, Marmaduke Stephenson and Mary Dyer into his custody and them forthwith by the aid of Captain James Oliver, with one hundred soldiers taken out by his order proportionately out of each company in Boston, armed with pike and musketeer with powder and bullet, to lead them to the place of execution, and there see them hang till they be dead, and in their going, being there, and return, to see all things be carried out peaceably and orderly. Warrants issued out accordingly.'"

Then the jailer turned and left his prisoners in the dark.

Ah, thought Mary. They have arrested Brothers William and Marmaduke. They went to Salem to preach and specifically to provoke Governor Endecott and his deputy, Simon Bradstreet, in their benighted, desolate territory. Tomorrow we go to trial, though our conviction and sentence is already concluded.

Several of the women wept, but Mary stood up in the stinking straw and began to recite scripture: "'I reckon that the sufferings of this present time are not worthy to be compared with the glory which shall be revealed in us… As it is written, For thy sake we are killed all the day long; we are accounted as sheep for the slaughter. Nay, in all these things we are more than conquerors through him that loved us. For I am persuaded, that nothing shall be able to separate us from the love of God, which is in Christ Jesus our Lord.'

"And we have a word of encouragement from George Fox. He, like us, lies in prison for boldly speaking the gospel and acting according to the Light within him. He said, 'Stand still in that Light which shows and discovers; and then doth strength immediately come. And stand still in the Light, and submit to it, and the other will be hushed and gone; and then content comes.'"

*****

The eighteenth of October was a busy day for the General Court of Massachusetts Bay Colony. They took actions on petitions, made numerous court orders about the nearby towns and security, entered their justification for executing Quakers in the record, and set a handsome annual salary of sixty pounds for Secretary Edward Rawson. Because Mary Dyer and her Quaker friends kept coming to the prison and conversing with prisoners, they ordered that there should be a sufficient fence erected around it that would debar them from doing so, and that the cost should be borne half by the colony and half by Suffolk County.

Christopher Holder, having had his ears cut off and having been banished to England, had returned without permission of the court, so they considered it appropriate to banish him again upon pain of death. Until his ship sailed for England, he would remain in prison.

Finally, as Edward Rawson recorded in the colony records, "William Robinson, Marmaduke Stephenson and Mary Dyer, banished this jurisdiction by the last Court of assistants, on pain of death, being committed by order of the General Court, were sent for, brought to the bar, and acknowledge themselves to be the persons banished."

The marshal tied Mary's hands together, and he took her, dirty and unkempt from a week in the dark, cold cell, to the courthouse. She saw Brothers Robinson and Stephenson tied together like horses, hatless, being prodded along the muddy road by the jailer coming back from the courthouse. Mary and the Friends didn't speak aloud as they passed, but there was an unmistakable light in their countenances. Her heart beat faster for the life and energy that coursed in her veins. She was certain they felt the same way.

She and the marshal climbed the wooden steps to the porch of the courthouse, and waited for a moment to be called inside. At the end of the room was a low platform with a skirted desk, behind which sat Endecott and Bellingham. Flanking the dais were benches on both sides of the room, where sat the other members of the court: magistrates, ministers including John Norton and John Wilson, and Suffolk County men who had been elected by their communities to represent their rights and their business interests.

The marshal escorted her to stand before the judges' bench, and she stood as straight and tall as she could. She was not ashamed of her behavior or her prisoner status; nor was she fearful of the outcome of the hearing.

Mary knew this poured coals of fire on chief magistrate John Endecott. It was one thing for Robinson and Stephenson to stand before him, wearing their hats instead of removing them in respect. But her proud appearance as a daughter of Eve, whose rebellion led all humanity into sin, was a bitter gall to him.

"Do you own yourself to be Mary Dyer, the person banished from this colony on pain of death if you returned?"

"Yes, you know that I am that Mary Dyer."

"Why do you return to this jurisdiction, knowing you are under sentence of death?"

"I came in obedience to the divine call."

"Mrs. Dyer, there is nothing of the divine with you. You have listened to the devil, to the peril of this life and for eternity. We do not desire your death. Why do *you* value your life so lightly?"

Mary didn't answer.

"Take her away to the prison."

October 19, 1659
Boston, Massachusetts

This being the lecture day when criminals were publically whipped and ministers like Wilson and Norton stirred the emotions of their congregations to a fever heat, the General Court met after the service to continue their business.

Rawson wrote: "After a full hearing of what the prisoners could say for themselves, it was put to the question whether William Robinson, Marmaduke Stephenson, and Mary Dyer, the persons now in prison, who have been convicted of being Quakers and banished this jurisdiction on pain of death, should be put to death according as the law provides in that case."

What he didn't write was the underhanded way in which the sentence of death was made lawful, by only one vote. The legislature's magistracy, including Governor Endecott, Deputy Governor Bellingham, and the other assistants, had written the law and submitted it to the elected representatives from surrounding towns, but had done so when an opponent of the law was sick, and they prevailed upon others to change their votes, so that what had been a slight majority of those opposed to the death penalty for Quakers was turned to the minority. The death penalty passed into law.

Again, the three Quakers were brought to court: the men together, and Mary alone.

The governor asked, after the Bay had made laws to keep the Quakers away from them, why whipping, banishment on pain of death, imprisonment, crippling fines, and other punishments couldn't keep the Quakers away from this colony.

"In the past," said Mary, "God revealed his truth by his prophets and priests. But now, we have a better word—the Holy Spirit in our hearts. He has revealed himself to us, and called us according to his purpose."

Endecott sucked in a great gasp of air in rage and horror.

"You have ever been a woman given to revelations. That is why you were driven from Boston twenty years ago! Now give ear, and listen to your sentence. Mary Dyer, you shall go from whence you came and from thence to the place of execution and there hang till you be dead," the governor pronounced.

Mary remembered her revelation of long ago, that she would climb the scaffold to be hanged, but would feel no fear, only fulfillment.

"The will of the Lord be done," she answered.

"Take her away, Marshal Michaelson!" said Governor Endecott. His face was full of loathing for the wave after wave of devilish heretics that would not stop trespassing in his domain.

"Yes, and joyfully I go!" Mary said brightly, without the slightest tinge of sarcasm.

She turned to Edward Michaelson, the marshal general, expecting to be escorted back to the prison. He bent over and picked up the end of the rope that tied her hands together in a loop. Mary followed him like a lamb.

There was a small group of curious townspeople outside the courthouse. Mary Dyer was well-known, still, as the woman who gave birth to a monster twenty-two years ago, a hideous creature with a face but no forehead or neck, and open wounds and horns on its back like a sea monster. It had been buried somewhere on the Common, and some said that no grass would grow on the place for the abominable corruption below.

The marshal parted the crowd with only a look, and he led Mary by a slack rope.

"It is unnecessary for you to guard me to the prison," she said. "I am here in Boston, here in your hands, because I have come at the Lord's command. Laws, commands, rules, and edicts are for those who have not the light which makes plain the pathway. He who has God's grace in his heart cannot go astray."

"I believe you, Mrs. Dyer, but *I* must do as *I* am commanded."

October 26, 1659
Boston, Massachusetts

FROM MARY DYER TO THE GENERAL COURT now this present 26th of the 8 month 59 assembled in the town of Boston in New England,

Greetings of grace, mercy, and peace to every soul that doth well: tribulation, anguish, and wrath to all that doth evil.

Whereas it is said by many of you that I am guilty of mine own death by my coming (as you call it "voluntarily") to Boston: I therefore declare unto everyone that hath an ear to hear: that in the fear, peace, and love of God I came, and in well-doing did and still do commit my soul and body to him as unto a faithful Creator. And for this very end hath preserved my life until now through many trials and temptations, having held out his royal scepter unto me by which I have access into his presence, and have found such favor in his sight as to offer up my life freely for his truth and people's sakes. Whom the enemy hath moved you against without a cause, to make such laws as by him is intended which the Lord hath blessed for ever, called by the children of darkness "cursed Quakers," for whose cause the Lord is rising to plead with all such as shall touch his anointed or do his prophets any harm.

Therefore, in the bowels of love and compassion, I beseech you to repeal all such laws as tend to this purpose and let the truth and servants of God have free passage among you. For verily, the enemy that hath done this cannot in any measure countervail the great damage that will fall upon you if you continue to keep such laws. Woe is me for you.

Was there ever the like laws heard of, made by such as profess Christ came in the flesh? Have such no other weapons to fight with against spiritual wickedness, as you call it? Of whom take you counsel? Search with the light of Christ in you, and it will show you of whom, as it hath done me, and many more who hath been disobedient and deceived as you now are; which secret light as you come into and obeying what's made manifest to you therein, you will not repent that you were kept from shedding blood though 'twere by a woman. It's not my own life I seek, for I choose rather to suffer with the people of God then to enjoy the pleasures of Egypt, but the life of the Seed which I know the Lord hath blessed, and therefore seeks the Enemy thus vehemently, the life thereof to destroy, as in all ages he did.

Oh, hearken not unto him, I beseech you, for the Seed's sake, which is one in all and is dear in the sight of God. Which they that touch, toucheth the apple of his eye and cannot escape his wrath—of which I, having felt, cannot but persuade all men that I have to do withal: Especially you, who nameth the name of Christ to depart from such as bloodshed, even of the saints of the Most High. I have no self end, the Lord knows, for if this life were freely granted by you, it would not avail me to accept it from you, so long as I shall daily hear or see the suffering of my dear brethren and sisters, with whom my life is bound up, as I have done this two years, and now it is likely to increase even unto death, for no evil-doing but coming among you.

Therefore, let my request have as much acceptance with you (if you be Christians) as Esther had with Ahasuerus, whose relation is short of that which is betwixt Christians. And my request is the same that hers was to the king, who said not that he had made a law and it was dishonorable for him to revoke it. But when he understood that these people were so prized by her and so nearly concerned her as in words of truth and soberness I have here expressed you that these are the same to me. You know by the history what he did for her.

Therefore I leave these lines with you, appealing to the faithful and true witness of God which is one in all consciences, before whom we must all appear, with whom I do and shall eternally rest in everlasting joy and peace. Whether you will hear or forbear, I am clear of your blood, but you cannot be of ours, but will be charged therewith by the Lord before whom all your coverings will prove too narrow for you. But to me to live is Christ and to die is gain, though I had not had your 48 hours' warning for the preparation of the cruel and (in your esteem) cursed death of me, Mary Dyer.

Know this also, that if through the enmity you shall declare yourselves worse than this heathen king, and confirm your law though 'twere but by taking the life of one of us, that the Lord will overturn you and your law by his righteous judgments and plagues poured justly on you, who now, whilst you are warned thereof and tenderly sought unto to avoid the one by removing the other, will neither hear nor obey the Lord nor his servants. Yet will he send more of his servants among you so that your end shall be frustrated that think to restrain them you call Quakers from coming among you, by anything you can do to them. Yea, verily, he hath a Seed that suffereth among you for whom we have suffered all this while and yet suffereth, whom the Lord of the harvest will send forth more laborers to gather out of the mouths of the devourers of all sorts, into his fold where he will lead them into fresh pastures, even the paths of righteousness for his name's sake.

Oh, let none of you put this good day far from you, which verily in the light of the Lord I see approaching to many in and about Boston, which is the bitterest, darkest-professing place and so to continue so long as you have done, that ever I heard of. Let the time past therefore suffice of such a profession as brings forth such fruits as these laws are.

In love and in the spirit of meekness I again beseech you, for I have no enmity to the persons of any; but you shall know that God is not mocked, but what you sow that shall you reap from him that will render to everyone according to their deeds done in his body, whether good or evil.

Even so be it, saith

MARY DYER

Who also desireth that the people called Quakers in prison or out of prison that's in the town of Boston at the time of our execution, may accompany us to that place and see the bodies buried.

*****

October 27, 1659

Boston, Massachusetts

Boston was still a small town, thought Mary as she and her brothers were roughly shoved from the board porch of the courthouse, out into the strong morning sun. To stay together while they were herded down the path, the three joined hands, with Mary in the middle of the two young men. Their hearts were light, and filled with joy, knowing that soon they would be entering the Light of the Savior.

William Robinson projected his voice above the din of the shouting crowd. "The streams of my Father's love run daily through me, from the Holy Fountain of life to the seed throughout the whole relation. I am overcome with love, for it is my life and length of days; it is my glory and my daily strength. I am full of the quickening power of the Lord Jesus Christ. I shall enter with my

Beloved into eternal rest and peace, and I shall depart with everlasting joy in my heart and praises in my mouth."

The court had ordered that Marshal-General Edward Michaelson should command his red-coated, helmeted militiamen to carry pikes and muskets with powder and shot, and to keep spectators well away from the condemned prisoners for the one-mile march to the fort on Boston Neck. Executions often attracted three to six thousand spectators, and even more if a woman was condemned.

In consequence, seventy-two pikemen marched in six ranks of six in front and back of the ranks of thirty-six musketeers, with the three Friends in the very center. If needed, the pikemen with their ten- or fifteen-foot spears could protect the musketeers, as they reloaded their powder and shot to fire another volley.

Captain Oliver signaled the drum major to strike up an execution beat loud enough to drown out any utterances of the three Quakers.

At other executions or corporal punishments in both New England and Old, the crowd would be in a festival mood, and it was customary to throw rocks and dung, and shout insults at the condemned. But something was different about this occasion. Many of the people of Boston, Dorchester, Roxbury, Charlestown, and other settlements were angry, but not at the Friends. They resented the heavy-handedness of the government in such small crimes as preaching, providing for the needs of prisoners, and quoting familiar scriptures.

The two young men, a Yorkshire plowman and a London merchant, had done nothing worthy of death. The quiet, modest, Christian mother of six (even though she'd been the mother of a monster once upon a time) and wife of an attorney did not fit the role of an adulteress or murderer.

The three Friends, walking hand in hand with heads held high as if going joyfully to a wedding, were at the center of more than a hundred soldiers, and thousands of colonists. It struck her that far from demonstrating the power of the state as intended, or keeping the three meek prisoners from escaping, the militia were there to stop the crowd from rioting or rescuing her and Brothers Robinson and Stephenson.

The minister, John Wilson, was so delighted to send his condemned to their deaths that he darted into the center of the ranks, shook William's hand and taunted, "Shall such jackasses as you come in before authority with their hats on?" and plucked off Robinson's hat to be trampled by the soldiers.

Robinson answered in a measured, reasonable voice, "Mind you, it is not for putting off the hat that we are put to death."

The procession moved slowly as the spectators pressed in from the sides on Tremont Street, and eddied and rippled like sands in a tide to the edges of the Common grazing grounds.

Mary looked toward, but couldn't see, the house in which she and William had lived with dear Liza, and where she'd borne Samuel and her stillborn daughter. Then, as a member of the First Church of Christ in Boston, she'd had little hope of salvation for herself, and none for her deformed baby, who had not been baptized before John Cotton buried her somewhere on this Common, and John Winthrop exhumed her with such glee. Now, Mary rejoiced that in a few minutes, she would be in the presence of the Lord, and would meet her daughter, who would have been twenty-two, and her first son, who had been buried at St. Martin's on this very day twenty-five years ago. She felt euphoric about what was to come.

After the procession crossed over the training field on the Common, the marshal directed the troop to form a wedge as they neared the fortified stockade on the Neck, so that they could pass through the portal before the majority of the crowd did. He commanded them with a laugh, "Mind the pit by the marsh, men! If you fall in, we won't come back for you until we dump the heretics' carcasses in."

Michaelson noticed that the three were still holding hands, and walking with a light step instead of trudging to their deaths. From his saddle, he asked Mary, "Are you, a matron with grown sons, not ashamed to walk so happily, hand in hand between such young men?"

Mary answered brightly over the sound of the drummers beating the execution rhythm, "This is to me an hour of the greatest joy I ever had in this world. No ear can hear, no tongue can utter, no heart can understand, the sweet incomes and the refreshings of the Spirit of the Lord which I now feel."

The words had sprung freely from her heart. This was the twenty-sixth anniversary of her wedding to Will, and that was the second-greatest joy of her life. She breathed one more prayer for comfort for his grief, and thanked God for the gift of such a man. But by faith, she had left William in God's hands. Onward she walked toward the Light.

The Neck was a strip of land surrounded by sea marsh that connected Boston, which was very nearly an island, with Roxbury and mainland Massachusetts. The colonists had placed the gallows on a low hillock, to stand high for onlookers to see and take notice of what happened to criminals, as a deterrent to crime, and a warning to live uprightly. The two upright posts and the lintel were reminiscent of a portal to hell.

At the edge of the Neck, there was a pit into which the executed bodies were tossed for Nature to take care of: carrion birds, tidal seepage, rainwater—it was illegal to remove the bodies for burial elsewhere. They were to remain there as a lesson to all who passed by.

The executioner, by tradition, formally apologized to Mary, and quietly indicated his instructions were for her to climb the ladder to the scaffold first. Without a word, she gathered up her skirts in one hand and climbed the steps, holding the ladder with her other hand. The narrow wooden platform had no rail. She stood passively while her hands were tied before her, and her feet were bound at the ankles. Her hat was removed, though her coif was left to her to cover her ragged crop. The noose was placed over her head to lay on her shoulders like the chain of authority she'd seen on court officials when she was a young woman.

Then she was left there to stand and watch her Friends die before her own execution.

William Robinson climbed the ladder and turned to address the crowd. He saw there his Friends from Sandwich, Salem, Newport, Boston, Providence, and the other towns where he had been called to speak the gospel. Some were weeping, and others stood with pale faces and cold hearts, shoulder to shoulder with the rabble who shouted curses at the law-breakers.

Reverend Norton read the sentence of the court on the prisoners, detailing their crimes of sedition and heresy, and repeated disobedience against the court's banishment orders. He took pains to explain to the onlookers that the prisoners had, in mercy, been offered a conditional release—if they would only leave Massachusetts forever—but the prisoners had refused and thus chosen to die.

The tendons on his neck stood taut and his hatred stretched his face to a skeletal look, thought Mary.

He neglected to say that it was he, Norton, who had incited the court to execute the three heretics, and had said that they looked peaceful and happy now, but hanging would certainly change their visage. And that bloody priest Wilson had said at the same time, "I would carry fire in one hand, and fagots in the other, to burn all the Quakers in the world. From the devil they came, and to the devil let them go!" But now, pastors in front of the vast audience, they had hypocritically softened their tone.

"We suffer not as evil-doers," cried Robinson, "but as those who have testified and manifested the Truth."

He turned to the two Puritan ministers. "This is the day of your visitation, and therefore I desire you to mind the light of Christ which is in you, to which I have borne testimony, and am now going to seal my testimony with my blood."

John Wilson, the pastor of Boston's First Church of Christ for nearly thirty years, hissed at Robinson, "Hold your tongue. Be silent, or you will die with a lie in your mouth."

The executioner placed the circle of rope around his neck and tightened it with the noose under one ear, so there was a greater chance of quick death than of strangulation. Robinson shouted for the onlookers' benefit, "Now are ye made manifest; I suffer for Christ, in whom I live, and for whom I die!"

A hood was placed over his head which muffled further words, and at a signal from the marshal, Robinson was pushed off the ladder. His neck broke. The crowd roared—but not in approbation.

"'Tis wrong!"

"He was no heretic! He was a good man!"

"Murderers!"

The executioner left Robinson hanging to be sure his heart had stopped, for even though he wasn't breathing, he might not be quite dead.

Marmaduke Stephenson climbed the ladder and stood between Robinson's hanging corpse and Mary. He also spoke to the spectators while the executioner adjusted the cruel halter: "Be it known unto you all this day that we suffer not as evil-doers, but for conscience' sake. This day shall we be at rest with the Lord, whom I trust to be husband to my widow and father to my children."

At this, there was a gasp from several women in the onlookers.

"Give ear, you magistrates, and all who are guilty; for this the Lord has said concerning you, and will perform his word upon you, that the same day you put his servants to death, shall the day of your visitation pass over your heads, and you shall be cursed forevermore. The mouth of the Lord of hosts has spoken it. Therefore in love to you all, I exhort you to take warning before it be too late, so the curse may be removed. For assuredly by putting us to death, you will bring innocent blood upon your own heads, and swift destruction will come unto you."

The executioner tightened the rope around Stephenson's neck, made sure the young man's hands and feet were tied, and at Wilson's signal that he'd given the man up for a heretic's death, the executioner turned Marmaduke Stephenson off the ladder. The body dropped and the rope tightened under his weight, and he died. Again the crowd shouted and the military men, looking uncomfortable, drew their rank tighter about the gallows.

"For shame!"

"You make widows and fatherless children today!"

"Cursed Quakers! Huzzah!"

"Wicked, ruthless judges!"

After a few minutes to be sure Stephenson was dead, the rope was cut on Robinson and Stephenson so that they dropped to the ground. Robinson's skull broke. The men's clothing was cut off, and two soldiers carried their naked bodies to the pit and heaved them in without a shroud or anything to cover them or lend a shred of dignity to their remains.

Reverend Wilson offered no prayer or comfort for the damned Quaker heretics. Instead, in an ecstasy of righteousness, he sang a song of joy at the men's deaths.

The only thing that really bothers me, thought Mary, is that I should be laid in the pit with no cover. I care not what happens to my flesh, for my spirit shall be with the Lord presently. But what will my children hear or believe of this time?

The hangman pulled the noose tight under Mary's ear, until its prickly fibers were snug against her neck, but he seemed hesitant, as if he were waiting for something.

And he was.

The wicked priest Norton had some things to say while he had a huge audience holding their breath.

"Here is a woman who had every advantage: she had a husband with a substantial estate and a child. But she had a weak mind, and followed that seditious heretic, Mrs. Hutchinson. God smote Mary Dyer with a monstrous birth, proof of the corruption she carried within, the whoring after false religion. She ran away to Aquidneck, the Isle of Error, where she could blaspheme God with her disobedience, and presume to interpret the Bible. Then she went to England, leaving her husband and children for years, to commit more monstrous error by trailing, like a camp follower, after those wretched Quakers. She entered Massachusetts to infect you with her disease, and we banished her on pain of death if she returned, the latest only last month. She just couldn't stay away from her lovers, those Quakers now dead."

Suddenly, from outside the militia escort, came a loud voice, interrupting Norton. "Stop! She is reprieved!"

Mary, who had been in prayer and had not listened to Norton, heard that voice. It jarred her from her trance, and pulled her away from the Light to which she was already drifting. No, no, no, she protested, and felt her heart tear. This was the voice of her son. It was William Dyer the Younger, born nineteen years ago. She had turned her face from her family, and left them in the care of God. How could William be here, keeping her from the calling of God? Was this a test? A temptation of the evil one?

She stood very still, calling on the Lord for an answer. And heard nothing. The glorious Light had retreated, and she was left in the dimness of Boston's midmorning sun. For the sun in the autumn sky held little radiance compared to the tangible Light of God.

The hangman loosened the bindings that kept her skirts tied at her ankles, and told her to get down. But she stood fast.

John Wilson, who had hovered around the pit in exultation, sprinted back to the gallows and swarmed up the ladder. Out of breath, he said in a theatrical voice that carried on the onshore breeze, "Mrs. Dyer, you're not going to heaven as you thought. And you're not going to hell as we would prefer—at least, not yet. Your punishment was that you were to stand here with the rope around your neck and watch your friends die. Your protest has failed."

He laughed in short exhalations, with a mad gleam in his eyes. "With this humiliation, you have joined the ranks of O'Crimi, an Irish servant who attempted buggery with a cow. Anna the Negro, who was suspected of murdering her bastard child. Alice Thomas, a vile prostitute. And a veritable parade of adulterers and blasphemers and witches. For you have committed adultery against your membership in the Church of Christ, whoring after the devil."

Even the marshal thought the cruelty had gone too far. "Mrs. Dyer," he said gently, "Come down now, or we'll take you down by force. I'm to conduct you back to the prison. Your son will receive you."

She spoke again, for the first time since she had come back from heaven's gate. "I'm willing to suffer as my brethren did, unless you will annul your wicked law. I came here at God's command."

"And you will leave here at *my* command. Come down," he repeated.

"I desire to stay a little and inquire of the Lord," Mary said with a small, ragged voice. For the first time, there were tears in her eyes.

But some of the mockers nearby were struggling to get through to the ladder to drag the Quaker down. Captain Oliver ordered the pikemen to form a barrier by extending their long spears, and he chose four men to take Mary down forcibly. This was no time to let a riot begin. Two soldiers grabbed her by her arms and lowered her roughly to two more men on the ground, who set her on her feet.

Her son spoke to her quickly, "Mother, I'll follow you to the prison, where we'll talk." He was shoved away as the musketeers and pikemen reformed their ranks.

As the company passed over the Common lands again, some of the crowd followed, though only a handful this time. Dimly, Mary recognized some of them as Friends, though she didn't know them personally. The others must be Boston sympathizers.

Though it was yet before noon, Mary was exhausted. She hadn't slept because she'd written the letter to the court, spent time in silent worship, and in fellowship with the women Friends in the prison. They had been ecstatic at her expected entrance to eternal life. Now she was trembling for two reasons: that her heavenly journey was not begun, and because she was deeply angry with the members of Boston's court.

Nay, three reasons. Her husband had again thwarted her mission, this time by using their son, his namesake, to announce her reprieve and keep her from her mandate to die in the cause of conscience. A nineteen-year-old boy would never have had the authority and presence to persuade the court to free her. This had her husband's signature written all over it, even down to the name of their son, otherwise, why not come himself or send Samuel? Or Edward Hutchinson? Or ask another Rhode Island attorney to plead for her?

When the procession reached the prison, Mary entered the building with Marshal Michaelson while Captain Oliver dismissed the militia to their respective churches for the weekly lecture, which they were required to attend. The marshal gave Mary's custody back to Jailer Salter, who put her in a tiny cell to wait for her son.

*****

When William entered the visitor cell, Mary's heart lurched in grief and remembrance. Here was the babe born healthy and whole, whom Anne had delivered, the child who proudly sailed his mother to Dyer Island, the boy she had treated for sunburns and bee stings, the youth who welcomed her home when she returned from England. She embraced her son, but stiffly, and then she backed away. She'd made her sacrifice already. It was too difficult to go through that again.

"Mother," he said, choking back tears. "We found your letter almost as soon as you left. Father solicited the support of Governors Winthrop and Temple weeks ago, and he's sent money with me to redeem you from prison."

"Oh, William. I came here to offer up my life for God's people. It was at God's command that I came, knowing full well what he expects of me."

"But how can you leave your family? You left us alone for so long while you were England, that the younger ones hardly remember you. Despite our need for you, you've left us again and again. Do you not love us? The Bible says that he who does not love, does not know God, for God is love."

"William, you tempt me to be a mother and wife, but God has called me to be a witness for him. I will *never* stop loving you. Remember that. Teach it to your brothers and sister. What I do is from a love I pray that you'll grow to understand: that no one will dictate what you, and generations to follow, should or should not believe about God. That spiritual matters be kept separate from civil matters, lest you see the zealous, corrupt, mad bloodlust of this city spread across America, and men and women are persecuted and repressed for following God's commands.

"When I heard the order of reprieve, it was a disturbance to me, for I was so freely offering up my life to him who gave it to me. To answer your charge about love, this is how you know that I am in God, who is Love, and he in me. If I say I know him and keep not his commands, I'm a liar and the truth is not in me. But if I do keep his word in my heart, the love of God is perfected. Christ fulfilled the law, and gave only one command, that we love one another as God has loved us, even unto death on a cross."

William reached out to catch his mother's hand, but she pulled back instead of accepting his gesture. "Are you not afraid of hanging?" he asked, "or whipping? Or of what your undeserved penalties will inflict on your family?"

"My son, I fear not for myself, and I fear not for you and Samuel and the children because both your fathers, the Lord and Will Dyer, will continue to care for you and hold you precious. God gloriously accompanies us with his presence, and peace, and love. I have rested from my labor, in Jesus Christ. For *he* is my life, and the length of my days. You should not think of me as mother."

Mary's heart softened at the look of devastation and the effects of rejection on her son's face. "You are so young yet, you have lived your short life in safety and comfort, and you enjoy liberty of conscience, and freedom to do as you wish so long as you do no harm to others. You do not understand the nature of love as a mature, godly man does. Nor do you understand the depths of hate men are capable of."

"With wicked hands they have put to death two servants of God, men who were filled with love and meekness. The court has hindered my request to annul their law and stop their evil treatment of the Friends. But they are fighting a mere battle. God has won the war already. We only wait to see the victory."

"How can you call it a victory when you are dead?" asked William in a bitter voice.

"Ah. Do you remember the chapter in Hebrews that begins, 'By faith?' The writer tells of their famous deeds in the power of God. Then the writer tells us something surprising: that in their lifetimes, they experienced terrible pain and loss, but never saw the promises fulfilled. But they had their eyes on what could not be seen, and held up their hands, like little children, trusting that God would grasp their hands and guide them. They believed that the invisible and intangible were better than what they had on earth, and in that realm they found power to perform the tasks assigned them. Now they are at the right hand of God, waiting for all to be fulfilled. We are even now, by faith, receiving a kingdom which cannot be taken away. This is why I do not fear, William. I've been to that kingdom, and I will return there. When you return home, more a man that you came here today, I charge you to strengthen your father and your brothers and sister with my words."

As William, agitated, paced around the cell while Mary spoke, he looked to her like a dark silhouette before the small, barred window, with the midday light glowing strong behind him. Mary stopped for a moment, surprised at the images God was showing her: William was a middle-aged man wearing military attire in a courtroom. He was defending himself before the King, and being acquitted.

"Someday you will be unjustly charged with a capital crime," she said. "The Lord has shown me this. When that time comes, you must appeal your case to England, and remind the King of my Friends, and of me, and the merciless cruelty and corruption of New England courts. You will prevail.

"Now, dear, return home, knowing that I am grateful for your respect and love. I am in God's will and in his hands. There is no better place to be, I assure you."

"Nay, Mother, not yet. I will obey Father and pay your ransom, and see you are released to my custody."

"So be it, William. I have a letter brewing in my mind, meant for the General Court. Would you please purchase the paper and writing materials from the jailer? Oh, and bread and cheese and apples for my Friends still here in the prison. Salter would separate body from spirit before the hangman has his chance."

*****

William had come back with the materials and the food, but Mary couldn't eat any of it. She was terribly thirsty, though, and cider revived her. She was compelled to write before this day left her ill or senseless, and she had the use of the room while it was light.

She didn't know if her anger with the Court gave her strength, or where this energy came from. She thought of several opening volleys, but after a few starts in her mind, she set the quill to the linen paper and wrote in her neat, even script.

> "ONCE MORE THE GENERAL COURT, assembled in Boston, speaks Mary Dyer, even as before:
>
> My life is not accepted, neither avails me, in comparison of the lives and liberty of the truth and servants of the living God, for which in the bowels of love and meekness I sought you; yet nevertheless, with wicked hands have you put two of them to death, which makes me to feel, that the mercies of the wicked are cruelty. I rather choose to die than to live, as from you, who are guilty of their innocent blood. In due time, you will see whose servants you are.

> Like Esther before Ahasuerus, I have stretched out my hand, and no man regarded it. You have refused your reproof. Then shall you call upon the Lord, but he will not answer. You will eat of the fruit of your own way.
>
> In obedience to the Lord, whom I serve with my Spirit, I can do no less than once more to warn you, to put away the evil of your doings, and kiss the Son, the Light in you.
>
> When I heard your reprieve order read it was a disturbance unto me, that was so freely offering up my life to him that give it me, and sent me hither to do, which obedience being his own work, he gloriously accompanied with his presence, and peace, and love in me, in which I rested from my labor—till by your order, and the people, that I should return to prison, and there remain forty and eight hours; to which I submitted, finding nothing from the Lord to the contrary, that I may know what his pleasure and counsel is concerning me, on whom I wait therefore.
>
> For he is my Life, and the length of my days, and as I said before, I came at his command, and go at his command.
>
> MARY DYER

Mary sanded the letter to dry her ink. All her life, she had held back her emotions, and disciplined face, mannerisms, and breathing not to show anger, because it would show vulnerability to those who would hurt her. Now, she felt herself weak because of the fury in her blood.

Last night she had written a passionate letter to the court, aching with hope not only for her own cause, but for the salvation of their souls, that they would turn aside from the malevolent course they had chosen to persecute God's own children. And her letter had failed. Had they even read it? Or had they read it and mocked God and sent her and her Friends to the gallows anyway?

And just think of the behavior of their "priests," Wilson and Norton. Both men were popular with their churches in Boston, which should be shocking for the distance they stood from Christ-likeness—but the apparent glee they took in the hangings today had sickened her.

Seeing her friends die was even more sickening. She knew their spirits were now with the Lord, and she wished she were there, too. This world was so dark and dreary, like an oppressive rainy season, compared to the Light and peace she was drawn to. But the way the Boston court had so cruelly killed the men—for what should have been a misdemeanor—and discarded their bodies was wicked. Even so, the point had been made with the people, who saw two gentle, inoffensive Friends slaughtered merely for offending the pompous politicians and preachers. Endecott and Bellingham had shown their fear of the Friends by setting such a large guard on the procession and execution. Showing fear, of course, made them even more desperate and dangerous. Their efforts to eradicate the Friends would escalate.

Her own death would seal their disgrace, she knew. The Lord had commanded her to come here and offer up her life, but had stayed the hand of the executioner. What did he mean by that? Was this like the sacrifice of Isaac—just to test her obedience and faith? How could that be, when God knew all things, and knew her faith?

She would have to wait for an answer.

*****

TO WILLIAM DYER, delivered to your hands by your son
28th of October 1659
My old friend,

Knowing that you are disconsolate over the late events, I remind you of our many years of fellowship in happier times, and assure you of my continued love for you. Indeed, your dedicated efforts to save your wife have succeeded, because of the esteem for you and your wife from Governor Temple of Acadia, who offered to provide house and sustenance for a year for Mary and your family, and from John Winthrop of Hartford, who wrote on Mary's behalf, begging her life, he said, as if on his bare knees before the court.

Yesterday was a regular lecture day in Boston. After the hangings at the fortification, and Mary was pulled down from the scaffold and conveyed to prison, the ministers called their flocks to their churches, undoubtedly to speak of the lessons to be learned from the disobedient, and exhort their members to perfect keeping of the law. I know that's what Reverend Wilson did at First Church.

Afterward, when a large number of the crowd crossed over the inlet on the North Street bridge to North Boston, one end of the drawbridge came up and broke, and many were injured as they fell on one another or the bridge fell upon them. One of the women who mocked the Quakers loudly yesterday was so severely bruised that she probably will not live, which calls to mind Stephenson's curse that "now is the day of your visitation." Some are already saying that it was either the court's fault for ordering the executions, or that it was Stephenson's curse that caused it. But I remember that two years ago, the governor, assistants, and court discussed the complaints of too few bridges in Boston and Charleston, and what bridges there are, are old and rickety. The court decided that the existing bridges were sufficient and no funds would be allocated for repairs or new bridges. Then they made land grants to several of their number. They are perpetually short of coin, but rich in rewards to their own faithful.

They say that these Quakers have violently and willfully rushed into the colony, and thereby become felons, and they declare that the sparing of one, upon the intercession of your son, will manifestly evince that the court wishes their lives absent, rather than their deaths present.

It would seem that this justification was necessary to be made public at the time, in order to subdue the clamors of the people. That is, the clamors against the General Court—not against the Quakers. Endecott and his court performed a morality pageant to escape the wrath of the Bay's citizens, though I think they sailed in very shallow waters, as demonstrated by the large military presence armed for action.

They believe that they are justified by having taken the example of England in their laws against Jesuits, in declaring banishment on pain of death.

I leave it to you to discuss with your wife, but I learned that there was no intention to execute her. *Nine days before*, at a court session, they determined that she should be carried to the place of execution, and there to stand upon the gallows with a rope about her neck until the others be executed, and then to return to the prison to remain for forty-eight hours until she should depart from Massachusetts. After that time, she will be forthwith executed if she is found here.

I urge you to use all means to keep her away from here, Will. Perhaps she would consider a return to England, or a winter's stay in Barbados until the dust settles. Now that several of the most radical Quakers have prudently returned to England, languish in prisons around New England and New Amsterdam, or have been hanged, the members of the court believe they've won the war. The Quakers, including my Scott relatives, can live safely and quietly in Rhode Island.

As you know, the Bay's charter does in no degree give authorities the power to enact new laws that are contrary to ancient principles of English jurisprudence or liberties. When they act on their own authority, they do so with the knowledge that they are committing treason, but they are relying on the turbulence of our home country's government and the ignorance of this colony's citizens to do their own furious will.

When events settle down, perhaps you would join a deer stalking with Richard Scott and me, though we'd understand if you had to put it off to next year.

I hope plans for the betrothal of Samuel and Anne will not be interrupted by these events. It would be a tragedy to delay the commencement of their marriage because of politics.

May God bless you and those you love. Unless I hear otherwise, I shall see you at the handfasting.
CAPTAIN EDWARD HUTCHINSON

*****

November 8, 1659
Newport, Rhode Island

She'd come home on All Souls Day when their son came into Newport Harbor, having sailed from Boston around Cape Cod. He'd embraced his wife to welcome her home, but she was almost a stranger. He saw love and sorrow in her face, but she kept herself very separate and formal. When they shared their enclosed bed at night, they might as well have had a bundling board for all the physical contact. She made herself as small as a child and slept with her back to him.

Though it was cold, she spent hours out on the cliff above the surf, walking, praying, or looking out to sea as if expecting a ship to carry her away from her home of twenty years.

Still, there was family business to conduct, as if Mary had never walked away from her family, and gone to the gallows. Before she'd left for Boston, the Dyers and Hutchinsons had planned a betrothal ceremony for their oldest children.

Samuel had completed his nine years of apprenticeship with Ed Hutchinson and was now allowed to marry. Men outnumbered single women four to one in Virginia Colony; but if one included the indentured women servants, the ratio in New England was less than two men to one woman. Many men, like Governor Coddington, had gone back to England to find a bride, either for their first marriage, or subsequent to the death of a wife because of childbirth complications or disease. But Samuel had laid eyes on Edward Hutchinson's daughter Anne several years ago, and the two fathers had known what would bond their friendship in blood ties. The problem was that Anne was still so young, barely sixteen.

The answer was to contract the two young people to a near-future marriage. The betrothal ceremony, conducted by a person of gravity and experience, would espouse the couple in a knot. In the presence of family and friends, they would take one another by the hand in the manner of their ancestors and say, "I, Samuel, take thee, Anne, to be my wife and none other, and do faithfully promise to marry thee in times meet and convenient, in token whereof is this: our holding by the hand." Anne would promise the same. Performing the ritual and speaking the promises before witnesses would lay a foundation for faithfulness in marriage.

Because of Mary's sentence, and the unspoken desire to put all things Boston out of their minds, they held the short ceremony and feast in Newport. Edward and Abby and their children came from Boston, and Susanna Cole and Bridget Sanford and their families sailed into Newport. The Dyer home was bursting with children of all ages.

William Dyer marveled that Susanna was a matron of Boston society, for she was the only survivor of the children who had been with their mother Anne when the Siwanoy massacred their family and servants in 1643. Nine-year-old Susanna had been taken captive for almost four years, and had barely spoken for months after her redemption, leading some to think she'd forgotten her native English language. But living with her brother Edward's family had gradually replaced her fears with trust, stability, and normalcy.

Now, with the ceremony and feast behind them, and everyone home, William and Mary settled into their cupboard bed with wrapped, heated bricks at their feet, and pulled the curtains for warmth.

"It was wonderful," sighed Mary. Even in the dark, William could hear the smile in her voice. "Our eldest son, and Edward's eldest daughter, just as Anne foretold, many years ago."

William was surprised. "You never said anything in all that time?"

"When I was carrying Samuel, Anne had a revelation that has given me peace: that our son and her granddaughter would marry and have a large family."

"I meant that you didn't see fit to tell me."

"William, there are many things that I don't tell you."

"Such as being taken with sudden whims to defy laws where you have no business? New Haven, Boston—thrice—what's next?"

She was silent. He knew the smile was gone.

"If you can't abide in your own home, Mary, where can you be happy? I can't allow you to go back to Boston, and I love you too much to tie you down like a boat in the harbor. What about a stay on Long Island? No, that's back in Davenport and Endecott jurisdiction. Shelter Island?"

"I'll seek the Lord's will on that, but Shelter might be best. There are Friends there."

William felt her rejection as a blow to his chest. "Then you really can't live with me and your own children, Mary? You've chosen God above the family that he gave you?"

"Do you know who Jesus called his family? Those men and women who shared the road with him. Those who were loyal to his mission to heal and comfort and bring the Light to the darkness. This is what happened to some of my family in September and

October: They were sentenced to be confined for two months and then received further punishments—Daniel Gould thirty lashes; Robert Harper and William King fifteen each; Margaret Smith, Mary Southwick Trask, and Provided Southwick ten lashes each, and recommitted to the prison for an undetermined time, though the slush and snow have set in. Alice Cowland, Hannah Phelps, Mary Scott, and Hope Clifton were delivered over to the Governor to be admonished.

"The Lord has called me to my destiny, William. I'll not disobey. I'll pray that you accept both God's will and my faith in his promises."

"Why does his will always end in death?" he asked bitterly.

"My love, death comes to everyone anyway, but Jesus said that he was the resurrection and everlasting life. I have nothing to fear, dear one. I have seen the Light."

He answered, "I wish you feared breaking my heart. And making your children motherless. How can you pass out of our lives? How shall we live without you?"

"If I had died in childbirth, or of plague or smallpox, you'd have found a new wife to mother our children. That is what we do in this life, for comfort, for mutual support, for companionship. William, you have been everything to me that you've promised. You have treated me honorably and fairly, you've protected me to the best of your abilities, and you've cherished me. In the cherishing, I have been the most favored of women."

"Wife, you're speaking as if this is your deathbed, and not a reprieve with a new life ahead of you." He carefully regulated his voice, and was glad that in the dark, she couldn't see the streaks of tears on his cheeks.

But her hand reached over and with the back of her fingers, she tenderly brushed away the water on his face.

"It's not my deathbed, William. But you must let me go. I feel like I'm not of this dark world, and I don't know how to get back. So I will walk into the Light that I *can* see."

November 13, 1659

Sandwich, Plymouth Colony

Mary dismounted her borrowed horse at the farm of Friends Robert and Deborah Harper. Her fellow traveler, Thomas Greenfield, a recent immigrant from England, had brought her in a fishing boat from Newport, along the rocky southern coast of Plymouth Colony, past Dartmouth, and eastward up Buzzard's Bay. The passage had been fast as the captain made the most of gusty early-winter winds.

At the head of the bay, Thomas collected the horses he'd left there on his trip to Newport, and they'd ridden eight miles to the town of Sandwich, on Cape Cod Bay, where he had a property. As they'd followed the road along a river, the almost-snowflakes left nearly-imperceptible droplets of moisture on their cloaks. The storm passed into the Atlantic and left a few debris clouds for the sunset to gild.

The Harpers had traveled to Boston three weeks ago, to protest the imprisonment of all the Friends in Boston, to remonstrate with Endecott, to support Stephenson, Robinson, and Mary, and bear witness to their persecution and martyrs' deaths. Robert had suffered fifteen stripes from the thrice-knotted catgut whip. They'd returned to Sandwich in sorrow and fury, determined to resist evil and wait for the Lord's next calling.

Mary, submitted in silent worship before her Maker, had heard God's call to go to Sandwich, on the southwest coast of Massachusetts Bay in Plymouth Colony, and encourage the Friends there. Recognizing Thomas Greenfield at a Friends meeting in Newport, she had asked him to take her to Sandwich.

Her husband had arranged for her to take ship to Shelter Island, but knowing that he'd never agree to this mission to enemy territory, she had slipped away while he was working.

Greenfield and Robert Harper greeted one another with clasped arms, not the usual clap on the back in recognition of Robert's recent whipping, and took the horses for a grooming and some sweet hay. Deborah Harper, a woman in her late twenties, took Mary into the modest farmhouse and gave her some warmed cider by the kitchen fire.

Two little girls with messy faces sat stock-still at a low table, spoonfuls of porridge frozen halfway to their mouths at the entrance of the stranger. Deborah chuckled as she dabbed the smeared porridge, and Mary took up a spoon and helped the baby finish.

"How old are these little Friends?" asked Mary.

"Mary is nearly three years old, and Experience was twelve months last week."

"They're lovely girls," Mary mused. She stopped for a moment and closed her eyes to savor the Light that sparkled inside. It showed her that Experience, the baby, would be the mother of a young man who would marry one of Mary's granddaughters.

What blessings the Light gave her, with no notice. Just love-gifts, like the countless thoughtful gifts Will had given her over the years. Her son Samuel would marry a Hutchinson and carry on the Barrett and Dyer inheritance. And now she knew at least one of her other descendants would marry into these passionate, committed Friends. She nearly chuckled when she realized that she and the Harpers would be grandparents-in-law, as she would be related in a similar way to Anne Hutchinson. But she kept these things to herself as usual.

Deborah mistook Mary's sudden stillness for exhaustion. "Mary, you must be very tired of the journey, and we've yet to hold our Meeting this evening. Let me help you rest and refresh for a few minutes."

November 14, 1659

Sandwich, Plymouth Colony

Sandwich was a mostly-Quaker town, having been evangelized by Marmaduke Stephenson, William Robinson, and William Leddra, but the Pilgrim descendants and their Governor Prence who ruled Plymouth Colony would not tolerate such an abomination in their midst. The General Court issued an order that any Quaker coming into Sandwich was to be arrested. There were so many Sandwich Quakers that when they went up to Boston, and were known to be of that town, they were arrested and jailed—on suspicion only. William Newland was tried, but no evidence could be found that he was a Quaker. If he had been convicted, he would have been whipped.

The many Friends adherents of Sandwich held frequent meetings for which they were fined heavily. When they ran out of silver or cabos, their livestock were confiscated, then their properties. They suffered a whipping every time they were arrested and sent to prison.

At least twice a year, the Plymouth general court required the men of Sandwich to make an oath of fidelity to Plymouth's government and to the English Commonwealth, so that they could serve on juries or in the Assembly. The Friends refused on the grounds that Jesus Christ had said not to swear at all. For this disobedience, each man was fined five pounds, the value of a cow and a calf, "to the good of the colony."

Even Isaac Robinson, whose father John Robinson was still esteemed as the Pilgrim Pastor forty years on, had been punished for protesting the ill treatment of Friends and Baptists. The next offense would mean disfranchisement, and because he stood fast on principles of justice, he knew he would lose his civil rights. He was not a Friend, but he could not countenance the vicious and venal treatment of his harmless neighbors.

"Woe be unto you stiff-necked Pharisees," declared Isaac when he was fined. "Have you forgotten the admonition of John Robinson when the Pilgrims set off for America? He said, 'The Lutherans cannot be drawn to go beyond what Luther saw. Whatever part of His will our God has revealed to Calvin, the Lutherans will rather die than embrace it; and the Calvinists, you see, stick fast where they were left by that great man of God, who yet saw not all things. This is a misery much to be lamented.' And you, who sought liberty in America, have borne that intolerance here. You've stayed inside your Calvinist walls and shut out the Light of God."

Tuesday, the fourteenth of November dawned clear and frosty, with only a few shreds of mist on the ponds. Farmers went about their business of feeding and milking and turning their animals out to pasture, most the swine having been slaughtered recently.

The sun rose over Cape Cod and the Bay, but on this morning at a little after seven, it cast its shadows as indistinct crescents where it showed through foliage. The sky, instead of lightening to pale blue, kept its twilight hue for more than two hours, as eight-tenths of the sun was obscured.

Mary and Deborah were out in the herb garden this morning, gathering leaves and seeds to use as medications over the winter, when the neighbors began gathering, looking for wisdom about the darkened sun. Such a thing had never been seen in their lifetimes.

Robert Harper spoke, from scripture he'd memorized; words that were in all their hearts. "Immediately after the tribulation of those days, the sun will be darkened and the moon will not give its light; the stars will fall from heaven and the powers of the heavens will be shaken. The sun shall be turned into darkness and the moon into blood, before the coming of the great and awesome day of the Lord."

"What does it mean, Mistress Dyer?" asked one woman. "Is this a judgment of God? The end of the world?"

Mary hesitated. She wasn't a preacher, but here was a crowd who looked to her for what to think about a sign from God. She knew God had asked her to visit and encourage the people of Sandwich, perhaps for such an event as this.

"It's an eclipse of the sun, a naturally-occurring event in the heavens, but used by God to warn his people and speak to our hearts," she said. As she spoke, her voice gained power. She was more sure of herself.

"The sun represents the light of the New Covenant gospel. What is the gospel? It is the glorious news that Christ obeyed, fulfilled with his death, and made obsolete the Mosaic law, and has written a new law on our hearts and minds. The dark New Moon represents the old Jewish law of sin and death, which the Massachusetts governors have raised as an idol, serving their false god of self-righteousness. Their law calls for the persecution and death of the saints, like our Friends Stephenson and Robinson three weeks ago. Their law would extinguish the Light if it were possible."

At this, someone shouted, "Praise God that he saved you, Mary Dyer!"

She continued as if she had not heard. "But you see today that the moon does *not* fully obscure the sun. Governor Endecott, who denies the Light and dwells in darkness, killed our Friends eighteen days ago, and it was a dark day for we who remain. But Governor Endecott or your Governor Prence cannot quench the gospel. And see now, the sun shines again in full strength. It is God's intent to restore men, through Christ, to the pure Light he has placed in our hearts. The Holy Ghost teaches you righteousness and holiness that come from Christ, not by your own futile works. Seek the Spirit's counsel, and obey. Remain in the Light.

"Though the children of darkness pursue us, the Lord will send more of his servants among them so that their end shall be frustrated if they think to restrain us from coming among them. We start a fire and leave it burning."

The Quakers held hands and prayed silently for a few minutes. But then Marshal George Barlow came from behind the small crowd, laid his hands on Mary's arms in a rough manner, and propelled her to the small jail in the town. Barlow had standing orders from the General Court to arrest Quakers coming into Sandwich. He was also the man who collected the fines and confiscated livestock. Mary noticed that he forbore whipping her—her husband's word had reached even here. Only one year ago, the missionary Friends, Copeland and Holder, had preached here in Sandwich, and they'd been whipped thirty-three times with a three-fold lash, until their torn bodies ran with blood.

Nevertheless, she had obeyed God's call to visit the Friends of Sandwich and encourage them in their faith—and even bring attention to the cause of Christ by her notorious imprisonment. Sitting on the floor of the jail, she stifled a laugh of delight that God would use her, out of all the men and women in the world, to minister to his people at this day, this hour, this unique heavenly event.

November 20, 1659
Long Island Sound

Thomas Greenfield was also taken to the jail, but refused to talk. He was interrogated about his residency, but he wouldn't reveal if he was from Sandwich, from England, or Rhode Island, and he was returned to his cell to await trial. At Plymouth's

December 7 general court, a Sandwich man claimed that Greenfield was a neighbor, and Greenfield was ordered released after he paid thirty shillings for expenses, and the price of Mary Dyer's incarceration and the boat passage to take her out of Sandwich. He refused to pay for his own incarceration, but Friends raised the fees to allow his release and removal from the colony. He went back to Newport.

Mary stayed in the jail only six days before her release. Rather than go back to Newport to live with William and the children, she resolutely turned her face to her next mission, which God had whispered to her through a ray of dust-laden sunshine that stabbed the darkness of the cell.

The Friends supplied her with a hired sloop and a captain to sail her away—but Mary didn't go to Rhode Island. After writing a short note to her husband, she made for Shelter Island, a small place at the east end of Long Island. Her captain was Tristram Hull, a mariner of Barnstable who had moved his family to Newport five years before. Mary was pleased to recognize a man who provided succor to the Friends when he could. Like Isaac Robinson, Hull wasn't a Friend, but he was outraged at the fanatical persecution in New England, and it was his pleasure to help.

Shelter Island, formerly called Farrett's Island, was owned by English sugar planters from Barbados, the Sylvesters, who were sympathetic to Friends, though they hadn't embraced the tenets of George Fox. The island was named for the sheltering arms of Long Island, but it was becoming known as a refuge for persecuted Quakers, among them the elderly Southwick couple of Salem.

After being rowed to the marshy shore from the sloop in the harbor, Mary and Captain Hull stepped out onto a dock and walked past the warehouses there, and up a path through the naked November woods to a farmhouse. It was not unlike the Dyer house at Newport. Though she'd been able to wash away the prison dirt during the voyage, she wished she could have changed her clothes and coif and hat, for she knew she must look like a London beggar. The day was blustery and cold, and she pulled her heavy cloak closer to hide her dishevelment.

The farmyard was busy, with servants and slaves packing barrels of salt pork, dried venison, milled grains, and other foodstuffs to be shipped to Barbados, for this island farm supplied food for the Sylvester family there. A man who looked to be Mary's age detached himself from the laborers and hurried over to Hull and Mary.

"Tristram, you old pagan!" exclaimed the man. "You're early by four days for your shipping run down to Barbados. What are you trying to do to me? The cooper is still building barrels for the cargo my men are packing."

Hull replied, "Perhaps I came early to partake of your bountiful harvest. Have I timed my arrival for some new-smoked sausage?" Hull was done with jolly greetings, though. He turned toward Mary.

"Nathaniel Sylvester, may I present Mistress Mary Dyer, wife of Captain William Dyer of Newport."

Sylvester swept his hat from his head and bowed. "Mrs. Dyer, what an honor you do the Sylvesters and our island farm by your presence. I have heard many good things about you from our mutual friends, John Rous and Christopher Holder and others. And my brothers in Barbados have done business with your husband on several occasions. I have made the acquaintance of your husband at the admiralty court, when my ship wrecked at the entrance to Narragansett Bay and the captain made off with some of my goods. The commissioners found in my favor, and I have much admiration for your husband."

Mary inclined her head and said, "You're very gracious, Mr. Sylvester. Your providing a haven for Friends has surely saved their lives and allowed them to heal and resume their ministry in New England. In fact, that's why I've come to visit Shelter Island—with your permission, I hope. I would like to meet with the Southwicks, and serve and support them if I may."

"You're welcome to stay here, Mrs. Dyer, as long as you like. But I fear that the Southwicks will never return to Salem or resume their business. They're not long for this world, since Governor Endecott had his way with them."

Mary's eyes welled with tears. "I've seen the sick and the abused restored to health by God's miraculous power, and I've seen them die in the assurance of eternal life. We know not which gift God will appoint them, but in the meantime, the Lord has asked me to be a comfort to the sick and an encouragement to the imprisoned."

"My wife Grissell will arrange a comfortable place for you here," said Nathaniel, "so you can feel welcome, and minister to the Southwicks. And there's a growing group of Quakers nearby on Long Island, so you'll have fellowship for your Meetings, if you so desire."

At this exchange, Captain Hull looked like the cat that ate the songbird, for this was the result he and Mary had hoped for by bringing Mary to Shelter Island. "I'll need to stop over for the night, Nathaniel, with those freshening winds and the storm clouds," he said. "Looks like I'll get that smoked sausage one way or the other before I go back to Newport and kiss my wife and children on my way to the Caribbean."

Sylvester gestured for Mary to follow, and they entered the large farmhouse. He introduced his wife Grissell, who was half his age. Mary noticed that as young as Grissell was, she had a bright girl of five and a toddler boy who were the very images of their parents. The age difference in mates was a common theme in Europe and America, but Mary was glad she and Will had been close in age.

As Mary had had Eliza Stansby to teach her the supervision of a busy home and farm with many servants, Grissell had her staff as well, and they were instructed to bring a wide, shallow foot basin, soap, and warm water for Mary to bathe. When Mary had changed into fresh clothes, her stained and dirty ones were carried away to be laundered and mended. When she'd left Newport for Sandwich, she'd only carried a few items in her bag; warm, serviceable clothing meant for travel and practical tasks. If there were a special need, the Lord would provide.

Now, refreshed and ready to move and work, Mary asked to meet the Southwicks. Grissell took her up to the gabled attics, where a small but comfortable room had been furnished for the couple under the thatch and near the kitchen chimney.

Near the one glassed window, there was a table for Lawrence to read and write, for Cassandra to keep her sewing, and for them to take meals—when they could sit up, as they were this afternoon. But Mary could see that they were crippled after their many severe whippings. Their muscles had atrophied and contracted in painful strictures without the benefit of medical care during their imprisonment. But Mary was surprised at their relative youth. She had expected the Southwicks to be about seventy, but they were only ten years her senior.

Grissell introduced them to Mary, but the introduction was not needed.

"Our sister," said Lawrence Southwick. "You were sent here for such a time as this."

"What do you mean?" asked Mary.

"The Lord asks you to bear witness to the suffering of the Seed, and to record it for others' instruction and inspiration."

*****

TO CAPT. WILLIAM DYER IN NEWPORT
November 23rd, 1659
Dear William,

A note to boast of a court victory yesterday. I represented my father's brother, Richard Hutchinson, in his appeal against Capt. Thomas Clarke, concerning his part ownership in the ship *Exchange*, which is used primarily as a transport ship for carrying goods and large numbers of Irish to Massachusetts and Virginia. The Irish are sold into indentures to pay for their passage. When the Court heard arguments from Clarke and me, they voted to overturn their previous judgment and instead of the eighth part of the *Exchange*, to give the ship *Goodfellow* to my uncle as compensation for the dispute, as well as the court cost and financial damages in the amount of fourteen pounds, fifteen shillings. Would my father not have been proud of a large ship and trade that the Hutchinsons have acquired? The *Goodfellow* can carry up to 300 passengers, and some cargo as well.

There are not many who would understand, so I beg your forgiveness for my outburst.

With much affection, I remain
CAPT. EDWARD HUTCHINSON
Boston

January 1660
Sylvester Manor, Shelter Island

Mary stamped the snow from her boots and shattered the sheet of ice from her skirt hems, and blessed her husband again for having sent winter clothes to her at Shelter Island. This wasn't the coldest winter she'd experienced, and the seas around Long Island moderated the air temperature a bit, but the wind was constant, and drove the chill right into her bones.

She had just returned from a visit to the Indian village on the island, where she had visited a sick woman who had recently given birth. The wigwam was a familiar style to Mary, who had lived in a wigwam when the Hutchinson party had left Massachusetts and founded the towns on Aquidneck Island. This round dome house was temporarily set apart as sick quarters.

How the Indian men and women dressed so scantily and survived New England's blizzards and nor'easters, Mary could not understand. Tunics and trousers clothed both men and women, and with an English trade blanket slung around their shoulders, that was enough. Only occasionally did they add fur pelts to their outer wear.

Visiting the Indian women with a translator, Mary exchanged herb lore with them, and learned how they treated disease and injury: by vigorously exercising themselves until the sweat ran from their bodies and the fevers burned out.

One of the young Friends from England wintering on the island, John Taylor, described a healing ritual he'd seen across the narrow strait on Long Island. "There was a great man's house next to the King, and he was very ill, but by and by, there came in a great many lusty proper men, Indians all, and sat down. Everyone had a short truncheon stick in their hands, pretty thick, about two foot long. They began to 'pow-wow' as they called it, and it was thus. The sick man sitting up as well as he could and had a dish or calabash of water in his hand, he supped a little of it, set down the dish, and spurted it with his mouth into his hands, and threw it over his head and naked body (for all of them sat naked on their seats), and beating himself with his arms, and clapping his hands, till he was all of a foam with sweat.

"They all spake with one voice and knocked on the ground with their truncheons so that it made the very woods ring and the ground shake. My Indian guide, Robin, said this would make the sick man well, and that something would come and tell them what to do. For they converse sometimes with dark infernal spirits.

"'Nay,' said I. 'I will speak to them.' With much urging, he desired that they should listen to him after he heard my words. 'Nothing will come while the English man is here,' he said. This was all in the night and eight or ten miles from any other English. I told them what they could do for the sick man, and that I would find one that should cure him, which I did.

"When I traveled that way again, he was well, and exceedingly glad to see me. So then I had an opportunity to declare the truth to them, and to turn them from darkness to the Light of Christ Jesus in their own hearts, which would teach them, and give them the knowledge of God who made them. And they heard me soberly, and did confess to the Truth I spake. They were loving and kind afterwards to Friends."

Mary had observed long ago that preaching to people in the marketplace was not the effective way of winning over new Friends. People only gathered to watch for the spectacle and the novelty, and the ones who converted were at best unstable, and at worst, mad—the kind who latch on if one merely looked them in the eyes and smiled kindly.

But if there's a relationship, God's Spirit would do all the work of sowing, tending, and harvesting. The important thing was the friendship and finding ways to be helpful. In contrast to the English colonists who treated the Indians as barbarians and a slave class, Mary went to the Indian women to sew garments, treat the sick, and tell stories. No one turned down an offer to pray for their healing or safe delivery of a baby.

Her male translator would have nothing to do with Mary's meetings with the Indian women, so they made do with demonstrations or quiet fellowship if they must. But the storytelling was popular with everyone, and Mary learned to use words and concepts that would be easily translated and understood.

John Taylor and other Friends from Shelter or Long Islands held Meetings at Sylvester Manor when they came together after short trips to the English towns on Long Island. During the winter, they met in the parlor, and Grissell told her that in warm weather, they met in the open air of the woods, like the Friends did at Sandwich.

Recently, the men had carried Lawrence and Cassandra Southwick down the stairs for a Meeting in the parlor, but it was more of an ordeal for their twisted bodies than it was peaceful time waiting for God to speak.

Mary warmed herself for a few minutes at the kitchen fireplace, a huge fieldstone cavern with a single chimney. There were several small fires of different temperatures in the hearth, for keeping the pottage warm, and baking meats and stews in large kettles. The bread oven was cool now after a dawn baking for the needs of the family, guests, and servants.

She sliced some sausage thinly, added some soft white cheese and bread, then poured off some small beer into cups and carefully carried a tray up the stairs to the Southwick's room.

"I've brought you your meal," she said.

Cassandra, the talker of the family, nodded cheerfully from her padded chair at the table by the window. "Good food for a hard day's work—and here we sit idly."

"Sister Cassandra, I've thought of an occupation, if Grissell agrees. You could teach little Grissell her beginning embroidery stitches. In turn, the little one's company will substitute for your grandchildren at Sandwich. And you can tell her stories while she does it."

Lawrence brightened to see Mary, but was constrained by his injuries from arising from his bed without help. Mary put her arms around his frail chest and slipped a hand under his hip while he put his arms around her neck. In that way, she was able to lift him to a sitting position. She stacked and punched the goosefeather pillows behind him until they resembled a bolster, then offered him a portion of food.

"And Mr. Southwick, I've considered what might occupy your hands. There are only so many hours you can read in a day, and I know you miss the labor of glassmaking and farming, which, to be candid, are no longer possible. Would you consider carving? The cooks need long spoons and ladles for the kettles. And workmen's tools need handles."

"Such a task," he answered, "is suited for a boy—but my wounds have purged me of any pride in strength or skill, and I will do what I can with pleasure." His dark green eyes sparkled.

"I'm glad to have an occupation, my dear. How are you coming with yours?"

March 19, 1660

Portsmouth, Rhode Island

Now that the worst of winter had passed, his work load picked up speed like a runaway horse, William thought. Not that he was complaining: the long, comparatively inactive winter often bored him. But starting in March, there were meetings in Newport and Portsmouth, at the same time he needed to plow for spring planting, and the ewes and heifers were dropping their young. He was glad of the indentured laborers he'd purchased, but he wished he had a steward, a job Mary had ably performed for years, arranging the workers' schedules, buying and selling, and managing the resources. He'd taught some of these things to Maher and Henry, but they didn't have the authority or experience of an adult.

He'd received a letter from Harry Vane, carried privately by his son William on one of his trading voyages so that it wouldn't be intercepted by the spymaster Thurloe, who knew everything about every man—and Sir Henry Vane was a watched man. After his imprisonment under Oliver Cromwell, he'd been released and stood for Parliament again, and had regained his position on the national councils after the abdication of Cromwell's son Richard. With Charles II invited back to England's throne, there were many matters to arrange as they rebuilt a government to resemble the Commonwealth before it became the Protectorate in December 1653. Parliament reappointed Sir Henry to the committee of safety and to the Council of State to manage foreign affairs and remain on peaceful terms with other countries.

Still, William knew, politics in England were volatile and treacherous. When the king returned to the throne, would the republican officials keep their positions—or their heads? Harry had been on both sides of the civil war: a royalist fifteen years ago, and then a Commonwealth government minister—even president of the

Council of State. His career could go on like this for years, or he could be tossed back in prison. The latter was more likely, as William couldn't imagine Harry not speaking out or not writing inflammatory booklets, and quietly squiring his properties in retirement. He hoped Harry would remember his wife and children instead of chasing after a cause that would leave them widowed and fatherless.

There was still no letter, no message from Mary, who had spent the winter months on Shelter Island, only seventeen leagues away from Newport. The same blizzards or thaws, the same sunsets and moon phases, the same bird migrations, or first bulbs rising through the snow. The woman he'd married, but who had left him for another Lover.

He turned his attention back to the business at hand and signed his name as witness to a property transfer. William Brenton of Newport for full satisfaction hath sold unto Thomas Ginings of Portsmouth on Rhode Island eight acres in Portsmouth bounded on the south by the land of Thomas Ginings lately Gyles Slocum's land, on the north by the land of Henry Pearcy lately Nicholas Browne's land, on the east and west by the Common with all houses, fencings…

*****

TO MARY DYER AT MR SYLVESTER'S HOUSE ON SHELTER ISLAND
19 March 1660
My dear sister in Christ,

I send you greetings of love from my family, and from yours. Richard corresponds with William and he will pass on your assurances of safety to him as you asked. Please also give my respects to the Southwicks.

We rejoice that you've had safe harbor with the Sylvesters on Shelter Island during this harsh winter. A severe storm yesterday has left a thick blanket of snow on everything, and frozen the creeks which had only recently thawed. Does it not remind you of our departure from Boston in 1638, when the snow lay drifted in the forest though it was April?

There is recent news from Plymouth that Isaac Robinson has been convinced of the Truth. Whether it is truly a new faith, or disaffection with the old one, I know not. Last year, he was appointed to endeavor the conversion of the Friends, but the result has been the reverse, and he seems to have turned to our faith. He has written a letter to the Plymouth Court that the court says is scandal and falsehood. I'm certain he will be fined again and again for his disaffection to authority, but they may forego corporal punishment for the sake of his father.

Your namesake Mary and I are to take ship for England in a few days, where I'll leave her a married woman. She's younger than I'd like, not quite 18, but I'm delighted that she'll wed Christopher Holder later in the summer. He's full of the Love and Light of God, and they will raise up godly children. Richard has been to England, six years ago, but I've not been back to my native land for 26 years.

My dear friend who is closer than a sister, the Lord has not shown me what our futures hold, but I know your determination, and I can guess what might happen. I will hold you up in prayer continually, as 'when Moses held up his hand, Israel prevailed: and when he let down his hand, Amalek prevailed.' Ex. 17:11. If we are separated by death, my dear, we shall be reunited in God's presence.

Until I return from England, or until that glorious day, I know not. But we rest in the Light and abide in the Love.
KATHERINE SCOTT

*****

May 12, 1660

Shelter Island, Long Island

Mary was exhausted. She was not in the mood to hear or make another condolence. She didn't want to hear, much less feel, more angry words about the wickedness of the colonial governments against the Friends, not in New England, and not in Virginia. She wanted something, but what?

This morning, she and the Shelter Island Friends had gathered for a blessedly-silent Meeting and then a burial service for Lawrence and Cassandra Southwick. Both of those dear people had died this week: first Cassandra and then a day later, Lawrence. Though Mary had done all she could to loosen the terrible knots under their skin caused by the triple lash, and soothe their pains by gently working scented and pain-relieving balm into their scars, all it took in the end was a respiratory fever. Once Cassandra was gone, Lawrence gave up and followed her. Again, Mary thought of the life force in a human being: sometimes it was strong, like a mighty river current, and other times, it was merely a trembling leaf on an aspen. The sixty-two-year-olds could endure savage beatings, they could tolerate the loss of every material thing they'd worked so hard for, they could hear of their adult children sitting in dark, cold prison, and grieve that their adolescent children had barely escaped being sold as slaves. But finally, they had left behind their torn old bodies for freedom and eternal joy in God's presence.

She wasn't sure whether to rejoice or to weep, or to nurse a very natural fury at the evil that could inhabit the governor, assistants, and ministers of Boston, Salem, and Plymouth, who claimed to speak for God but were voracious lions seeking to devour harmless lambs.

Nathaniel Sylvester hadn't been convinced of the Friends' teachings when Copeland, Holder, Robinson, and others visited here in previous years. Perhaps his sympathetic support of the Friends had something to do with his Barbados partners and past experience with Friends there—and something to do with his antagonistic attitude to the New Haven Colony which administered the English settlements on Long Island and had so gravely injured the Quaker missionaries.

But something had changed. Perhaps it was Lawrence and Cassandra, perhaps it was Mary herself, for now Sylvester was in a hot lather to send a letter to the General Court at New Haven and declare himself a Friend. An outraged Friend, furious about the unwarranted, malevolent persecution by New England's governments. How dare they, to hold Mary Fisher and Ann Austin in prison for five weeks, and inspect their naked bodies for marks of witchcraft or imp teats, to threaten death, and then ship them off to Barbados. Ann had said that though she'd borne five children in

England, she'd never suffered as much as she had under those barbarous and cruel hands.

Mary already knew what the false minister Davenport would say: that Nathaniel was slandering New England's godly magistrates and himself in particular, and blaspheming God with his pernicious doctrines, and that he was entertaining members of a cursed sect. There would be fury, accusations, and perhaps arrests. These were the people who had begun their bloody work with Humphrey Norton.

New Haven. Davenport. The earthquake. Was it really only two years ago? How the faces had changed in that time. Some had gone back to England. Sarah Gibbons drowned. William Robinson and Marmaduke Stephenson hanged. Richard Doudney, Mary Clark, and Mary Wetherhead all drowned in a shipwreck off Barbados. Anne Robinson dead of a fever in Jamaica. Now the Southwicks. And soon, Mary Dyer. She felt it. She knew the time was near, for the madness and hate of New England were still not ripe.

But did she mourn her Friends? Deep down, no, for she knew that their salvation was secure and they were now part of that great cloud of witnesses. Instead, she mourned the suffering of the converts who were only obeying the quiet voice of God, and acting as scripture prescribed: to visit the sick and imprisoned, to be just, merciful, and humble, to love one another. She mourned for the families and children who didn't understand where the hate came from, and why their naked, bleeding mothers had been dragged out to the wilderness and left to die, or suffered the winter in Boston prison, with no heat and little food. And because these women were not well-known, were not as educated or experienced as men, and to be honest, not as privileged and connected as Mary Dyer, they needed an obelisk or flag to rally around. They needed an advocate, and someone important enough to draw the attention of Endecott and Bellingham away from the outrages they visited upon the faithful. They needed the hearts of the people of New England turned from bloodthirst to pity and charity.

And that Mary could do by God's grace. She would have done it last October, but the Lord in his wisdom had used his two willing servants, Robinson and Stephenson, and reserved Mary's sacrifice for such a time as this, when it would have a greater effect.

Ah! That's what Mary had been longing for. Not the prison and hardship, but knowing that every moment, she was fulfilling God's will. She longed for the kingdom that was closer and more real than this world, and being in that place of perfect love.

The annual Court of Elections would be held in Boston in ten days' time, and she would be there. Even in taking the Southwicks home and releasing Mary from their care, the Lord was preparing her way. She had nothing to fear.

*****

Captain Hull's ship appeared in the harbor that evening, and he rowed the small boat into the inlet and its dock near the manor house.

"Nathaniel," he said at supper, "I've unloaded a cargo of sugar and molasses from Barbados at Newport, and before I take on the cargo for a return, I wonder if you have goods to ship."

"I think we can send some salt meat again this time. My men will have it ready by morning."

"Mr. Hull." The men turned in surprise to the usually-quiet Mary. "The timing of your arrival is provident. I need a passage to the town of Providence as soon as possible. Will you take me?"

"Wouldn't you rather go back to Newport, to your family and neighbors? You'd be safe there, as safe as you are here at Shelter Island."

"I didn't come to Shelter Island to be safe. I came at the Lord's command, and he has shown me what to do. And now I go to Providence at the Lord's command.

"Do you think that your arrival today is accidental, Mr. Hull?"

"I'm beginning to think that it was not, Mrs. Dyer." He grinned at Nathaniel, then sharpened his gaze at Mary. "You'd be safe at Providence, too, if that were your final destination. But I suspect you mean to go on to Boston. Am I correct?"

"The Lord requires me to visit Massachusetts, to finish my sad and heavy experience in the bloody town of Boston. He has set me apart for a holy purpose: to turn the hearts of people against the governor and assistants in their persecution of the saints."

Grissell Sylvester, already on the verge of tears from mourning Lawrence and Cassandra, reached for her wine cup, but at Mary's words, knocked it over on the white tablecloth. It spread like a bloodstain.

May 13, 1660
Long Island Sound

Nathaniel's barrels of salt meat and fish were loaded onto Hull's sloop before dark. No one slept well that night, and the dawn was a relief. They broke their fasts as a mere ritual, not because they were hungry.

Mary left her winter clothes and shoes with Grissell for some other woman, some other winter. She had no other possessions she needed to take with her but the outdoors clothing and shoes she wore, and a few grooming articles such as soap and a hairbrush.

She also left a manuscript of stories of the Friends, a testimony of the providences God had worked with them, with Nathaniel. "Give them to whichever man the Lord will show you, so that the witness of these people will not disappear from the earth. Do not say who wrote them, for the readers' sakes." Even now, and perhaps for decades to come, the monster birth stories would follow her and distract listeners and readers from God.

Grissell was heartbroken at the boat dock on the inlet. "You've been like a mother to me," she whispered, and clung to Mary until Nathaniel peeled her gently away.

"No, Sweetheart," Mary answered. "We are sisters. We shall ever be sisters, in this life and the next."

Nathaniel embraced Mary, and said to her, "John Taylor wrote to me from Barbados that he's returning to Shelter Island soon. In his letter, he said that you are 'a very comely woman and grave matron, and even shined in the image of God. We had several brave meetings there together and the Lord's power and presence was with us gloriously.' I hope that will encourage and strengthen you for the trials ahead. Go in the Light of God."

He turned to Tristram Hull. "Some men may think this a superstition, but I prefer to pray for safety before making a voyage. This is part of a long prayer by Samuel West:
'Grant o most gentle Savior, that whensoever any troublesome tempest, arise upon the Seas so that such as are in danger by calling on thy holy name with true faith may find favor at thy merciful hands to be delivered out of all perils and dangers and being preserved by thy heavenly power may make happy and prosperous voyages.'"

Captain Hull replied, "Amen," and helped Mary step into the ship's boat. From the bench with the shipped oars, he added, "I'm glad 'twas only a short blessing, because I don't want to miss the tide. Cheers until next time!"

With strong pulls on the oars, Hull quickly reached his sloop, and handed Mary up the rope ladder to his first mate. She was given a tiny cabin, hardly larger than a kitchen fireplace, but fit with a tiny bunk.

With the speed of long practice, Hull and his two crewmen raised the anchor and set the sails on the single mast, and with the captain at the tiller, they made their way out of the harbor and into the larger waves of the Long Island Sound.

Mary came out on the deck then, mindful of the boom and the shifting sail and ropes. "How long do you expect our journey to take, Mr. Hull?" she asked.

The corners of his eyes creased even more than the sun and salt had done over the years. "You sound like a child, if you don't mind my saying so, asking if we're there yet."

Mary smiled. Yes, it had been so with her children, as well.

Hull eyed the western and northern skies, which bid for chill winds and rain squalls later in the day. "All things like tides, currents, and winds being *perfect*, we could sail into Providence in twelve hours. But all things being *usual*—you should double that. It's safe to say that we won't make port until this time tomorrow morning. Mrs. Sylvester sent a box of victuals, and I'll have your cabin made more comfortable. There's no point in making your journey as miserable as a pilgrim dragging himself to Santiago Compostela."

Mary watched as they sailed out of Gardiner's Bay, and she squinted through the marine fog, trying to see the coast of

Connecticut, but today wasn't as fine as a hot July day. It was chilly, and the rain squalls came and went. The waves were darker than the sky, and the sloop tilted up until they could see only storm clouds, and then downward until she wondered if they'd dive under the wave's crest. Captain Hull wasn't worried; in fact, he was enjoying the challenges of the day. This was his life. And Mary was comforted by trusting.

May 14, 1660

Providence Plantation, Rhode Island

Captain Hull asked if Mary would like to detour on the eastern, Newport side of Narragansett Bay, or take the channel past Kingstown and Warwick. It was a temptation to see her farm and home once more, and imagine her children and husband going about their lives. Samuel and William were away from home now, working in their trades. The younger ones would be in school, and Marie was fostering in a friend's home. Her husband would be at the general court in Newport or Portsmouth at this time of year.

Her heart contracted painfully, thinking of her family. And her home, set in such a lovely place with vegetable and herb gardens, orchards and meadows running down to the rocky shore, and paddocks of foals and lambs. It wasn't the possession of it that lured her. It was the knowledge that it had been home and it could be again. The years of hard work and starting over in a wilderness had paid off in a gracious, comfortable life if she chose it.

They were still miles off when Mary asked Mr. Hull to keep to the west channel, what the Indians called the Salt River. Straight on to Providence. She had made her farewells a long time ago. And convinced of her command from God, there was no time to spare for sentimentality or regret.

She would not fall into the sin of ignoring the world of fear, pain, anger, and hopelessness that she had been appointed to change. Mary Dyer had a calling, a command. She had been given a part to play in the divine orchestration of the liberation of her people. Men and women must have the right to obey their consciences without threat of persecution and death.

Even nonbelievers, pagans, and heretics knew that there is no law on earth against the virtues of love, joy, peace, patience, gentleness, goodness, faith, meekness, and temperance. Yet her Friends like the Scotts, Perrys, and Harpers followed those principles and were fined, beaten, and imprisoned.

The sloop rounded the point and headed north into Narragansett Bay. To the port side, Mary saw rocky beaches, and above them, low hills covered in forest; and before the bow she could see the profile of Conanicut Island.

Captain Hull, in familiar waters and currents, navigated the sloop through the bay's islands and up the Seekonk River to the Providence Harbor, and then a few hundred yards up the Providence River.

Hull refused payment for the passage, saying, "Mrs. Dyer, you had your command, and perhaps I had mine and didn't hear it over the roar of the waves. But it is my pleasure and my honor to be used by Almighty God for such a time as this."

"God bless thee and thy family, Mr. Hull. Walk in the Light, and you shall not stumble."

As she had done eleven months before, when Sarah had drowned, Mary transferred to the longboat to be rowed to the landing near Roger Williams' home. As she sat there in the boat, she looked across the small river to the farms on the south side, as she had done so many times before. This time, though, she had a revelation of the future, that there was a road there, part of a city harbor, she thought. The street sign had the name "Dyer" on it. And then the vision was replaced by the waterfront farms with docks and shallops. If it was the future she'd seen, the place must be named for one of her descendants. Still, she was happy now that the Lord gave her revelations. When she was a girl, she had wondered if she was mad or a witch, to have seen things that weren't there.

When the boat landed and she had her satchel, Mary walked around the narrow home lots to the street where the Scotts' home backed up to Roger Williams' lots. At this hour, late morning, the roads were busy with ox-carts and tradesmen. No one lived idly, with so much work to do: baking, brewing, tanning, shipbuilding, butchering, and so much more.

The Scott home was as busy as any other, and there was no need to knock to announce her arrival—the servants were working there, as were Hannah and Patience Scott.

"Mrs. Dyer, how wonderful to see you here!" said sixteen-year-old Hannah. "I'm sorry my mother and Mary aren't here to greet you."

"That's all right, dear. I received your mother's letter a few weeks ago. I pray they'll arrive safe in London in a week or two."

"Father and John are out at the farm, but they'll be home in a few hours. Would you like to take luncheon with Patience and me?"

She was rarely hungry, and meals were more for sociability than eating, but Mary nodded yes. Richard Scott was one of the most prosperous men in Providence, but the midday meal was like any meal in any home: bread, cheese, beer, and a ladle of vegetable, herb, and meat stew that always simmered at the fire.

Mary made herself busy with Katherine's mending, and greeted people she knew from a bench under a shade tree, until Richard and his son John came home from the farm.

Richard took her hands and greeted her. "Mary, my heart is glad to see you—and at the same time, I can guess why you're here and I'm saddened that this may be the last time. Have you seen Will? Does he know?"

"No on both accounts. I came straight from Shelter Island after the Southwicks went home to the Light, and I go on to Boston, where the court sits in a few days. This is the appointed time."

"Oh," Richard said dejectedly. "Lawrence and Cassandra." He was quiet for a few moments. "It feels like I've lost a limb. Endecott murdered them, and has grievously wounded all of us in the process."

Mary said softly, "The only way I don't go mad with vengeance and hate is to remember that they are in the presence of the Lord, that they are blessed to have been persecuted for the Name's sake, and they were faithful to God's voice."

Richard agreed. "I'll meditate on that, Mary. Shall we have a Meeting tonight? I assume you'll leave in the morning for Boston."

"I'd like that. We must pray for the hearts of John Endecott, Richard Bellingham, John Wilson, and others, that their hands will be stayed in their persecution of the saints.

Richard answered, "The monster of iniquity directed the constable at Salem to apprehend William Leddra, and transport him to Boston to appear before the court. If you are arrested, you'll be in good company."

*****

The Friends of Providence gathered at the Smiths' large home, and sat down, men on one side, women on the other, to silent contemplation, waiting for God to whisper to their hearts, or reveal a scripture to them. This was the time the Friends felt God's presence and boundless love, and they trembled in awe.

After nearly an hour had passed in deep peace and joy, Patience Scott stood silently, indicating that she had a word to impart. Her father nodded that she had permission to speak.

In the voice of the twelve-year-old child she was, Patience said, "I am called to attend Mrs. Dyer on her journey to Boston."

The silence in the parlor continued, but this time because they all held their breath. The girl had been imprisoned for more than two months last summer, for accompanying Robinson and Stephenson and testifying publicly about the cruel laws. But she'd been released to Edward Hutchinson, her cousin, because of her age.

Mary stood up to speak. "If I fall, it will be as a seed falls to fertile ground. The Seed in me will spring up to greater fruit and more seeds. Patience will be safe in Edward's care."

One of the Friends said his heart was at peace in this matter. Richard, Patience's father, looked stricken. His wife and daughter were gone to England, and Patience, his youngest, would be going to Boston, leaving only Hannah and John at home.

He swallowed his fear for his daughter, who had proven her maturity even at such a tender age. "Patience has a powerful anointing on her from the Lord. She may go with Sister Mary, with my blessing and my prayers."

May 20, 1660
Massachusetts

The woman and the girl walked out of the deep woods and through a meadow where honeysuckle vines covered a low rock wall. The first clusters of blossoms showed golden against the dark foliage. Mary motioned for Patience to stop, for she heard a slight hum and saw a flash of iridescent green in the dappled sunlight.

It was a humbird, that tiny miracle of jeweled beauty she'd read of as a young woman in England, and seen for the first time in Boston. The bird was darting among the flowers, but then flew a zigzag pattern toward Mary and hovered before her, looking curiously and fearlessly at her face before vanishing in a sudden vertical ascent. Mary and Patience laughed in delight.

"Patience," said Mary as they walked, "hear this poem that I learned when I was a young mother, and read again during the past winter. It was written by a godly man, George Herbert, and teaches us of this temporal life, and of the eternal life hereafter. For those who walk in the Light, death is not to be feared."

Hark, how the birds do sing, and woods do ring.
All creatures have their joy: and man hath his.
Yet if we rightly measure, Man's joy and pleasure
Rather hereafter, than in present, is.

To this life things of sense Make their pretense:
In th' other Angels have a right by birth:
Man ties them both alone, And makes them one,
With th' one hand touching heav'n, with th' other earth.

In soul he mounts and flies, In flesh he dies.
He wears a stuff whose thread is coarse and round,
But trimm'd with curious lace And should take place
After the trimming, not the stuff and ground.

Not that he may not here Taste of the cheer,
But as birds drink, and straight lift up their head,

So must he sip and think Of better drink
He may attain to, after he is dead.

But as his joys are double, So is his trouble.
He hath two winters, other things but one:
Both frosts and thoughts do nip, And bite his lip;
And he of all things fears two deaths alone.

Yet ev'n the greatest griefs May be reliefs,
Could he but take them right, and in their ways.
Happy is he, whose heart Hath found the art
To turn his double pains to double praise.

"Sister Mary," said Patience, "I can clearly see the center verse in my mind. When a bird drinks and then lifts its beak to swallow, he looks to heaven from whence the blessing came, and he gives thanks and praise."

"That's right, child. We go to Boston at the Lord's command, and we drink the cup he has offered. For you, it will be to observe and testify what you have seen. For me, that cup will be my death—but I have seen Paradise, even been there in my spirit, and that is a sweet drink, not a bitter one. In my life, I have indeed tasted of joy and love, and the sweetness and beauty God intended for our happiness. But there is no comparison to the love and the Light that we will encounter in his presence."

At about half-past six, as near as she could tell by the lengthening shadows, Mary stopped their walk, and they prepared a camp. The road had been cleared along a high bank over a river, but they'd never sleep at the side of the road, for it was too exposed to travelers, both English and Indian. They weren't far from the town of Dedham, but they didn't want to be discovered or disturbed—or delayed—from their purpose.

Mary found a circle of trees and brush, perfect for a deer's daytime hideaway, and they tied a canvas sheet over two bushes for a roof against dew or rain. They settled down to eat their supper of dried venison and Indian corn cakes.

Patience had been on this road last year, and she knew they were still about two hours' walk from Boston's gate. "There are

Friends near Dedham," she offered, "who would harbor us for the night."

"We shouldn't put them in danger, nor can I afford a delay for hospitality's sake. The Boston General Court is in session, and I must be there for the appointed time. Remember, you are not to stay with me once we reach the town. You go straight to Edward's house and keep quiet, no matter what happens. You were banished last year, and you must not be seen again. Edward will make sure you get home safe again."

"I understand." Patience was quiet for a time while they piled pine needles to form a mat under their blanket and settled down to sleep. "What religion is George Herbert? Is he a Friend?"

"He died before his poems were published, but he died in faith that joy and pleasure, being in the presence of God, would be his in Paradise. He believed that God was faithful and just to forgive his sins and cleanse him from all unrighteousness. He was a protector and supporter of the poor and the widows and orphans in his parish. Now, does his religious label matter?"

"No, I suppose not," Patience said slowly. "The scriptures say that pure religion is to help the widows and orphans. But it seems to me that war is fought in the name of religion: Catholic against Protestant, Christian against Jew or Moor, Anglican against Presbyterian and Puritan, Puritan against Friends and Baptists. And the ones who suffer most in war and persecution are the widows and orphans, for they have no defenders. Why, then, does religion matter so much to man?"

"Religion," Mary answered, "is constructed by sinful, inadequate man to create a barrier of distance between us and the holy and perfect God. It is settling for a vision of Paradise, and not claiming the whole of Paradise as the rightful heir of Christ. It is human nature to assign classes and to place strong walls around their creeds to separate themselves from those they consider corrupt or unworthy. But in a revelation to the prophet Daniel, the Lord showed himself as a boulder that would smash the iron and clay structures of nations and their religions. The Lord's coming will put an end to those divisions."

Suddenly, the entire countryside was lit like daylight, and there was a deafening crash before it went black again.

There was no rain—yet—but the lightning and thunder increased in intensity. Patience instinctively backed herself up to a tree trunk, but Mary told her sharply to lie flat under the canvas, and not touch the trees, which might be struck by lightning. Mary and Patience lay together under their shelter and held each other for warmth and comfort.

"Mary," said Patience, shivering, "how can you be so calm, with the storm raging around us, and facing the wrath of the Boston court when we arrive there in a few hours?"

Mary smiled and pulled the girl closer in her mothering embrace. "Ah, my girl, you are wise beyond your twelve years, and you have your life stretching ahead. You're a worthy successor to your aunt Anne Hutchinson's and your mother's scholarship and ministry. Here is something that Anne taught me by example, and that I've learned by experience. Let go of your fears, and don't let them control you. Instead, submit to God and embrace his adoration of you as his child, bought with a great price. Therein is great joy! I'm not afraid of the storm, for I know he has plans for me. And I'm not afraid of his plans for me, for I know that I shall have eternal life in his presence. He is love, and perfect love casts out all fear.

"You will see by contrast that the men of the Courts of Massachusetts have none of that perfect love; they are full of fear. Fear that they are not in control of their lives—which they are not!—and fear that they will be lost in the flames of hell because they can never be good enough to merit salvation. They know their sinfulness, but they don't claim the grace of forgiveness, nor the peace that follows.

"When we part in the morning, it may be in a rush, with many distractions. So no matter what we say between now and then, let these be my last words to you, the only commandment Jesus gave to his followers: '*Love one another, as I have loved you.*'"

For six hours, until about three o'clock, there was continuous lightning and thunder over coastal Massachusetts between Boston and Salem, as if the towns were being visited by the wrath of God.

May 27, 1660
Portsmouth, Rhode Island

As he sat in court proceedings for the colony business, William Dyer noticed a young man standing in the doorway, fidgeting and uncomfortably shifting from one foot to the other.

A young clerk came and tapped William on the shoulder, indicating that the business at the doorway concerned him. Leaving his documents on the table, he stepped out of the assembly chamber and spoke to the messenger. "Well? What calls me from government business?"

The messenger placed an envelope in his hands and stepped back a pace to wait for a reply.

Will opened the envelope to find a short letter from Edward Hutchinson.

CAPT WILLIAM DYER IN PORTSMOUTH
25 May 1660

My dear brother Will,

Your wife has come under arrest in Boston, and lies in the prison with others of her religion. I hear from Patience Scott that she sailed from Shelter Island, landed in Providence, and walked to Boston. She next was seen visiting at the boarded-up prison windows with the Quakers, and from thence arrested and imprisoned. I fear for her life. They won't let her go a second time. I shall do what I can, but you must come.
EDWARD HUTCHINSON

His heart hurt so that he nearly clutched at his chest. Returning to the council chamber, he gathered his papers into a folio, begged their leave to recess, and left. He stopped at a tavern and purchased a flask of rum, and carried it up to his room at the inn.

Richard Scott could have stopped Mary. He could have sent word. But he didn't. Instead, he lent his daughter for this foolish death drama. May the same grief attend upon Richard Scott as William now faced.

Will sank down onto the mattress and took a swallow of the rum. *Could she not have stopped to see me or the children? Could she not have written a letter to say goodbye? She's had six months to meditate with her friends. Six months to play the enclosed hermit or to satisfy her need to be with the Quakers. But instead of working it out of her system, she's become more firmly entrenched.*

I've loved her without reserve. I prayed to God to show me how to love her more, to get her back. But every day that passes, she's more distant, and I'm lonely. And empty.

He took another swallow of the drink, but corked it because he needed a clear head to do what he must to save Mary.

Oh, Mary, why is my love insufficient for you? How can you do such violence to me, to our love? You stop my breathing, you stop my heart, my blood riots, my tongue cleaves to my palate. And you move past me without a glance, without a word, going to your Lover's arms. You are faithless to me. And I'm a fool to drag you back.

With a heavy heart, Will sat up and forced himself to focus on another defense for Mary. There was no defense but emotion this time. She had deliberately broken a law, and would not repent of her transgression. He could only ask for undeserved mercy. The grace of God. And he knew that Endecott had none of that in him.

From his folio, he removed a large sheet of linen paper, and set his fine-tipped quill pen to the ink and then the paper.

> "Honored Sir,
>
> "It is not little grief of mind, and sadness of heart that I am necessitated to be so bold as to supplicate your honored self with the Honorable Assembly of your General Court to extend your mercy and favor once again to me and my children. Little did I dream that I should have had occasion to petition you in a matter of this nature, but so it is that through the divine providence and your benignity my son obtained so much pity and mercy at your hands as to enjoy the life of his mother, now my supplication your Honor is to beg affectionately, the life of my dear wife.
>
> "'Tis true I have not seen her above this half year and therefore cannot tell how in the frame of her spirit she was moved thus again to run so great a hazard to herself,

and perplexity to me and mine and all her friends and well wishers.

"So it is from Shelter Island about by Pequid Narragansett and to the Town of Providence she secretly and speedily journeyed, and as secretly from thence came to your jurisdiction."

Here, William pressed his pen boldly, and laid the ink more thickly on the page, thinking of his friend of more than twenty years, Richard Scott.

"Unhappy journey, may I say, and woe to that generation, say I, that gives occasion thus of grief and trouble (to those that desire to be quiet) by helping one another (as I may say) to hazard their lives for I know not what end, or to what purpose.

"If her zeal be so great as thus to adventure, oh let your favor and pity surmount it and save her life. Let not your forewanted compassion be conquered by her inconsiderate madness, and how greatly will your renown be spread if by so conquering you become victorious.

"What shall I say more, I know you are all sensible of my condition, and let the reflect be, and you will see what my petition is and what will give me and mine peace.

"Oh, let Mercy's wings once more soar above Justice's balance, and then whilst I live shall I exalt your goodness—but other ways 'twill be a languishing sorrow, yea, so great that I should gladly suffer the blow at once much rather.

"I shall forebear to trouble your Honor with words, neither am I in capacity to expatiate myself at present; I only say that yourselves have been, and are, or may be husbands to wife or wives, so am I. Yea, to one most dearly beloved. Oh, do not you deprive me of her, but I pray give her me once again and I shall be so much obliged forever, that I shall endeavor continually to utter my thanks and render you Love and Honor most renowned. Pity me, I beg it with tears, and rest you

most humbly suppliant

W. Dyer

Portsmouth 27 of May 1660

Most honored sirs, let these lines by your favor be my Petition to your Honorable General Court at present sitting.

W.D."

It galled him to submit to those devils at Boston, but to be heard and heeded, he must write in courtly language. The letter was William's last arrow in the quiver. The bloody-mad Endecott wouldn't find mercy and justice if it were borne to him in the angel Gabriel's hands. Mary would not accept her husband's rescue attempt even if he carried it there personally, and when she was executed, he could not stand in the jeering crowd to watch. No, he must remain here for their children's sake. And his own sanity's sake.

For Mary had left him, and her children, for another. She did not want him there. He would, with broken heart, allow her that dying wish.

He enclosed the letter. He drank some rum. And he wept for his most dearly beloved dead.

May 31, 1660

Boston, Massachusetts

Mary opened her eyes after several hours of exhausted sleep interrupted by vivid dreams. One didn't sleep well in a prison, being mindful of rats and vermin, the permanent chill, and the lack of a bed and pillows. She knew that her days and even hours were limited, and sleeping to preserve her health and strength was unnecessary.

She'd been confined in the prison for ten days and eleven nights, having been arrested immediately on her entrance to Boston and deliberate appearance at the prison gate. Meanwhile, the General Court was meeting for its annual elections (John Endecott was returned as governor), superior court deliberations, and legislation.

Rhode Island and the other colonies were doing the same, as required by their charters. William would be in session in Portsmouth.

It was early, and the dawn light did not penetrate her cell. She sensed the hour by the barking of a dog and the crow of a rooster in that very normal world outside her boarded window.

She had dreamed disjointed scenes, not a story. In one dream she had seen her old friend Sir Henry Vane, reuniting with Lady Francis and the children after his release from prison. But Mary knew that his freedom, and his life, were only temporarily reprieved.

In another dream, she had seen her beautiful friend, Anne Hutchinson, on trial at Cambridge. Mary hadn't attended that trial, but Anne had told her of it.

And she'd seen her husband and children, on a carefree day of sailing on Narragansett Bay. That one was perhaps the greatest temptation to recant her actions now, because it wrung her heart dry to see their innocent faces. With effort, she put that memory aside and thought about what would happen today. And then she sought the Lord in prayer, as was her custom.

In prayer, in that quiet communion with God, there was no prison or dark. It was light everywhere. She sensed that every being in that place seemed to glow as if lit from within, but not like candle light—they glowed with love. Whether they were souls, or angels, she didn't know. It was indescribable because such a thing could not exist on earth.

With the greatest difficulty, she returned to her world. The light faded slowly, until she was again conscious of her prison cell and the two strips of morning sunlight that came through the boards over her window.

Jailer Salter clattered his way through the women's cells, overseeing his servant, who was carrying the buckets of water and a sack of bread heels to the cells containing prisoners of the General Court.

His skeletal face leered at Mary in the gloom. "You're to appear at the court this morning, so be sure to wear your nicest vestment." He laughed loudly at his own joke that prisoners had only the clothes on their backs because he sold their belongings to pay for their keep. He poked the servant with his baton and moved on.

Mary used a bit of her water ration to wet her face, and she dried it with the underside of her overskirt, a part that wasn't too soiled from her walk from Providence and then nine days in prison. She gnawed at the hard bread not because she was hungry, but because she knew she'd need some strength to meet the General Court today.

The marshal, Edward Michaelson, arrived with the warrant from Rawson, and she stood quietly while he tied her hands, and took the long end of the rope to lead her like a horse or cow. A small group of tradesmen and servants who were about the area on business observed the transfer, and followed the pair, talking in hushed voices.

Among the cases on this day's agenda were the organization of the town of Marlborough and another called Stony River, cutting back militia training days from six per year to four, and defining a freeman: the court declared that "no man whatsoever shall be admitted to the freedom of this body politic but such as are members of some church of Christ and in full communion, which they declare to be the true intent of the ancient law."

Again, thought Mary, the church ultimately governs the state by amassing its power with voters "owned" by the ministers like Norton and Wilson, who held eternal life and death in their hands.

They waited outside. Neither the marshal nor Mary said a word, but Mary's heart was at peace. She gazed around the familiar town with interest. There was the familiar flutter inside, as if a babe somersaulted in her womb, and she heard the voice, not quite audible, but clear and strong, in her body: *"They will deliver you up to the councils, and they will scourge you; and ye shall be brought before governors and kings for my sake. But when they deliver you up, take no thought how or what ye shall speak: for it shall be given you in that same hour what ye shall speak. For it is not ye that speak, but the Spirit of your Father which speaketh in you."*

Finally, her case came up on the agenda, and she was escorted through the chamber. She stood below the bench on the same raised platform as she had last October. John Endecott, as governor, sat in the middle. There were several rows on each side of the room, where the magistrates, ministers, and elected freemen sat. She knew by English law there should have been a jury of twelve men deciding her case, but when had Massachusetts Bay operated by established law? Instead, it was the entire assembly. Just as in England, she had no defense but her own testimony, and it was her own responsibility to prove her innocence if she expected acquittal or mercy.

But that was not Mary's desire. She was there to be noticed and remarked upon. She prayed that some of the freemen here today would see and hear, and be convicted in their consciences, and the Light would gain entrance in all the communities of Massachusetts Bay.

Endecott looked pointedly at the rope that bound her hands. "Are you the same Mary Dyer that was here before, who rebelliously after sentence of death passed against you, returned into this jurisdiction?"

He knew the answer, of course. He recognized her from last autumn, and remembered her as Anne Hutchinson's accomplice in heresy in 1637. Not to mention that uncomfortable visit from William Dyer three years before. The William Dyer whose letter had arrived this very morn by messenger.

She replied, "I am the same Mary Dyer that was here at the last General Court."

He asked if she considered herself to be a Quaker.

Like Jesus at his trial, when he was asked if he were a king, she replied, "This is what *you* reproachfully call me." And it was not lost on the ministers and magistrates of the New Jerusalem, the City Upon a Hill. They were the new Sanhedrin.

The governor glanced uneasily at his deputy, Richard Bellingham, Simon Bradstreet, and the other members of the court, then spoke. "The doctrine of this sect of people tends to overthrow the whole gospel and the very vitals of Christianity."

He turned to face Mary. "Why should not your former sentence of death be executed upon you?"

"I deny your law. I came to bear witness against it and could not choose but to come and do as formerly," she answered.

"I must then repeat the sentence pronounced upon you. You must return to the prison, and there remain until tomorrow at nine o'clock. Then from there you must go to the gallows, and there be hanged till you are dead."

"This is no more than you've said before." Like the last time they sent her to the gallows and then pulled back.

"But now it is to be executed; therefore, prepare yourself for nine o'clock tomorrow."

Mary spoke more boldly this time. "I came in obedience to the will of God, to the last General Court, praying you to repeal your unrighteous sentence of banishment on pain of death; and that is my same work now, and earnest request, although I told you, that if you refused to repeal them, the Lord would send others of his servants to witness against them."

Endecott taunted Mary. "Are you a prophetess?"

"I spoke the words which the Lord spoke to me, and now the thing has come to pass, just as it did for Anne Hutchinson, so cruelly persecuted by this very Court more than twenty years ago."

Mary didn't believe in ghosts, for souls went to heaven or hell when they were judged by God. But she felt a presence with her now; perhaps it was an angel of God.

Her eyes flashed fire at the men who had been responsible for the deaths of her friends, and whipped the Southwicks nearly to death, rained blows on Herod Gardner and her tiny baby, beat William Brend to pulp, and sliced the ears from Christopher Holder and others. Surely the Sanhedrin, the Jewish council of the Pharisees, priests, and scribes, had never been as bloody.

"That good woman said then, 'Therefore, take heed how you proceed against me. For you have no power over my body. Neither can you do me any harm, for I am in the hands of the eternal Jehovah my Savior, I am at his appointment. The bounds of my habitation are cast in Heaven. No further do I esteem of any mortal man than creatures in His hand, I fear none but the great Jehovah, which hath foretold me of these things, and I do verily believe that He will deliver me out of your hands. Therefore take heed how you proceed against me; for I know that for this you are about to do to me, God will ruin you and your posterity, and this whole state.'"

Endecott was shaking with rage at this witch, this bride of Satan. "Away with her!" he cried, with a wave of the hand which glittered with his signet ring, the skull and crossbones.

"The said Mary Dyer, for her rebelliously returning into this jurisdiction (notwithstanding the favor of this court towards her), shall be by the Marshall General on the first day of June, about nine of the clock in the morning, carried to the place of execution and according to the sentence of the General Court in October last, be put to death. That the Secretary Mr. Rawson issue out warrant accordingly, which sentence the Governor declared to her in open court. Also, warrant issued accordingly to Edward Michaelson, Marshal General, and to Captain James Oliver and his order as formerly."

Marshal Michaelson picked up the end of Mary's rope, and she followed him out of the courtroom to the porch. He had several armed men there to escort her back to the prison. "For your protection, Mrs. Dyer," he explained.

There was a crowd of curious men and women, some of them hoping for a spectacle of a public whipping or abusing a prisoner in the stocks. Rather than look in the faces of people eager to see her shame—of which she had none—Mary looked up to the clear blue sky as she walked in the middle of the cluster of guards. In the bright southern sky, she could just make out the slim crescent of the last-quarter moon.

After the moon had set and the sun was low in the sky that evening so near the summer solstice, Mary was allowed a visitor, and she was brought into the jailer's office.

Edward Hutchinson stood there, holding a paper in his hands that he rolled and unrolled. "We are watched," he said in a low voice. "But as an attorney, I have permission to see you. How do you fare?"

"Well enough, my friend. And on the morrow, I shall enter Paradise, of which I have had glimpses already."

"You know how it is with your husband, who is distraught. Have you heard his latest letter to the General Court? I've brought a copy."

"No. And I don't want to read it. It would only serve to make me miss him more—or make me resentful. Have you spoken to him recently? Have you seen Marie and the boys?"

"Not recently, no. Will and I have exchanged letters. Samuel is building his mercantile in Kingston, south of Providence, and after they marry, he and Anne will move there."

Mary's face softened. "May I tell you a secret I've held since your mother told it to me?"

A shadow fell across his face for a moment. Mary was one of the few people who had known and loved his mother. And Mary would be no more, after tomorrow. But he nodded agreement.

"The day I felt Samuel quicken within me, your mother foretold that he would marry her granddaughter, and that they would have seven children. I've always considered your little Anne as my daughter."

The two were constrained by the circumstances and the watchful Jailer Salter, and fell silent. When Salter shifted impatiently in his chair, Edward spoke sorrowfully: "Do you need anything? Food, or blankets? Shall I bear a message to Will?"

Mary stood taller. "No, my brother. I have no needs now." She smiled. "You may become known as a Quaker sympathizer, Ed, by helping your Aunt Kathy, your nieces, and me."

"You leave me no choice," he said gruffly. "Between my loyalties to family and my own conscience, I cannot be silent, even if I choose not to convert to your beliefs. There is too much of my parents in me to turn my back on the truth."

"Yes. I see now that though you could have stayed in Newport, the Lord led you back to a difficult situation in Boston. To bring succor to the Friends in prison and under persecution. For such a time as this."

Edward had had his eyes on the floor, but he looked up suddenly. There was something about her tone, something about her face, that reminded him of his mother.

Mary continued, "As for a message. You may tell William that I've always loved him, and I love him still; I expect him to find a new mother for our children, and live a long and productive life. He should not blame God for this, but embrace the Light and submit to the love. I will be there in the midst of it."

Some small part of her wanted Edward to stand in for her husband and take her in his sheltering arms for comfort and peace and strength, but with Salter there to twist the truth and report it to the court, they remained apart. Finally, she turned away and walked back through the prison door.

June 1, 1660
Boston, Massachusetts

Mary spent the night in prayer and silent communion. Her companion was Margaret Smith of Salem, who had spent many months in both Salem and Boston prisons for being in the presence of other Friends when they were arrested. Like Mary, she hadn't preached. There were no charges, but to satisfy the zeal of Endecott and the ministers Norton and Wilson, the mother of young children had been whipped ten stripes in the open marketplace, when the snow drifted against the buildings and fell on her bare skin, wetting her as the flakes melted. The whipper, in his haste to finish the job and go someplace warmer, had ripped her clothes as he bared her back and breasts. People in the crowd had laughed and urged him to go ahead and tear the rest of her clothes off. She'd been returned to the jail soaking wet and bleeding from the three-stranded, knotted lash.

"Mary, if you have second thoughts," said Margaret in the morning, "you can still avoid the gallows and live to testify of the Seed in another place."

"No, my sister," Mary said calmly. "I am here to obey the Lord's command, and having had no other word, I will walk into the Light. I prefer his glorious presence to this dark world, and he will raise up more servants to bring in the harvest. It may be that my notoriety as the mother of a monster, a heretic, a 'cursed Quaker,' and the respectable wife of an important government servant will bring an end to Endecott's beastly war on the saints."

She fell silent for a few moments. "Years ago, Endecott, John Winthrop, John Wilson, and many others wanted to build their Zion here, with the Old Testament as the law. They wanted to hasten the coming of the Lord by proving to him that they were worthy of salvation. But behold, they have instead become the beast of Revelation, pursuing the church, the bride of Christ, into the wilderness. Margaret, remember: we will overcome them by the blood of the Lamb, and by the word of our testimony; because we loved not our lives to shrink from death."

She remembered again the vision she'd had many years ago, a vision of her execution in which she felt no fear, only a strange exaltation, and the knowledge that of all the countless people in this world, at this moment *she* was chosen by the King of kings to be his maidservant, to bring about laws protecting liberty of conscience, and "to proclaim liberty to the captives, and the opening of the prison to them that are bound."

In the prison yard outside the boarded window, they heard the militia arrive with a clatter of boots and weapons. Marshal Michaelson strode into the prison and came to Mary's door, which Jailer Salter unlocked.

"Let us go, Mrs. Dyer, to your appointed place."

"But sir, it is not yet nine o'clock. Stay a little, and I shall be ready presently."

"I cannot wait upon you. You should now wait upon me. My orders are to bring you to the place of execution by nine o'clock, and that means we must leave now."

Margaret was incensed to see such hard-hearted treatment of her friend. "We have not finished our farewells, because you are too early. You should be ashamed to take an innocent woman to her death by obeying the unjust laws and proceedings of Massachusetts."

"Mrs. Smith," said Michaelson, "you shall have your share of the same. Stand away."

He took the rope and looped it in a figure eight about Mary's wrists, and held the long end in his hands. They walked out through Salter's office and into the morning sunshine.

As she had been last October, Mary was surrounded by a troop of more than a hundred musketeers and pikemen who were there to protect the officials of the court from the angry mob. Captain Oliver was the officer in charge of the guard today.

Word had spread quickly overnight, and this day thousands of men, women, and children were spread out along the streets as if for a parade. Others waited at the gallows for the spectacle to come to them. Should she attempt to speak, before and behind her, military men beat the slow execution drum call to drown out the sound of her voice.

Brrr-tap-tap-rest. Brrr-tap-tap-rest. Brrr-tap-tap-rest. Brrr-tap-tap-rest.

The monotonous, repetitive beat set the pace for the walk along Tremont Road, part of the Common, and finally, to the fortification and gate of the city of Boston. Then they were out on the isthmus, or Boston Neck, where the road led to Roxbury. Hundreds more people surged up from the towns of Roxbury and Weymouth.

Mary remembered that the last execution here had been a chilly autumn day, appropriate, perhaps, for the murder of the two dear young men. Today, though, was a day at the height of spring, with daisies on the Common turning their faces toward the sun, and dandelion seed puffs drifting on the breeze from the bay.

It was just such a day, exactly twenty-two years ago, that the great earthquake had rumbled across New England, and the little group of people praying with Anne Hutchinson had felt the Pentecostal filling of the Holy Spirit.

And thirty years ago this day, Mary remembered seeing the noon-day comet that marked the birth of the future King Charles the Second, and presaged war, famine, and plague. What was it that John Donne had preached at St. Paul's? That

> "all mankind is of one author, and is one volume; when one man dies, one chapter is not torn out of the book, but translated into a better language; God's hand is in every translation, and his hand shall bind up all our scattered leaves again, for that library where every book shall lie open to one another."

Like all memories, these flashed through Mary's mind in still pictures, like landscape paintings. One could view the scene all at once, or stop and decipher the symbolism. She had lived them and learned from them, but were they connected with today?

She and the guard and drummers, and all of Boston behind them, arrived at the gallows. Michaelson ceremoniously handed the end of her tether to Edward Wanton, the man at the foot of the gallows.

Mary climbed the ladder, the drumbeat ended, and she stood ready.

The crowds of men and women, packed shoulder to shoulder on the slim neck of land, jostled one another and a few on the edges of the marsh actually trod in the mud.

"Mistress Dyer," a man shouted over the din of the people, "if you'd only leave this colony, you might come down and save your life!"

As beautiful as this world is, and as much as I love my life with family, friends, health, and prosperity, what does it avail? How does it compare to the Paradise I've already glimpsed? If my momentary death can shine Light on the human right to worship and obey God, then let it be. I shall be with the Lord.

She answered, projecting her voice while she motioned for silence, "No, I cannot, for in obedience to the will of the Lord I came, and in his will I abide faithful—to the death."

The man in charge of her execution was Captain John Evered-Webb. She recognized him from 1635, when he and his shipmates had been caught in the great hurricane as they approached Massachusetts, but miraculously avoided shipwreck and limped in with broken masts and mere rags of sails. He and his sister and her husband had settled near Salem, and that made Webb one of Endecott's men.

He stood on the platform and shouted to be heard. "The condemned woman has been here before, here on this very gallows. She had the sentence of banishment on pain of death, but she has come again now and broken the law. Therefore she is guilty of her own blood. The executioner shall not ask her forgiveness as would be customary."

The masked hangman bowed as if he were an actor.

At this insult, some in the crowd grumbled at Webb's lack of godly grace. The angry murmur spread through the crowd like a wave as the nearest told their neighbors behind them what they'd heard.

Mary answered, looking pointedly at Reverend Wilson, Major-General Humphrey Atherton (an assistant to the governor), and others of her accusers, "No, I came to keep blood guiltiness from you, desiring you to repeal the *unrighteous* and *unjust* law of banishment upon pain of death, made against the *innocent* servants of the Lord. Therefore my blood *will* be required at your hands, who willfully do it; but for those that do it in the simplicity of their hearts, I desire the Lord to forgive them."

She raised her voice to a victorious shout. "I came to do the will of my Father, and in obedience to his will, I stand even to death!"

"'Tis wrong to murder this innocent woman! Take her down! Let her go home!" came the shouts from every direction.

Edward Wanton tied Mary's legs together with the rope over her skirts for modesty when she'd be dropped.

John Wilson, the man who had examined Mary and William for church membership, and baptized her baby Samuel nearly a quarter-century before, put on a dramatic act for the audience, far larger than any Sunday congregation he'd ever preached to. He added a sob to his voice: "Mary Dyer, O repent! O repent! And be not so deluded, and carried away by the deceit of the devil."

It was difficult to control her facial expression at this hypocritical display of concern for her soul, but Mary answered, "No, man, I am not now to repent."

One of the ministers asked if she would have the elders pray for her soul, if she would not pray for herself. They meant an appointed elder of the First Church of Christ in Boston.

She said, "I do not know of a single elder here." She meant she didn't recognize their elders as having authority over her. As Anne Hutchinson had rejected the authority of that body over her.

"Would you have *any* of the people to pray for you?"

"I desire the prayers of all the people of God." As she looked over the crowd, she recognized Friends, including Robert and Deborah Harper of Sandwich. She knew they kept her in prayer continually, and being encouraged, she felt warmth and strength fill her.

A scoffer from the church cried out, "It may be she thinks there is none here!"

Mary replied softly, "I know that there are only a few here."

The Light became brighter now, Mary thought. She was closer to heaven than she'd ever been.

Another from the crowd below her urged, "Woman, you're about to die, and a heretic at that. Don't throw away your soul. Ask for an elder to pray, that his effectual, fervent prayer will be heard by God."

Mary answered, "No, first a child, then a young man, then a strong man, before an 'elder' in your Church of Christ."

"What?" called the critic. "You said 'an elder in Christ Jesus?' You don't want a Christian man to pray for you? If not an elder in Christ Jesus, you prefer to go, then, with your master the Devil?"

She said, "It is false, it is false; I never spoke those words. I said an elder in the church."

"Are you not afraid to die, knowing that you are a cursed Quaker? A heretic?" said the minister Norton.

"The Lord has said to me, as to all who come to him in repentance and humility, 'Today shalt thou be with me in Paradise.'"

"You and the dead Quakers said last time that you *have* been in Paradise."

"Yes, I have been in Paradise several days," she said with a blissful smile.

John Wilson, who had a look of fear on his face now, produced a handkerchief from his coat, and young Wanton draped it over Mary's face and tucked it under the rope before than hangman made it snug.

She remembered what Sir Harry Vane had said, "Death does not bring us into darkness, but takes darkness out of us, us out of darkness, and puts us into marvelous light."

As she spoke further of the eternal happiness into which she was now to enter, Mary felt that familiar buoyancy of light and love, as if she were being borne away by angels.

"Mary."

"Yes, Lord?"

*****

TO WILLIAM DYER AT PORTSMOUTH
1 June 1660

My brother, it is with heavy heart that I relay to you the things said and done this day. I shall tell you more details when we meet, if you can bear to hear them, and if you have not already heard from other witnesses.

I visited your wife the evening before—I can hardly bear to say her death—and she told me to assure you that she had always loved you, that you should carry on, and that she would be surrounded by the Light of God. I do believe that is the truth.

She mounted the ladder and stood ready, calmly answering the taunts of the people and of Reverend Wilson, saying that she was obeying the Lord's command, and she was already in Paradise. Indeed, there was a look of rapture on Mary's face that I saw on my mother's face when God revealed his will to her. There seemed to have been a radiance like a halo in a painting, but it could have been my imagination and grief.

Perhaps I did not imagine it alone. Instead of using the executioner's hood, Reverend Wilson was quick to produce his own handkerchief to cover Mary's face. She appeared to glow with a supernatural light. I was reminded of Moses coming down from Mt. Sinai, his countenance glowing from the reflected glory of God, and they veiled his face as the light faded away.

When Mary was turned off, there was no struggle, and surely she felt no pain. I believe that she had already left us, William, and as she said, walked into Paradise.

The righteous perish and the merciful are taken away, and no man takes notice that God is taking them away from the evil to come. But they now rest in peace.

After it was done, Mr. Atherton scoffed, "She hangs there as a flag for others to take example by." Though he is a miserable man, he may be a prophet, for if I know you and Roger Williams and John Clarke, Mary's witness and martyrdom will be an ensign for religious freedom in both America and the Commonwealth.

You know what usually happens with the bodies of the condemned, but I took advantage of Endecott's fear of you, Johnny Winthrop, and Governor Temple, and I took legal possession of your Mary, saying that it would be best that she not become an object of pilgrimage for Quakers or other malcontents. She will be returned to you for burial as soon as possible. She will not go down to the pit, nor under the grazing Common. I hope, dear brother, that this will be a comfort to you and your children.

There were many times, William, that I observed you with your wife, and saw a full measure of godly love and pride in your eyes. I say this before God: you can be proud of Mary in her last days and hours.

Until I see you again in a few days, I remain your brother from the shire,
EDWARD HUTCHINSON

*****

EPILOGUE

This timeline of events will tie off storylines and characters of the novel. Author's Notes follow the Epilogue.

1660

From **George Fox's** journal in 1661: ...we received account from New England that the government there had made a law to banish the Quakers out of their colonies, upon pain of death in case they returned; that several of our Friends [William Robinson and Marmaduke Stephenson], having been so banished and returning, were thereupon taken and actually hanged, and that diverse more [Mary Dyer] were in prison, in danger of the like sentence being executed upon them. When those were put to death I was in prison at Lancaster [in 1659-60], and *had a perfect sense of their sufferings as though it had been myself, and as though the halter had been put about my own neck,* though we had not at that time heard of it.

> http://www.ushistory.org/penn/margaret_fell.htm 1659: Two weeks after the restoration of Charles II, soldiers appear at Swarthmoor and arrest George Fox on charges of treason. Fox is imprisoned at Lancaster Castle dungeon for 20 weeks [5 months]. Margaret Fell left Swarthmoor in the **summer of 1660** to visit the King and secure Fox's release accompanied by fellow-Friend Anne Curtis (whose father was executed for Royalist sympathies during Cromwell's time). They secure Fox's removal from jail to London to answer the charges there. Full liberty was then ordered for Fox by the King.

Edward Wanton, the militia man on duty at Mary Dyer's execution, became a Quaker before 1661. He went home and said, "Alas, Mother! We have been murdering the Lord's people," and taking off his sword, put it by, with a solemn vow never to wear it again. Within two years, he was arrested for holding a Friends Meeting in his home in Boston. His descendants helped form Rhode Island policy.

William Dyer Sr. of Newport challenged John Porter as to "ye proporiety of our lands and libarties of ye people." Author Jo Ann Butler wrote: On May 28, 1660 the town of Portsmouth, Rhode Island votes "that a challenge from Mr. William Dyer of Newport to Mr. John Porter of Portsmouth about ye propriety of our lands and liberties of ye people within the jurisdiction of Providence Plantations be publicly read in the assembly, to be answered with writing." Mr. John Porter accepts of it and is resolved to answer it in writing." Porter's response was read at

Portsmouth on June 4, but the records don't say what the challenge was about. –PUBLICATIONS OF THE RHODE ISLAND HISTORICAL SOCIETY NEW SERIES Vol. V January 1898 No. 4, Whole Number, 20

Sir Henry Vane was expelled from office and banished from London in January 1660. He was then imprisoned in Tower of London after Restoration. He petitioned for his life, and permission was granted.

Spymaster **John Thurloe** was accused of treason and arrested in May 1660, when Charles II was restored to the throne. He was released in June. Thurloe died in February 1668 at his chambers in Lincoln's Inn, London. His state papers, hidden in a false ceiling at his chambers, weren't discovered for 30 years. Now they're freely available online.

King Charles II was greeted with joy in the streets as he made his triumphant royal entry into London on 29 May 1660. It was planned to coincide with his 30th birthday and the 1630 comet.

In the fall of 1660, **Samuel Dyer** married **Anne Hutchinson II**, daughter of **Edward**, granddaughter of Anne Marbury Hutchinson. They lived in Kingston, Rhode Island, and had seven children.

Roger Williams said in a letter of September 8, 1660 to **Governor John Winthrop Jr.,** of Connecticut: "What whipping at Boston could not do, conversation with friends in England and their arguments have in great measure drawn her [**Katherine Scott**] from the Quakers and wholly from their meetings." **Richard Scott** remained a Quaker.

Isaac Robinson, son of the late Separatist pastor John Robinson who was minister of the Pilgrims before 1620, was disfranchised in Plymouth Colony for advocating a policy of moderation to the Quakers.

October 16, 1660. Did Mary Dyer have a legal trial by a jury of twelve men? Apparently not. This law plugs a hole after the fact, as so many of Boston's laws did. From Boston court records: "For explication of the law or laws referring to the manner of trial of such persons as are found in this jurisdiction after banishment on pain of death, this [Massachusetts Bay] Court doth judge meete to declare that when any person or persons banished on pain of death shall, after the expiration of their time limited for departure, be found within the limits of this jurisdiction, all Magistrates, Commissioners, Constables and other officers of this jurisdiction, do use their best endeavors for their apprehension and conveying to safe custody, and being there secured, such person or persons shall at the next Court of assistance [sic], whether in ordinary or specially called, according to direction of the law for calling of such Courts**, have a legal trial by a jury of twelve men**, and being found by evidence of their own confession to be the person or persons formerly sentenced to banishment on pain of death, shall accordingly be sentenced to death and executed by warrant from the Governor or Deputy Governor, directed to the Marshal General Edward Michaelson, unless they be regularly reprieved in the meantime."

On **October 18, 1660**, the General Court of Commissioners met at Warwick, Rhode Island, with 24 members present. A letter was read from Dr. John Clarke, telling of the Restoration, and a copy of the letter of King Charles to the House of Commons, with his declaration and proclamation. The Rhode Island commissioners ordered that King Charles the Second should be proclaimed on October 19, at eight o'clock in the morning, in the presence of the Court, and the officers and company of the train band of the town of Warwick. It was also ordered that on Wednesday next, each town in the Colony shall at the head of the Company of each train band, solemnize the proclamation of the Royal Majesty, "if the weather doe permitt; if not, it is to be done the next fayre day, and that all children and servants shall have their Libertie for that day."

When the Massachusetts freemen complained of the vicious laws and executions of the General Court, the executives wrote *The humble Petition and Addresse of the General Court at* Boston *in* New-England, defending their actions and motives in the deaths of Robinson, Stephenson, and Mary Dyer, and had it sent to London to King Charles II.

Edward Burrough, a 27-year-old Quaker minister living in London, wrote a response that was successful in stopping the capital punishment of Quakers in New England. Burrough characterized the Boston pamphlet as "divers Calumnies, unjust Reproaches, palpable untruths, and malicious slanders, against an Innocent People, whom they scornfully call Quakers, whom, for the Name of Christ's sake, are made a Reproach through the world, and by these Petitioners, have been persecuted unto Banishment, and Death."

The restoration of **Charles II** was celebrated on the Brenton estate in Newport. A bonfire was lit at the Lime Rocks, Brenton's Cove, and Cromwell in effigy, threatened by Satan with a spear, was carried by a crowd with kettledrums, handbells, and fifes, while someone declaimed—

"Old Cromwell! man! your time is come,
We tell it here with fife and drum;
And Satan's hand is on your head.
He's come for you before you're dead,
And on his spear he'll throw you in
The very worst place that ever was seen,

For good King Charles is on his throne,
And Parliament now you'll let alone."

However, the restoration of King Charles II was *not* pronounced in Massachusetts Bay, according to historian Thomas Hutchinson (**Anne Hutchinson's** great-great grandson through her son **Edward Hutchinson**), because there had been such great upheaval in England between the death of the Protectors Oliver and abdication of his son Richard Cromwell, and temporary rule by the Council of State, that Boston's leaders (Gov. Endecott, deputy Gov. Bellingham, et al) were afraid to write an address or position statement to the new king, only to have him overturned and they'd be left hanging in the wind, showing their partisan colors.

James Nayler, the volatile, fanatical Quaker preacher who had been severely punished for his Messianic ride into Bristol in 1656, was released from hard labor in prison in 1659, physically broken. He reconciled with George Fox, and in 1660 was robbed and left for dead. He was rescued and left a touching deathbed testimony before passing away in October. Nayler was 42.

John Taylor, Quaker missionary from York, continued his Atlantic crossings for years, preaching the Quaker message in southern New England, the West Indies, England, and Ireland on his trading trips before settling down with his wife. He died in 1709 at age 70, in his native shire.

"In 1660, occurred an eruption of Vesuvius, and of a volcano in Iceland. The year was very tempestuous, and **earthquakes shook England, France, and America**. In 1661 appeared a comet." *~The British Critic and Quarterly Theological Review, Volume 16*

1661

William Dyer married a woman named Catherine probably in winter (7-10 months after Mary's death), their baby Elizabeth Dyer was born in same year.

William Dyer was member of General Court.

Son **Henry Dyer,** age 14, old enough to begin apprenticeship or farming (probably farming, because he had a tobacco house on Dyer lands).

Henry Vane taken back into custody. Imprisoned in Scilly Isles off Cornwall.

William Leddra, last Quaker hanged in Boston, in March. Was given choice to return to England, refused, saying he had no business there.

Edward Burrough, a Quaker preacher in England, takes eyewitness reports of the executions of Robinson and Stephenson, and of Mary Dyer, and writes a pamphlet about Quaker persecution to the sympathetic King Charles II, newly restored to the throne. He presents it to the king in about January 1660. Charles II sends an order to John Endecott at Boston:

> CHARLES R.
>
> Trusty and well-beloved, we greet you well, Having been informed, that several of our subjects among you, called Quakers, have been and are imprisoned by you, whereof some have been executed, and others (as has been represented unto us) are in danger to undergo the like; we have thought fit to signify our pleasure in that behalf for the future; and do hereby require, that if there be any of those people called Quakers, among you, now already condemned to suffer death, or other corporal punishment; or that are imprisoned, and obnoxious to the like condemnation, **you are to cease to proceed any further therein**; but that you immediately send the said persons (whether condemned or imprisoned) over into their own kingdom of England, together with their respective crimes or offences laid to their charge; to the end such course may be taken with them here, as shall be agreeable to our laws and their demerits. And for so doing, these our letters shall be your sufficient warrant and discharge.
>
> Given at our Court, at Whitehall, the 9th day of September, 1661, in the 13th year of our reign.
>
> To our trusty and well-beloved **John Endicott**, Esq., and to all and every other the governor or governors of our plantations of New England, and of all the colonies thereunto belonging, that now are, or hereafter shall be; and to all and every the ministers and officers of our plantations and colonies whatsoever, within the continent of New England.
>
> By his Majesty's command,
>
> WILLIAM MORRIS [Secretary of State]

Of the receipt of this mandamus by the Governor, George Fox in his Journal gives the following account. The commander of the vessel, Ralph Goldsmith, and Samuel Shattuck, a Quaker who had been banished from the Massachusetts Colony, "went through the town (Boston) to the Governour's John Endecott's door and knocked. He sent out a man to know their business. They sent him word their business was from the King of England, and they should deliver their message to none but the governour himself. Thereupon they were admitted in, and the governour came to them; and having received the deputation and the Mandamus, he putt off his hat and looked upon them. Then going out he bid the [Quaker] Friends follow. He went to the Deputy Governour

[Bellingham], and after a short consultation, came out to the friends, and said, "We shall obey his majesty's commands."

When Charles II was restored to the monarchy, the regicides who executed his father, Charles I, fled to Massachusetts and were welcomed at first by prominent members of the Massachusetts Bay Court. When it appeared that Charles II was securely on the throne and would not be overturned, Massachusetts thought it would be better for Endecott, Bellingham, Bradstreet, and other prominent Bay politicians, if the regicides would flee to Rev. Davenport's protection at the colony of New Haven. They protested ignorance of the regicides' whereabouts, and finally acknowledged the king's authority.

In August 1661, they could delay no longer. "Forasmuch as Charles the second is undoubted King of Great-Britain and all other his Majesty's territories and dominions thereunto belonging, and hath been some time since lawfully proclaimed and crowned accordingly; We therefore do, as in duty we are bound, own and acknowledge him to be our Sovereign Lord and King, and do therefore hereby proclaim and declare his sacred Majesty Charles the second, to be lawful King of Great-Britain, France and Ireland, and all other the territories thereunto belonging. God save the King."

1662

William Dyer member of General Court of Rhode Island.

A new charter combines the colonies of New Haven and Connecticut into an officially recognized colony of Connecticut.

Henry Vane returned to prison at Tower of London in April. On June 2, he was convicted of high treason in rigged trial. On June 14, Henry Vane was beheaded at the Tower. Trumpets drowned out his speech. Samuel Pepys said Henry "died justifying himself and the cause he had stood for; and spoke very confidently of his being presently at the right hand of Christ; and in all things appeared the most resolved man that ever died in that manner, and showed more of heat than cowardize, but yet with all humility and gravity." High treason conviction could end in hanging, drawing, and quartering, so beheading was a quick death.

Anne Burden (now Richardson), who had been imprisoned at Boston with Mary Dyer in 1657, returned to New England as a Quaker missionary. In December 1663, she wrote to George Fox from "Kittery Eastward in New England," situated between the Atlantic Ocean and the Piscataqua River just north of the New Hampshire border. She appears to have ministered in Maine and northern Massachusetts for several months, and for a time, to have been joined by Elizabeth Hooton and

Jane Nicholson (Jane was in Boston prison at the time Mary Dyer was executed).

1663

Rev. Samuel Stone died in Hartford on 20th July 1663, aged 61. There had recently been witch trials at Hartford.

With no evidence, only informed speculation, I believe **William Dyer** went to England to participate in the granting of the royal charter to Rhode Island. This is the charter that **Dr. John Clarke** had labored for, for more than ten years. There are provisions that William probably insisted upon, including rights of free passage in other colonies (because Mary had been forbidden entry to the other colonies). Notice that other First Founders of Rhode Island are mentioned in the list on the charter, but Richard Scott's name is missing. I suspect that William gave the list to Clarke. Was Richard Scott left out because William was still angry about Richard sending Mary on to Boston in May 1660? Benedict Arnold's name was the first in the list of charter members of this great title of freedom, with Brenton, Coddington, Easton, Baulston, Porter, Smith, Gorton, Weeks, Williams, Olney, Dexter, Coggeshall, Clarke, Holden, Greene, Roome, Wildbore, Field, Barker, Tew, Harris, and Dyer. William Dyer's name being last suggests that he was the one who provided the list of names. This charter was an inspiration and guide to the Declaration of Independence and to the State Constitutions of every Commonwealth in the American Republic.

1664

William Dyer member of General Court 1664-66. Lost suit against Coddington regarding trespassing. October, William was one of a committee "to ripen the matter about people voting by proxies."

Son **Maher Dyer**, age 20-21, in Plymouth court regarding purchase/exchange of boats--he wins.

1665

Early in 1665, **Anne Burden Richardson**, who had been Mary Dyer's shipmate in 1657, was engaged in Quaker ministry on Rhode Island.

John Hull, master of the mint at Boston, wrote in his diary on March 15, 1665, the date of **John Endecott's death**: *Our honored Governor, Mr. John Endicott, departed this life, - a man of pious and zealous spirit, who had very faithfully endeavored the suppression of a pestilent generation, the troublers of our peace, civil and ecclesiastical, called Quakers. He died poor, as most of our rulers do, having more* *attended the public than their own private interest. It is our shame: though we are indeed a poor people, yet might better maintain our rulers than we do. However, they have a good God to reward them.*

May elections: **William Dyer** is Solicitor General for Rhode Island Colony.

Great Plague in London kills 75,000.

Boston opens the first almshouse for poor.

Capt. John Underhill is delegate of Oyster Bay to the Hempstead Convention in 1665. At the close of the convention, Underhill was named High Constable and Surveyor-General.

1666

March 27, **William Dyer** proceeds in case against **William Coddington** for killing a mare.

May 7, William Dyer sues Coddington for "uttering words of contumacy" and loses.

Capt. Tristram Hull dies in Barnstable. He knew Dyers, their grandchildren married.

"In 1666 another considerable earthquake happened in New England; and in this year was the drought." ~*The British Critic and Quarterly Theological Review, Volume 16*

September: Great Fire of London.

1667

Anglicanism reestablished in England.

Rev. John Wilson of Boston's First Church of Christ died August 7 after prolonged illness.

1668

William Dyer is Solicitor General for Rhode Island. He probably began his survey of New Hampshire and Maine, which he'd write, have printed (probably in London), and send to the king in 1670.

April 3, a strong earthquake in New England lasted for two minutes.

Son **Charles Dyer**, aged 18, married Mary Lippett. Their children were born at Little Compton, Newport, RI (on mainland toward Cape Cod). Charles is husbandman (probably horses).

In December, New Haven Colony minister **John Davenport** was installed as minister of Boston First Church of Christ, following John Wilson's death the year before.

1669

In May, **William Dyer** was elected secretary to the council. He was 60 years old in September. October 18, 1669, testimony was given in his behalf by **Governor William Coddington**: "I do affirm that we the purchasers of Rhode Island (myself being the chief), William Dyer desiring a spot of land of us, as we passed by it, after we had purchased the said island, did grant him our right in the said island, and named it **Dyer's Island**." Others so testified also. Deeds northern part of farm to son Henry Dyer.

Son **Samuel Dyer** is Conservator of the Peace (constable), Kingstown, Rhode Island..

Rev. John Davenport died in Boston of stroke on March 15, 1670, and was buried in the same tomb as Rev. John Cotton, in King's Chapel Burying Ground. Gov. John Winthrop and Rev. John Wilson were also buried there. In 1686, the graves of the Puritan founders were covered by the King's Chapel, an Anglican church. Some people think the irony was intentional because the colony was then governed by the royal appointee, Edmund Andros.

1670

Son **Maher Dyer**, a tobacco farmer and ship owner (sloop and shallop) died at age 27. He left a young widow and no children.

On 25 July 1670 **Samuel & Henry Dyer** were charged by their father to post a £300 bond to ensure the inheritance of £100 due their eldest sister, **Mary Dyer**, and £40 to their half-sister, **Elizabeth Dyer** (Rhode Island Land Records, 1648-1696 [Ms at the Rhode Island State Archives], 414).

> Wm. Dyre to Henry Dyre.
>
> William Dyre of Newport Gent granted to my sonn Henry Dyre into that part of my Farme lyinge at the northerly and there of : to witt, from the Stone Ditch, as alsoe from the tree where my sonn Mahers Tobacco house stood, from the Cave to and by that tree upon an Equi distante line from the said Stone Ditch downe unto and through the swamp unto mr, Coddingtons line by the brooke (the fence is equally devided) percell of Land.... so bounded with a free Egress ingress and regress to and through the Land of my sonn Samuells but in case my sonn Henry should have Isue only Femailes then my sonn Samuell after the death of the said Henry shall Give one hundred and fifty pounds starllinge the eldest to have a double portion the rest an equall dividend of the Residue, but if only one all to her &c besides the Valluation of the. . . .houssinge .... .thereon built the Land to return to Samuell
>
> 7th day of July 1670. William Dyre.
>
> Wit.
>
> The X marke off. Robert Spinke.
>
> John Furnell.

William Dyer Sr. deeded **Dyer Island** to son William. He may have become quite ill in the spring, because people generally made their wills shortly before they died. Perhaps he had malaria or a stroke.

William Dyer Sr. had a pamphlet printed to propose the purchase of parts of New Hampshire and Maine by King Charles II, to rein in the arrogant Massachusetts men from their imperialism. See my book, ***The Dyers of London, Boston, & Newport*** for a chapter on this remarkable document.

1672

Captain John Underhill died aged 75 years, a Quaker, on 21 July 1672 and is buried in the Underhill Burying Ground in Locust Valley, New York.

1673

Son **William Dyer Jr.** was appointed to the military service under the crown and proposed the conquest of New York from the Dutch in 1673.

1674

Son **William Dyer Jr.** takes up residence in New York. He was a member of the governor's council.

1675

Daughter **Mary Dyer**, aged about 27, marries Henry Ward of Cecil Co., Maryland and Newcastle, Delaware. They may have settled on land obtained by her brother Maj. William Dyer, who was a major landholder in the area.

Aug. 19, **Edward Hutchinson** dies aged 62 at Marlborough, Massachusetts Bay Colony, leaves special bequests to his daughter Anne Hutchinson Dyer and his sisters.

New England hurricane causes extensive damage in Connecticut, Rhode Island, and Massachusetts.

King Philip's War between Indians and settlers begins.

> JoAnn Butler writes: Dec. 19, 1675: A force of Wampanoag and local Narragansett Indians attacked Jireh Bull's fortified home on the bank of the Pettaquamscutt River, near the Porter-Gardner settlement. Bull's garrison house was burned and fifteen unidentified men, women and children were killed. The Porters and Gardners, like most English settlers on the western side of Narragansett Bay, had already taken refuge at Newport or Portsmouth. On December 19th the Narragansett's fort in the Great Swamp, about twenty miles inland from

Narragansett Bay, was reduced to ashes and many of its defenders killed by a Massachusetts and Plymouth army. The Indians were scattered, and the war continued as a guerrilla action until King Philip was killed on Aug. 12, 1676. Two escaped from Bull's Garrison, reputed to be James and Daniel Eldred, originally from Connecticut, then of Wickford.

Samuel Dyer, constable, rescued mainland Rhode Islanders from danger in King Philip's War by sailing them across the Narragansett Bay to Aquidneck Island. 27 June 1675 Roger Williams writes from Richard Smith's home at Wickford, Rhode Island, to John Winthrop Jr., "Just now comes in **Sam Dier** in a catch from Newport, to fetch out Jireh Bull's wife & children, & others of Pettaquamscutt." (Page 371 of *The Letters of Roger Williams*, edited by John Russell Bartlett 1874.)

1676

Dr. John Clarke, author of the Rhode Island charters, Baptist minister, and friend of William Dyer, died. They were born within a month of each other.

John Winthrop the Younger, born in 1606, was governor of Connecticut Colony from 1657 until his death in April 1676.

Sgt. John Plympton abducted from Deerfield, Massachusetts, and burned to death by Indians in Canada.

Rev. Johannes Theodorus Polhemus, Dutch Reformed minister in Brooklyn who opposed the Quakers there, died.

Both adult sons of **Richard and Katherine Scott** were killed in 1676, related to King Philip's War.

1677

Son **Major William Dyer Jr.** was customs collector-general in New York, accused of illegally impounding trading goods, sent to England for treason, exonerated. Treason was a capital offense, so his appeal to England (based on Charles II's directive following Mary Dyer's death) and subsequent acquittal saved his life.

Son **Henry Dyer** granted 100-acre tract in East Greenwich, Rhode Island, for services rendered during King Philip's War.

Daughter **Mary Dyer Ward**, who had married in 1675, gave birth to one son named Henry, and a daughter, Rebecca. She died at age 30, in January 1678, perhaps of childbirth or its complications. Rebecca died at age 17, and Henry lived to marry and have one child.

William Dyer Sr. died this year sometime before December 24, aged 67-68 years old. Burial ground on Dyer farm, at the extreme end of Old Newport, opposite Coaster's Harbor Island [now the Naval War College], on Narragansett Bay.

Book at Newport Historical Society: "A Record of the death of Friends & their Children." It dates to the late 1670s, but records earlier events that were important for the community. The following entry is about two thirds of the way down the first page:
"Dyer a Martyre 1660 Mary Dyer the wife of Wm Dyer of Newport in Rhode Island. She was put to death at the Town of Boston with the like Cruelty hand as the Martyers were in Queen Mary's time, and there buried upon the 31 day of the 3rd mo 1660."

The will of Gov. Benedict Arnold of Rhode Island, written Dec. 24, 1677: "Item. Unto my beloved daughter Penelope Goulding, ye wife of Roger Goulding I give and bequeath a certain parcell of land being and lying in ye precincts of ye Town aforesaid, ye said land by me named Scirt field, and is that **which I purchased of Wm. Dyre sen'r., now late deceased,** containing by measure two and twenty acres and a half, and is bounded as followeth, that is to say, on North by land in ye possession of Peleg Sanford, or his assigns, on ye East by ye Great Common aforesaid as also on ye South by ye same common and on ye West partly by **land now or late in ye possession of ye assigns of Wm. Dyre aforesaid, deceased**, the premises to be and remain to ye only use and behoof of my said daughter Penelope Goulding and her heirs forever."

William Dyer Sr.'s widow **Catherine Dyer** had her dower set off by order of Newport's Town Council in 1681, and she was alive six years later. As William's widow, Catherine Dyer and widow **Anne Hutchinson Dyer**, Samuel's relict [Samuel was William's oldest son and by primogeniture inherited a larger share], battled for three years in the courts over a "breach of covenant" before the justices saw fit to "cease the action."

At the May 12, 1679 court, "upon indictment by the General Solicitor against Catherine Dyer of Newport for misbehavior she being in court called, appeared: pleads not guilty and refers for trial to God & the country. The Court upon serious consideration of the matter see cause to quash the bill." Catherine Dyer was not through, however, and went after her stepson **Charles Dyer** in 1682 in a £30 complaint of trespass, in which the jury found against her. These actions may represent the attempts of Catherine Dyer to gain possession from the children of William Dyer's first wife, Mary, of the estate that she felt belonged to her child with him. There is no record of Catherine's surname before she married William Dyer Sr., nor is it known who her family were or where she came from. I used author's license to suggest that Catherine was an indentured servant who had finished her contract and was young enough to marry and have a child.

1679

Richard Scott of Providence died before July 1, at about age 73. His estate was the second-largest in Providence.

1680

Estate of **Samuel Dyer** (oldest son, heir of parents) taxed 15s 6d. So he must have died between 1678 and 1680, aged 44-45. His widow, **Anne Hutchinson Dyer**, remarried to Daniel Vernon.

Nathaniel Sylvester, Barbados and English trader and the owner of Shelter Island where Mary Dyer spent her last five months, died at age 70.

William Dyer Jr. made a will.

1681-83

William Dyer Jr. mayor of New York City.

1683

Roger Williams died between January and March.

1685

Feb. 6: death of **King Charles II**. His brother James, the Duke of York, ascended the throne as James II, but abdicated in 1688.

1687

Katherine Marbury Scott of Providence, aged about 75, died in Newport on May 2, 1687. Her daughter, **Patience Scott Beere**, lived in Newport, so Katherine may have been living with her daughter's family after Richard Scott died in 1679.

1688

William Dyer Jr. died between 1688 and 1693.

1709

Charles Dyer, youngest son of William and Mary Dyer, died at age 59 in Newport, Rhode Island, six months before his father would have been 100 years old.

AUTHOR'S NOTES

Mary's whereabouts in the 1650s: There are no records of what she did between her arrival and departure in England. She wasn't arrested with other Quaker women for preaching or attending Quaker meetings in England. No one knows if she had any relatives living in England, and after reading about epidemics and the short life spans of people then, my opinion is that she had no relatives even in 1635, since she was executrix of her brother's estate. That Mary stayed with the Vane family during her sojourn in England was my conjecture. Sir Henry Vane had been a friend from at least the 1630s when they emigrated to Boston. He named a child Mary, and she named a son Henry in a similar time frame. Those are common-enough names, but neither had Marys or Henrys in the family to honor with the naming of a child. Vane continued to advocate religious liberty throughout his life. He was wealthy and connected to government and society, and he would be an ideal protector for Mary, that would have been approved by William Dyer.

The court case of Richard "Long Dick" Chasmore is true, and it was presented in Newport in the spring of 1657, about the time Mary Dyer was imprisoned in Boston. Chasmore, who had been accused of buggery with his cattle by two Indian men who witnessed it, was found not guilty because the Indians' testimony would not have been accepted in a court of law. You can read the short book, online: http://bit.ly/1nJ5ckN

Earthquake of April 1658: This very strong earthquake did occur, and Mary Dyer was in New Haven in the same month to protest the torture of Humphrey Norton. I don't know if the two events coincided, but for dramatic effect, I put them together. The waters of the Massachusetts Bay were said to rise 20 feet, and large stands of trees fell down with the shaking.

Henry Vane's description of meeting George Fox: I claim author's license! The true description was actually written by George Fox in his journal, and I turned it around to be Henry's words because he's the character in my narrative. The meeting took place in the summer of 1657, after Mary Dyer had returned to America. I imagine Vane and Fox were cut from ends of the same bolt of cloth, but neither would admit it; and somewhere in Paradise, they sit down and feast together.

George Fox and Mary Dyer: It's likely that Mary would have heard Fox speak on at least one of his preaching and lobbying trips around England. But he didn't mention her in his journals, even when he described the vision he had of Marmaduke Stephenson and William Robinson being hanged at Boston.

Was Mary Dyer a preacher? Several of the Quaker historians said that she was, but they don't record what, when, or where she preached. The women who *did* preach were stripped to the waist and beaten as much for their heretical words as for their crime against "teaching" men ("But I suffer not a woman to teach, nor to usurp authority over the man, but to be in silence." 1 Timothy 2:12). Katherine Marbury Scott, wife of a wealthy man of Providence, was whipped for speaking against the Boston court. Mary was imprisoned for visiting Quakers at the Boston prison, not for preaching or disrupting services, and there is no record that Mary was ever beaten. It may be that she had some immunity because of her husband's position, but I doubt that would be enough to stop the bloodthirsty Endecott and Bellingham. My conclusion is that if Mary was a teacher, it was to women only, and that she wasn't a preacher at all—that the title the early Quakers assigned her would have been an honorific, like what we would consider a deacon or elder.

Was Mary Dyer a midwife? I've portrayed her as a midwife's assistant in both novels, but there's no evidence that she was licensed or that she delivered babies. However, as a woman who gave birth eight times, with six who lived to adulthood, and as a friend and protégé of Anne Hutchinson (who was a midwife), Mary would have attended many, many birthings. And it was a perfect occasion to teach and testify to women with no interference from men. Midwifery in England was an honored profession regulated by civil and ecumenical councils.

Solar eclipse on 14 November 1659: "An eclipse of the sun began 'presently after seven o'clock in the morning, continued till half past nine; digits eclipsed nine.'" (Salem records.) Seventy-three miles south, in Sandwich, where Mary Dyer was staying, the solar obscuration was 82%. The 20 May 2012 evening eclipse at my home in Arizona was 83%, making it a cinch to describe what Mary Dyer might have observed in 1659. Dr. Jay Pasachoff, an astronomer who has written for *National Geographic* and many other prestigious publications, confirmed my guesses in an email: "[Salem] shows an 87% coverage of the diameter by the Moon [magnitude at maximum], so that is close to 90%, which is probably what is referred to. The eclipse was in the early morning, with the maximum about one palm's width above the horizon and the end about two palms width (each palm width is about 10°)."

The thunderstorm on the night of 20-21 May 1660 was noted in Salem annals, as continuous thunder and lightning from 9:00 pm to 3:00 am. The annals didn't usually record weather events unless they were very severe; the severe events were considered to be messages from an angry God. The record didn't connect the storm with Mary Dyer's arrival in nearby Boston. She would have spent the night near Boston, and would have either experienced the storm, or seen it at a distance. But Mary was arrested in Boston on 21 May, which I believe she timed to coincide with the sitting of the General Court.

The correspondence in this novel, and in the first novel, *Mary Dyer Illuminated,* is mostly of my composition, though some letters are absolutely real, particularly the letters of Cromwell and Thurloe, Katherine Scott's letter to John Winthrop Jr., the first letter of Mary Dyer written from Boston prison, and the two letters to Massachusetts General Court written by William Dyer. Other real letters appear, from Roger Williams, Henry Fell, John Taylor, and John Copeland. If the style is stiff and formal, it's more likely to be a real letter than if I composed it.

THE AUTHOR

Christy K Robinson is published in the inspiration genre (***We Shall Be Changed***, 2010), and has edited and contributed to a number of other books during her career as a magazine and book writer and editor. ***Mary Dyer Illuminated*** and ***Mary Dyer: For Such a Time as This*** are her first biographical-historical novels. She's also written a nonfiction book of her research on the Dyers and their world: ***The Dyers of London, Boston, & Newport***, published in 2013. For updated (nonfiction) research on William and Mary Dyer's world, other books, or to contact her, visit her website: http://ChristyKRobinson.com

If you are an author considering self-publishing, or polishing your manuscript for submission to agents, please contact Christy Robinson about her editing and proofreading services.

book series without a "day job" in an ongoing economic depression (Cindy Manning, Carla Lidner Baum, Donald and Verona Robinson, Robert and Lillian Johnston, Angelica Kim, Ellie Lewis, Sondra Hadley Leno, Jeff and Bernadette Allen, Kevin and Sharon Crockett Walker, Glenn and Bonni Brown Polyak, and my invisible friend, "Anonymous").

Some are the nameless university and library volunteers who have scanned, digitized, and archived countless antique books, documents, annals, and court transcripts for free use on the internet.

Some are the thousands of social media "friends" of Mary Dyer whose search terms on my Dyer blog and questions in Facebook informed me of the level of interest in the Dyers.

I hope my efforts have lived up to the trust you've placed in me.

Thank you.

PREFACE

Who was Mary Dyer? And who was the man who married her? Very little has been known for sure, except that Mary was a wife and mother, and eventually was hanged in Boston in 1660 for her strong beliefs. Legends have sprung up since then, and religious and women's-studies writers have used her few words on record to further their own messages.

William Dyer's name is all but forgotten for several reasons: the destruction of Rhode Island court records on behalf of William Coddington, and the loss of vital records of the colony during the Revolutionary War. Additionally, his nonconversion to Quaker practices and beliefs meant that he was not much of a consideration in the works of Quaker historians. But William Dyer was a significant member of the Rhode Island government, and he was most worthy as a husband for the famous Mary Dyer.

In fact, William was Mary's greatest supporter during her life, and even after her death, by his influence in the 1663 Rhode Island charter that guaranteed separation of ecclesiastical and civil powers, and freedom of conscience. These principles were a model for the American Constitution's Bill of Rights, which in turn has been a model for civilizations around the globe.

While we don't find much direct evidence of Mary's life and thoughts, we can look at the culture, politics, religions, natural history, sociology, genealogical records of their associates, and journals and letters, of the friends and family—and enemies—surrounding the Dyers. As I researched the backgrounds of the characters, real and imagined, I was shocked to learn that most of these people had known each other for good or ill for generations in England before they emigrated to America. Rev. John Donne's sermon containing the words "No man is an island" would have been reassuring and comforting, reminding congregants of their blood and cultural ties, and that they had temporal and spiritual responsibilities to one another.

All those pieces, when placed in parallel timelines and looked at with logic and some healthy skepticism of biased reporting or fiction that's been presented as fact, create an ink drawing, and in some places a painting, of the woman only glimpsed in the journals of others or in court records of the day.

As you'll see from the cast of characters in this book, I only invented a few people for dramatic purposes. Most of the extraordinary people and their stories are true, and worthy of resurrection and exposition. Their deeds and beliefs created societies and laws on both sides of the Atlantic that influence us today.

This two-part novel of the Dyers is not written for a religious or inspirational genre, but because of the nature of the 17th century and its highly charged atmosphere, the reader will understand that religious beliefs were paramount to every Western culture at that time. The Separatists who became the Pilgrims fled the Anglican repression under King James; the Thirty Years War, between Catholics and Protestants, raged across Europe during the Dyers' lives; the Jews of the Iberian peninsula, even if they converted to Catholicism, were still burned as heretics if they didn't escape the country; the English Civil Wars of the 1640s and 1650s were fought over Anglican-versus-Puritan issues; the Dutch West Indies Company, which colonized the Caribbean, Brazil, and parts of New England, provided their settlers and military forts with Dutch Reformed ministers. In every comet, eclipse, earthquake, or plague, the priests, ministers, and rabbis in Europe and America saw the hand of God. There was no secular or sacred segmentation: all was one fabric, and that was sacred fabric. They believed that the short years they were on earth were a preparatory time for eternity. Religious issues and morals weren't "lifestyle choices," but eternal matters. Strict adherence to biblical law and punishment of heretics concerned the entire community. Religious liberty was worth dying for, and in some cases, worth killing for. In today's secular society, few authors have tackled writing about John Winthrop, Anne Hutchinson, and Mary Dyer because it's all so complicated! I had no religious soapbox, but attempted to show the beliefs through the characters' eyes. I hope I've simplified it for the 21st century.

Whether you practice a religion or denominational affiliation, or you believe that there is a universal spirituality, or you believe there is no god at all, you can thank Mary Barrett Dyer for giving her life to win religious liberty for all—the right to exercise your beliefs, and the right not to. These liberties are still under attack today; when organizations seek to blend religion with politics or government, repression will be the result. That has been the case in every society, for thousands of years.

If you'd like a look at some of the cultural research I've done as background for the Dyers' story, visit http://ChristyKRobinson.com.

Made in the USA
Lexington, KY
30 January 2015